6/18 Ingram 26⁰⁰

Broken Places

Broken Places

Tracy Clark

MYS CLARK

KENSINGTON BOOKS
www.kensingtonbooks.com

KENSINGTON BOOKS are published by

Kensington Publishing Corp.
119 West 40th Street
New York, NY 10018

All Kensington titles, imprints and distributed lines are available at special quantity discounts for bulk purchases for sales promotion, premiums, fund-raising, educational or institutional use.

Special book excerpts or customized printings can also be created to fit specific needs. For details, write or phone the office of the Kensington Special Sales Manager: Kensington Publishing Corp., 119 West 40th Street, New York, NY, 10018. Attn. Special Sales Department. Phone: 1-800-221-2647.

Library of Congress Card Catalogue Number: 2017955284

ISBN-13: 978-1-4967-1487-9
ISBN-10: 1-4967-1487-3
First Kensington Hardcover Edition: June 2018

eISBN-13: 978-1-4967-1489-3
eISBN-10: 1-4967-1489-X
Kensington Electronic Edition: June 2018

10 9 8 7 6 5 4 3 2 1

Printed in the United States of America

Thanks

Heartfelt thanks to my hardworking parents for all their sacrifices on my behalf. I saw you. I know what it took to get me here, and you have my undying love, respect, admiration, and gratitude, always. But a special shout-out to my wonderful mother, who didn't freak out at the weird kid holed up in her room surrounded by books, pens, and balls of crumpled paper. Many mothers would have shooed the kid outside to get some air, jump rope or chase the ice cream truck, but my mom somehow knew the weird kid wasn't just wasting daylight, and even if she didn't, she was okay with it. To the rest of my family and friends, also, thanks for spurring me on, even though none of you saw a single word I was writing.

To my aunt, Pat Clark, my first real reader, who from 2,000 miles away in sunny California encouraged me to keep writing, even when the rejection letters kept piling up and writing was the last thing I wanted to do. She coaxed Cass Raines and her friends out of my bottom drawer so that I could start over . . . many, many times. You'd likely be reading someone else's book right now, if she hadn't.

I would also like to thank Detective Gregory Auguste, of the Chicago Police Department, and the best brother-in-law *ever*, who helped me out with information on the inner workings of cops. I may have deviated a bit from the way he said things work in the real world, but only because the deviation made for a better story setup. For those sticklers for accuracy who might take exception to my flights of fancy, I offer a sincere *my bad*.

Thanks to Cal Thomas, who thought my work was good and took an interest in how it was coming along. He also kindly introduced Cass to his agent, Margret McBride, who graciously gave the book a critical read. Thanks for taking the time.

And to the late writer Eleanor Taylor Bland, who thought my work "impressive." I came to consider her a friend and thank her here for her grace and generosity of spirit.

I am also most grateful to my agent, Evan Marshall, for his enthusiasm and stewardship, and to my editor, John Scognamiglio at Kensington Publishing, as well as the entire Kensington family, for setting me off on this grand adventure in very good hands. A special thumbs-up to production editor Robin Cook, who provided invaluable feedback to help in my polishing efforts, and to my publicist, Lulu Martinez, for getting the word out.

All of the characters are completely imaginary, though I *may* have borrowed a distinctive walk, mannerism, or character flaw from some of those around me. Sorry, that's what writers do. It feels great to finally get these characters on the page after having them in my head for so long. They're still rattling around in there, of course—talking, sending me lunging for notebook and pen at odd hours, but they're out in the world at last, and now I'm pretty sure I work for them.

And now to Mary Carter—author, mentor, writer whisperer, friend—who quite literally taught me how to put a story together. As a member of Mary's writers' workshop, The Writers' Loft, I sweat it out (literally) every Wednesday for more than two years while she deftly broke my work down page by page, chapter by chapter, graciously offering the many years of experience under her belt to show me what worked, what didn't, and, more importantly, why. She was right every single time. Mary carried Cass Raines over the goal line and continues to be her most ardent supporter, and mine. Plain and simple, I couldn't have done it without her. Thanks also to the feedback and discerning eye of my fellow writers at The Writers' Loft for pointing out the rough spots and helping me through the dreaded draft phase. I hope I was able to do the same for all of you.

That's it. *Broken Places* is here; I'm here; Cass is here, and so are Pouch, Whip, Barb and the whole motley crew. It took a village. I hope you enjoy the ride, because I sure will.

Chapter 1

Chicago cops had to be on the lookout for any number of nefarious mopes eager to take a potshot, but this morning my biggest enemy was turning out to be the scorching rays of the summer sun. I slid into the driver's seat of the unmarked car and cranked the windows down, balancing a rapidly melting iced tea, extra ice, between my thighs. A few feet away, my partner, Detective Ben Mickerson, stood in front of the Dairy Queen basking in the hellfire. "Vitamin D," he said, ruddy face pointed skyward. "Soak in that vitamin D."

"You say vitamin D, I say skin cancer," I groused. The hot vinyl seats nearly seared through my blazer and pants—and they were both summer weight. I checked myself in the rearview. The little makeup I'd started the day with was long gone now, melted away by flop sweat. I flicked at the sweaty ringlets at the nape of my neck and wiggled uncomfortably in my bulletproof vest, my breasts pressed flat, as though squeezed between the hot plates of a waffle iron. I looked like I'd gone through a car wash, and it was just ten AM. No great loss, though. Five minutes tops was all I ever invested in primping. I didn't have the patience for it, and in the long run it seemed rather silly. Thugs and killers didn't care what I looked like. They spotted the cop car, they ran, then I had to run after them. I'd be thirty-five in the spring. Eyeliner and blush weren't going to make the running any easier.

"The sun is going to kill you," I yelled out the window.

"Tell that to my ex-wife," Ben yelled back as he continued to sunbathe. "She thought it'd be this job."

Summer in Chicago was no joke. They say black don't crack, but it does wilt, and I was wilting. Days like these I imagined all the career paths I could have gone in for. I could have been an oceanographer, swimming with friendly little dolphins in cool, blue water. Or a research scientist stationed in the Arctic. I'd die to be in the Arctic right now. Or even in a bank. Cass Raines, bank manager. Banks had AC, unlike this smelly cop car that would run hot as Hades until January, then cold until summer rolled around again. Or Cass Raines, astronaut—one of only a handful of African-American women ever to go up in space, a footnote in history, just like Sally Ride. Space was cold, wasn't it?

My tea was a watery mess. I was about to nag Ben to get back in the car so we could get rolling, when I saw him take a call. I watched as a grin broke out on his face and he pumped his fist. It was one hundred freaking degrees. What was he so happy about? Maybe he won the Powerball. If he won, I'd be happy for him, of course. What kind of partner wouldn't be happy? But I was also going to be a little pissed off. Millionaires didn't sweat their asses off in hot unmarked cars, their tits smashed between two boiler plates. Millionaires could buy enough ice to fill Wrigley Field and then hire the US hockey team to skate all over it.

"What?" I said as Ben slid into the passenger seat, buckled up.

"Uh-huh. Uh-huh. We're on it." He ended the call, slammed the door shut, and flashed me a triumphant grin. "Somebody just saw Jimmy Pick sneaking into his mother's house. We got him."

I flicked a look at my silent radio sitting beside me. "Why didn't we get it over the radio?"

He held up his phone. "Because they tagged another unit and they're already rolling on it, despite the fact that it's our case, can you believe that? That was Smitty doing us a solid."

I actually felt a shiver. "She's on Sangamon, right?"

Ben stared at me. "Still freaks me out that you got a memory like an elephant."

I shrugged. "It's a blessing and a curse." I meant it, too. I didn't want to remember half the things rattling around in my brain.

"Go. We gotta catch up."

I pulled out of the parking lot and shot out into traffic, lights and siren going, the heat no longer a concern. Jimmy Pick was the cold-blooded killer who'd been eluding us all summer; no one who knew him would give him up. Snitches get stitches. It was the way of things. "Who ratted him out?" I asked, scanning the streets.

"Anonymous. Tip line call. They even sent a photo of him waltzing through his mama's front door." He held his phone up for me to see. It was Jimmy, all right. He was young, but hard with a lifetime of street etched on his face.

"Maybe he missed her home cooking."

Just nineteen, Jimmy had a juvie record as long as my arm: assaults, car thefts, and drug possession, but he graduated to homicide this past Fourth of July when he walked up behind a gang rival and blew his brains out. Then he ran. Because that's what nineteen-year-olds do once the bravado wears off. The gangs had been sniping back and forth at each other for weeks— one side pulling off a drive-by, Jimmy's side retaliating by shooting up a park, then a gang brawl to retaliate for the retaliation. All of it was senseless and stupid and utterly maddening. Four other young men were dead now because of Jimmy's holiday kill, and we were just shy of Labor Day. Jimmy needed to be off the streets. I pressed my foot to the gas and punched it.

I ran through red lights, rolled through stop signs, my eyes checking the street for distracted pedestrians. I glanced over at Ben. "Who're we meeting up with?"

"Solis, Lyles, Grimes."

Cops worked in teams. Like salsa dancers and doubles partners. Ben was one short. "I can count, you know."

Ben sighed. "Farraday. And there's no point whining about it."

I groaned. Farraday wasn't a cop you wanted watching your six. He was pigheaded, haughty, and woefully slow on the uptake, but what he lacked in skill and temperament, he more than made up for in clout. Farraday was from a family of high-powered cops—sergeants, lieutenants, commanders, and chiefs—who'd paved the way for him. He'd risen through the ranks on the shoulders of giants. There seemed to be no mistake he could make egregious enough to derail his ascent; Farraday knew it and acted accordingly.

"But if he so much as blinks funny," Ben said, "I'll shove him down a sewer hole . . . Ferragamos last."

The Pick house sat as dejected as a whipped dog, one of many that sat on a block of bedraggled frame houses subsidized by the government. The house, crudely painted lime green, appeared to lean to the left, as if an unkind fate had sapped the straightness right out of it. Instead of grass, a rusted car sat atop oil-stained cinder blocks. It was a place dreams went to die. I rang the bell, but no one answered. Solis and Lyles were at the head of the street. Farraday and Grimes were out back covering the alley. Farraday didn't like it, but Pick belonged to Ben and me, and he knew it. Unfortunately, we didn't have a warrant, so the porch was as far as we were authorized to go, unless there were exigent circumstances, and I couldn't see any through the tattered bedsheets that passed for window drapes. I rang again, waited again, as Ben and me melted like butter pats in the midmorning heat, our bodies angled so we could watch both the street and the door simultaneously.

Something rattled around the side of the house. Ben and I exchanged a look, then carefully leaned over the wobbly railing just in time to see Jimmy sprint out the side door, fly down the gangway, and scale his mother's back fence.

"Son of a bitch." Ben took off down the steps with me right behind him. Jimmy crossed into his neighbor's yard, hopped another fence, and took off down the alley. Ben relayed Jimmy's description over the radio—approximate height six feet, wearing black track pants and a sleeveless yellow shirt. Jimmy, half a block ahead, saw us chasing him and sped up. It was too hot to run, but Jimmy was making a race of it, a race Ben and I could not afford to lose.

"Stop!" I shouted, digging in. "Police!" My holstered gun and radio bounced at my side. I caught up to Ben and passed him. Behind me, I could hear him puffing like a steam engine, but he kept it moving. He was knocking on the door to forty and in pretty good shape normally, but wind sprints in a heat-wave would have been too much even for Usain Bolt. "Where are Farraday and Grimes?" I yelled. And where were the sirens? There should be sirens by now. Jimmy clambered over a row of garbage carts and scaled another fence. I called out the address so Ben could call it in and then grabbed a handful of chain link, prepared to scramble up and over, but the gate swung free in my hands. Spared the awkward climb, I shoved the gate open with more force than I probably needed, but now I was mad. I barreled through the yard, my eyes boring holes into Jimmy's back.

"Jimmy, stop!" *Goddammit.* He glanced back, sneered, kept going. He flew through the yard and jumped another fence into the alley. Ben and I went up and over, but Jimmy was well ahead of us. We were losing him. I ramped it up, my legs wobbling from the effort.

"Where the hell's our backup?" Ben yelled.

I scanned the alley. No Farraday. No Grimes. No Solis. No Lyles. "Don't worry about it. Go." But I did worry about it. I worried about it a lot. Jimmy rounded a corner, and I lost sight of him. I took the corner with Ben right behind me. The alley dead-ended. We skidded to a stop. East and west, apartment buildings loomed over the narrow alleyway. Ben and I stood facing south. Jimmy was nowhere. We were boxed into a canyon of apartment windows, the sound of our heavy breathing echoing off the dirty glass. Was someone lurking behind them? Watching? Were they armed? Did they hate cops? Ben and I moved in circles, checking every opening, looking for movement, praying we didn't find any. It felt as though we were being tracked by a thousand eyes. "See anything?"

"Can't depend on that," Ben answered. "Left," he called out, indicating which side of the alley he'd take. That meant the right side was mine to lock down. My eyes swept over every shadowy spot, every window, every alcove, my heart racing, my fingers suddenly cold. Minutes ago I'd been begging for relief from the heat, now I didn't need it quite so much. In my head, I clicked through procedure, bracing myself for whatever came next, hoping to God I made the right choices and held up my end.

"Right," I confirmed in a tight, clipped voice, my mouth bone dry. No backup. No backup? It was inconceivable but here the two of us were, alone . . . in an alley . . . in active pursuit. There was plenty of police chatter on our radios, but none of it pertained to us. What bizarre world had Ben and I stumbled our way into? Where was everybody?

"Stop! Police!" The brusque command rang out from above us. Ben and I looked up at the same time, drew our weapons and trained them in the direction of the shout.

"The roof," Ben yelled. "The six-flat. There." We bolted for the building. We found the ground-floor door unlocked, and barreled through, rushing into the darkened stairwell, blinking to adjust quickly to the dark. From the street, finally, sirens.

"I said, stop!" Again, the roof, but this time I recognized the voice. It was Farraday. My heart leapt into my throat.

"Holy shit," Ben muttered. "How'd he get past us?" The door behind us flew open. We both reeled. Detective Grimes. "What the hell?" Ben's eyes were wide, hyperalert. Mine were, too. "Why aren't you with your partner?"

"He told me to cut off the alley," Grimes said. He bent over to catch his breath. He was just two years out of uniform, still green, which accounted for the look of terror on his face. "He jumped out of the car and took off. I sped around, but then ran into the dead end. I left the unit and doubled back. Where is he?" Ben pointed toward the roof and we all three raced up the stairs. We had six flights to climb. Farraday was not the cop you wanted to leave alone on a roof with a kid who felt cornered. Our job was to serve and protect, using force only when necessary. With Farraday it was force first, always. He was a cowboy who wanted to be the hero and score bones with his family. Not the best motivators for a good cop, lethal motivators for a bad one. The more stairs I climbed the more there seemed to be. Ben lagged behind, but not by much. Grimes fell in behind him. Do not kill this kid, I prayed silently. *Do not kill this kid.*

Chapter 2

We heard banging above us, a noise none of us could readily identify. Still three flights to go. Sirens blared outside—the cavalry at last. "Open the door!" Farraday shouted. "Now!"

Ben and I exchanged a foreboding look.

"Go!" I yelled, hoping to spur us both on. Two more flights. "Farraday! Stand down!" I called out, my voice reverberating off the dirty walls along with the banging from up top.

"What *is* that?" Ben asked.

"Sounds like somebody trying to push a door in," Grimes offered, his sweat-soaked red hair plastered to his head. The three of us hustled up the steps double-time, finally reaching the last flight. When I rounded the final landing, I saw Farraday, his back pressed to the door jamb, sunlight streaming in from the roof. He'd gotten the door open, but it didn't look like he was in any hurry to burst though it alone. It was the first smart thing he'd done all day. Farraday saw us there, his expression practically gleeful. It turned my stomach. "He's out there." Farraday kept his voice low. "I got him boxed in."

Ben looked as though he might shoot Farraday himself. "How the hell did you get ahead of us?"

Farraday sneered. "I saw him shoot out of the yard. I took off after him. Not my fault you two are slow."

Ben's eyes flashed danger. "You took off without your partner?"

Farraday's eyes darted toward Grimes. "He had the car. I got this."

"I hear you all out there!" Jimmy yelled from the other side of the door. "You all need to back up. I ain't going down. I ain't going to jail!"

"Cover me," Farraday said, pulling himself away from the door. "I'm going in."

I grabbed him by the arm, pulled him back. "Like hell you are. We're not killing this kid, you hear me? Now back off."

Farraday pulled his arm free. "He's my collar. I ran him down."

Ben faced him. "Are you really that far gone that you're itching to be the white cop who guns down a poor black kid on a rooftop?"

"Fuck you, Mickerson," Farraday spat out. Ben looked as though he wanted to pound Farraday into sand; instead, he simply turned his back on him.

I turned to Grimes. "You hold the spot. He holds it, too. Understood?" Grimes looked as though he might faint, but he nodded a confirmation and held.

"This is bullshit, Raines, and you know it," Farraday hissed.

My eyes held his. "I'll tell you what I know. I know I'd better not see your stupid face on the other side of this door until we get this kid off the roof. Period. Now get the hell away from me!"

Farraday slunk back, seething, as Ben and I counted off three and then eased through the door a half step at a time. Maybe Jimmy had a gun, maybe he didn't. I hoped he didn't. The tar-covered rooftop seemed to sizzle under my feet and cling to the soles of my shoes. Guns up, we stepped farther out, checking everywhere for Jimmy Pick. We found him along the building's edge, his back to us, as though he was thinking about jumping. His hands weren't visible. My heart seized. Ben and I fanned out. He took right this time.

"Hey there, Jimmy," I began, fighting hard to keep the quiver out of my voice. "Mind if we talk?"

"Ain't in a talking mood, especially not to no cops." Ben and I each took a step forward, flanking him. We exchanged a look, and Ben nodded, giving me the okay to take the lead on talking Jimmy down.

"I can respect that. A man's entitled to talk to whoever he wants." I slid another glance toward Ben. I had no idea where to go with this. Sweat pooled on Ben's face, his jaw clenched tightly, as though it were chiseled in stone. "See? Thing is, Jimmy? You're making a whole lot of people real nervous. I'd like to get you off this roof safe and sound, but I also need my partner and the other cops down there to be safe, too."

"You don't give a shit about me being safe."

I balanced evenly on the balls of my feet. "That's where you're wrong, Jimmy. I'd like us all to be safe."

"But I'll be the one going to jail."

I swallowed hard. There was no use lying to the kid. "Yeah, that's true. . . . This is how it goes, Jimmy. You'll put your hands way up and out where me and my partner can see them clearly. Then you'll turn around really, really slow, facing us. We'll ask you to get down on the ground, spread eagle, and then lace your hands behind your head, again, real slow, real easy. Then the cuffs go on, we stand you up, and take you down to the car. That's it. That's all. That's how it has to be." My gun weighed heavy in my hands, my palms sweating. "No one wants to hurt you, Jimmy." God knows I didn't. "But I'm going to need you to put your hands up and out now, just like I said. Up and out."

Jimmy did not comply. He barely moved. I couldn't be sure he'd even heard me. I wet my lips. Out of the corner of my eye,

I could tell Ben was bracing himself for what we both hoped wouldn't come to pass. "Nobody has to die here today."

Jimmy said nothing. He was likely watching the squad cars multiply down in the alley. He had no place to go. He had to know it. He had to feel it. "You cops like shooting black folks in the back," Jimmy said. "So go ahead."

Beads of sweat dripped into my eyes, and I quickly wiped them away with the sleeve of my blazer. "You're wrong about that," I said. "We don't want to shoot anybody." I shifted into firing position, my heart beating so wildly it seemed to ram against my rib cage. "Up and out . . . then around slowly."

"Then what?" Jimmy asked.

My fingers tightened on the grip of my gun, my eyes pinned to Jimmy's back. "Then on the ground, spread eagle, cuffs. Just like I said."

"Then what?" he asked again. He was toying with me, goading us. *Shit. Shit. Shit.* Jimmy began to slowly turn, his hands still down.

"Hands up! Do it now!"

Ben and I shouted together. "Now!"

Jimmy slowly raised his hands, a contemptible scowl on his face. "I ain't dying today, cop. I'm going to let you take me in." He held his hands out to his sides. "You don't shoot me, I don't shoot you. Fair deal."

"Down! Hands behind your head!" Niceties were done. Every cell in my body was operating in overdrive. I could hear the blood rushing through my veins, the valves in my heart opening and closing. I could count every pimple on Jimmy's face. His pockets hung heavy. There could be a gun in one of them, or a cellphone. I couldn't let his hands get anywhere near his pockets again.

Ben drew forward. "Get down. Face in the dirt. Now!" Ben and I made eye contact. He knew I had his back. I watched nervously as Ben slowly approached, keeping a safe distance.

Jimmy, seemingly resigned now to going to jail, prepared to plaster himself to the rooftop. He'd just started his descent, when the door to the roof banged open, and Farraday barreled through like a runaway freight train.

"Down, you asshole!" he barked, gun drawn, his feral eyes boring into Jimmy's confused ones.

"Farraday, stop! What the hell are you doing?" I yelled, but Farraday kept coming. I watched in horror as the expression on Jimmy's face flipped from resigned acceptance to primal ferocity. We'd had a deal and this wasn't it. He looked at me as though I'd betrayed him. I saw in his eyes the very moment he made up his mind to kill us all.

"Jimmy, don't," I pleaded. "Don't do it." Ben peddled backward, caught off guard by the sudden shift in activity. He dropped his handcuffs, raised his gun. A couple more minutes and we'd have had Jimmy cuffed and off the roof. Now this. "Farraday! What the hell? Back the fuck up!"

Jimmy let out an angry wail. "You lied!"

What happened next happened all at once and, seemingly, at twice the speed of light. Jimmy's arms, once held in surrender, shot down to his sides, and his right hand plunged into his pocket. I registered the glint of shiny silver. Ben was exposed, caught flat-footed partway between the safety at my side and the danger Jimmy posed. Time meant nothing. *Gun. Gun. Gun.* It was all I could see; it was all my brain could process. *Gun.*

I fired. Jimmy fired. Ben fired. Farraday fired. The acrid stench of spent gunpowder and the heart-sickening sound of rapid gunfire ricocheted off the sides of the grimy buildings, whipped around my ears, and then hung in the air eerily suspended before melting away to nothing. The dizzying progression from glint of metal to muzzle flash seemed to take no more than a finger snap. I suddenly felt a sharp, searing pain in my chest so intense that it knocked me backward and off my feet. Time, which had raced like a thoroughbred horse just half a second earlier, stopped dead. Just stopped. Dead. Nothing moved, no one moved as the world beyond the rooftop fell away.

I began to fall, feeling myself go, my back crashing against the hot, sticky tar, my gun tumbling out of a hand that could no longer grasp it. I lay there stunned, my chest burning, and stared up at the clouds, watching as a bird flew overhead. These would be the last things I ever saw, I thought, the last things my senses would touch. Bile rose in my throat. I could feel warm blood pooling at my neck. The smell of my own sweat mingled with the metallic stench of fresh blood, my blood. The vest protected my chest—my heart, my lungs, the things that counted— but Jimmy's bullet had caught me just above where the vest ended. It was my bad luck. Two minutes. Two seconds. No difference. There was no real time, only the rooftop and gunfire reverb, blood, sweat, gunpowder, bile, fear. Dammit. I was going to die today. Ben's head shot into view, blocking out the sky. The stricken look on his face told me all I needed to know. It was bad. I felt for him. I didn't want him to be the cop who lost a partner on a roof. It was a rough road to travel on. Still, I wanted the clouds back. I'd even take the bird, though I'd never liked them much. Way too chirpy.

"Hey, Cass," Ben said, feverishly checking me for signs of life. My eyes were open. Weren't they open? I could see the clouds, right? "Stay with me. Shit! You're all right. You hear? Keep breathing. Farraday, you son of a bitch!" My eyes blurred, watered. Nauseous, I clenched my eyes shut, waiting for the worst to pass. It didn't. Wouldn't. I'd planned on pizza for dinner, and now I couldn't catch my breath. I'd miss Christmas, I'd never have children, and I left dirty dishes in my sink. "Breathe," Ben ordered, tears flooding his eyes. Wasn't I breathing? I thought I was breathing. I watched, my vision fading, as he struggled out of his blazer, balled it and pressed it to my neck. A couple millimeters left or right and I'd have walked away from this. Ben's efforts sent a fresh wave of agony through me, but I didn't let on. I didn't want him to feel bad. He'd never be able to wear the jacket again, of course. He'd never get my blood out of it. "Officer down! Officer down!" Ben shouted into his radio. I watched the clouds. I wanted them to be the last things I took in.

"Jimmy?" I croaked.

Ben shook his head. "You got him."

But I didn't want to get him. He was bad news, but he was just a kid. I wanted him to live. I wanted us all to live. What happened? Where had it gone wrong? Then I remembered.

Farraday.

The chatter over the radio sounded like it was coming from the end of a long tunnel, and I couldn't make sense of it. I turned my head only as far as I could manage and there was Farraday, his face as pale as a ghost, but very much alive and well. Jimmy Pick was dead. I was dead, too. But there he stood. I heard the paramedics coming, but it didn't feel as though I could wait for them. I managed just one more half inhale before the sounds of salvation faded, and my field of vision shrank to the breadth of a pinprick. Calmly, silently, I let go of the world. I was cold at last and hadn't even needed to go to space for it. I thought I had more time. I hadn't planned on dying today.

Chapter 3

"Wouldn't you rather sit, Detective?" Dr. Voigt asked. "I don't charge for the use of the chair."

Dr. Nelson Voigt, dressed neatly for autumn in a white oxford shirt, navy knit vest, and black slacks, smiled and eyed me keenly from his overstuffed chair, his right leg crossed languidly over the left, his lean body perfectly still. Penetrating gray eyes that gave nothing away peered out of a narrow, clean-shaven face. Voigt, who appeared to be in his mid-fifties, didn't strike me as a careless man, yet his socks were mismatched, one black, one navy blue. It was a small thing of little importance in the grander scheme, yet there they were.

"Good to know," I said. There were just twenty-two minutes left in my fifty-minute session, and I was choosing to spend them as I'd spent the first twenty-eight, staring out of the police psychologist's window at a sterile courtyard with its faux serenity fountain and small waxen trees meant to ape the real thing. Beyond the courtyard, a tree—a real one—had gone from crimson to brown, as trees did in fall. A cardboard skeleton dangled inside a window across the street, a reminder that Halloween was just a week away.

"Cass?"

I watched a skittish sparrow light on the limb of one of Voigt's bogus trees before it suddenly flitted away again. I envied the bird. "I'll stand."

Voigt's ballpoint pen scratched across the notepad on his lap. The scratching stopped. "Tell me about Jimmy Pick."

I stiffened, took a moment. "He's dead." Jimmy had died where he fell. Two rounds from my gun had pierced his aorta. One of his had narrowly missed mine, leaving damage. My left arm was now weaker than it had been, and rehab was slow. I thought I would die, but I didn't. Instead, I spent weeks in the ICU, tubes sticking out of me everywhere, the steady beeping of the monitors my only assurance that I was still among the living. Now I was here watching birds. *Tell me about Jimmy Pick?*

"How do you feel about that?" Voigt asked as though he were asking me how I felt about losing a pair of gloves on the Red Line. The bird was back, or maybe it was a different bird. "Anger would be a normal reaction," Voigt prodded. "Anxiety, fear, even guilt for not being able to change the outcome are also normal. We haven't talked about the shooting. Maybe we should?" Silence hung like a heavy mist. I didn't feel compelled to break it. "So, what happened out there?" Voigt said gently after a time.

Farraday happened. I could have brought Jimmy in. I nearly had him. But Farraday wanted the collar; he wanted to be a hero. He didn't give a fig whether Jimmy Pick lived or died. Apparently, he felt the same about Ben and me. I squeezed my hands into angry fists. I could feel Voigt's eyes on my back, hear him scribbling. What was he writing down? What did he see that I couldn't? "You read the report."

Voigt paused for a moment. "The details were there, not your feelings."

I rolled my eyes. *Feelings.* Damn it all to hell and back. "I gave my statement. I *feel* that's enough."

More scribbles. I wondered why Voigt pressed the pen so heavily against the paper that I could hear the scratching clear across the room. Was he afraid the ink would fly away? "Tell me about Detective Farraday. His account was rather different."

I reeled to face him. "That's because he's a lousy liar." The words shot out of my mouth before I had a chance to edit them, as rage blasted up from somewhere deep. "That kid would be alive, if not for him. He nearly got us *all* killed!"

Voigt watched me intently. "It was ruled a justifiable shoot."

I squeezed my eyes shut, seething. Even thinking about James Farraday was almost too much. I opened them again, a little calmer, but not by much. "They gave him a commendation. Never mind the dead kid. Nobody wearing a star died, you see. That's all that counts."

"You backed up your partner. You did your job."

"Did I? Tell that to the protestors marching in front of the district. Their signs have my picture on them. KID KILLER. KILLER KOP." I took a breath, two. "I got a commendation, too, and so did Ben. You want to know why?"

Voigt stared at me intently. "Sure."

"Because they couldn't just give Farraday one, and they really wanted him to have it. A commendation looks good on your record. It's what they look for when they move you up."

"They?"

"Brass," I said. "They've got plans for Farraday no matter how many times he gets it wrong, no matter how many kids die."

"You take issue with how the department handled the situation."

I inhaled deeply. "Maybe it takes almost dying to lower one's tolerance for bullshit."

"How's the Xanax working?"

The little brown bottle was tucked inside the front pocket of my jeans. I could feel it there, pressed snugly against my right hip. I reached down and felt for it, disturbed by the level of comfort it gave me. The bottle was still full. "I don't need pills."

"It's not a battle, you versus the pills. Taking them is not a sign of either weakness or surrender." He was wrong. For me, taking even one would be exactly that, surrender. Every day I didn't open the bottle was a victory, and I needed the win no matter how small it was. Each pill-free day got me through to the next twenty-four hours and the twenty-four after that. Soon, I wouldn't need to chalk up the score; I wouldn't need to carry the bottle. Soon, but not today.

"Are you sleeping?"

Sleep? How could I sleep when every time I closed my eyes I saw a dead kid? We'd had a deal, Jimmy Pick and me—up, out, down, safe. I couldn't get his look of betrayal out of my head. Would I ever? I'd promised him he'd be safe. Now I was a kid killer.

"Like a baby." The lie came out easily. The truth was I couldn't remember the last time I'd slept more than an hour or two at a stretch. How could a kid killer sleep? "Do you have the time?"

Voigt glanced at the digital clock sitting on his desk. "We've got a few minutes more. I'd like to keep going."

"How many minutes exactly?"

"Eight."

I felt like a big bird trapped in a tiny cage with not enough room to flap my wings or hop on the perch. Eight minutes.

"You're seeing someone. A cop. Everything okay there?"

"I ended it. Let's not talk it to death."

I could feel Voigt watching. The bird on the branch took off. My wistful envy gave way to a slow and bitter resentment.

"Why?"

"I couldn't breathe." I slid him a sideways glance. "I'm speaking figuratively."

Marcus wanted to fix things, fix me, and cling while doing it. I wasn't a clinger. I'd lost too much to make that a thing. My mother was gone, father and grandparents, too. I'd lost them all by the time I was twenty-five. It was the way of things. Friends came and went, lovers, too. Only a fool tries to hang on to impermanent things. I learned early to take life as I found it and to keep moving forward, giving only as much as I could bear to lose.

"I backed away," I said. "I'm still doing it."

Voigt's pen attacked the paper. When he'd made his notation he said, "There has to be more to it than that."

"Why? We weren't married. We didn't have to split a kid down the middle. It got too complicated, so we each took our marbles and went home."

I padded over to Voigt's desk and fiddled absentmindedly with a glass paperweight sitting there. The entire desktop was littered with strange little knickknacks and baubles nervous Nellies could hold, caress, toss, or squeeze for comfort and ballast during a fifty-minute head-shrinking session.

"Tell me about your family. Your mother died of cancer. You were twelve, a tough age for that to happen. Your father wasn't in the picture. You were raised by your grandparents."

I bounced the paperweight from one palm to the other. *In the picture?* I almost laughed. A month after my mother's funeral, my father had packed me up and dropped me off at my grandparents', then left town for good. He'd yammered something about it being temporary, that he'd be back soon, but I knew he was lying. I always knew when he was lying.

"Does everything have to lead back to that?"

Voigt said, "Does it?"

"I hate it when you answer a question with a question. It's irritating. Where are you going with this, anyway?"

"Do you always have to know where things are going?"

I turned to look at him, my frustration building. "Yes."

Voigt steeple his fingers under his chin. "It's safer knowing, isn't it?"

I glowered at him. "That's the head-shrinking stuff, right?"

Voigt smiled. "I wouldn't be doing my job if I didn't try a little of it. We'll come back to family. Can we talk about your partner? I've spoken to him. He's having as rough a time as you are. You mean a great deal to him, and he obviously means a great deal to you."

I shook my head. I didn't want to talk about Ben. It was too close, too raw. I'd seen the look in his eyes on that rooftop, and I felt guilty for being the one to have put it there. He saved my life, I saved his. We were bonded, but neither of us could face what might have been. Not yet.

"Might be helpful," Voigt said.

"Not to me."

"You hate being pushed. That's something I've learned about you. Unfortunately, I'm kind of in the pushing business."

I ignored him.

"Your partner," Voigt gently pressed. "Or your parents. Your choice."

The dying tree beyond the courtyard had offered up its last mystery, and there were no new sparrows to divert me. I weighed my options. I had a lot of them, yet I didn't move.

"Why did you become a cop?"

I turned. Our eyes held. "Why do you keep asking me that?"

Voigt shrugged. "Because I want to know, and you won't tell me."

A moment passed, two, before I spoke. "Lunchbox."

Voigt looked confused. "Want to explain?"

"No," I said.

Voigt chuckled. "My mistake. *Will* you explain?"

I slammed down the paperweight and padded back to the

window, my back to Voigt. Still no birds. They were probably off somewhere crapping on someone's car. "There was a bully at school, a big oaf of a kid, a mean, nasty piece of work. He made it his life's mission to pick on this one kid half his size—Adam Lychee. Funny, how I still remember his name.

"The oaf took Adam's lunchbox—Spider-Man. God, I remember that, too . . . He held it up over his head and made him jump for it in front of all the kids in the schoolyard. He laughed; they laughed. I can still see the look of humiliation on Adam's face. It made me angry, so angry I shook with it." I slid Voigt a look, watching as he scribbled feverishly in the notepad. "I got the lunchbox back but ended up in the principal's office. I got a three-day suspension for bloodying the oaf's nose.

"I don't like bullies. I didn't like them in the schoolyard then, I don't like them on the streets now, pushing old ladies down in the dirt for their Social Security money, preying on those who can't protect themselves. They're cowards. Someone has to stand up to them."

Voigt looked up. "You?"

"Me. Someone else."

"Just curious. Was the bully bigger than you?"

I shrugged. "I guess."

"But that didn't stop you from confronting him. Why do you think that is?"

"You're the doctor. You tell me."

Voigt chuckled. "My theory, and it's just that, is that you felt compelled to right a wrong because so many things had gone wrong for you. You couldn't do anything about your mother dying or your father leaving, but you *could* face the bully, get the lunchbox back. It was a need to create order where there wasn't any, to fight for someone because your father didn't fight for you. The bully's size would have been irrelevant."

I faced him, frowned. "They pay you for that psychobabble?"

He smiled. "Quite well, actually."

"My theory? The kid was a jackass who needed his bell rung. Nobody else was willing to do it, so I stepped up. Why do you have to chew things to death?"

"Black and white, no gray?" he asked.

"Sometimes it's just that simple."

"You've lost both parents. That would likely be a devastating thing for most people. Which one did you love the most?"

I reeled. "What the hell?"

He grinned impishly. "That got your motor revved up. Your mother died. Your father left you behind. There must be some anger buried somewhere."

"You can't blame a person for dying. Leaving voluntarily by Amtrak? Who would you be angry at?"

He angled his head. "I think your father would be the winner there. If you had to describe each of your parents in one word, what would that word be? Your mother first."

I rolled my eyes, sighed. This was the longest eight minutes. I reached up and fingered the gold chain around my neck. At the end of it was a ring my mother had given me when she knew she didn't have long. She'd kissed it first, and then pressed it into my palm. My remembrance, my link.

"I'm not going to say this is fair," Mom said, her weary head lying on the starched white pillow. *"It isn't. I wish things could be different."*

"But they aren't," I said.

"We'll just have to make the best of the time we've got, that's all." She forced a smile. I could tell it cost her. *"C'mon, scooch closer.... I'll make you a deal. I'll tell you everything about me, and won't leave a single thing out, if you'll tell me all the things you think I don't know about you. That way, when we meet again, all we'll have to do is catch up a little bit.... How's that sound?"*

I reached over to trace my fingers along the protruding veins in her frail hand. "Not a single thing?"

"Not one. Pinkie swear."

"Cass?" Voigt's voice drew me back. "One word to describe your mother?"

"Present," I said. "That meant everything."

"And your father?"

I released the chain. He hadn't left much behind, barely even memories. He was supposed to be there, but he wasn't. He didn't have it in him, I figured out much later. But the world kept turning; I didn't break. One word? I looked over at Voigt, thought about the question. "Cornered—not up for the hard stuff. It was like he was always on the wrong side of every door, in when he wanted to be out, out when he wanted in."

"Then maybe he did you a favor by leaving?"

I smiled a little. "That thought came to me much later. At twelve, it felt more like a sacrifice, my life for his."

Voigt nodded, scribbled. "Interesting." He looked up, snapped the cap back on his pen. "Good start. We'll pick up there next session."

I shook my head. "No thanks. I'll go the rest of the way on my own." I walked toward the door.

Voigt stood. "But these are mandatory sessions, Detective. I can't clear you for active duty if you terminate them prematurely."

I stopped, my hand on the doorknob. "I won't need that clearance. I turned in my star a couple of hours ago. . . . Now you'll ask me why."

Voigt stared at me, an expression of concern on his face. "Consider it asked."

I opened the door, stopped. "I burned that commendation they gave me. Farraday framed his." I shut the door behind me.

Chapter 4

I hooked my bike onto the repair stand and grabbed an Allen wrench out of the set, humming while I worked. The rear brake pads needed to be tightened or my next morning ride down the lakefront would be my last. I'd just closed a case, the check had cleared, and I had no new clients lined up. It was April. The sun was high, the air light and clean. Heat and humidity were months away. I was a rare thing, indeed—a PI with money to keep her office lights on and time to putter around the house on a lazy afternoon. I twisted the bike's barrel adjustment and kept the humming up. I liked humming; it lifted the spirit. Old Motown and '70s soul, mostly, songs with words instead of grunts, sung by singers who could hold a note without having to strip bare-assed naked, paint themselves blue, or swing from construction equipment. I looked up from the bike, rolled my shoulders. Maybe I should go into the office, I thought, do something that made money? I shook my head. Nope. I'm good.

I tested the brakes, but the pads still wobbled. I checked the cable attachment and found some give in it, so I applied the wrench and hit the adjustment again, stopping after a time to shake the numbness out of the fingers on my left hand. "Damn it," I hissed, flexing every digit.

The rooftop was two years ago, but I still carried Jimmy Pick with me. He was in the scar on my chest, in the numbness in my fingers, in every sleepless night, every night terror.

The red Bianchi Lupo was the gift I'd given myself after I handed in my star. Some cops bought sailboats when they retired, some invested in lakeside property. I bought a bike, though it took months before I could ride it. I tossed the wrench aside and ran my fingers over the spot just above my left collarbone where Jimmy's bullet had caught me. The scar was the easy part. I'd taken a life to save two others, three if you counted mine, but that didn't minimize the enormity, or the finality, of what I'd done. I would always carry the weight of it. That was the part that was hard.

I shook out my hand to get the feeling back. I'd finished rehab six months ago, but the bullet had nicked the nerves, leaving my left arm a little weaker than the right, at least for now. To get it back, I rode the bike, lifted weights, and spent time at the shooting range. It was slow going, but it was going.

"There," I said when I got the brakes fixed. "All better." A leaky faucet was next on my To-Do List. This wasn't the life I'd imagined for myself, but it was okay. I kept it moving.

I owned the modest three-flat I lived in, left to me by my grandparents. It had been their stake and legacy, and I fussed over it as they had, babied it, really, mindful of the sacrifices made on its behalf, and mine. I'd lost my grandmother my senior year of high school, my grandfather my second year on the force, but I held fast to the building. It was my last tangible link to either of them.

The third-floor apartment came to me rent-free as a gift when I graduated from the U of I, and I accepted it gladly at the time, only to balk a few years later when I got the entire building after my grandfather died. The building wasn't the same without them to watch over it, but I couldn't bear the thought of selling it, knowing how hard they'd worked for it. So now I was landlord and super to three and a half tenants—Mrs. Vincent, a widow who'd worked with my grandmother at the phone company, and the Kallishes—Stuart, Marie and four-year-old Nate. Nate was the half. Mrs. Vincent had wonderful old stories about my family, and when I needed to hear them she gladly retold them over homemade shortbread.

Mrs. Vincent lived on the first floor; the Kallishes lived between us. The building didn't pay for itself, mainly because I didn't force it. Mrs. Vincent got by on Social Security and her late husband's meager pension. The Kallishes, both doctoral students at the University of Chicago, studied between jobs that didn't pay nearly enough. I liked having them around, so I ate the rent they couldn't pay, taking on a few more jobs to make up the difference. It was a system that worked.

I grabbed my toolbox and *Plumbing for Dummies*. How hard could a little leak be? If I could bust up a riot with only a night stick and a can of Mace, I could certainly stop water from dripping into an old lady's sink.

When I hit the second-floor landing, the Kallishes' door swung open and Nate jumped out into the hall in rain boots, sweats, and a Transformers T-shirt, his wild mop of curly black hair matted from his afternoon nap, his moon face, dimpled at the cheeks, the color of soft sand. He stood there watching me, not saying anything.

"Hey, Nate."

"I'm going to playgroup today." His honey brown eyes stared up at me, unblinking.

"Me too," I said.

He frowned. "You can't. It's only for kids."

I squinted at him, the toolbox heavy in my hand.

"Who says?"

His little arms flew out wide. "The world."

"Big people go to playgroup all the time. It's called work. Ask your mommy."

I could see the wheels turning in his little head; he angled it. "Do you get animal crackers?"

I smiled. "You got me, Nate. Big people do not get animal crackers when they go to work."

He grinned, unable to hide the gloat, sure he'd bested me. "Ha. See?"

"Nathan Marshall Kallish," his mother, Marie, yelled from inside.

Nate jumped, scurried back inside, and slammed the door in my face. If I were a parent, my four-year-old unlocking the door whenever the mood struck him would worry the hell out of me, but Marie, apparently, rested quite well at night.

She told me once that Nate only opened the door when he heard me in the hall. I had no idea how he knew when that was, but I imagined him lying on the floor on his side, ear pressed to the carpet, one squinted little eye peeking out from the inch and a half of clearance, listening for my footfalls. He was either a cop in training, or a stalker in training. I hoped it was the former.

"Come on back," Mrs. Vincent said when she let me in. "You know where the kitchen is, and I got fresh muffins out there for you. Grab one." She surveyed me intently, frowned. "Or two."

She wasn't anyone's real grandmother, but she was a great stand-in with her steel-gray hair pulled back in a neat bun, a generous bosom, and a smile as warm as fresh-baked cookies. She never missed church on Sunday or bingo on Saturday night, and in all the years I'd known her, I'd never heard her utter an unkind word about anybody. She came with the building, she liked to tell people, and it was true. She was here before I moved in, and she was here now. If things kept on like they were going, she'd likely get the building in my will.

"Just started dripping, huh?" I said.

"Last night. It was like that Japanese water torture. *Drip, drip, drip.* It about drove me crazy."

I was pretty sure she meant Chinese water torture, but I let it sit. That drip wasn't going to fix itself. I padded back to the kitchen and got to work, the smell of the cooling muffins vying for my attention. It felt like forever that my head was under Mrs. Vincent's sink. I ate three muffins while trying to decipher *Plumbing for Dummies,* but I thought I finally had it. I crawled out from under the sink and called for her.

I heaved out a sigh. "I think that does it."

She clasped her hands together. "I knew you'd get it."

I reached for the spigot. "Let's test it."

I turned the handle slowly, cold water, not hot, and braced myself. The water poured out smooth as anything, and a giant smile crept over my face and Mrs. Vincent's.

"Your granddaddy would be so proud of you."

Suddenly, the pipes began to make a horrendous sound, like a wildebeest in heat, then the fixtures began to shake and groan as an impressive eruption of violent water shot up out of the drain and soaked me through and through. I yelped. Mrs. Vincent yelped. Scurrying under the sink again, I twisted the cutoff valve and shut the water down, but it was too late for my clothes or Mrs. Vincent's kitchen drapes.

Slowly, I tossed my tools back into the box, shut it, and squished over to the phone hanging wet on the wall. Mrs. Vincent stood there, nice as anything, wringing water out of her housecoat.

"Who're you calling?" she asked.

"A plumber."

I backed out of Mrs. Vincent's door with a $250 receipt from Speedy Plumbers clutched in my hand, my feet squishing inside my Nikes, and two more of her muffins in my toolbox. I should have gone into plumbing instead of investigations. It paid better and nobody told you to mind your own business. The knock at the vestibule door startled me, and I turned to find Father Ray Heaton standing on the other side, smiling sweetly. I opened the door.

"Pop, what're you doing here?"

He noticed the soaking, shot me an amused grin. "I was in the neighborhood. What in blue blazes?" The sounds of New Orleans tripped off his tongue as easy as anything; his eyes twinkled mischievously. "You been swimming somewhere?"

We had a standing date for chess and life talk every Wednesday night that had been going on since I was a kid. Twenty years on, we were still keeping it up, though the chitchat part had graduated from peer pressure, homework, and high school, to more adult subjects, which sometimes got a little dicey when you were discussing them with a priest. Pop had helped my grandparents raise me, offering guidance, counsel, and perspective to all of us when we needed it most. They'd lost their only child and never got over it, holding tight to me, her facsimile, as though that would give them a little bit of her back. Meanwhile, I kicked out at grief in ways that sometimes overwhelmed them, never by design. My childhood was rough, the last two years rougher, but Pop was always there to make sense of it; he remained a constant, my North Star. Today was Tuesday, though, not Wednesday, and he wasn't holding his lucky chessboard.

I smiled. "Mrs. Vincent's sink. Unintentional."

He was dressed in his black suit and clerical collar and swinging his black umbrella, the only one I remember him ever carrying. The vinyl canopy was a bit beaten up and the wooden crook handle was worn smooth by decades of Pop's hand gripping it, but it still kept the rain off, and so he would not part with it, despite the number of fancier umbrellas people gifted him with every birthday and Christmas. The black suit paired with the old umbrella made him look a little like the Penguin, minus the waddle, the nose, and the psychotic propensity for mayhem. He stepped inside.

"I'm sure it's one heck of a story. I can't wait to hear it."

He followed me upstairs to my apartment and hooked his umbrella on the hat rack by the door as he'd done a million times before. I tossed *Plumbing for Dummies* into the wastebasket, never wanting to see it again, and set my toolbox down by the door. "What's up? Want a ginger ale or something?"

He waved me off. "I'll get it myself. You go get out of those wet clothes before you catch your death. I'll meet you in the kitchen. Hope you have some of those cookies I like."

I smiled, peddling away toward the bedroom. "Cabinet on the left. Back in a minute."

I was back in five, having had to hang my sweat socks over the bathroom towel rack to dry them out. I swapped wet jeans for dry ones and my tried-and-true U of I T-shirt for the one I had on. I ran my fingers through my choppy hair, but left it to dry on its own. I felt renewed as I padded into the kitchen to find Pop on a stool at my kitchen island munching on a Milano cookie, a cold ginger ale there to wash it down.

"So? Why were you wet?"

I grabbed a cookie from the bag, took a bite. I deserved it. I'd nearly drowned on dry land and had to pay a plumber $250. I took a second cookie. I deserved that one, too. "A leaky faucet downstairs turned into an eruption."

"Ah, that's okay then. I was worried it was work related." He shook his head. "I still can't begin to understand what you do for a living now. The police work was nerve-wracking enough. This PI thing is dangerous, and you're out there by yourself."

I smiled. "I could say the same for you, you know—battling Satan, dunking warm babies into cold birdbaths."

He chuckled, shrugged. "Somebody's gotta do it." He watched me intently. "How're you getting along?" Since the rooftop, he'd asked the same question every time he saw me; every time I gave the same answer.

"The pills are still in the bottle."

He nodded, smiled. We were quiet for a time. It was an easy silence.

"This is Tuesday. You didn't bring your chessboard. What's wrong?"

He glanced over at me. "A detective at work?"

"It's not like I can turn it off."

I watched as his hand hovered over the bag of cookies, and then drew away without taking one. "Mind if we talk for a bit?"

He'd turn sixty-nine next March, and didn't look it, despite the thinning gray hair. But now, really looking at him, he appeared older than he had even last week, as if something were bothering him, something big. My gut clenched. "Of course not."

He hesitated just slightly, but it was enough to send a niggle of dread sliding down my spine. "Pop?"

His eyes met mine. I waited, my pulse quickening. He was sick, I thought. Cancer. Again. He was going to die of cancer, like my mother, and didn't know how to tell me. I held my breath, my brain sputtering, my fears taking on a life of their own.

"I need a detective, or think I do."

I wasn't sure I heard him right. "What?"

"I need a detective."

I paused, relief flooding over me. I was a bit startled by his directness, but too relieved he wasn't dying to worry much about it. My appetite for the cookies was gone, though. I pushed them aside, focused in. "Why do you need a detective?"

He got up to pace the floor. "I've never been one to spook easily. Maybe it's just me getting old, but . . ." His voice trailed off. "I've got the sinking feeling that somebody's watching me."

I didn't know what I was expecting, but it hadn't been that.

Who follows a priest? Why bother? "What makes you think that?"

"Besides the feeling?"

I nodded.

"That's not the only strange thing. My car's been broken into, fires set in our garbage carts, a couple of busted windows in the rectory. Kid stuff, I told myself, but then I got to thinking, what if somebody got hurt? A parishioner or one of the kids at the school?"

"When did all this start?"

Pop shrugged, turned his back to me—avoidance. I knew the signs. I'd perfected them in Voigt's office. "A few weeks, maybe."

I stood. "Then why am I just now hearing about it?"

He turned to face me. "Because I didn't want to worry you over it, that's why."

"A fire? A break-in?"

"A *little* fire and a *little* break-in."

"And you reported this to the police." It was not a question.

He waved me off. "Let's try not to make a big thing out of this. I ruffle feathers, you know that. I'd just like it to stop is all. I thought maybe you could poke around like you do. See if anything jumps out at you."

I grabbed a notepad from a drawer, mostly to keep my hands steady. Just the thought of anybody harassing Pop made my blood boil. "Who do you think it is?"

He fell silent. "Truthfully? It could be any number of people."

It was true. Pop was a burr in a lot of sides. He harassed slumlords, linked arms in human daisy chains to block neighborhood crack houses. Every news station in the city had B-roll of him sitting in at hooker pickup points or staring down grungy cashiers behind the counters of filthy stores that sold beer and crack pipes to children along with the expired milk and overpriced toilet paper. "Who recently?" I asked.

"I don't always see eye to eye with everyone on everything. Doesn't mean people want to do me harm."

"And yet someone seems to want to do just that. Give me a name."

"I've chosen forgiveness and understanding. My primary concern is the safety of the parish, like I said."

"I need a place to start, Pop. Your forgiveness and understanding are not going to help me here." He looked away. He was probably reciting a prayer in his head. That's what priests did, wasn't it? Turn to divine guidance. I wanted to scream out in frustration, shake him. "Pop?"

He turned back. Our eyes held. His were full of kindness and compassion. They were patient eyes. It slowly dawned on me that we weren't talking about some unknown stalker; he knew who was doing these things. Soon after that revelation came this one—he wasn't going to tell me.

"I've given you enough to get started. I've seen you do more with less."

I sputtered. "What? You've given me *nothing*. I need information. I get you're—" I stopped midsentence. "You won't tell me because you can't. That's it, isn't it? Someone confessed to you, and now you're bound by that seal thing. Is that it?"

Pop's eyes twinkled; he smiled. He didn't have a mean bone in his entire body. "Fire's a very dangerous thing, Cassandra. The church could catch, or the school. These are my people, my kids. I need them safe."

The kitchen phone hung from the wall. I picked up the receiver, dialed.

"Who're you calling?"

"The police." I got the desk sergeant at the Third District on the line and then handed the phone over to Pop. "Tell them everything."

While he talked, I paced. The call seemed to go on forever. Each detail Pop relayed felt like a stab to my heart from a hot knifepoint. I wore a path in the linoleum between the island and the dishwasher across the room. The pacing got a little monotonous after a while, but I was too keyed up to sit, too angry to stand still. Something Pop said to the cop on the phone, however, stopped me cold. The incidents had been going on not for a few weeks, but for three months.

I faced the kitchen window so he wouldn't see how startled and hurt I was that he'd kept all of this from me. How could I stop this? What did I need to do to find some nameless, faceless person? Pop couldn't help me; he was bound by the Seal of the Confessional. That left me next to nothing. I worked to keep my breathing steady. What could anyone have against a simple parish priest anyway, against Pop? How far were they willing to take it? When Pop's call ended, I turned back to him. "Three months?"

He exhaled. "Don't parents try and keep the hard things to themselves? Besides, you've got enough on your plate with the rehab and the new direction you're going in."

"I'm not a child anymore, Pop."

He slid his hands into his pockets, smiled. "Age doesn't make a bit of difference, that much I do know."

I cleared my throat, trying to dislodge the lump in it. "We can talk about that later, and we *will* talk about it. What'd the police say?"

"They'll have a car swing by the church a few times tonight to make sure everything's all right. Somebody will be by in the morning to take a report. The officer recognized me by name, turns out. I've been detained over there a few times, you know. Nice bunch of folks."

"You were arrested, not detained."

He shrugged, grinned. "I think detained sounds friendlier, don't you?"

I couldn't think clearly about much at the moment; I was too worried. "I'll follow you home, check the place, and make sure you're all locked in." These were things I could do now, things I knew how to do. Pop opened his mouth to argue. I narrowed my eyes. "That's nonnegotiable."

He sighed. "And just like that, the child becomes the parent."

"I'm going to find out who's doing this," I told him, as though issuing a challenge.

"Then what?"

"Then I'll make them knock it the Hades off."

He smiled, amused. "You could've said Hell. I'm familiar with it."

"You're wearing the collar. It didn't seem right."

We padded out. I grabbed my car keys from the bowl in the entryway. Pop grabbed his umbrella from the rack. "It'll be good to get in early. There's a whopper of a storm coming."

I flicked off the lights and locked the door behind us. "You're right," I said, my jaw clenched. "There is."

Chapter 5

St. Brendan's Church, cross shaped and gray stoned, sat stoically on a good half block of land at the head of a quiet T-shaped street dotted with single-family homes and three-flats. The rectory, fashioned from the same stone, sat next door, the two buildings separated by a small courtyard with a well-worn statue of St. Brendan in its center.

I followed Pop inside the rectory and checked the ground-floor windows and doors to make sure they were locked and secured. Then I went outside and walked the perimeter with a Maglite, training its beam into every shadow and under every scraggly bush. A black wrought-iron fence about six feet high separated the church and rectory from a narrow alley, which was particularly murky at dusk because of the impending storm, and also because someone had busted out a couple of the alley lights.

Across the alley stood more brick three-flats, their sooty sides facing the church's back fence. A block north on the main drag, CTA buses lumbered up and down the wide street at irregular intervals like tired mastodons with miles to trek to the nearest watering hole, their slow progress announced by rude engine burps, hydraulic hisses, and the stench of diesel exhaust.

I jiggled the latch on the back gate. It was a joke, but it would have to do until Pop could get someone to shore it up. Looking for places someone unhinged might duck and hide behind, I checked inside every trash cart and every alcove and nook, but found nothing but a lot of smelly garbage and a couple of stray cats hoping I had a juicy morsel to share.

Pop was standing in the rectory doorway when I made my way back, the door open wide, the light from the foyer shining down on his head like a halo. He couldn't have made himself an easier target if he'd actually worked at it. I said, "I asked you to stay inside."

"How could I when you were out there by yourself with nothing but a flashlight?"

I flicked off the light, slid it into my left pocket, my right pocket hanging low from the weight of my Glock. "I have more than a flashlight, Pop."

He held up a hand. "Don't tell me. I don't want to know."

It began to drizzle. I flicked my hood up. "I'll keep watch tonight so I can be here when the police swing by."

Pop shook his head no. "No, ma'am, you go on home. I'll be perfectly fine all locked up inside. Thea will be here at six like always."

"Where's Father Pascoe?" I asked. He was the parish's new transfer, a vinegary, curmudgeonly killjoy, far too stodgy for someone twenty years Pop's junior.

"Personal business. He'll be here in the morning, too. Go on now."

A sudden boom of thunder and a streak of lightning lit up the courtyard.

"So, it's you alone in the house during a thunderstorm, and someone's after you?"

"I'm never alone, neither are you. Read your Bible."

I shook my head, a stubborn child digging her heels in. "I'm not moving from this spot till the cops get here in the morning."

Pop pulled a face. "You'll go now, or I'll call them back and tell them you're the one harassing me. It's a night in your own bed or one at the police station."

"You wouldn't."

"If it'll get you home warm and safe, I sure would."

I glowered at him, turned to leave, but stopped.

"Get walking," Pop said. "And, Cassandra, don't let me look out this window and find you sitting in your car watching my curtains. You did your search. I'm locked up tight as a drum. I'll see you tomorrow. Come early and I'll even cook you some breakfast before Thea shows up and throws me out of her kitchen."

I didn't move. Knowing the housekeeper would be there at six didn't make me feel any better about leaving. Suddenly, the light drizzle became a steady downpour. I stood there as still as a pillar getting soaked. Second time today. Two times too many.

"You should be walking."

"Fine, but the lock on that gate is pathetic. You need a sturdy padlock."

"I'll get somebody on that first thing."

"And it wouldn't hurt you to put some lights with motion sensors near the alley."

"That too," he said, shooing me toward the street. "Good night!" he called after me.

"Lock that door," I called back. "I want to hear it lock before I go a step further."

I stood there as he closed the door and locked it. Another clap of thunder rumbled overhead. I double-timed it to my car, dodging puddles. I pulled away from the curb reluctantly, and after one last glance at Pop's windows, I headed home. Pop was safe, for now. Tomorrow I'd make sure he stayed that way.

* * *

I spent a restless night punching pillows, watching my bedside clock mark time, and listening to the rain pelt against my windows as I thrashed away at Pop's problem, wondering what I was going to do about it. By three AM I was too anxious to even pretend I was getting any rest, but managed to last another two hours before I finally had to get up, get dressed, and head back to the church. The storm had moved on, and the weather was calm, the sun still hours from rising. I stopped on my way for a bag of Pop's favorite crullers. He'd promised breakfast, but cooking wasn't exactly his thing. The crullers were backups in case the eggs, toast, and OJ went horribly wrong.

Pop didn't answer the rectory bell, even after three insistent rings. Bewildered, I peeked through the side window. Through a break in the curtains I could see that the lamp in his office was on. I rapped on the window, but he didn't acknowledge that either. He was an early riser, and there was nothing wrong with his hearing. After the talk we'd had the day before and my fitful night, I began to worry.

I dug my cellphone out of my pocket and called inside. I could hear the phone ringing, but no one picked up. I ended the call, then turned to scan the deserted courtyard, noticing only then that the church's side door stood ajar. I breathed a sigh of relief. That's where he was. It was a little early for church praying if you asked me, even for a priest, but Pop was Pop. I headed over, more than a little put out, prepared to give him a good talking to. Honestly, sometimes adults acted more like children. If you think someone's stalking you, do you hang out alone in an empty church with the door standing open? No, you don't. Pop may as well have hung a sign around his neck reading: HERE I AM. COME AND GET ME.

I pulled the door wide open by its Gothic handle, the creaking noise it made resembling that of a warped prison door in a dank dungeon. "Pop? C'mon, you're killing me here." The church was dark, cold, and eerily silent, like no one had been inside it in a thousand years, despite the cloying remnants of candle wax, wood varnish, and spent incense. What had he come over here for? I stood just inside the door blinking into the shadows, waiting for my eyes to adjust, my ears peeled for any sound other than the ones I was making.

"Pop? Are you in here?"

He didn't answer. There was a small vestry out back. Its lights were on. That's where he had to be, I thought, relieved that I'd found him. But why was he here at the crack of dawn? Maybe he had a prayer emergency. Was there such a thing? Couldn't you pray anywhere? In the rectory, say? Where it was safe and the doors were locked? I felt my way along the dark wood paneling, my fingers skimming along the wall, heading toward the light. The crullers inside the bag I carried were getting cold. Who wants a cold cruller? Nobody, that's who.

"A little creepy, Pop, church or no church," I called out as I made my way back. "And just so you know? Your crullers are as good as hockey pucks now." I pushed the door to the vestry open, fumbling for the switch that would turn the lights on in the rest of the church. I stood in the doorway waiting as the old lights sputtered to life and the cavernous nave behind me emerged from darkness. I expected to see Pop sitting at his desk, engrossed in something, having lost all sense of time, but he wasn't there. An old institutional clock snicked time on the wall, the tick of its second hand the only sound in the close little room. Hymnals with frayed spines sat on cluttered bookshelves, vestments hung from hangers in a closet nook, and a large pedestal fan stood idle and cobwebby in a corner. But no Pop. The worry was back, joined by a healthy dose of foreboding.

I glanced out through a wide archway at the altar table— monolithic, incorruptible—covered in a white cloth embroidered in vibrant color at the borders. On top, the altar book lay open on a golden bookstand. There it was, I thought, the center, the lodestone, the heart of Saint Brendan's, the heart of any church. I turned to leave, but caught something out of the corner of my eye sprawled on the altar steps. I dropped the bag and drew my gun, my hands as cold as ice.

"Pop!"

I forced myself forward, my eyes, the gun, sweeping over the quiet church, my legs shaking, feeling already a growing weight crush hard against my chest. The blood trail began just shy of the altar table, droplets at first, widely spaced, perfect little circles of congealing crimson.

The dead boy lay at the foot of the steps, his black eyes half open, a bullet hole in his chest. Beneath him was a wide carpet of blood, nearly dry. . . . His arms were outstretched, Christlike, his long, tapered fingers fixed in open claws painted in the same horror. He'd reached for something before death took him. Before he ceased to be, he'd skimmed his fingers along the cool, marble floor, leaving ten perfect tracts of desperation as his final mark.

I scanned the church wildly, no longer breathing. Pop? Nothing. No one. I stared up at the figure of the crucified Christ hanging below the massive rose window, wondering where he'd been when the boy died. I stepped carefully around the blood pool. No gun. No weapon of any kind. Cop mode. I needed cop mode.

Hispanic, I noted, taking in the scene. Maybe eighteen, twenty. Where was Pop? Black hair. Black eyes. Olive complexion. Five foot eight, five foot nine maybe? Pop hadn't been in the vestry, but the light was on. I checked around the altar, up and down the nave, over the pews, the darkened choir loft. No Pop. Back to the boy.

Gang tats, banger standard issue—baggy pants, white T-shirt, boots. He was a Scorpion, according to the faded ink etched along his neck. Way off his turf. Why? Blood had soaked through his clothing, nearly covering everything, the blood dried stiff, more brown now than red. I'd never seen him before. I backed away, searching.

"Pop, Dammit, answer me!" I reeled 360 degrees, frantic. There was a dead boy in Pop's church. Pop was not in the rectory where I'd left him. A dead boy. In Pop's church. I shook my head as if to clear it. It didn't make sense. How could this make sense? How could there be a dead boy *here*? "Pop!"

I peddled back, away from the blood, the body, my stomach roiling, fear charging its way up my throat like a ravenous beast. I saw the shoe sticking out of the confessional box. A hard-soled shoe, like the kind Pop wore. I stumbled forward, gun still up, every neuron firing. I'd forgotten how to breathe. The shoe was attached to a leg, a leg in dark pants, like the kind Pop wore. My vision blurred, my heart pounded in my chest. My legs threatened to give way.

The body knelt slumped forward, the head pressed against the latticework in the narrow window that separated priest from penitent. I recognized the ear. It had listened to so many of my troubles over the years. Above it were the familiar flecks of gray, distinguished looking in a man of sixty some odd years. The right arm hung limp, streaks of dried blood mottling the graceful fingers. More blood had seeped between the slats of the hardwood flooring beneath. The gun just lay there. Matte black. A cheap throwaway. Discarded? Dropped?

My gun slipped out of my hand. I fell to my knees, my throat constricting, my insides on fire. The body was on its knees on the padded kneeler. I didn't want to look, to see, but I couldn't turn away. I could hear my own heartbeat echoing in my ears and the blood rushing through them like the crash of ocean tide. *No. No. No.* The word echoed in my head. Just the one; it was all I had.

I stood, or thought I did. I forced myself forward, or thought I did. I didn't want to see more, I didn't need to. I knew what it was before I saw it all. I could feel the stillness in my bones already, the loss in my heart. It was Pop.

I ran for the courtyard to be sick, and that's when my legs finally gave out. I fell to my knees in the grass and buried my head in my hands, rocking, trying to force myself to process, to think.

"Cass? What's wrong?" I looked up at someone. A woman. Someone I should know, but at the moment couldn't place. She looked worried, frightened. Who was she? "Cass?"

Thea. It came to me in a flash. It was Thea Bey, Pop's housekeeper. "Call 911," I croaked.

Her eyes widened, darted around the courtyard. "Why? What's happened?"

"Pop's dead. The boy's dead. Call 911, now."

I doubled over, my forehead to the cool grass, and wailed like a wounded animal.

From the window in Pop's office, I stood watching as a crowd gathered behind the police barricades. Ghouls, all of them, I thought, each one with a cellphone, each phone trained on the officers and paramedics milling around out in front of Pop's church. What were they hoping to see? Why didn't they just go home and leave him be? I eased down into his chair, ran my hands along the top of his messy desk. I wasn't sure how I'd gotten from the courtyard to here. I vaguely remembered Thea lifting me, but it all felt like a horrible dream. But I was awake now. Now I could think.

I looked around at the remnants of a vibrant life committed to service. A scuffed basketball shared a corner chair with a worn baseball mitt; Pop was the coach of both school teams. The overstuffed chairs held piles of books, all topics, and the bookshelves were filled to overflowing with more. Even along the windowsills, the book piles stacked up like wobbly towers. He read everything. He encouraged his kids to do the same.

Who would get Pop's things, I wondered. I looked around at everything and wanted it all—every scrap of paper, every pencil. I wanted this room to stay just as it was right now. I wanted no one to move a single thing in it. Who was that boy? What had happened here?

"Hey."

I looked up to find Ben, my old partner, standing in the doorway looking grim and heart heavy. He walked in and quietly shut the door behind him. "I came to take you home. You should get some rest."

I shook my head, stood, and turned back to the window, to the ghouls. "No."

Ben eased in beside me and quietly drew the curtains so I couldn't see the onlookers reveling in the street. I offered no protest. It's what I should have done. "They're not finished processing. It'd be better if you went home." Our eyes locked. "You know how this works. If I were in your spot right now, you'd be hauling my ass home, too."

"And you wouldn't go, just like I'm not going." I began to pace the floor. "Who's lead on this? I need to talk to whoever it is."

Ben avoided looking at me. "Cass, for the love of God, will you just let me take you home?"

"Who?"

He shook his head. "Farraday."

I heard myself scream, and it felt as though my feet lifted up off the carpet. Ben rushed over, gathered me up before I fell over. "I know how you feel, but this, right now, is not going to help anybody."

I fought against his hold, shoved him away. The thought of Farraday standing for Pop made me want to be sick all over again. To him, Pop would be just another case, just another body. I tried to step around Ben to get to the door, but he barred my way. "Dammit! Get out of my way!" I screeched, scrubbing my hands across my face. When he wouldn't, I retreated to a far corner. Ben watched me burrow in, knowing I needed the space. "I'm sorry. I didn't mean that," I said.

"I know."

We were silent for a time. I wanted Pop. I didn't want this.

"I'm not going anywhere. You tell Farraday that."

"I'll come and find you when it's done," Ben said. I nodded, not trusting myself to speak. "Or I can stay here, if you need me."

I did need him, but I wanted him with Pop more. I didn't want Pop to be alone with Farraday, not for a single second. I shouldn't have left Pop here alone, not after what he'd told me. If I'd stayed, he would be alive. "I'm fine. Go."

I could tell Ben was upset for me. We weren't partners anymore, but he still had my back, and I had his. We were still friends. He moved for the door, turned back. "What is there to steal from a church?"

"He came to see me yesterday. He thought someone was following him, but he couldn't tell me who."

"Following him? Why?"

I shrugged. Even that was an effort. "I wanted him safe, so I followed him home. I locked him in. I was going to stay and keep watch, but he wouldn't let me. I should have refused to go. If I had . . ."

"Stop it. This is not on you. We don't know what this is yet."

"And we won't. Not with Farraday on it. He won't be thorough. He won't get it right."

"Then we'll do what we always do, we'll work around him. I promise we'll figure this out. I've got him for you."

I smiled, or think I did. "Thanks, for everything."

"What're partners for?"

My eyes held his. "You've got a new partner now."

"Doesn't change anything for me. You?"

I shook my head slowly.

"Good. Then it's like I said."

Ben's assurances gave me some solace. That was something. "I'd like to see Pop before they take him."

"Sure thing."

I opened the curtains again to watch the death spectators behind the barricades, their greedy eyes glued to the spectacle, as though they'd paid their nickel and now wanted to see the bearded lady in the sideshow tent. Ghouls, all of them.

Chapter 6

I was able to see Pop when they wheeled him out. I said good-bye. Then I went back to his office and waited for Farraday to find me. It had been two years since I'd last set eyes on him, and when he walked in, I could tell in an instant that he hadn't changed. His dull face offered its usual haughty smirk, as though he smelled something foul in every room he entered, and his dark hair, cut short and heaped in product, framed a bulbous nose mapped by tiny spider veins that hinted at late nights of heavy drinking. His eyes, devoid of empathy, were as dark and as bottomless as a shark's. It was difficult to believe that anyone anywhere could find comfort in them. He hadn't aged well. Maybe Jimmy Pick weighed on him, too. His blazer and pants were still well tailored, and, as I remembered, his police star, hooked prominently to his designer belt, was polished so that it gleamed, as if to announce to the world: *Hey, look. I'm the police. I'm the police.*

"Raines," he said, his mouth twisted in a half grin. "Long time."

Long time? Two years, one rooftop, one dead kid. I stood to

face him, not wanting to give him the satisfaction of towering over me. Ben eased into the room behind him and stood quietly by the door; his new partner, Paul Helms, stood dutifully beside him. Farraday was here alone. Did he have a partner? If so, who was the unfortunate detective who'd drawn the short straw?

"I understand you knew the victim. Father, uh—" He flipped through the pages of his notepad, presumably searching for Pop's name.

"Father Raymond Heaton." I wanted to kill Farraday. I wanted it more than I wanted to take my next breath.

He looked up from the page as though we were discussing the latest Cubs score or the price of summer ham. "Right. Father Heaton. Mickerson says you were close. Sorry for your loss." He sped through the perfunctory condolence as though the words were hot rocks burning his tongue. "You seem to think this might have something to do with an enemy he might have had?"

The room fell silent. I stood listening to the ticking of Pop's old clock, breathing in the scents of his sweater slung over the back of his chair and the bowl of peppermints he kept on his desk for tongue-tied parishioners in for compassionate counsel. He'd never wear the sweater again, never enjoy the candy. I could feel tears coming, but I'd be damned if I'd cry in front of Farraday. I turned my back to him, faced Ben and Paul instead. "What can you tell me?"

Ben cleared his throat, stepped forward for the report. "Doesn't look like anything's missing, far as we can tell, but we haven't let anyone else in there yet who might know for sure. No wallet on either of them. We found Father Ray's in his room. Some kind of break-in, maybe, but that's preliminary."

"We're thinking maybe he hears or sees something and goes over to check it out," added Paul. "Things go bad after that."

Farraday moved around to face me, his eyes ablaze. "Hey,

I'm lead on this. I ask the questions. You met the vic last night, so what were you doing back here so early that you found the bodies?"

I stared at him for a time, but said nothing. *The vic.* It was Pop, not the vic. "I was coming for breakfast. He didn't answer at the rectory. I saw the church door open and went to check it out."

"Did you touch anything?"

The question was insulting. I could tell from his smug expression that he meant it to be. I turned away from him again, faced Ben. "No ID on the kid? Prints?"

"We bagged his hands, but we haven't run them yet. Right now, he's still unknown."

Farraday jockeyed around again, this time inserting himself between us, so close I could smell his cheap cologne. He reeked of it. "You don't hear so good, that it? This investigation is for stars only, and last time I checked, you don't have one, do you?"

I was on overload, on the verge of tears, my chest heavy with grief, shock, fatigue. Pummeling him would be the wrong thing to do, but it was all I could think about. I willed myself to keep my arms at my side. Ben and Paul stepped forward, but I held up a hand to stop them from engaging. We stood there waiting for Farraday.

"The gun next to Heaton is shy two rounds," Farraday said. "Seeing as it's with him, it follows he fired it. Obviously, the wound to his temple is self-inflicted. He catches the kid, they wrestle for the gun, the kid gets shot. Priest then, full of remorse, can't take the guilt and kills himself. Some kind of penance thing. Evidence should check out pretty neatly. Now I've got a few questions for you, since you stumbled blind into all this."

That was as much as I could take. "You haven't even finished processing the scene; the ME doesn't even have the bodies on her table. Nothing's certain, nothing's obvious. What's wrong with you?"

He smirked. "I know what I'm doing, and I plan on doing it without your interference. Despite what you think, I do have what it takes."

I watched him, acid and loathing eating away at the lining of my stomach. "You don't have what it takes to pull lead on a dog leash." I watched as his face flushed bright red. "This one I'm going to make sure you don't fumble. I'm on it every step of the way, star or no star. You want to get me off it, you're going to have to lock me up." I held up my wrists for the handcuffs. "Go on. Do it, or step off."

Farraday drew in closer, his voice low. "It's not my fault you blew a kid away. That's on you. I'm not the killer cop here." He backed away, flipped his notepad closed. "You stay out of my way." He glanced at Ben and Paul. "And that goes for everybody."

The dangerous smile Ben gave him was one I knew well. He took a step toward Farraday, Paul easing up beside him. Partners stuck together. Farraday was in trouble. "One more word, Jimbo," Ben said, "and you and me are going to have a problem your daddy can't fix."

Farraday grinned. "You threatening me, Mickerson? Because it sure sounds like you are."

The quiet face-off felt interminable.

"You're going to want to mosey on along now," Ben said finally. Farraday hesitated, then flicked me a disdainful look and sauntered quietly out of the office. The three of us stood in silence until we heard the hallway empty of cops and the front door slam shut.

"My blood pressure's got to be in the thousands," Ben said. "What a dick."

"He's a dick with a lot of other important dicks propping him up," Paul said.

"Doesn't mean I won't kick his dick ass," Ben said.

"Or that I won't help you," Paul said.

I stared down at my unfettered wrists. It was all too much. Pop was gone. Farraday was in charge of his case, and I was powerless to change any of it.

Ben gripped my shoulder. "Cass?"

I pulled away, looked up at him. "He got on the wrong side of someone. He told me in as many words. He asked for my help, and he's going to get it."

Thea stuck her head in the door, her eyes red rimmed, exhausted. "I started water for tea. A cup would do us both good." I shook my head no. I didn't have the patience for tea.

"Sit tight," Ben said. "We'll finish up, then I'll drive you home."

When they slipped quietly out, I slid down onto Pop's chair and placed my hands palms down on his desk, hoping to feel him radiating up from the wood, but the desk was cold. Someone had been following him, someone he knew. I pulled my hands away and began to rifle through his papers, looking for something, anything that would explain why he was gone.

"What are you doing?" Thea asked, a damp Kleenex wadded up in nervous hands. "The police said we're not supposed to touch any of his things."

I ignored her, squeezing my eyes shut when flashes of Pop's dead body intruded, causing my hands to shake. I'd never get that image out of my head. For a moment, I thought of Voigt's pills, now stuck in a drawer somewhere at home. I hadn't taken a single one after the rooftop, after Voigt's sessions. He'd been wrong. It *was* a battle of wills, me against them, and I'd won. I'd crawled my way back from misery without a single tablet. Right now, though, with Pop dead, I craved the momentary oblivion they offered. "I know what I'm doing. Go drink your tea."

Thea drew closer, watching. "It can wait."

The top of the desk offered up nothing interesting. I scanned the office. I knew it well. I'd been here many times before, for chess, for counsel. The mahogany table against the far wall held an often-replenished bowl of jelly beans, which neither Pop nor the school kids he welcomed in could get enough of. Behind the candy sat rows of framed photographs, a few with Pop shaking hands with local dignitaries, even the mayor. Those, however, were pushed well back behind the photos of smiling children: Pop's kids. What would they do now? What would I do?

I slid open the top drawer, quickly picking through pens, paper clips, and assorted dreck, but my mind was on the cops across the way, on Farraday. This was his job, I knew, but that mattered little. I started on the other drawers, finding nothing in the way of personal papers—no treasured birthday cards kept as a memento, no bank statements, no letters from old friends. Pop didn't hold onto stuff; he held onto people instead. The left bottom drawer held parish forms, phonebooks, carry-out menus, stacks of thank-you notes from churches—St. Ambrose, St. Rita, St. Margaret.

"He went everywhere," Thea said.

I looked up, having forgotten she was even there, then went back to searching.

"He liked to visit other parishes. That's how we started our homeless outreach. He saw it somewhere else and brought it here. We served lunch and made sure whoever needed it got a new pair of shoes, a sweater, or a referral to social services." She sniffled. "But you know all that already. I can't seem to stop talking."

Pop had been proud of the program, and he should have been. It did a lot of good. I kept looking. Finally, I pulled the handle on the last drawer, but it wouldn't budge. I yanked harder, feeling just a little give in the latch. It was locked, not stuck. With a little more effort, I could probably just yank it free, but not without busting the lock. Thea and I exchanged a wary look.

"Oh, please tell me you're not going to force that open."

I let the handle go, just for a moment. If there were keys, I'd have found them by now. I remembered I'd seen a letter opener and fished around in the top drawer again until I found it.

"Wait." Thea stepped forward. "This doesn't feel right."

I looked up at her, feeling her pain, knowing it matched mine, but Pop was dead, violently taken. And then there was the rage and the call of the pills and the incompetent Farraday. I popped the lock.

We stared at the gray lockbox, neither of us saying anything or making a move to lift it out of the drawer, cautious, as if it were a living, unpredictable thing capable of biting off a finger if you came at it wrong. When I finally lifted the box out and set it on the desk, Thea breathed a sigh of relief, and then moved in closer to see what else might be inside the drawer.

"Legal pads," I said, drawing out a stack of yellow pages. "His sermons, handwritten, going back months." I set them on the desk. There was nothing else in the drawer, so I shut it. The lockbox opened by sliding a tab to release the latch, but when I did that, nothing happened. Pop had locked that.

"The letter opener again?" Thea asked, pain creasing her face.

"You should go," I said.

She shook her head. "No, ma'am. I want to know what you know."

I thought for a moment, then carefully turned the box bottom side up, finding a tiny silver key taped to the underside by a short squib of masking tape.

Thea's face lit up. "How'd you know?"

"Small key. Easy to lose. This is where I'd keep it." I opened the box.

"His personal things," Thea said.

There was a passport inside, Pop's, a checkbook, credit card receipts. There was also a neat stack of business cards tucked up against the side, held together by a heavy rubber band. "Plumber. Notary public. Dentist."

Thea peered at them over my shoulder. "Dr. Mendel. I see him, too. Nice man."

I read through the old credit card receipts. There were a lot of charges from about a year ago for clothing and shoes from men's stores, which surprised me. Pop wore basic black almost every day. Where was this vast new wardrobe he'd gone into hock for?

There were also charges for airline tickets, dated last May. I couldn't recall him taking a trip or being gone for even a day. "The Red Roof Inn in Los Angeles," I said, reading the next charge down. "A two-day stay." I held the statement up for Thea to see. "What was he doing there?"

I could tell from her confused expression that she hadn't a clue.

I read on. "There's a charge for a single one-way ticket out there. Two days later there's a new charge for two tickets back to Chicago. Who'd he come back with? And why can't I remember him being gone?" Thea asked.

I sat holding the statement. I had no answers. The front door of the rectory suddenly creaked open down the hall. Probably Ben, coming back to collect me. I slid the receipts into my pocket, the sermons, too. "I'm taking these."

"But you know what the police said."

I stood, faced the door. "I'm still taking them."

Chapter 7

I was twelve and my mother was dead. The smiling priest stood over me, blocking out the sun. "Punch it," he said. I stared up at him as if he were crazy. I'd come to sit quietly on the bench outside the church, away from the oppressive sadness inside, away from my mother's body in the casket. I wanted to be alone. I wanted peace. I wanted to run until I ran out of road. I had had a good mother just over a week ago. She cared for me, knew everything about me; now she was gone. I felt untethered, set adrift in the world, lost.

He smiled, holding a pillow to his chest. I wondered briefly where he'd gotten it, then decided with a sigh that I didn't care. Adults were strange. There was no figuring them out.

I turned my head, ignored him. I didn't have time for childish things anymore. When I turned back he was still there.

He tossed the pillow to me. "You'll feel a lot better if you sock something. Really whale on it."

I threw the pillow back. "Go away."

"You want me to get your daddy for you? He's right inside."

I smirked. My father wasn't holding up. He didn't know how.

I shook my head, squeezed my eyes shut. When I opened them again, the priest tossed the pillow back. It was a stupid game.

"The point here, kiddo, is that you need to whale on it to get the anger out. Make room for other stuff. Go on. Take a shot."

I turned away from him again. He could eat the pillow for all I cared. I threw it down on the bench beside me. "Leave me alone."

"Want to hit me instead?"

I faced him, glowered. It was a tantalizing offer. "Who are you, anyway?"

He held out a friendly hand, which I stared at, but didn't take. "Father Raymond Heaton. I just transferred here." He scanned the courtyard. "Pretty place. I think I'm gonna like it." He beamed down at me, his face so open, so kind, I softened some in spite of myself.

"You talk funny."

He shrugged, smiled. "Could say the same about you. I hail from New Orleans. They call it the Crescent City. Best city in the world. . . . You ready for that pillow now?"

"Then will you go away?"

He chuckled, the corners of his eyes wrinkling in a comforting sort of way. He stood tall and straight, just beginning to gray at the temples. He was a good man. I didn't know how I knew it, but I did. "Sorry. I kinda come with the church now. Package deal, you could say."

"I can figure this out on my own."

He watched me, smiling. "I believe you can. But isn't it a wonderful thing that you don't have to?"

He picked up the pillow and tossed it to me a third time. This time I caught it.

"You're gonna feel a whole lot better. I guarantee it."

"And if I don't?"

He shrugged. "Then I'll just have to think of something else, won't I?"

I took the pillow and beat it until my knuckles ached, and a mound of goose feathers lay at my feet.

"Cass?" I jumped, startled at the sound of my name being called. I looked up into Thea's worried face. She eased down beside me on the bench and plopped her handbag onto her lap, her stout frame bundled into a warm sweater, wisps of black hair fluttering out from under a sturdy knit cap. It looked as though she hadn't slept in a hundred years. "You looked like you were a million miles away."

I offered a weak smile. I hadn't slept, of course. Instead, I'd poured over the things I'd taken from Pop's office the night before, but none of it meant anything yet. "I met him sitting right here. God, he pestered the hell out of me."

Thea smiled. She knew. "I like that pillow story. It's a fact he wouldn't let anything or anyone go. I'm living proof. I once begged him to leave me be. I was on the street, strung out, lowest I'd ever been, but he kept coming at me." She rapped her knuckles on the bench. "Fifteen years clean, all because of him."

I smiled. "You did the work."

She shrugged. "I couldn't disappoint him by *not* doing it." She was only in her early fifties, but it seemed as though she'd aged that and more since I'd seen her just a few hours ago. That's what grief does. It adds years and takes some away. She mournfully eyed the rectory door. "I don't think I can step one foot inside there again."

"You can. You will."

We both looked out onto the empty street. The school was closed. No kids to pile noisily into the building, just the birds in the trees and the two of us on the bench not knowing what to do with ourselves.

"There's still Father Pascoe to do for, of course, but Father Ray was the heart of the place."

"Pop said Pascoe had personal business to attend to. That's

why he wasn't here when I saw Pop home. Where is Pascoe now?" I didn't mean for it to come out as a condemnation, but it did.

Thea noticed. "He's not a bad man, just different. A little standoffish, sure, but his heart's in the right place."

"He never smiles. He acts like the parish is some alien planet he just crash-landed on. This is the South Side of Chicago, not Mars."

Thea shook her head. "Like I said, he's different. I don't know where he was, but I called his cell after the police showed up. I didn't want him to hear it from the news. He was so upset, he could hardly get a word out. I expect him anytime." Thea heaved out a weary breath. "He's in charge now, of course. And so you won't have to ask, I'll tell you. Before I found you in the courtyard I was at home, just me and my cat. He can't speak for me, but if he could, he would." Thea grew quiet. "I know it's hard for you to turn the cop off."

I stared at the yellow crime scene tape still strung across the side door of the church. The building would be off limits until all the evidence had been gathered. I burrowed into my jacket, trying hard not to think of the church as Pop's tomb. "He never said a word about the trouble he was having. . . . No one did."

Thea sighed. "You blame me."

Of course, it wasn't her fault. Not anyone's. Maybe not even mine, though it felt like it. Pop was stubborn and fiercely protective. Neither of us could have easily swayed him to do anything he didn't want to do. I put a reassuring hand on hers. "I don't."

Thea straightened. "You do, because *I* do. He kept saying it was nothing to worry about, that it would all pass. And I could be wrong, but it felt to me like he knew who was doing it, and he was trying to give them a chance to work it out for themselves."

"Did Father Pascoe know?"

She nodded. "And he wanted to call the police right away, but Father Ray wouldn't hear of it. He had to remind Father Pascoe that he was only the associate pastor." A faint smile swept over her face. "He didn't much like being reminded."

"You made Pop come to me?"

"I told him if he didn't, I would, and he knew I meant it." She blew her nose into a tissue. "I was scared for him, for all of us, and I didn't care how mad he got about it. You know how he was when he dug his heels in."

I nodded. "Unmovable."

"He could be a stubborn old cuss."

I chuckled, remembering. "Yes, he could."

"They wrote in the paper that he shot that boy, then himself. I know as sure as I'm sitting here that that's not true, and you do, too."

"Then who hated him enough to kill him?"

Thea turned, shock on her face. "You're asking me?"

"I found him in the confessional. Maybe he got there on his own, maybe he didn't. Maybe somebody thought he needed to atone for something. That feels personal. It feels close. You saw him every day. I need a name. Someone he got on the wrong side of."

Her eyes skittered away. "I don't know anyone who'd want to kill that man."

"Someone with a grudge."

Thea paused, her expression grim. "Folks can argue without being killers."

"Then whoever it is won't have anything to worry about."

She shot up from the bench. "I'd be naming somebody who probably didn't have a thing to do with this."

I stood. "Or you might be giving me the name of the person who killed him."

She stood there fretting over what to say, what to do. "It

feels like you're asking me to go behind his back." She shook her head. "I can't do that. He trusted me. You know what I owe him."

Thea turned on her heels and headed for the rectory. I followed. "I know you're loyal. I know you wouldn't dream of gossiping if he were here, but he's not here. He's dead." The words landed like daggers. "I need your help."

She turned to face me. "And what if I tell you, and it turns out they're innocent? Then what?"

"Who's they?" She moved to tear away from me, but I grabbed her arm lightly. "Thea, *please.*"

"I need to think this over." She pulled her arm free and walked away. Again, I followed. She unlocked the door and plowed inside. I rushed in after her. The empty feeling of the place nearly knocked the wind out of me. Thea headed full speed toward the kitchen out back, her domain. I matched her step for step. She slammed her bag on the kitchen table, shimmied out of her sweater. "Everyone has disagreements."

"Who did he have disagreements with?"

She threw up her arms in frustration. "Half the city, from the mayor on down."

"Thea, the mayor didn't sneak over here in a rainstorm and kill him."

"You're making a joke, but this isn't funny."

"Tell me about it."

We each took a step back, composed ourselves. We'd suffered a loss and hadn't yet found a way to deal with it. I gave her some space; she did the same for me. Finally, I saw her square her shoulders. "People expect their privacy to be protected. He took that seriously. He made me take it seriously, too."

"I understand, but he needs your help now. I need it. I'm asking for it."

She stood quietly, twisting the rings on her fingers, biting her lower lip. "I'm not some gossipy woman listening at key holes."

I nodded, but didn't speak, waiting for her to make up her mind.

"Sometimes you hear things." She hesitated. "Anton Bolek. That's a name. School's janitor. Something about him worried Father Ray, but before you ask, I don't know what that was. I know he discussed it with Father Pascoe, so you'll have to ask him."

"I will. Who else?"

Thea looked as though she were on the horns of a great dilemma. I felt like a heel for putting her there, but pressed on.

"George Cummings. He's a new parishioner, nice enough. He came in like gangbusters, though, volunteering right and left, a real old-fashioned kind of guy. He didn't much care for the modern Masses Father Ray went for, and told him so. I'm of the opinion that if you're the last one in, you should have less to say about how things are done, but it's clear he thinks differently." Thea made a face.

"And?"

"Nothing," Thea said. "He's a good family man."

"There's a but, Thea, I can see it on your face."

She sighed. "He's a little bossy, for my taste. I had a man like that once. Had to know everything all the time or he wasn't happy, and if he wasn't, I sure wasn't going to be. Men like that have to tell you how, when, and why to do a thing. They always have to be in the driver's seat." She shrugged. "That looks like love to some women. Janice Cummings seems to be one of them, but it's up to her what she settles for."

"And he and Pop had a problem?"

Thea nodded. "Something happened a couple months ago that Cummings got real upset about. He and Father Ray really went at it in his office. I could hear the yelling all the way in the kitchen. Afterward, he and his family stopped coming to church. Father Ray reached out after a few Sundays and things seemed to go back to the way they were with them working together, just like always." Thea turned her back to me, pulled the teakettle from the cabinet, and set it on the stove. "Maisie Ross. You know her." She had owned a store that sold alcohol and drug paraphernalia to kids, until Pop organized the community and closed her down.

"Pop got rid of her."

"And she held that against him, but it didn't stop her from opening up a store someplace else. He told you about the break-in a couple weeks ago?"

I was stunned. "He didn't tell me it was so recent."

"It was. Happened while Mass was going on. Well, they only took one thing—the Bible his mother left him."

"And you think that was Maisie?"

"I know it was her. She called for days afterward. She kept asking him, *'What's it say in the good book?'* She knew he wouldn't call the police. It wasn't his way, even for Maisie. She's a nasty piece of business, that one." Thea sighed. "He didn't take it half as bad as I did. All he said was he hoped she'd get good use out of it."

The revelation hit me like a boulder to the chest. He didn't tell me he'd lost his Bible. It seemed now he didn't tell me a lot of things. Pop's Bible. Now Maisie had it. He might not have wanted it back, but I sure did.

"I got the feeling there was something going on between him and Father Pascoe . . ." Thea added. "I could feel the tension. That's it. That's all I know."

It was a start. "Thanks, Thea." She nodded, her arms folded across her chest. "I didn't mean to push. I'm sorry."

"Yes, you did."

I thought for a moment before coming to terms with the truth of it. She was right. I would have pushed her to Gary and back if I had to. I was just sorry I had to. "I'm sorry just the same."

Thea's glare turned slowly into a smile. She shook her head. The smile grew. Just like that, she'd forgiven me. I breathed a sigh of relief. "You're just like him when you get all het up about something. God help you in getting along with that Detective Farraday."

"That'll never happen." I grinned sheepishly. "Bright side. You're inside the house."

Thea looked around. "I am at that." She faced me again, her arms down, a solemn look on her face. "I think, maybe he just panicked? That a horrible thing happened that went against everything he believed in, and he couldn't handle it."

I zipped up my jacket and felt for my keys, resolution straightening my spine. "He didn't. He knew I was coming. He had his faith, he had me. Someone did this, and I'm going to prove it." On my way out, I passed the church door and stopped to stare at the crime scene tape, shocked even now to see it there. Even through the heavy oak door, I could feel Pop's absence, and the loss of him cut right through me. I flipped up my collar and walked away.

Chapter 8

The parish school was closed in deference to Pop's passing, so I couldn't start with Anton Bolek. Thea knew where George Cummings lived and that he owned his own business in Englewood. I wasn't surprised that she knew that address, too. There was little that went on, in, or around St. Brendan's that Thea didn't know about, so whatever Pop had stumbled into, whatever trouble he'd kicked up, he scored big points for keeping it to himself, though it went without saying that I wished he hadn't.

I sat in my car, hands tight on the wheel, and stared blindly ahead. Farraday had been on the case just over twenty-four hours, and already he'd set about tying it up in a neat little bow. As far as he was concerned, Pop stumbled in on a burglary, and what happened after that was an inevitable end. Cue the press conference. But it wasn't that easy or that clean, nothing ever was. I knew that as surely as I knew the earth was round and oceans ran deep. There was someone out there who had met the dawn thinking they were free and clear of murder. I started the car and pulled out into the street headed south. Whoever it was, they were dead wrong. George Cummings's modest bungalow sat in the middle of a quiet block where all the houses looked the same, except for the color of the curtains. The yards were neat, lawns cut and edged, and the houses well maintained. No one answered the bell when I rang it. The curtains were drawn, the driveway empty. I pressed my ear to the door, but heard nothing from inside. The garage had room inside for two cars, but when I peered through the garage windows, I saw only one brown Cutlass Supreme inside, and it looked like it'd been there a while.

"Looking for something?"

I whirled around to face an old black woman, thin, bird-like, her arms crossed over a scrawny bosom. She stood at the foot of the driveway, staring me down, her fingers poised over the keypad of a cellphone. "I know you don't live there, so you got no reason to be peeking in the windows. We got neighborhood watch, just so you know."

"I'm looking for George Cummings. He doesn't answer."

"So you thought you'd trample all over his grass and press your nose to his windows?"

I smiled. "Occupational hazard, I guess." I pulled my business card from my bag and handed it to her. "I'd like to ask him a few questions about the trouble over at the church two nights ago."

The woman slid the phone into her pocket. I guess I no longer looked like someone she'd need to call the cops on. "Those sirens woke me out of a sound sleep. What's the world coming to when you can't be safe in church? But what's that got to do with them?"

"They're parishioners."

"I didn't know that, but I wouldn't. They're new, and they keep to themselves. I know, because I live right next door and they won't give me the time of day."

"Did you hear them go out that night?"

"He didn't, as far as I can tell. You can hear that old van from a mile away. Bad muffler. Don't think they've moved the car in days. Besides, she's gone. I saw the three of them leaving early one morning, luggage and all. They got into a car, drove off. Family vacation, I thought, but he was back that night, same as always. Guess he didn't go."

"When was this?"

The woman thought about it. "A week maybe, little over; it was a Thursday, I know that. From the number of bags, it looked like the trip was going to be a long one. I'm not nosey, mind you, but I am curious, so I asked him about it. He said Janice, that's the wife, decided to take Skeeter down to see her folks in Tuscaloosa. That's what they nicknamed their daughter, 'Skeeter.' Wouldn't have been something I'd do, but folks do what suits them, not you."

"Tuscaloosa?"

The woman shrugged. "And it doesn't seem like he's making plans to join them either. He comes in, goes out, just as always. Don't know why the house stays so dark, though. Maybe he doesn't see the point in turning on the lights for just him."

"About what time did you see them leave?"

The old woman beamed. "Know that for a fact. Four-thirty. That's when I get up to let the dog out, and I drink my morning coffee. Four-thirty every day, no earlier, no later. Howard's got a bladder that runs like clockwork. He's my Pekinese."

I pointed to the house next door, "That's your house?"

"For near on thirty years," she said.

"Living so close," I said, "you'd hear if they weren't getting along?"

Her eyes narrowed. "I'm no eavesdropper, Missy, and to tell you the truth, I don't know if I feel all that comfortable telling a lady detective somebody else's business. What do you want with them anyway?"

"They knew the priest who was killed. Maybe they know something that could be important to the case."

She rolled her eyes. "Well, you'll have to get whatever you need directly from them. Besides, if you don't mind me saying, you don't much look like a PI." She gave me a good, long once over. "You could be George's side piece, for all I know. Might explain why his wife up and left him."

"Is that what you think happened?"

"Not my business to think about it at all, but he wouldn't escort her to the airport or wherever if she was leaving him, would he? At least that's not how we did it in my day."

"You're sure it was them leaving?"

"Came out of their house, didn't they? Saw her and Skeeter plain as day, didn't I? He had on a black coat and hat, so I couldn't see his face, but who else would it be? He was holding little Skeeter's hand just as sweet. Kind of surprised me, though; he never struck me as being the mushy type. Real strict with the rules, it seemed. And you never did answer about the side piece."

I frowned. "I didn't think I needed to."

The woman's lips twisted into a contemptuous smirk, studying me from tip to toe. "Guess you look too smart for it, anyway. Still, I wouldn't put it past a man to have one, married or not."

"I'll slip my card in their mailbox. If you see him, tell him I stopped by."

"I'll do that. Name's Lillian Gibson, by the way. And I'll keep you in mind if I ever need someone to peek into a window for me, as long as your rates are reasonable. That Rockford on TV charges $200 a day, plus expenses. I'm on a fixed income."

I thanked her for her time, then backed away, hoping she never called me. I didn't like peeking through windows. What consenting adults did in the privacy of their bedrooms was none of my business, and that's the way I liked to keep it.

I smiled. "I'm in the book." *And I screen my calls.* That last part I kept to myself.

The sign on the fence in front of the repurposed gas station on West Sixty-Third Street read CUMMINGS CONTRACTING CO. Two vehicle bays fronted by rolling metal doors with grimy glass faced the busy street; splotches of old motor oil on the cracked concrete resembled a Pollock painting. A six-foot chain fence marked off the perimeter, a shiny padlock dangling at the open gate. There was a white van parked inside, its hood up, a man leaning over working on the engine.

"George Cummings?"

The man's head popped up. He was a husky black man, dressed for manual labor in jeans, boots, and a flannel shirt, his large hands covered in motor oil and grease. He looked terrible, as though he'd slept in his clothes, or worse yet, tried to sleep in them, and couldn't. His eyes held mine for a time, suspicion in his steady gaze. "That's me, pretty lady." He adjusted the bill on his cap, pulling it farther down over his eyes, and shot me an evaluative look. "Who's asking?" He had an easy drawl, one that rolled off his lips like honey off a warm biscuit.

"Cass Raines. I'm a private detective." I held out a hand to shake his, then thought better of it and pulled it back. "I'd like to ask you a few questions about Father Ray Heaton."

His eyes widened, and his smile lost some wattage. "I heard the news this morning, but I just can't get my thick head around it. That poor man. Is there anything new? Do they know what happened?"

"Nothing yet. It's early."

"You said private detective, not police detective."

"That's right. I'm also a friend of his."

He nodded slowly, his expression souring, as though the mention of Pop's name caused him physical pain. "He had a lot of friends. I was pleased to count myself among 'em. I don't think I've had the pleasure of seeing you around, though."

I shrugged, my eyes on his. "Different schedules, I guess." I didn't recall Pop ever mentioning Cummings, but he wouldn't have. When we got together, we didn't talk about church business. "Did he mention having trouble with anyone recently?"

"Trouble? No, don't think so, but, to be honest, it's likely any trouble he had is trouble he started himself. He was like a bantam rooster always itching for a good fight. If it wasn't him up against the city or the drug dealers, it was him up against somebody else. He was an equal opportunity rabble-rouser."

He was right, of course. That was Pop. "Just as many fans as enemies?"

"I hate to say it, but it's true. Still, I can't recall anyone in particular giving him the business."

"You two had a disagreement. Mind telling me what that was about?"

His smile faded some, but Cummings kept it on his face. "Where'd you get that?"

"It isn't true?"

He stared back at me. "Look, I may be an old country boy, but I catch on pretty quick. Someone told you me and him had it out, so now you're thinking maybe I had something to do with what happened to him?"

"I'm just asking questions."

"Well, nothing personal, little lady, but shouldn't it be the police asking them?"

I angled my head, studied him for a time. "Would you rather it be the police asking?"

His full smile returned. "I'm not saying I haven't committed a sin or two in my lifetime, but killing folks? Well, that there's going way too far, especially killing Father Ray."

"So what did you argue about?"

Cummings took a moment before he spoke. "I really got to get this van squared away. I need it for a job. You mind if I work while we talk?" I didn't and moved around to the opposite side of the truck as he went back under the hood with some kind of silver tool. "It was a simple difference in the way we saw things, I guess," Cummings said as he tinkered. "I wasn't the only one on the lay committee who saw it my way, but I guess I was the only one who blew it way out of proportion."

I stared down into the van's engine compartment. I didn't know a lot about cars. I picked out the engine and the fan belt, and the tank where the washer fluid went, but everything else was a mystery. I stood well back to keep from getting grease all over me. "Blew what out of proportion?"

The tool stopped turning. "Don't get me wrong, I'm as civic minded as the next Christian. I tithe like I'm supposed to, I go to Mass on Sunday, I even pay it forward, like they say, mentoring at-risk kids in summer camp and working with folks who need a leg up. I'm all for helping out, but I just felt he was trying to do too much, putting the whole church at risk, so I said something."

"Putting the church at risk how?"

"He practically opened up the place to the homeless. There were meals for them in the school hall, clothes drives, food giveaways. He even let them sleep in the pews when it's cold out. I didn't think it was safe, is all. We have to worry about the kids at the school. A lot of these homeless people are mentally ill. It just isn't a good mix, and I told him so straight out. Mind handing me that torque wrench?"

I stared at him, stymied by the request.

"That one," he said, pointing at a long silver thing sitting on the ground near my foot. I bent down and handed it to him. "What'd he say?"

"He said, basically, to mind my own damn business, is what he said."

"That doesn't sound like him."

Cummings banged the wrench against a fan-looking thing. "Maybe he didn't say it quite like that, but that's what he meant. I'm pretty new to the parish, so I don't have the right to say how things go, but I figured I'd feel a lot better if I said what I felt instead of waiting for something bad to happen, then wishing I had, you know? Now this." He shook his head. "I just hate being right, but I *was* right."

"We don't know that the boy found with him was homeless," I said.

"Thief, homeless, what difference does it make now? It's all the same in the end. Bad mix." Cummings paused, took me in again. "You're his friend, so you're taking a personal interest. Good. That means you'll work hard to find out what happened."

"You stopped coming to church. Was that about the disagreement?"

He grinned. "Somebody sure has been wagging their chin, haven't they? It's true what they say about church people." He stepped back, took off his cap and ran his forearm across his sweaty scalp. "My Mama always said I was as ornery as a mule. I like things my own way. Long story short, I got my feelings hurt about us not seeing eye to eye. I got it in my head I wasn't being appreciated and went home to sulk about it." He grinned. "I came around eventually. Father Ray agreed we could work on a plan that'd work for everybody, and I was looking forward to it. . . . I'm sure gonna miss those fights. He always gave you a good battle."

"Maybe you went to confession to put it to rest?"

Cummings laughed. "Probably should have, but I'm way behind on my atonement. Haven't been inside the sweat box in years. You?"

"I'm sure I've got you beat. I like your accent. Where you from, if you don't mind my asking?"

He chuckled softly, his face brightening. "Durham, North Carolina, but I've been here long enough now to consider this home. Came up here, found myself a nice woman, and started raising a family. Fell in love with that church the minute I saw it. The people were nice, too. A lot of that had to do with Father Ray."

"So you married a northerner?"

"You'd think so, but no. My wife hails from Tuscaloosa, Alabama." He chuckled. "It's true what they say, you know, it's a small world."

"How does she like the church?"

He looked up, smiled. "Janice? Oh, she likes it just fine."

I watched him work, not the least bit interested in what was going on under the hood. "How do you get along with Father Pascoe?" Cummings straightened up, then buried his hands in his pants pockets. I took a step back, braced. It was a learned response. Hands in pockets were a cop's worst nightmare. I no longer wore a star, but I couldn't imagine a day when my heart wouldn't seize when someone's hands were hidden. Cummings's hand came out clutching a black rosary; only then did I breathe again. I watched, waiting for my pulse to slow, as his thick fingers slowly worked their way along the decades.

"I'll just say, I'm really gonna miss Father Ray. I regret that I wasted all that time not speaking to him. It didn't help my temper any that I was stressed out about this place. Business isn't good; money's tight. It looked like I might go under, but this place and me seem to have more lives than a cat's got whiskers. Matter of fact, a job came in just a couple days ago. I guess God really does come through in his time, not yours. Maybe Father Pascoe will grow on me."

"Father Ray thought someone was following him. Any idea who that could have been?"

Cummings frowned, slammed the van hood closed. "He never mentioned anything like that to me. Who'd want to follow a priest? What'd he have that anyone would want?"

"He asked me the same thing the night he died."

Cummings tossed his tools into his toolbox. "I hate to say it, but you don't think it could be one of the people we've been feeding and housing?"

I shrugged. "Anyone in particular?"

"I don't know their names, but one stands out. Big guy. He wore an old Army jacket all year round, no matter the weather. Talked to himself. Came and went as he pleased, wouldn't let anybody near him. It's been a while since I've seen him, though. Maybe he's moved on."

I dug into my pocket for one of my cards, handed it to him. "Thanks for your time. If you think of anything else that might be helpful, I'd appreciate a call, day or night."

Cummings read the card. "Sure, no problem. And you let me know if I can help you, okay? We have to get this guy."

"I will." I turned to leave, then stopped. "Did you and your wife hear the sirens the night of the murders?"

He shook his head. "I had my place soundproofed years ago, had to with all the loud music playing and motorcycles revving at all hours. We slept right through it."

I nodded. "Thanks again."

We. I headed back to the car, thinking of Lillian Gibson's account. She said she saw Janice Cummings and her daughter leaving with luggage more than a week ago. Had Gibson remembered the details incorrectly? Had Cummings misspoken? I glanced back at him as I pulled away. He'd gone back to working on the van. I wondered which one was telling the truth.

Chapter 9

I still had friends in the department. It took a few calls, but I got an address for Maisie Ross and headed over. Even if Thea hadn't mentioned her, Maisie definitely would have been on my short list because of all her run-ins with Pop. She'd opened another store west of the Dan Ryan, well out of Pop's parish, but not off his radar. Months ago, he'd mentioned getting a group together for a new assault to shut her down again. He wanted her out of business and away from kids, and there was no distance he wouldn't travel to make that happen. If I had to answer the question—who in the world would kill a priest?—a woman who steals Bibles and sells drugs to children is definitely at the top of the list.

Sitting in my car, curbside, I could see her store was closed. Rusted bars fronted a grimy door and even grimier windows. The plastic clock face on the front sign was missing its hands, so I had no idea when the store would open—maybe noon, maybe midnight. I checked my watch. It was just after eleven. Nearly lunchtime, if I'd had an appetite.

Ross lived in apartment 2B above her business. I glanced up

at the second story, staring at ripped window blinds in the apartment facing the corner, wondering if it was hers, trying to decide whether to go up or wait.

I scanned the block, watching as a CTA bus lumbered up to the corner and stopped. Squares of cardboard bordered in duct tape stood for window glass in many of the nearby storefronts, vandals or wayward bullets most likely the cause. There was no grass anywhere, just patches of parched, naked earth that got water only when it rained. Maisie Ross couldn't have found a more depressing spot to hang out a shingle.

There was no lock in the front door to Ross's building, only an empty circle where the hardware used to sit. I pushed the door open, and it swung back lazily. No lock, loose hinges. The vestibule reeked of reefer and fast-food, and the mailboxes had been ripped from the wall, leaving only the metal recesses stuffed with discarded potato chip bags and flattened McDonald's cups. I wondered where the mailman put the mail.

The inner door should have had a door-length plate of glass in it, but there was nothing there but a gaping hole. I stuck my arm through to the other side, wiggled my fingers. Then, for the heck of it, I tried the knob. The door was locked. As I stood there wondering what sense it made to lock a glass door with no glass in it, a lanky teenager came barreling down the stairs and stepped straight through the gap without a moment's hesitation.

He scowled, taking a long survey of me. "You got to be lost."

"I'm not. I'm looking for Maisie Ross. You know her?"

"Nope."

"Upstairs. 2B. You just came from up there."

"Nope."

He eased through the door headed for the street. He could have been one of Maisie's kids, for all I knew, but no one talks

to cops or ex-cops, and there was no law written that compelled them to talk to PIs. We're always on the outside looking
in, until someone needs us.

I pressed the bell for 2B, expecting a buzz, but got nothing. I
sighed and stepped gingerly through the gap, taking the sticky
stairs two at a time. No one answered Ross's door after several
hard knocks. I knocked again. Again, no answer, but this time
the door across the hall opened.

An old woman peered out of 2C. She'd opened her door just
a smidgen, the security chain still on.

"They ain't home," she said. She spoke to me through the
crack. I could see one brown eye, one wrinkled cheek, and half
a head of blue hair. "Who you looking for?"

"Mrs. Ross," I said. "Maisie Ross? Do you expect her
soon?"

"She ain't no Missus," the woman said, frowning, though I
could only see half the expression. "And I don't know as I expect her at all. My business is over here, not over there." She
stared at me suspiciously. "You from the welfare?"

"No, ma'am, it's a personal matter."

She paused to assess. "You don't exactly look like you could
have personal business with old Maisie. You look like you're an
educated woman with steady work. Old Maisie's about as banged
up as a ten-cent can of sauerkraut. Two different worlds, I'd say."

I would have handed her one of my business cards, but
truthfully, the less Maisie Ross and her band of crime-prone
misfits knew about me, the better I liked it.

"When does the store open?"

The old woman snorted. "Whenever the spirit strikes. It ain't
like Macy's."

"I heard some folks were trying to shut it down," I said casually. Apparently, 2C knew a lot about Maisie's business,
which could work out well for me.

"Yeah, somebody sent flyers around, and she was fit to be

tied, let me tell you. You wouldn't believe the cussing and banging coming out of that apartment. I'm a Christian woman and that mess sent me straight to the Good Book. But, like I said, I keep to my side of the hall."

"It got loud, huh?"

The woman rolled an eye. "Did it? It was all, *'He's at it again!'* this and *'That meddling SOB'* that. Whoever the SOB is, ole Maisie's got no love for him, that's for sure."

Pop, I thought. That's who Maisie had no love for, but was she angry enough to kill him? People killed for all kinds of reasons. It wouldn't surprise me that Maisie would kill to keep her store running, but would she have done it herself? Had she gotten one of her thug friends or relatives to do it for her? And where did the Hispanic boy fit in?

"Was Maisie home two nights ago?" I asked.

"Couldn't tell you; I sleep like the dead. But I know she keeps all hours. She comes and goes as regular as planes at O'Hare, that one."

"She has a son. When's the last time you saw him?"

Her brown eye widened in shock and the door slammed shut. I'd asked one question too many, and she was suddenly done talking. Or maybe I'd asked the wrong question. Maisie was a bad apple, her son was, too. Maybe he'd taken it upon himself to come to his mother's defense?

"Thanks for your help," I said through the door. "Why don't I just come back then?"

"I wouldn't," she called back. "But if you're just bound and determined to, you might want to bring somebody bigger than you back with you. After dark, Maisie's ain't no place for a woman alone."

I came back the next morning, and the store was open. Through the window, I could see Maisie manning the register. I recognized her from all the sit-ins and marches Pop had organized in front of her old place. She couldn't have been much older than forty, but she looked twice that—well-used, grizzled and flinty, the result of a lot of hard living. I walked in to find her holding court behind a counter crowded with candy and cigarette lighters, chips and air fresheners, mini flashlights, and bottles of Glue Be Gone. "Hello, Maisie."

She turned to face me, straggly hair extensions in an unnatural shade of clown red hanging from her pinhead. The gap-toothed smile on her face melted away, replaced by a virulent sneer, followed close behind by an aggrieved groan. "I don't wait on cops in here. Read the sign." She pointed to a small hand-lettered sign sitting on a shelf behind her. Propped up against a dusty display of five-hour energy drinks, it read simply: No cops. No soliciting. No dogs. No exceptions.

I was a cop the last time we saw each other, but I didn't see the need to correct her now. Let her believe I had the full weight of the Chicago Police Department behind me. And, though I was no longer on the job, I still took offense at the sign. I smiled, though it was the last thing I felt like doing. What I felt like doing got folks five to ten in state prison. I walked up to the counter, aware that there were others in the store watching. "It's been a long time."

Her lips curled back like a mangy dog's. "Not long enough. I got nothing for you."

I placed my hands palms down on the counter, mainly to keep from wrapping them around Maisie's throat. I drew in a breath and dove in. "Father Heaton was killed. I'm sure you've heard by now. You two weren't exactly on good terms. I'd like to know where you and your son were when he was killed."

She smirked. "You don't hear so good, do you? I said I got nothing for you." She slid a glance toward the others in the store. Playing to the crowd, she leaned over the counter, her throat dangerously close to my hands. "Now get going before I call my lawyers and sue for harassment. I know my rights."

"You should. You've certainly had them read to you enough. When was the last time you saw Father Heaton?" I didn't expect her to answer. Maisie Ross had been in and out of the system her entire life. She ate intimidation for breakfast. You could probably waterboard her, and she'd come up from the bucket defiant as all get-out.

Her feral eyes narrowed, and her lips clamped shut. I stood there staring at her, wondering how she got through a day in her skin. If I'd still had my star, I'd have marched her off to the station by now. Without it, here I stood staring at her, wondering if she had it in her to kill a priest and then come to work the next day as though nothing had happened.

"Your son around?"

"I got nothing to say."

"Me knowing your whereabouts when a man you hated is murdered is kind of important. If you won't tell me, then . . ." I spotted a worn Bible with a red cover on the shelf behind Maisie's left shoulder, the initials RMH embossed in gold down the spine. RMH—Raymond Martin Heaton. Pop. I turned back to Maisie. No smile this time, only contempt. My palms came off the counter. "That Bible doesn't belong to you."

She began to laugh. "Says who?"

My body smoldered as though I might actually combust and take the entire store down with me. "It was stolen from Father Heaton's rectory."

She jabbed a nicotine-stained finger at the book. "He gave it to me, and you can't prove different. So unless you got a warrant in your pocket, you can just get the hell out of my place!"

The few patrons milling about the dirty business heard the words "cop" and "warrant" and quickly hustled out and scattered, leaving just the two of us.

I smiled. "Your customers don't like cops?"

"Hell, *I* don't like cops! And I like any cop-friend of that trouble-making priest even less!"

"You called him after you took it to gloat and rub his face in it. They recorded the calls, Maisie. That proves it was you." Her eyes widened. There were no such recordings, but she didn't have to know that. The lie was leverage, the only leverage I had, but it still might not work. Maisie didn't spook easily. She lived her life playing the angles. "So, where were you and your son? Or would you like another chance to hear your rights read to you?"

She laughed, but she seemed slightly less confident about it this time. "I say he gave it to me. It stays put. I like knowing I got it. Kinda like a trophy. Besides, I figure he owes me that and more for what he did to me and mine." She crossed her arms over her chest and stuck her chin out in an act of childish defiance. "Now, do I call my lawyer, or are you getting out of here?"

If I moved around the counter and snatched the book from her, that was theft, and I jeopardized my license. If I slid across the counter and tackled her to the ground, same result. I'd have to bide my time, wear her down.

I shrugged. "I'll wait. Word about me has probably gotten around the block by now. Me sitting out front is bound to discourage a few of your regulars from conducting their usual shady business."

Maisie lifted a bat from behind the register, slammed it down on the counter. "I ain't scared of no cop."

I smiled, eyed the bat. "I can see that." I turned and headed for the door. "Have a profitable day, Maisie."

I sat in my car at the curb watching Maisie through her window. No one went in. I honked a couple times and waved at her when she turned my way. She answered with her middle finger. I kept an eye out for her son. He'd be in his early twenties about now. I couldn't remember his name. If he was bold enough to kill Pop to defend his mother's interests, he wouldn't be above taking a swipe at me sitting at the curb, but hours went by and nothing happened. A few hours into my sit-in, a police cruiser rolled up. Maisie had called the law, which was rich when you thought about it. Here was a woman who likely hadn't done a legal thing in her entire life, calling the police to report being harassed. I slid a glance toward Maisie's window. She was watching. The cop riding shotgun rolled down his window. I rolled mine down, too.

"You on the job?" he asked. He was a big man who barely fit in the cruiser, more fat than muscle.

"Retired," I said. "PI now." I held up my license for him to see.

"Lady says different."

His partner peered over at me, sizing me up. I glanced back at Maisie. She grinned triumphantly, having sicced the cops on me. She really was a stupid woman. I smiled and waved at her, then turned back to the cops. "Lady's nuts," I said.

"So, what's going on?"

"I'm wearing out my welcome. The store owner, Maisie Ross, took something that didn't belong to her. I asked her to return it no questions asked. She told me where to get off and then brandished a bat. Now I'm sitting here hoping to weigh on her conscience."

The cops laughed in unison. "What'd she take?"

"A Bible . . . and she took it from a priest."

Both cops grimaced. It was gratifying to know I wasn't the only one who thought the crime particularly uncivilized. Some things you just didn't do. Apparently, Maisie hadn't learned that lesson.

"Hey, I remember you," the cop in the driver's seat said. "You're Mickerson's old partner. I worked with him once. I'm Bo Kleist."

"Vince Turner," shotgun offered with a friendly wave.

"Nice to meet you guys."

Turner said, "Lady says you're stalking her and turning business away."

"She sells alcohol to minors and steals from priests. I'm proud to turn her business away."

"Want us to go in there and get it?" Kleist asked.

"It's my fight. I want to break her."

"You plan on sitting here long?"

"Public street. Legal spot. I figure till closing time today."

"Then what?" asked Turner.

I smiled. "Back tomorrow."

The window to the cruiser rolled up, and I could see the two conferring. I blew Maisie a kiss; she shook her bat at me. Moments later the cop window rolled down again.

"You sure it's the priest's Bible?" Turner asked.

"It's got his initials on it. RMH. Father Ray Heaton."

"Heaton? That's the priest caught up in that break-in?"

I nodded. "I'm a friend of his. That Bible was a gift from his mother. I want it back. More importantly, I don't want *her* to have it."

The cops exchanged a look.

"All right," Kleist said. "Keep your eyes open. This isn't Main Street Mayberry you're sitting on. We'll swing by on the regular to give you some cover." He slid his CPD business card out of the window. "You need anything sooner, call."

I propped the card up against my dashboard. "Thanks, guys."

"Tell Mickerson he still owes me fifty on that Bears game," Kleist said.

I chuckled. "Hate to tell you, but you'll grow old waiting for it. Ben's a double-or-nothing kind of guy."

He grinned. "Figured as much."

The cruiser eased off and disappeared around the corner. Maisie looked disappointed I wasn't going to jail. I waved again, and she turned her back to me. I notched my seat back to recline and propped my legs up on the dash, next to Kleist's card. Cozy as anything, there I sat watching Maisie watch me until she closed up the store at midnight. I got out of the car and watched as she locked up and toddled off to her apartment.

"Where were you when Father Heaton got killed, Maisie?" I called out to her.

She glared at me. "Minding my own business!"

"Want to hand over the Bible now?"

"Go to hell!" she yelled back.

When the lights to her apartment flicked on, I got back in the car and drove away. I didn't know why people were always telling me to go to hell, but the sentiment didn't worry me much. Hell was as good a place as any.

Chapter 10

True to my word, I was back the next day. The store was open, and Maisie stood behind the counter with no one to wait on. I brought along a couple of donuts and a big bag of McDonald's goodies for lunch. I ate the donuts while reading the paper on my phone. I also brought a couple of books and snacks for when the donuts wore off. In between eating and watching, I studied the street, making sure no one snuck up on me. Nobody Maisie knew would be averse to smashing my windows in, slashing my tires, or worse. My gun was within reach, but I didn't want to have to use it.

A couple of kids strolled into the store after school, but they only came out with bags of chips and cans of pop. Maisie would be hard-pressed to turn a profit on that. The kids eyed my car as they passed it, giving me and it a wide berth. Yep, word had gotten around, all right. The police cruiser crept by about every half hour, each pass pounding another nail into Maisie's coffin.

By five o'clock it looked like a McDonald's had blown up in the back seat, but there I sat, watching Maisie stand guard over her empty store. No one came by to bust out my windows. Maybe I'd overestimated her access to muscle? If Pop were here, he'd tell me to let this whole thing go, but I just couldn't. My getting the Bible back felt like I was doing something constructive, even if it came too late for it to matter overmuch.

When Maisie closed up for the night, I drove away, but then had a paranoid thought that maybe she was waiting until I pulled off to open the store again, and so I doubled back around 2 AM just to check, but the store and her apartment were both dark.

Ella Fitzgerald blasted out of my radio midway through the next day. "Cow Cow Boogie" was in full swing when Maisie marched out of the store with Pop's Bible. I rolled down my passenger window and waited. When she got close, she tossed the book onto the seat. "I was at the casino in Hammond!" she yelled.

"Your son?"

She glowered at me, biting back rage. "Renauld's been inside for three months! Check, if you don't believe me. Now get the hell away from my place!" She turned on her heels and stomped back into the store.

I picked up the Bible, confirmed it was the one I wanted, and then drove away as I'd promised I would. I felt satisfied that I'd accomplished at least a little something for Pop. Now I could move on to finding who killed him.

Pop's Bible lay in my lap, my fingers tracing gently over his golden initials. I supposed it was mine now, at least I thought he'd want me to have it. Maisie had stolen it just for spite, teasing him with it over the phone with her prank calls. When she saw that it wasn't working, did she follow up face-to-face and somehow it went horribly wrong?

Maisie was mean, but she wasn't physically imposing; Pop was old, but he wasn't by any means feeble. He could have easily defended himself against Maisie Ross without hurting her, and she wouldn't have been able to carry, drag, or coax him into the confessional and force him to put a gun to his own head. And, again, I kept stubbing my toe on the same rock. None of it, the break-in, the confessional, the Bible—explained the dead kid on the altar steps.

I looked around my living room at the lamps and tables and throw pillows and such. Bay windows overlooked trees just beginning to bloom for spring, double pocket doors of solid wood separated the large room from a dining room I rarely used. It's where I kept my grandmother's dining room table, a dark, polished monster of a thing that felt and looked like it weighed a ton, made back when things were expected to last long enough to be handed down to somebody. I used it now as a catchall space for spare bike gear, backup running shoes, unread mail, and magazines I'd never have time to get to.

Just inside the front door, a warmly lit long corridor ran east and west. In the front hall sat a narrow table with an old artisan bowl on top. It's where I dumped my keys. The hardwood floor was covered by a paisley runner—swirls of deep burgundy, black, gold, and red. My bedroom, a guest room, and a full bath were to the west; to the east were an underutilized kitchen and a neat storage alcove where my bike lived. The apartment was way too big for just me, but it suited me fine. I felt close to my grandparents here.

I was stalling, of course. I didn't need to take inventory. I'd lived here more than half my life. I could walk the entire building blindfolded. I opened the Bible, the paper-thin pages crinkling when I turned them. I started with the Old Testament and made my way forward, checking for special notations Pop might have made. It was likely a long shot, but what else did I have? I fingered my way through, losing track of time, getting caught in the words. When it became hard to see them, I looked up to figure out why. The sun was setting, and the room had gone dim. I turned on a lamp, and went back to it. If I hadn't, I might have missed the yellow sticky note.

It was stuck to the page next to Romans 12:17. There wasn't much written on it, but what was there was in Pop's handwriting: 430/HWY, 150-DB. I sat bolt upright. What was it? Someone's initials? An abbreviation? Four hundred and thirty. What was that? Was HWY short for highway? There was nothing written on the back, but Pop had underlined the Bible passage: "Repay no one evil for evil, but give thought to do what is honorable in the sight of all. . . . 'Vengeance is mine, I will repay, says the Lord.'"

Sure sounded like Pop, but why underline it? Whose vengeance? Whose evil? I clawed my hands through my hair in frustration. Pop often wrote little notes to himself, sticking them everywhere as reminders to do something or go somewhere, but something about this note, here in the Bible, felt purposeful. And I wasn't getting it. I closed the cover and lay the book down next to me on the couch. I was too tired to think anymore. I lay down just for a moment to rest my eyes and promptly fell asleep.

I was startled awake at six A.M. by someone ringing my bell. Ben's voice boomed over the intercom, and I quickly buzzed him up. Maybe he had something new to report. I waited anxiously at the door for him as he climbed the three flights, using the time to smooth down a major case of pillow head.

"What have you got?" I asked as soon as he stepped inside the apartment.

Ben stared at me intently.

His full attention had me taking a step backward. I folded my arms protectively across my chest. "Stop looking at me like I'm about to jump off a ledge, or something." My eyes skittered away nervously. "I'm fine."

He kept staring. "You were getting fine, but now you're not, which is why I'm here." He lifted a white deli bag stained with grease. "Bagels. Still warm. And it looks like you could use one."

"Do you have a lead? Information? Anything?"

Ben shook his head. "Not yet."

I knew it was too soon, but I deflated nonetheless. Knowing how things worked, how slow they could move, didn't keep me from being disappointed by the lack of progress. Pop's killer was out there, and it was making me antsy. Why were we wasting time with bagels? "I'm not hungry, but thanks."

"You don't have to be hungry to eat a frigging bagel. You just open your mouth and pop the damn thing in. It's like gulping air or scarfing down cotton candy." He snapped his fingers. "Like nothing."

My eyes narrowed, suspicious now. "This is not about the bagels, is it?"

He shrugged. "If you want to get some things off your chest while you're eating it, I won't stop you."

"And if I don't?"

He smiled. "You do. You just don't know it."

I led him back to the kitchen. "I'll make coffee." I didn't drink it, but I kept it around for those of my friends who couldn't seem to meet the day without it.

"Nuh-uh, I'll handle it. You tea snobs don't know shit about coffee beans."

"Did you come over here just to insult me?"

"Not just," he said, giving me a playful shove. "So, you want onion or sesame seed?"

Ben tossed the bag of bagels on the counter and padded over to the coffeemaker. I grabbed orange juice and a bag of ground coffee out of the fridge and tossed the bag to him.

"Bring me up to speed," I said. "There has to be something."

Ben went to work on his coffee—filters, water, it was a process. "No burglar tools on the kid—no picklocks, no screwdriver—and no keys on Father Ray. The door to the basement was jimmied, so you'd think that's how the kid got in, but it's sooty and dirty as hell down there. That old church still uses coal, if you can believe it. But there was no soot or coal dust on either of them. You saw that for yourself."

I pulled a juice glass from the cabinet, thought it through. "There were no sooty footprints anywhere near that altar. I'd have noticed." An image of the bloodied bodies flashed in my head, along with the horror and panic I'd felt. "At least I think I would have. And Pop would have had his keys. He'd have known the church was locked. He saw me check it."

"But it was open when you got there," Ben said. "So where'd his keys go?"

"Someone took them or tossed them. Maybe they figured the jimmied door would be enough for the police to jump to the same conclusion Farraday did—a simple break-in gone bad. Taking the keys was a mistake."

He scooped coffee into the filter. "There could have been two kids. The other one jimmies the door, crawls through the soot, opens the door from the inside for the one we found dead, and that's what Father Ray walks in on. First guy shakes him down, takes the keys and whatever else is in his pockets. Dead guy goes for something else, a candlestick, a chalice, there's a struggle, the gun goes off. The guy in the soot books it, leaving the scene like you found it."

I shook my head, unconvinced. "He did *not* kill himself. You're still operating like this was a burglary. It wasn't."

"Then *you* explain the dead kid."

"I can't. Not yet, but I will." I told him about Cummings and Maisie and Pop's Bible. I showed him the sticky note. "This is just a start. There's bound to be more."

"Aww, this could be anything—a shopping list, a reminder to a dentist's appointment."

"It feels important."

The coffeemaker began to burp and bubble, filling the kitchen with the aroma of brewed coffee. Ben stood there, his back to me, not saying what I knew he wanted to say. He wanted me to stand down, but not because of Farraday's threat. He knew how important this was to me, how much it would cost.

"I know what I'm doing," I said, busying myself so I wouldn't have to look at him and make a big thing out of it.

"I know." He tossed me the bag of coffee, and I put it back in the fridge.

"Maisie Ross had good reason, at least in her mind, to want to hurt him," I said. "You could check the casino's surveillance cameras to verify her alibi. As for Cummings, he admitted arguing with Pop, but he seems to have gotten over it. Besides, wrangling over how best to tackle a problem hardly seems like a reason to kill. Maybe he was home that night and didn't hear the sirens, but, if I believe his neighbor, and I have no reason not to, his wife wasn't there with him. So why'd he include her?"

"But if you're right, somebody didn't just kill him, did they? They made it look like he killed *himself*. That's a lot of rage. A Bible, a shouting match over feeding the homeless, and a couple of initials on a sticky note don't lead us anywhere we want to go, at least not yet."

I grabbed a bagel from the bag. Sesame seed. "Then I keep digging. I still have the janitor to talk to."

Ben pulled down a coffee mug from the shelf, his expression pensive. "You're on a collision course with Farraday, you know that, right?"

"I don't care about Farraday."

He sighed, filled his cup. "What if I ask you, pretty please, to back off?"

I pulled a face. "What grown man says pretty please?"

"One who's trying to keep his partner out of jail for interfering in a police investigation."

I slowly poured myself a glass of OJ. "I'd do anything for you, you know that."

Ben squinted, his gaze anticipatory. "Why do I sense a 'but' coming on?"

I shrugged, smiled sweetly. "Well, if you sense it, I don't have to say it." I handed him the greasy bag. "Onion bagel?"

Nancy Akers, the school's receptionist, was a big, startled-looking woman with auburn hair pulled back into a severe bun. Her green eyes were red from crying. She couldn't believe Pop was dead. I knew, because she kept repeating "I can't believe he's dead." When I told her why I'd come, she was finally able to pull herself together enough to summon Anton Bolek over the PA system. It was going to be a long day for the both of us.

I'd seen Bolek before, but this would be our first time meeting formally. Pop never said too much about him, but Thea had come up with his name pretty quickly when I asked if Pop had had a problem with anyone close to home. Again, something else Pop didn't feel it necessary to mention to me. I was beginning to see a pattern forming and didn't like it much. I waited for Bolek in the rotunda, anxious to get it done, so that I could move on to the next thing. When the side door screeched open, I turned to watch him lumber in. As he drew closer, I wondered what he'd done to get on Pop's bad side.

He was portly, pockmarked, and dressed in a dark green janitor's uniform. He was maybe in his early sixties, if I had to guess, and nearly bald, the top of his head freckled from the sun. Bolek walked deliberately, at half pace, as though he was counting every step. His work boots skimmed the carpet, barely clearing the nap, and he listed slightly to the right as he ambled forward, a massive key ring clipped to his belt, the keys jangling like wind chimes.

He shot me a long, calculating look. "You're the detective they called me for?" He emphasized the first word, which immediately got my hackles up. His small dark eyes, like inky dots, narrowed. "I've seen you around, haven't I?" He nodded. "Sure, you were with Heaton. Detective, huh? Go figure." His eyes darted around the circular room, landing on nothing in particular, until finally making their way back around to me. "What's this about then?"

"Father Heaton's dead," I said, watching, sizing him up. "You worked with him. I'd like to ask you a few questions."

Bolek's eyes widened. "What kind of questions?"

"Whether you noticed anything out of the ordinary, saw anyone hanging around, or could tell if Father Heaton seemed upset or distracted. General questions. How you two got along."

According to Thea, they didn't. In fact, she painted Bolek as a very difficult man to get along with. Pop, I knew, would have made the effort, and would have kept on making it.

Bolek glanced around. "We weren't exactly drinking buddies. It's a job. I come in, I do it, I go home. That sums it up."

"You're here every day?"

"I don't do weekends. I'm in at six A.M. on the dot, and I'm out the minute that bell rings at three o'clock. They can't pay me enough to stick around here after the sun goes down. Once it does, this neighborhood turns into a regular shooting gallery, what with the gangbangers and such, no offense."

"Good people live here, Mr. Bolek. Not everyone's in a gang."

Bolek snorted. "Tell that to the police blotter. That's what happens when you turn the zoo over to the animals. I knew this neighborhood back in the day when it was all Irish. They had nuns here then, real ones, not these others they got now." He chuckled meanly. "You could say I knew it when."

Our eyes held for a time as I worked to tamp down a growing desire to take Anton Bolek's ring of keys and shove them up a dark and narrow place. He knew I was black, right? I mean, I was standing not two feet from him. Who would not take offense? "Let's get back to Father Heaton. When's the last time you saw him?"

Bolek blinked, thought for a moment, and then I could almost see the light bulb go off in his head. "Oh, hey, I get it. You guys need somebody to pin this whole thing on, and you're going for the white guy in the basement, that it?"

He started to sweat, damp circles forming under his armpits. I watched as he checked out the rotunda again, as though there might be a hidden camera somewhere. Cops learned to read body language. Bolek's wasn't hard to decipher. He was guilty about something. "Look, I was way in my own neighborhood when all this went down, and I got plenty of witnesses who can prove it."

"I'm not accusing you of anything."

"A cop asking you about a killing? I know how that goes."

"I'm a private investigator, not a cop. I'm looking for information, that's all. Perhaps there was someone around paying close attention to Father Heaton's comings and goings? Maybe you know someone else he had a beef with?"

He appeared to settle down some, though his eyes stayed squirrely. "A private dick? That's all? You had me worried there for a second, doll, not that I have anything to worry about, mind. It's just I'm no fan of cops. I hate 'em, matter of fact."

I glared at him with hard eyes, not bothering to smile this time. "That so?"

A slimy grin revealed double rows of nicotine-stained teeth. "Never met an honest one my whole life, and that's a true fact."

Bolek's picking away at my good graces was beginning to wear thin. First, the swipe at the neighborhood and the people in it, then the sexist labels, now the swipe at cops. Thea had pegged him right. Bolek was old school, his teeth cut on generations of prejudice, fear, and a warped sense of how things should go and what type of people they should go for. He was entitled to his narrow-mindedness. If the situation were not what it was now, I'd even call him on it, but Pop was dead. I needed Bolek's cooperation, no matter how much it pained me to stand here and angle for it.

"Then it's a good thing I'm not one," I said, forcing a weak smile. "So? Anything you noticed?"

He crossed his short, chubby arms across his chest. "You don't see much from the basement. I start these crap furnaces first thing, then walk the place all day tinkering with old pipes, then I hightail it out of here while it's still light out. Same every day, come Hell or high water." Bolek stared at me with a look of trollish cunning for a moment too long; he gave me the creeps. I wondered about the safety of the children he came in contact with every day, and wondered what I could do about it.

"And you and Father Heaton?"

"Didn't like him, and I'm not ashamed to say it. I don't like anybody who looks over my shoulder all day like I don't know what I'm doing, even if he is a priest."

"What about you didn't he trust?"

A hateful smirk spread across his face. "Guess you'll have to ask him. Besides, seeing as you're no cop, I don't have to tell you anything, do I? Bottom line, he's gone, I had nothing to do with it, and I got work to do."

We stood quietly for a time, Bolek appearing satisfied that he'd said his piece. I recognized a brick wall when I came up against it. I'd get nothing useful from him, not without police powers. I handed him my card. "If you remember anything else."

He took it, slipped it into his breast pocket without reading it. "Don't think I will."

I slanted him a look. "It's possible you might."

He shook his head, snorted derisively. "You and the cops, you're all the same."

I headed for the door.

"You got killers all over this neighborhood," Bolek said to my retreating back. "Try looking at one of them instead of trying to stitch me up. I got rights, nonalien ones. It says so in the Constitution."

I rolled my eyes and, for a fraction of a second, considered turning around and correcting him, then decided not to bother. Life was too short, and I'd wasted too much of it already on Anton Bolek.

Chapter 11

Pop had no blood family, only the family he'd fashioned for himself. Hundreds had shown up for his funeral and burial, but they were gone now. I stood alone at the gravesite in St. Kevin's Catholic Cemetery well past my time, surrounded by an unnatural quiet, my heels sinking into the moist grass. I stared down at the mahogany casket covered by a large spray of white hydrangeas, remembering all the other caskets I'd tossed flowers on before walking away and leaving a piece of myself in the hole. Time didn't exist inside cemetery gates. The dead had forever. The lives of those who stopped to visit also seemed to halt for a time, as they reverted back to the moment of loss. It was dead time kept on a clock with no hands.

It had been six days since Pop was killed, and still the cops had nothing of substance. Thanks to Ben, though, I at least knew they had a few more details and an ID on the dead boy. Cesar Luna, eighteen, was a low-level gangbanger from the far Southeast Side, and the throwaway gun found next to Pop was thought to be his. Farraday's theory still stood. Why not? It was neat, tidy, easy. That's how he liked things.

But easy and tidy didn't mean right. Farraday didn't know Pop, I did. Pop wouldn't have wrestled over a loaded gun. If Luna had come to rob him, Pop would have emptied his pockets and given him whatever he asked for. He would not have taken a life, not even his own. I wiped away a tear and tossed a single white rose onto the floral spray. It was both an end and a beginning.

Earlier, I'd checked the crowds at the church and here for Maisie Ross. I figured she'd show up just to gloat, but I didn't see her. I was thankful she stayed away. There was also no Anton Bolek, but it was obvious after speaking to him, that he didn't care enough about Pop to want to honor him in any way. George Cummings had given a reading at the service and wept through half of it, then solemnly helped to carry Pop's casket to the hearse. Even some of the homeless Pop had helped showed up to pay their respects. Pop would have liked that.

"Hey, Bean."

I turned to face a man standing behind me. Only a handful of people had ever called me Bean, a childish nickname short for String Bean, and I hadn't heard it in years. I stared into the man's face and slowly recognized the young boy behind the grown man's eyes.

"Whip!?"

He smiled broadly. "You remembered!" He didn't look much like the thin, wiry boy with the mop of black curly hair I used to pal around with. This man was well over two hundred pounds, broad at the shoulders, narrow at the waist, husky. His dark face, once bright and youthful, was now pale and tired looking, the boyish dimples now filled in, his thin hair cut short. Deep lines spread out from weary eyes that looked as though they'd seen too much.

His real name was Charles Mayo Jr., but no one from the old neighborhood ever called him that. He was Whip, because he was always as thin as one. We grew up on the same block, and his mother died just a few weeks after mine, leaving us mother-less children in a world that suddenly seemed too big and too cold. My grandparents loved me and took great care of me, but Whip's father, well, that was a different story. My father left by Amtrak train, but Whip's father, a mean, hopeless alcoholic, stayed, though Whip often said he wished he hadn't. Mr. Mayo used cruel words instead of fists to beat the light out of his son. We clung to each other then, as though we shared the last life preserver on a sinking ship. Both of us, eventually, found our way to Pop's door.

We hugged and held on, Whip's winter-blend suit coat straining at the back as though it were a size too small. "I saw you standing here, but I didn't want to bother you. I hung back, over there by that tree."

"Why?" I asked, bewildered.

He shrugged, but didn't answer. He stared instead into the grave. "I can't believe it. Father Ray . . ." His voice trailed away. He gave me a playful grin. "You look good. Still don't know what to do with your hair, though. Looks like you comb it with a rake."

We shared a hardy belly laugh, which culminated in another bear hug. I'd forgotten how much I cared for Whip, and he for me. Time and distance had a way of dulling the pull, until time and distance fell away, and you were right back where you started, as though you'd been together the whole time.

"Last time I saw you," Whip said, "you had just graduated and were off to the Peace Corps. How long did you stay in?"

"Two years."

"Making the world a better place, huh?"

"One well at a time. What did you end up doing?"

Whip looked past me. "I stayed around. . . . Pontiac Correc-tional. In and out—mostly in."

The news made my heart sad. "What for?"

"Stealing cars, burglary. I've tried a little bit of everything.

But I'm out now, and I plan on staying out. Hell, I'm thirty-five. I got to get myself ironed out before I kick it, right?" He smiled broadly. Then he glanced over my shoulder, and I turned around to see what he was looking at. We were the only ones there. "Hey, Bean, I know cops when I see them, and there were some big ones hanging around over there, watching you like you boosted something. I wanted to stick around in case you needed me to run interference or something."

The cops had been Ben and Paul. "They're friends of mine. Just here for support."

"Cops as friends. Never thought of that before. I have a whole different kind of relationship with them. . . . So what'd *you* end up doing with yourself?"

I smiled, anticipating his reaction. "I became a cop."

Whip nearly choked on his tongue, which made me laugh till I cried. It felt good to laugh. Pop would have appreciated the joke.

"Aww, man! Don't tell me that, Bean. Really?" The pained look on his face made me laugh even harder.

"I went private a couple years ago, though. I run my own one-woman agency now."

He swiped a hand though his hair. His knuckles were scarred and calloused, boxer's knuckles. "Well, I'll be damned."

We started walking slowly toward our cars. "What're you doing now that you're out and staying out?"

"I'm a cook. Work at a little joint called Creole's over on the West Side. It's nothing fancy, but stop by sometime and I'll cook you up something good."

I looked at him closely, seeing clearly now the boy I'd known. "I'll definitely do that."

Whip stopped walking, placed a hand on my elbow. "I know you said those cops were friends of yours, but I got a bad vibe off one of them. The white guy? Big dude. Fancy duds? He was standing away from the other two. How good a friend is he?"

My stomach turned. Farraday. "He's not a friend. He's the detective in charge of Pop's case."

"Then what's he doing here? He should be out there beating the bushes."

"He's here making sure I stay out of his way. This is him letting me know he's watching."

Whip pulled a face. "See, just when I was starting to think differently about cops. So what are we going to do about all this? How're we going to set this straight? Because no way is Father Ray a suicide."

"I'm going to see what I can turn up. Go back to the beginning and try to figure out what happened."

Whip stared at me. "I said 'we,' Bean."

"You're staying out of this. I'm on shaky enough ground as it is; you're on even less than that."

"Don't get it twisted. I'm ready to go all in. This is family we're talking about."

"I'll call if I need you."

He looked as though he didn't believe me. "You never were any good at passing the ball, Bean."

"I will. I promise."

"Do that. I mean it. You need me, you call me."

"Same here," I said. "And no more Pontiac."

He chuckled. "Ha! That'll be a first, me calling a cop."

"Ex-cop," I said.

He waggled a finger at me. "Ain't no such thing. It's all in there. Cop eyes. Cop brain. Nobody sees it clearer than somebody with a rap sheet as long as mine."

We shared a good laugh, then exchanged numbers and parted. I watched as he got into a beat-up Kia and drove through the cemetery gates. Pop would be glad to know that Whip was doing well. Maybe he did know. As I drove through the gates, my mood, which had lightened some at seeing an old friend, darkened again at the thought of Farraday shadowing me.

I checked the rearview, watching as the graves got smaller and smaller the farther I got from them, knowing that I would carry one of them with me always. "Going all in, Pop."

Civilians walk in and out of police stations every day, but it seemed like ages since I'd walked through the doors of one without a star, a gun, and an assigned battered desk with all my stuff crammed inside. The experience felt otherworldly, as if I'd traveled light years and back, returning a stranger to a world that had pressed on quite well without me.

Cops milled around the ground floor of CPD's Area 2 Headquarters like they did in every police station anywhere, their eyes watchful, the centurion intensity not matched by their unhurried steps. Sweat and body odor at varying degrees of ripeness comingled with the essence of well-polished holster leather and poorly ventilated air. Somewhere in the building, someone was getting locked up while someone else was being let go. Only the cops stayed put, moving as though they had years to get where they were going, shoveling smoke for city pay and the promise of an adequate pension.

The desk sergeant called upstairs to tell Ben I was there to see him. I waited on a blue plastic chair, one of many in a row anchored against the wall so belligerent drunks couldn't hurl them through a window, and watched as activity pulsed around me. Cops. Perps. Marks. All here. All joined together in a free-form dance where the music never stopped, and only half the partners matched the tempo. I didn't know these particular cops, and they didn't know me; I was thankful for the anonymity. Ben stepped off the elevator, and I stood, waiting for him to reach me.

I could read his face. He was worried about me. I didn't want him to be, but there was nothing I could do to stop it. The worry flowed from my end too. Being a cop was dangerous work, now more than ever, and he had to work with Farraday. It made me nervous.

His smile reached me before he did. "The funeral was yesterday. What took you so long?"

"I'd like to see what you've got."

He searched my face, and I tried working up some happy to plaster on it, but I don't think I succeeded.

"You're white-knuckling it."

I met his gaze. "That counts."

"I've kept you pretty up to date."

"I'd like to see the file."

He let a beat pass. "You're not going to pay any attention to what I'm about to say, but I'm going to say it again anyway. Step back. Take time to get your head back on straight. Nothing good's going to come from you pushing on this."

"Got it."

He sighed, rolled his eyes. "Don't know why I bothered."

"Look, another set of eyes and a fresh pair of legs can't hurt, right?"

An angry man stormed through the front doors muttering profanities, a bloody towel pressed to his left eye. Ben and I tracked him all the way to the desk sergeant and assumed defensive positions, our backs to the wall. Force of habit.

Ben planted his hands deep in his pockets, percolating the coins inside the polyester blend. His eyes met mine. "There's a reason surgeons don't operate on their own mothers, you know that, right?"

"I do. But I can't sit back and do nothing while Farraday's out there grandstanding and kicking dirt under the rug. Pop had enemies, lots of them. It can't be that inconceivable that one of them might have wanted to do him harm."

"The gun was next to him, Cass. His prints were on it."

"And it's also not impossible for someone to force a person's hands on the grip."

"Maybe, but you sticking your nose in can't end in a good place. You know that. Our files are CPD property, internal use only, and you know that already, too. Still, here we are."

We stood facing each other, neither of us speaking.

He heaved out an aggrieved breath. "And if you don't get anything now, you'll turn up again tomorrow and the next day, until either I go nuts or Farraday tosses you into a cell and swallows the key."

I held my ground. "So why are we still talking?"

Ben hesitated. "I wouldn't be standing here if not for you. That factors in. Pick had me cold. My back was to him."

I shook my head. I didn't want to talk about Jimmy Pick. "You'd have done the same for me. I'm looking for a little professional courtesy, not payback."

Ben scrubbed his hands across his face. His eyes narrowed as he surveyed the lobby as though searching for enemy agents crouched behind the potted palms. "I'll give you ten minutes. Follow me. If anybody asks, you're my sister."

"What?"

"From another mother. It happens. Just keep your head down and move like you own the place. Should be easy for you. You do that second part anyway."

The small interview room had only a sorry-looking metal table and two battered metal chairs in it, and along its back wall a metal bench with a bar behind it to clip handcuffed perps to so they couldn't do a runner. But what more did you need, really? Cops asked questions, those who weren't cops answered them. The cop needed a pen and something to write on, the perp a place to sit and cry his or her eyes out. The setup was simplicity itself. Ben closed the door behind us.

"You want something? Herbal tea?"

I shook my head, then thought about the offer. "Since when do cop houses have herbal tea?"

"That tree hugger Gleason's got a stash of the stuff in his

bottom drawer. Looks like weed to me but, hey, if he says it's tea . . . it's tea. Park it. I'll be back in a second."

"Wait. Could you run a name for me?"

His eyes narrowed. "You're really pushing it, aren't you?"

I smiled my sweetest smile. "You have the resources. I don't. I talked to the handyman at the school. Anton Bolek. He and Pop butted heads about something, but he wouldn't tell me what. I got a vibe off of him that I didn't like. He's hiding something. I'd like to know who I'm dealing with before I take another run at him." I spelled Anton's name for him to make the lookup easier.

"What the hell kind of name is Bolek?"

"I didn't ask."

"Sit tight. But we're going to discuss who'll be taking that run."

Ben eased out of the room, closing the door behind him. I'd have looked around again, but didn't need to trouble myself—there was only the table, the two chairs, and a grimy window encased in wire mesh. This is where I'd be spending a lot of my time, if I continued to run up against Farraday. I thought about whether or not that concerned me, deciding finally that it didn't. Ben was back in less than a minute's time with the case file, which he dropped like a stone on the table before taking a seat across from me. He slid the file, thick with detail I wasn't sure I was ready for, into the center. I looked at him. He looked at me. I waited. He waited.

"Are we waiting for a starter pistol?" I asked.

· He pointed at the file. "That's not for civilian eyes."

"So you thought you'd walk it in here and taunt me with it?"

"I'm gonna get up and stretch my legs, look out that window." He cocked a thick thumb toward the grimy opening. "Do not rifle through that while my back's turned."

I glanced at the window. I knew it faced nothing more interesting than the cop lot. "How long are you going to be preoccupied?"

"You got a safe ten. What you don't want is to be sitting there when Farraday prances his prissy ass back in here. If you are, I may just have to punch his lights out, and I wore my good shirt today. Besides, there are way too many guns in this building to guarantee any kind of showdown ends well."

"How can you work with him knowing what kind of cop he is?"

Ben's eyes bore into mine, suddenly serious. "I watch my back. I take his word for nothing. He nearly got my partner killed. That's not something you forgive a guy for."

I sighed, let a moment pass. "I can do ten. Unless, while I'm sitting here not rifling, I come across something I have to go over twice."

"I could stretch it to eleven, if you need the extra time."

"Then why not make it fifteen?"

"Is that how long it takes you not to rifle through shit?"

"I've never actually timed it."

Ben shook his head. "Well, take my advice, rifle fast." He walked out of the room again. Screw Farraday. I knew my lawyer's number by heart and knew whatever I got charged with, I'd likely skip on. What I didn't want to do was jam Ben up and put him in his boss's crosshairs, so I would stick to the time he'd given me and get on my way. I readied my pen and notepad, then closed my eyes and breathed. This was it. Once I opened the file, there'd be no turning back, no stopping, no matter what Farraday threatened me with. I needed the truth.

Chapter 12

"I'm conducting an interview in here, Hallstrom," Ben announced to the hall when he came back in. "Give me fifteen." He locked the door behind him.

He strolled in with a small bag of potato chips and what smelled like a pastrami sandwich on rye. Winking slyly, he nudged his chair over to the window and sat down with his back to me, unraveling the plastic wrap around his sandwich. "Whatever you do with that file is between you and your higher power. And while you're sitting there *not* reading it, be sure *not* to pay particular attention to the ME and ballistic reports."

I pulled the file toward me. "You missed your calling. You should have taken to the stage."

He turned to wink at me, his mouth full of deli meat. "Right? I certainly have the looks for it. I'm ruggedly handsome."

My hand hovered over the file too long. Ben noticed. "Forget how?"

"I'm a little rusty. Are you going to tell me it's just like riding a bike?"

"Hell no. What's a bike got to do with anything?"

"This is Pop."

"Which is why I get it, but, me to you, we're beating every bush, we're running this by the book, and we're coming up cold. You won't want to hear this, but the evidence fits a determination of an interrupted burglary, struggle, and accidental weapons discharge. Father Ray's reaction might not jibe with the man you knew, but trauma makes people act differently than they normally would. Maybe there were people out there that didn't care for him, but I can't see a shopkeeper with questionable morals or a good ole boy contractor with an ego beef going off the rails like this, can you?"

I didn't know. I couldn't say. All I knew is I couldn't stop, not until I had the truth, and I didn't think Farraday or Ben had it, not yet, no matter what the evidence said. I placed my hand on the file folder.

"You don't have to do this, if you're not up to it," Ben said. "There's no dishonor."

"I do have to," I whispered. "Someone killed him. Someone killed Cesar Luna. And I'm going to prove it."

Ben turned back to the window. "Then open the damn file."

Speechless, I opened the damned file.

With the crime scene photos laid out in front of me, I again stared clinically into Cesar Luna's dead eyes as I'd long ago learned to do. He was a crime victim. These were crime photos—stark, basic, lacking aesthetic value. They were an official record of violent crime for the express purpose of investigation, nothing more. I inhaled, detached, and started the clock on my fifteen.

Luna had bled out, a single bullet to the center of his chest. His face was badly bruised, his lip busted and swollen, and he had a deep, fresh scratch, approximately three inches in length, staggered across his right cheek. I remembered the injuries, the metallic scent of Luna's blood.

"Luna was a Scorpion," I said. "Pop's parish is way off his turf. What was he doing there?"

Ben shrugged. "Nothing good. He's got a sheet a mile long."

I flipped the pages. "But for assault, gang activity, gun possession, not for robbing churches, and he hadn't been picked up for anything in more than a year. Isn't it a little strange to you that a hardcore banger would be shot dead in a church way off his home turf, alongside a priest he had no obvious connection to?"

"Maybe he's passing by, sees the lights on, and figures he can score something."

"But the lights weren't on, except in the vestry. I had to turn them on myself. When I left Pop, he was locked in for the night. It was raining. Why venture outside again? Why enter the church and leave the lights out? He wouldn't have done that. He promised me he'd stay put until I got back in the morning to meet the police."

"Maybe he decided to go over there to pray."

"That morning, for a moment I thought that, too. But Pop promised me he'd stay put." I searched the report. "You told me the back door was jimmied. Pop wouldn't have been able to see that from the rectory. So what drew him over? And you still haven't found his keys." I fingered through the pages. Pop's photos were missing. "Where are his photos?"

Ben slid me a glance. "I pulled them."

"What? Why?" My voice rose, indignant, aggrieved. "They're part of the evidence."

Ben stood, dragged his chair to the table and sat. His sharp gray eyes watched me closely. "If my father died the way Father Ray did, I'd hope to God you, or somebody, would have the decency to do the same for me. You found him. You saw. That's enough. Everything else we've got is there. You have questions? Ask me, and I'll answer them. Right now, though, you're eating up your time. Being pissed off at me can come later."

I stared at him. "I hate being handled."

"Who knows that better than I do? But I guarantee you you'd hate those photos a lot more."

I reached for the file again. Ben watched me read through the text-only portion of the ME's report on Pop. I exhaled deeply. "He didn't suffer." Until that moment, I hadn't realized how much not knowing that had gnawed at me. I wanted to know, needed to know, that Pop had not languished in pain, that death was quick. Knowing for sure came as a great relief.

"One bullet to the right temple. Residue on his right hand, his clothes," Ben said. "If you were in my spot, and you were two years ago, what would you come up with?"

"I don't care what it says. There's another explanation."

"Now you're refuting stone cold forensic evidence? Come on, Cass."

"I knew the man!"

"Nobody knows everything about everybody they know. Hell, the shit you don't know about me would take the curl out of your hair." The room fell silent. He was right, but I was also right. I knew the man. I was certain I'd known him well. "Is there anything else you'd like to know?"

His eyes met mine. "Yeah, everything." Ballistic reports, interview statements, CSI reports—I raced through them all, jotting down notes, committing the rest to memory before closing the file, my heart racing, my mouth dry. It took a moment before I found my voice again. I cleared my dry throat, wishing I had water, fearing an ocean's worth wouldn't be enough. "Pop didn't own a gun, obviously."

Ben nodded. "We figured as much, but we can't link the gun to Luna. It was unregistered, a cheap .25-caliber throwaway. Striations on both bullets match. Luna was shot close range, consistent with a struggle. Father Ray, well . . ."

"Pop was a pacifist," I argued.

"Nobody's a pacifist when they're grappling for a gun and their life is at stake. And pacifism as a defense doesn't fly when both their prints are on the gun."

I shoved the file away from me. "Then we're missing something."

"Not if we're talking physical evidence. Techs logged in a butt load of crap. But, again, we can't link any of it to either Luna or Father Ray." Ben slid the file toward him, opened it. "I mean look at the stuff people left behind—hand fans, a pack of gum, eyeglasses." He thumbed his way down the list. "A paperback novel, a handful of beads, a candle in a bag, socks. Volunteers clean the place pretty often, so this stuff wasn't hanging around long." Ben slid the file back into the center of the table. "It was all over the place, under the pews, near the altar, behind it. Even found a couple of plug nickels in the donation box. Chances of narrowing down any of that to anybody are nil."

I glanced at my watch, my time almost up. "Pop didn't give Luna that beating."

"No," Ben said. "His knuckles were clean, and, well, he's a priest. Except for the wound to his head, there wasn't a mark on him. Besides, the ME determined Luna's bruises were at least a few hours old. Also, there's no trace of anyone else on the gun or on the bodies. Luna and Father Ray are in the church, however it happens. Luna's shot. Father Ray's shot. You can twist the kaleidoscope anyway you want, but the picture always comes out the same. We got nothing else to go on, not yet. The Scorpions aren't talking. There were no witnesses, at least none that came forward. If we had another card to play, we'd play it."

"Nobody talks to cops."

Ben snorted. "Till they need one, then we're everybody's best pal. Cass, we can't prove Heaton was being followed. Nobody who would talk to us admits to harboring any deep resentment toward the man. The three names you came up with show nothing promising, not really. His community work was ruining a lot of shady business in that neighborhood, but as far as we found out, all they wanted was for him to knock it off and move on to the next sap. And none of that had anything to do with Luna."

"So you're letting Farraday's stupid burglary theory stand?"

"It's the department's theory. We're still working it, but, the truth? Nothing's popping. Nobody saw anything, nobody knows anything."

"And you've got other cases to work, not just this one."

"Right now, somebody's out there tossing homeless guys, and if we don't shut that down quick, somebody's going to get seriously dead."

"And Farraday?" I asked.

Ben scowled. "Probably already halfway through his victory lap, crowing about how he closed this one in record time. He's all about the clearance rate. Look, I promised you I'd work this hard, and I will, I am. Heaton was a good man. If there's an opening in the evidence, I'll dig on it."

Our eyes held.

"I know you will. Thanks." I rose, pushed my chair in. Ben did the same.

"What about you?" he asked.

"I'm going to help you. I'm going to talk to Cesar Luna's family. If they know something they're not saying, I'm going to find out what it is. Luna didn't just pick that church out of thin air. He was there for a reason. Then I'm going to talk to Hector Perez."

Ben grinned. "I guess I shouldn't be surprised you got through *all* the interview statements."

"Guess I wasn't as rusty as I thought." According to the file, Hector Perez was a fellow Scorpion who'd copped to being with Cesar Luna hours before he ended up in the church.

"I doubt Perez will talk to you either. He only copped to seeing Luna after we threatened to violate his probation and send him back inside. You don't have that kind of pull. He claims Luna left him nursing a Negra Modelo at some hangout of theirs. Other than that, he doesn't know where Cesar was headed when he left, and he didn't ask. He also said he didn't know what Cesar was into or up to. In short, he don't know nothing from nothing. All of it's a crock of shit. Bangers like to jerk cop chains just for the hell of it. Makes 'em feel all manly. You going over there on your own might not be too smart. Perez hates cops, and he hates outsiders. You used to be one, you're still the other."

I slipped my pad and pen into a pocket. "I've got this."

"There's not a doubt in my mind about that. Just do me a favor and don't go empty-handed."

I zipped my jacket. "I won't. Thanks for the look, partner."

Ben moved around the table, and pulled me into a bear hug. "Anything you need. Just be careful. You don't have me on your six anymore."

I leaned into the hug, my face buried in his shirtfront, determined not to break down into an ugly cry.

"But thank me again," he said, "and I'll mop the floor with your lanky ass."

I sighed, no threat of tears now. "I just love these Hallmark moments, don't you?"

He let me go with a playful shove. "Get out of here, wiseass." He unlocked the door, opened it. "Word of advice? Farraday may be a prick, but he's like a scent hound when he sniffs out a chance to get his name in the papers. He's done everything but circle this case three times and piss on it, so you might want to tread a little light and pray he doesn't smell you coming. I'm too pretty to go away for murdering the son of a bitch."

"I'm not worried about Farraday, but how sharp is his new partner?"

Ben shrugged. "He runs through them like I run through socks, but the new guy seems decent enough. His name's Weber. Time will tell if he and Farraday gel. We got bets going around they won't. Weber doesn't say much, but he doesn't miss much either." He grinned. "Who's that sound like to you?" I just looked at him. "Hey, remember when you told Lieutenant Evans to go fuck himself? He'd transferred in all new and shiny and tried to make his bones by dressing you down in the middle of the squad because you were the only woman under him?" Ben slapped his knee. "The guy nearly choked on his breath mint. We thought we were going to have to call EMS." Ben wiped away a tear, sighed. "Those were good times, weren't they? You got a seven-day rip for that, but it was worth it just for the memories alone."

I walked out of the room smiling. "You're seriously twisted, you know that?"

"But you love me anyway," Ben called after me. "And if I weren't already in a committed relationship with Buster, it'd be you and me, kid!" Buster was Ben's fifty-pound English bulldog, a slobbering, lumbering fire hydrant with legs and an appetite to rival that of a T. rex.

"For the hundredth time, he's a dog!" I yelled back.

"Don't cheapen it!" Ben said. "We have something special, Buster and me."

"Seriously twisted," I answered as I turned the corner and headed for the elevator. I was practically home free, in and out without running into Farraday, when the elevator doors slid open, and we came face-to-face.

If it weren't for bad luck, I'd have none at all. Farraday's face went predatory as he slowly stepped out of the box and I stepped in, trying my best to ignore him. Just as the doors began to close, he grabbed them on both sides, holding them open, pissing off the three burly uniform cops in the elevator with me, who let out exasperated groans of irritation.

"What the hell are you doing here, Raines? Because I'm real sure I made myself perfectly clear the last time we met."

I fixed languid, unimpressed eyes on him. "I was mugged. I came to report it."

Farraday grit his teeth. "This is homicide, and you damn well know it."

"Then I was murdered and came to report it."

A cop snickered behind me. Farraday shot him a warning look. The snickering stopped.

"I told you I didn't want you nosing around. The case is off-limits to you. This building's off-limits to you."

"Oh, now you're claiming ownership of the entire police station? I didn't realize you'd risen so high, Detective Farraday. Congratulations. I'm curious, though. How many asses did you have to kiss to get crowned 'king of cops'?"

His chest heaved, his face got all splotchy. "One wrong move, Raines, just one . . ."

I cut him off. "Blah, blah, blah. Save the tough-guy act for someone who doesn't know who and what you are."

Farraday's eyes went to lizard-like slits, but if he had a comeback, he stifled it.

"Now let go of the door. You're keeping these fine policemen from their duties. And you're starting to make me physically ill."

Farraday leaned in, menacingly. "You're going to want to be real careful where you step from here on out."

I smiled. "I'm always careful, Detective. I'm careful on the street, on rooftops, and even in cop elevators like this one."

Moments passed without him making a move, then finally he drew his hands away, and the doors slowly began to close. My last look at Farraday was of him standing there, his chest heaving. He looked like he wanted to strangle me with his bare hands. The feeling was mutual. The elevator descended, and I stood there in the cramped box, eyes forward, mindful of the large cops crowded in around me. I'd just hassled one of their own, their brother in blue, and when you hassled one, you hassled them all. That's how it went. How would they take it? Would I now have to endure death by a thousand parking tickets? I waited, marking every second of our slow descent. One of the cops broke the silence.

"His daddy's not going to like that one bit."

Silence.

"His daddy can go screw himself," said another.

More silence.

"Six ways from Sunday," muttered the third.

The grin on my face stayed with me all the way down to the ground floor, through the lobby, and out to my car.

Chapter 13

The Chicago Skyway loomed over South Chicago, forming its western border. On the east, murky Lake Michigan served that purpose. The snaky Calumet River ran through it, reeking of sulfur and fish rot, a stink strong enough to water the eye and burn the throat as it blew through the neighborhood's cracked streets like a miasma of toxic pestilence.

Once an industrious steel mill community, South Chicago's silos were now reduced to hulking art-like installations towering over the flat landscape. The working-class Poles, Irish, and Italians who'd worked the factories and mills had fled farther south and west when the jobs dried up. Mexicans, blacks, Puerto Ricans, Dominicans and those too poor to pull up stakes and run, now tried to eke out a living at mom-and-pop *mercados*, sagging storefront health clinics, discount mattress emporiums, and payday loan places.

The report said Luna lived with his family at Eighty-Fifth and Muskegon. Father, deceased. His mother's name was Irma. There was no foot traffic on the street when I pulled up in front of the Luna's narrow clapboard house. Light blue paint had chipped away from the old façade, but the front stoop had been swept clean, the grass had been cut, and there were white lace curtains hanging from the front windows and colorful flower boxes outside, which told me the place was well cared for.

I scanned the houses of Luna's neighbors as wary eyes peeked at me from behind drawn curtains. In neighborhoods where bad things happened and no one in authority seemed to care about them, neighbors found it necessary to look out for one another. A stranger at one person's door was immediately a concern for everyone within eyeball range. You could almost imagine the conversations taking place on telephones all up and down the street. Who was that at the Lunas'? The police? Child Protective Services? The IRS? Could she be from INS? What did she want? Who was she looking for?

A little girl of about eight sat on a pink Barbie bicycle in the middle of the sidewalk in front of the Lunas', watching me as though she were waiting for me to do something miraculous, like sprout wings and fly. She barely blinked. Two houses up, an old man with a bushy white mustache stood sprinkling his grass with a limp garden hose and stopped to see what I was up to. I tried not to make any unnecessary movements and kept my hands completely visible, my body angled so I could see both the street and the Luna door, my eyes sweeping the sidewalk, the windows of the houses nearby, the little girl on the bicycle, the old man with the hose, my car. The reassuring weight of the gun in my clip holster gave me a peace of mind that money could not buy.

A half minute after I rang the bell, the Lunas' curtains parted, then stilled. I turned to face the window, hoping I looked non-threatening. From inside, I heard the muffled sound of a television but nothing else, until moments later when the security chain was engaged and the lock on the door slid free. I stepped back as the door opened and the top half of a woman's face appeared, her dark eyes cautious. "Yes?"

"Mrs. Luna?" I asked. "Mrs. Irma Luna?"

I could see a wall of suspicion rise. "Who are you?" she asked in accented English. "What do you want?"

When I gave her my name and a brief summary of why I was there, she slammed the door in my face, the force of it blowing my hair back. Feeling the neighbors' eyes on my back, I stood there for a moment doing nothing. The block was certainly getting their money's worth.

I rang the bell again, then eased back a couple steps and waited. It took almost a minute for Mrs. Luna to open the door again. Angrily, she stepped from behind it and stood in the doorway where I could see all of her, though she kept a tight grip on the door. She looked to be about five foot three, dressed in jeans and a short-sleeved pink shirt with pearly buttons and embroidered flowers along the bodice, her straight black hair pulled back in a neat ponytail. Maybe she was my age, mid-thirties, maybe a little older. Steady eyes staring out of a face with sharp angles told me I didn't have long before the door slammed shut again.

"Go away," she ordered. "I do not want you here. You and the police have done enough."

"Mrs. Luna, I understand you're angry, but I'm not with the police. I'd just like to talk to you about your son, Cesar. About what happened at St. Brendan's."

The caution in her eyes turned to something harder and much colder. For a while she didn't speak. "You look like police. You come to me like they come, and I've told them all I am going to. You are not interested in what happened to Cesar, only in what you say happened."

I lifted the bottom corner of my jacket to show her I didn't have a star. "I'm not with the police. I'm just here for the truth."

"The truth is that my son is dead! The truth is that no one outside of this neighborhood cares that this is so!"

"I care."

She eyed me skeptically. "I don't believe you. Leave my house."

The door began to close. "I was a friend of the priest who was killed along with your son. I do care, Mrs. Luna. More than you know."

The door opened wide again.

I dug into my back pocket, pulled out my PI's license and business card, and held them out for her to read. "I'm a private investigator. This is my card. This is a copy of my license. I am not the police. I want to find the truth. That'll be a lot easier to accomplish if I know more about your son."

Defiant eyes met mine. "And the police whose job it is to find the truth? What are they doing, besides blaming my son for such a terrible thing?" Her eyes bore into mine. The door wavered.

"Could you go to your grave in peace not knowing what happened to Cesar, Mrs. Luna? Because I sure couldn't. Father Heaton was family to me. I need to know how he died. Somebody has to pay for taking him." Mrs. Luna stood there saying nothing. "Sometimes people won't talk to the police," I said hurriedly. "But I was hoping you'd talk to me. I need you to tell me about Cesar."

Her dark eyes burned hot. "He was a gangbanger and a criminal, isn't that what they say?"

I hesitated. "Yes. That's what they say." Her eyes widened. I'd shocked her. She'd likely expected me to lie. "But I'm sure he was more than that to you, wasn't he?"

She thought things over for a time, and the door stayed open. "He would not have stolen from God's house. We are Catholic. But the police do not listen. The police say the priest killed my Cesar."

"I promise you. He did not."

"What can you do against the police? They are many. You

are just one." She wrapped her arms around herself, as though she'd caught a chill, her eyes still angry, wounded, defensive.

"A determined one can do a great deal against many, Mrs. Luna. And right now, no one is more determined than I am. I don't believe your son robbed that church, and Father Heaton did not kill him. If I'm right, if that's true, then there's somebody walking around out there who thinks they got away with two murders. I'm willing to do whatever it takes to make sure whoever it is pays for what they did. What do you want, Mrs. Luna?"

"Justice," she answered, her voice strong, resolute. She studied me for a moment without speaking. "My neighbors are watching. They do not like strangers."

I didn't bother to turn around to look. I could feel them watching. "I'm not too wild about strangers either."

"And yet you come here alone? A woman. You are either very brave or very stupid."

I smiled. "Probably a little bit of both."

Without another word, Mrs. Luna held the door open, stepped back, and let me in. "Then come. For Cesar, I will also be a little bit of both."

An old woman dressed in a yellow house dress and red slippers sat on a floral couch with a little dark-haired girl of about three, both of them watching a lively cartoon in Spanish. Neither looked up as I was led toward the back of the house. In the dining room, Mrs. Luna and I sat in two of the six chairs that surrounded a well-polished table covered by a large doily tablecloth. She offered me something to drink or eat. I politely declined. "My son was not a perfect son," she began. "But he was my son. Do you have children?"

I shook my head no. "Not yet." I could barely keep house plants alive; I shuddered to think how I'd handle a real live human.

She gave me a pitying half smile. "Then you cannot know." She pointed to a spot on the wall behind me. I turned to see a large framed photo of an angelic altar boy, his eyes cast heavenward, his small hands on a white Bible.

"Cesar?"

She nodded. "He was a good boy. But the world changes people. His father, my Jorge, died not long after that picture was taken. That is when Cesar began to find trouble. He turned away from the church, from us. But he was young. I hoped he would return, somehow become a good man."

"Do you know where he was the night he died? Why he might have ended up at St. Brendan's?"

Her lips twisted distastefully. "He often went out late. I could not stop him. He would give no answers. After a long time, I stopped asking, too afraid that one day he would tell me something I did not want to know. I continued to pray for him, to light the candles."

"Did you notice any changes in him?"

Mrs. Luna looked puzzled. "Changes?"

"Going out more often, or not as much," I prompted. "Did he seem angry, upset? Did he mention having a problem with anyone?" I recalled Cesar's bruised face, the beating he'd taken. "Any change at all."

"He seemed . . . less hard," she offered. "A few times they called for him, but he did not go. I was pleased. He even went to Mass with me. Not for a long time had he done this. I told him, with tears, how happy this made me. But again, he would go out."

"And the day he died?"

"I made him breakfast." Mrs. Luna smiled, appearing to recall the morning, but her smile quickly faded. "Then he went. The next time I saw my son he was dead, cold."

"There was a storm," I said.

"Yes. I worried where he was on such a night. . . . I always worried. I worry now, even though I know where he is."

"He must have been heading someplace pretty important to go out in that weather."

Her expression soured. "He was always with them—the men who are not men."

"None of them will talk to the police," I said.

She sneered. "Their precious code. They will not go against it."

"Even Hector Perez?"

"Not even him, even though he grew up with my Cesar. They were like brothers, both the same—boys without fathers looking for something in the streets that only God and family can give. Hector's mother feels as I do about the Scorpions, but what can we do?" From the front room, the music on the cartoon swelled to a crescendo. The toddler giggled wildly. Mrs. Luna studied me. "How is it you are so close to this priest that you would come all the way out here to do what the police won't? A friend, you said."

"More than that," I said.

She studied me. "But not blood."

I shifted in my chair, suddenly uncomfortable. "No, but the closest thing I had to it." I hesitated, resistant to sharing such a personal part of myself. Mrs. Luna sat watching my internal struggle, and I could see the barriers begin to rise again. Not sharing would close her down. "I lost my mother when I was a kid. Father Heaton helped me through it."

"Your real father? He did not help?"

I shrugged. "Took off. I guess the thought of being a single parent was too much for him."

"Do you miss him?"

"I stopped missing him a long time ago."

She nodded knowingly. "A familiar story, a familiar sadness." She sighed. "Then it seems someone has taken something

very dear to both of us, yes?" The silence hung in the air between us. Mrs. Luna stared off into the distance. She looked as
though she would never have another happy moment as long as
she lived. "I apologize for closing the door. You are different
from the others. Perhaps it is true we want the same thing. Still,
it is difficult to trust. People so often wear false faces."

I nodded, understanding completely. She rose from the chair
and pulled herself up to her full height. "I think it would help
you to see Cesar's room, to see who he was. Maybe then you
can find the person who did this to him and to your father."

I shot to my feet, surprised by the offer. "Yes, it would.
Thank you."

"But if you are not as you seem," she said. "If this is some
trick played upon me, I will not rest. I will not stop until I have
my justice. You understand this?"

I smiled. "Seems we are a lot more alike than we are different, Mrs. Luna." She led me back to a room set apart from the
rest of the house. She turned the knob on a narrow door,
opened it, and then stepped aside to let me through. She didn't
venture past the threshold.

"Everything is as it was," she said softly. "I cannot bring myself to go in, not yet." Her eyes blazed. "I would not let the police look. They showed no respect. They made up their minds
about Cesar before they even showed up." She hovered in the
doorway, her eyes avoiding her son's things. "For them, it was
all about the priest," she said, nearly in a whisper. She stood
there stoically, watching. "Do what you must."

I thanked her again and got to work. Cesar owned a pretty
impressive stereo system and a big-screen plasma TV, along
with hundreds of CDs and DVDs, which I slowly fanned
through. Most of the music was in Spanish, produced by artists
I didn't know. The movie titles leaned toward the car-chase-
creepy-vampire variety, top of the hit parade, I assumed, for
eighteen-year-old males. The walls were plastered with *Scar-*

face posters, and strands of multicolored Christmas lights hung from the stucco ceiling.

For nearly an hour, with Mrs. Luna standing as still as a sentinel, I searched on my knees and on tiptoe. I emptied drawers and filled them again. I picked through the closet, feeling down into the toes of boots and shoes, checking the pockets of shirts, pants, and jackets. I slid my hands along shelves, but drew back only dusty fingers.

Taped to the dresser mirror with narrow strips of clear tape were photos of Cesar's mother, the old woman, and the little girl in the front room. There was also a photo of Hector Perez, whom I recognized from his mug shot. In the photo, Hector posed rakishly with Cesar in a smoky bar, his arm slung fraternally around Cesar's shoulder. Hector, dark and covered in angry tats, might have been attractive if not for the malevolent sneer. A few of the tape strips didn't have photos attached to them.

I kept searching. I fluttered the pages of magazines and crawled beneath Cesar's bed, scraping up long-forgotten discards—an empty candy wrapper, a broken shoelace, an old issue of *Hot Rod* magazine. I ran my hands between Cesar's mattress and box spring. Nothing. I lifted the mattress, expecting well-thumbed issues of *Playboy* tucked away where Mrs. Luna wouldn't find them. Nothing. Then, by chance, I noticed a slit in the side of the mattress wide enough for a hand to fit through. I reached in and felt around, my hand bumping up against something solid, yet flexible. A book. I pulled it free. It was a Bible.

"What is it?" Mrs. Luna asked from the doorway.

I held it up. "Why would Cesar hide this?"

She peered at the book from half a room away. "I don't know," she said, her voice cracking. She looked puzzled.

I shook my head. I had no idea either. Why would anyone hide a Bible? I sat down on the mattress and opened it, fluttering the pages. I gasped when a photograph of a young black girl and a church bulletin from St. Brendan's fell on my lap. I shot to my feet, turned to Mrs. Luna, and held the bulletin up for her to see it. "St. Brendan's. He didn't just stumble on it. He'd been there before." He and Pop weren't strangers.

"How can you know this? Many people go to church."

"Father Heaton made it a point to meet every person who stepped inside his church. He learned their names; he remembered things about them, even if he only met them once. They knew each other. There was a connection." I held up the photograph. "Who's this girl?"

Mrs. Luna stared at the picture. "I have never seen her before. Why would Cesar hide these things?" I heard her, but didn't answer. My attention was drawn to the items in my hand, which, at this point, were more precious to me than gold. There were no handwritten notations scrawled in the borders of the Bible's pages, no highlighted passages, or turned-down corners anywhere. The bulletin, too, was unmarred. I noted the date, Sunday, December twelfth. I studied the photograph again. The girl looked to be about sixteen or seventeen, pretty. She smiled easily for the photographer. Had that been Cesar? "What does this mean?" Mrs. Luna asked.

"Nothing yet," I said, buoyed by the possibilities. "Do you mind if I take these with me?"

"You want to take Cesar's Bible?"

"I promise I'll return it to you."

She nodded, though she didn't look at all sure. I slipped the bulletin and photo back inside the book, then set the book aside while I continued my search with renewed vigor. What else would I find? Where else would it lead me?

Several bottles of high-smelling cologne and hair gel sat on the dresser, along with a couple dollars in loose change and a knockoff designer watch. A Bulls ashtray fashioned from cheap tin sat off to the side, the tray filled with some sort of ash. I picked it up, sniffed the debris, rolled the ash around on my fingertips.

"My Cesar did not smoke; he did not do drugs."

I held the ashtray out so she could see it better. "Not drugs, ash. But not tobacco. Something else."

She glowered. "But the something else always turns out to be something we must pay for, in money, in years, often both. The law is not blind when it comes to us."

I couldn't argue with her. She was right up to a point. Systems, legal or otherwise, rarely worked in favor of those with black and brown skin. For our communities, breaks and benefits didn't exist. Punitive punishment ruled, and it came down hard. I doubted Cesar ever got a single break his entire life. "May I keep looking?" I asked. "I won't without your consent."

She scanned the room, glancing at the Bible on the bed, the ash in the tray, me. Finally, she nodded. "Continue."

I plucked out a few of the larger pieces from the ashtray and cradled them in the palm of my hand.

"Paper," I finally decided.

Not writing paper, heavier.

I glanced back at the mirror and the empty strips of tape. Photographic paper. "He burned photos." I faced Mrs. Luna. "There are photos missing from the mirror. Can you remember what they were?"

She studied the mirror, bewildered. "His pictures of the Scorpions are not there."

"Why would he burn those?"

She shrugged, but did not look at me. Her eyes were locked on the Bible.

"He was reading the Holy Book," she whispered, her eyes flooding with tears. "My son would have been a good man."

"He left the photo of Hector Perez," I pointed out.

"I told you they were like brothers. That is a bond not easily broken."

"He may have been one of the last people to see Cesar alive."

She dabbed at her eyes with a Kleenex from her pocket. "How do you know this?"

"He gave the police a statement. He didn't tell you?" Mrs. Luna shook her head. "Do you think he'd talk to me?"

"No, he will not. . . . Does that mean you will not try?"

I shook my head. "No, I'll try."

Hopeful eyes held mine. "When?"

"Now."

"Then I will come with you. He will not talk to you, but he will talk to me."

I smiled. "Let's hope you're right. We're due for a break right about now."

Chapter 14

I pulled up in front of Hector's house and Mrs. Luna and I got out of the car and walked up to the neat red brick bungalow with white trim. The small front square of lawn was crowded with yellow plastic daisies stuck into the patchy grass. When the wind picked up, the petals would turn like tiny windmills. Today the air was still. Ankle-high chicken wire separated the neglected grass from the city's cracked and neglected sidewalk. On the front porch, I stood beside Mrs. Luna as she rang the bell. After a time, an old woman opened the door, staring rheumy eyed through a screen door that looked as if a dog had clawed at it one too many times. She looked at Mrs. Luna and smiled. Her eyes narrowed suspiciously when she saw me. Mrs. Luna spoke to the woman in Spanish, gesturing a few times in my direction. The woman listened, nodded, and then closed the door.

"Hector's grandmother," Mrs. Luna explained. "She thinks perhaps Hector is out working on his car. She will check for us." She drew her sweater in close against her body. I was sure there had been more to the conversation, but I kept my mouth shut. "She says you look like the police," she added sheepishly. "She doesn't allow the police into her home either. The police do not have the respect of the community."

Mrs. Luna started to say more but stopped when the door opened again and the old woman returned. This time she had a young boy about eight or nine with her. For a moment, the old woman stared at me without speaking, then said something to the boy that sounded like a command before she unceremoniously nudged him out onto the porch and closed the door behind him.

"This is Raffi," Mrs. Luna said. "Hector's nephew."

The boy stared at me for a moment, then jumped down off the porch steps and headed for the side gate, waving for us to follow. "Come on," he said.

There were no plastic daisies in the backyard, only a couple of knobby trees with a sagging hemp hammock twisted between them. The garage, one of those aluminum-sided, two-car, prefab jobs, sat at the end of a narrow yard bordered by chain link fence. The blare of Tejano music also marked the spot in case I missed the visual cue.

I stood quietly in the doorway of the small garage beside Raffi and Mrs. Luna, watching as Hector, dressed in chinos and a sleeveless undershirt, worked under the hood of a white, late-model Cadillac Eldorado. Off to the side, a plump, slope-eyed Latina, maybe about sixteen, sat in a battered lawn chair bopping to the beat of the music. As the girl moved, she twisted the dial on an old boom box in her lap, jumping from song to song, likely looking for one she liked better. On top of the radio, she'd propped a textbook—opened midway—and a bag of red vines. A school bag sat on the floor by her feet. Hector didn't appear armed, neither did the girl, but I had no way of knowing what might be hidden in the garage, in the car, or in the bag.

"Hector," Raffi announced. "Somebody to see you."

Hector turned, wiping his greasy hands on an oily rag he

pulled from his back pocket. He balked when he saw me. I noticed his knuckles were lightly bruised.

"Who the fu—?" he began, before spotting Mrs. Luna. When Hector registered her presence, his demeanor shifted instantly from ferocious to almost docile. He smiled warmly at Mrs. Luna and hugged her, as a son would a mother. Gently, she stroked his jet-black hair and kissed him on the cheek, as she no doubt wished she could still do with Cesar.

Spanish was quickly exchanged. Most of it I didn't get, but I got enough to know that she was introducing me. I was able to pick out the words detective *privado*, so Hector was learning I was a PI, not a cop, not that either profession would cut me much slack with him. While Mrs. Luna explained, Hector glared at me, and I could tell by the way he did it that he was trying to decide which way to play it—hard-ass, routinely reserved for outsiders, especially cops, or conciliatory, as his obvious bond with Mrs. Luna dictated. The distasteful frown he gave me was clear evidence of his inner struggle.

"Looks like cop to me," he said, his heavy-lidded eyes narrowing. "I don't like cops. I don't like white cops, black cops, dude cops, or chick cops." He stretched his arms out wide. "This right here is a no-cop zone."

I pulled out my card and laid it on his tool cart. "Like she just told you, I'm a PI."

Hector leered, then sniffed derisively. "Nah, I'm looking at cop. Don't matter what the card says."

I couldn't argue with him. Cops and robbers everywhere had a good nose for ferreting out the other. I could give the star back and walk away from the roll call, but even after two years I couldn't get the cop out of my head. Cop literally oozed from my pores. Cop was in the walk, in the talk, in the way I saw the world, in the wary way I approached Hector. Same held for him, I suspected. Gangbangers walked an opposite path and saw the world from the bottom side up. My eyes held his. I didn't take the bait. It was what it was.

"Please, Hector," cried Mrs. Luna, jumping in to end the stare down. "If there is something you know, you must say it." Hector appeared unbowed. "This is about what is right, about *familia.*" The garage got quiet, except for the music from the radio.

"I don't know nothing about Cesar and no church," Hector said.

I pulled a photograph of Pop from my pocket, the one he'd let me take last Memorial Day. "Maybe you've seen this man with Cesar?"

Hector gave the photo the briefest of glances before turning away, disinterested. "Nope."

I repositioned the photo so that it was directly in front of him. "This is Father Heaton. His picture's been in all the papers."

He shrugged. "Don't read the papers."

"You knew Cesar better than almost anybody," I said. "Like brothers, right? Why would he go to St. Brendan's?"

Hector slowly crossed his tatted arms across his chest. "Who knows? Who cares?"

"I care," I said.

Mrs. Luna turned to the girl in the chair. "This is Marisol, Hector's sister. Perhaps you know something, Marisol?"

I angled the photograph so the girl could see it. She shut her book and leaned in close for a better look, as did Raffi, who, apparently, didn't want to be left out of anything.

Marisol squinted. "I never seen him."

"Raffi?" I asked.

The boy pursed his lips, concentrated hard. "Nah, I never seen him either."

I turned back to Hector. "Cesar ever mention going to St. Brendan's?"

Hector chuckled. Raffi, taking his lead from his uncle, joined in. "Yeah, right," Hector said. "Like Cesar was some *mona-guillo.*"

I didn't know the term and turned to Mrs. Luna for help.

"Altar boy," she said, turning to Hector. "My son was good. He was reading the Bible."

I pulled out the photo of the black girl I'd found in Cesar's Bible, but got the same negative response from Hector.

"Cesar have a girl?" I asked.

"He had lots of girls," Hector said. "So?"

"A girlfriend," I said. "Maybe *this* girl?" I held the photo up again.

Hector took his time answering, his eyes dull, flat. He looked bored. He didn't want to help me. He didn't trust me. I didn't trust him. "Nah."

Marisol cranked up the volume on her radio, but there was something in the way she did it that piqued my interest.

"That true, Marisol?" I asked, angling the photo so she could see it.

Her head popped up. She blinked rapidly. "Huh?"

"I asked if Cesar had a girlfriend. Hector says no. Maybe this girl?"

Marisol and Hector exchanged a cautious glance. "Nu-uh, I never saw no girl of Cesar's around here."

Hector shot me a satisfied grin. He looked pleased I was coming up empty. "So, we done?"

"You and Cesar were close," I said. "Yet, you don't seem to care what happened to him."

Mrs. Luna jumped forward. "Yes, Hector. He was like your brother."

Hector began to slowly crack his knuckles, demonstrating just how disinterested he was in the whole thing. "Cesar's dead, and dead is dead. We all die. That's why you got to live hard, right?"

Mrs. Luna screeched and flung herself onto him, shaking him as violently as a five foot three inch woman could. "Enough!" she yelled. "You are going to tell me what I need to know, or I swear to all that is holy—".

Hector yanked his shirt free and sneered at her, his body coiled tight for a fight, but then he took one look at the grieving woman and appeared to melt into himself, his swagger gone. There was humanity buried beneath the toughness. I'd suspected as much. Most everyone had a spark of untouched humanness down deep that cruelty, dysfunction, or anger hadn't yet destroyed. Hector's guard was down, but it wouldn't stay down. I had one shot to get what he was willing to give. Mrs. Luna's nostrils flared, but she stood her ground, glowering, grieving. "Tell me about the last night you saw him."

Hector glanced at her, and then faced me. He looked like he'd rather cut off his own arm than help me, but after some hesitation, he squared his shoulders and began to talk. "We were at Angel's, all right? We drank some beers, then he got a call and left."

"Do you know who the call was from?" I asked.

His cold eyes grew even colder. I hadn't thought it possible. "No," he snapped.

"Long call? Short call?"

"Short. And none of my business. Or yours."

The garage was not big enough to give any of us room to breathe easily. Hector, Mrs. Luna, Marisol, Raffi, and I were far too close for anyone's comfort. The raw hate radiating off Hector's body seemed to heat up the place, but I pushed on. "What'd you two talk about at the bar?" I asked.

Hector didn't answer right away. He let my question lay there like a dead alewife washed up on the beach. This pulling of teeth was excruciating. Would the Scorpion code of silence win out, or would he tell Cesar's mother, and by extension, me, what we needed to know? Everyone waited for him to decide as the thump-thump of the music punctuated the awkward passage of time.

Finally, Hector shook his head, and the corners of his mouth turned up into a sly grin. He wasn't going to tell me, and there wasn't anything I could do to compel him. I couldn't arrest him. I couldn't call for backup. I opened my mouth to ask another question, but before I could get the words out, Mrs. Luna hauled off and slapped Hector across the face, leaving an imprint of her entire hand on his cheek. Stunned, he stumbled back but quickly regained his footing and lurched forward as though he were going to strike her back. Instantly, all the air in the garage got heavy. Marisol and Raffi gasped.

I quickly stepped in front of Mrs. Luna and pulled her behind me. "Stop! Right there! Everybody just stop!" Hector's eyes, black and dangerous, bore into mine. They were evil eyes. I extended one arm to hold him off, the other to hold back Mrs. Luna. "Back up! Right now! Hector, keep your hands where I can see them."

Mrs. Luna screeched from behind me. "I am not afraid of you! You are a boy, a child! I have nothing to lose!"

Rapid Spanish followed, none of it helping to squelch the fire. This was no place for a gangbanger face-off. If I had a gun, Hector likely had one. I motioned for Mrs. Luna to keep quiet.

"Let's everybody just calm the hell down," I said.

Mrs. Luna backed up. Hector backed up, then turned to pace the floor. It was a tiny garage. Bullets made big holes. I was working on three hours sleep and, dammit—I didn't want to die in a prefab garage listening to Tejano boom box music.

Hector stopped pacing, studied Mrs. Luna, then me. He stood straighter, lifted his chin. "What're you going to do?"

"That depends on what you do," I said.

Our eyes held.

"I got it covered."

"That makes two of us," I said.

Mrs. Luna kept at it. She may have been little, but she'd apparently found her voice, unfortunately, at the absolutely worst time ever. Hector began to ease over toward his tool cart, and my breath caught. His tools were there, possibly something else. A slap in the face was a difficult thing to let slide, especially for a hard man whose ego was so deeply tied to being perceived as such.

"Hector, whatever you're thinking about doing, don't!" I commanded. "Back away from that cart." I eased my right hand down to the holster at my back. "Let's all just dial this thing way back." Hector stopped, but didn't back away. He was still within range of the cart. He eyed it, but didn't move. This is how people died, I thought—one person strikes and won't back down, another feels disrespected, but doesn't have the emotional foundation to work it through. I held both my hands out in front of me to show they were empty, taking a chance I hoped I wouldn't come to regret. "Look. Look. Empty hands," I said. "We're just here to talk. That's all."

He breathed noisily, menacing eyes spitting fire. "She comes into *my* home like *this*!"

"Think, Hector. There are children here. Marisol, Raffi. And I'd really like it if we could all walk out of here alive and well."

Hector slid a glance toward Marisol and Raffi; both sat riveted.

"They got to learn how it is," Hector said. "How to be!"

My stomach lurched. "Not here. Not like this."

Mrs. Luna kept at it, ignoring the tension, the danger. "You would strike a mother? Is that how far you have fallen? What would your own mother say about that? I held you as a baby. I welcomed you into my home as a boy, and now you would do this to me?"

My eyes stayed trained on Hector's hands, as sweat ran in rivulets down my back. Hector appeared to think about his mother, about what she'd say. Maybe that would be enough to convince him to stand down. We all waited anxiously for him to cycle it through. Anxious moments passed before his shoulders relaxed, he moved farther away from the cart, and I gulped in air as though I hadn't had any in weeks.

Hector stared at Mrs. Luna. "For your disrespect, nothing. This I do in honor of Cesar. But only once." Then he turned to me. "Your lucky day, cop who's not a cop."

I barely heard him over the blood rushing in my ears. "I'll take it."

"Cesar wanted out," Hector said. Mrs. Luna drew in a quick breath and covered her mouth with hands that shook. "I told him he was loco. That there wasn't no out, but he wouldn't listen. He didn't want the life no more."

"When was this?" I asked.

He slid me a look that was hot enough to pierce a hole in a sheet of titanium. "Couple months ago."

That'd be February, I thought. The same month Pop began to notice someone following him.

"Who else knew about him wanting out?"

Hector chuckled bitterly. "Everyone knew. Cesar wasn't hiding nothing. I warned him, tried to get him to see, but Cesar was Cesar. He said he could handle what was coming down. Still, I'm trying to save his ass from a world-class beat down, or worse." Hector snarled, "Blood in, blood out. That's how it is."

"So you beat him," I said.

His eyes darted to Mrs. Luna. "I didn't say nothing about a beating."

"You didn't have to. I see your knuckles. The bruises are about a week old. I saw his face."

I could feel Mrs. Luna tense behind me, her rage nearly palpable. I motioned again for her to stay quiet.

"He was lucky it was me," Hector barked, half pleading to her. "He would have got worse from the others. I beat him, so they wouldn't kill him!"

I didn't know what to say. My "otherness" could never penetrate Hector's twisted value system. Gangs stitched together family from broken human pieces, creating an off-kilter patchwork with its own set of mores and strictures, incomprehensible to those who didn't belong. All you could see from the outside was the violence, the futility, and the waste. I suddenly felt an overwhelming sadness for the lives forfeited, including Hector's, evil eyes and all.

"So the Scorpions met not for beer, but to pile on Cesar," I said.

"He knew what had to happen. He wanted it. He was turning his back on family, so all of us took our turn, me first and hardest. We made it so he'd remember what he was giving up, but that's all. We had no part in what went down later. It's not on us that Cesar flipped and went after some priest."

"You lie," Mrs. Luna screeched. "He could not do such a thing to God!"

Hector's jaw clenched, but he didn't fire back; instead, he drew a half-empty pack of Marlboros from his left pants pocket, pulled one out, slid it into his mouth, and lit it with a cheap Bic he pulled from the right pocket. He was going for cool detachment. He got insolent four-year-old with candy smokes.

"We did what we had to, then we turned our backs like he did to us." He took a step forward. . . . "And we don't need no lady cop coming out here asking questions that don't have nothing to do with her. Now I'm done talking."

Mrs. Luna shook her head, pity on her face. "I hope you will someday see how foolish you are. I wish this, especially, for your mother. This is the end between us. From this time on, I do not know you."

She turned on her heels and walked out of the garage, back up the walk. I turned to back out after her, but stopped to ask one last question.

"What are you, a junior or senior at Cervantes?" I asked Marisol.

The girl's eyes narrowed. "How do you know where I go?"

I pointed to the school decal on the bag at her feet. "Junior? Senior?"

"Junior," she answered warily. "Why?"

I shrugged, smiled. "Just curious. Thanks for your time, Hector."

Raffi trailed me up the walk, flitting around me like a gnat. "Oh man, Hector is mad."

"Yep, I got that."

"It was like a real standoff! Cool, huh?"

"No. Not cool." I picked up my pace, but Raffi matched it. His eyes sparkled excitedly. "Can I see your gun? What do you got? A Glock?"

"I'm counting," I said. "When I get to five you'd better be far away from me. One . . . two . . ." Raffi took off running back to the garage. I headed for my car. "Thanks for your help back there," I said when I'd caught up to Mrs. Luna. "You were right. He wouldn't have talked to me without you there."

"I wash my hands. I turn my back on all of it. My son is dead. Whatever happens, he will still be dead." We got in the car and I headed back to Mrs. Luna's.

"What do you think really happened to Cesar?" she asked. "What do you know that the police do not?"

I slid her a sideways glance. "I know Father Heaton. I have a bulletin that suggests Cesar knew him, too. I know that people just don't stop being who they are at the drop of a hat, that pattern of behavior is important, and I know that there's more to uncover."

I could sense her watching me as I drove. "That is not much."

It wasn't, I thought, my eyes on the road, but it wasn't *nothing*, which is what I had yesterday.

"What would you have done if Hector pulled his gun? He had one. He always does."

"I don't want to think about it."

Mrs. Luna shook her head. "He won't talk to you again."

"I know. I'm hoping to have an easier time with Marisol."

She turned to face me, puzzled. "Marisol? Why?"

"I believe she didn't know Father Heaton, but she's seen that girl in the photograph."

Mrs. Luna stared at me, confused. "She said she did not."

"She looked away and began to fidget when she saw the photo. She recognized her."

"How can you know this?"

"Experience," I said.

Mrs. Luna looked as though she'd lost her last friend on earth. "She lied to me?"

I nodded. "And I'd like to know why, wouldn't you?"

Chapter 15

When the sun came up, I got my first good look at Miguel de Cervantes High. The four-story, sand-colored brick building took up the entire north side of the block. The sign on the brown grass out front announced upcoming local school council meetings and a dance for upperclassmen planned for Saturday. On the south side of the street sat an unassuming row of sagging shotgun houses and three flats, the modest homes of the working poor. There was nothing fancy about the southeast side. It was solid, proud, and as indestructible as cast-iron. It was pot roast and potatoes, spare change collected in old apple cider jars, church on Sundays, and dirty jobs that didn't pay nearly enough to send kids off to college. It was working class and steadfast. Even the beaters at the curb seemed to match their owners' unwillingness to give in or out.

Kids started showing up a little after eight, some dropped off by cars driven by parents in a rush, most dawdling up the cracked sidewalk under their own steam. Marisol was not among the early arrivals. There was a lot of pulling and pushing and horsing around, boys pulling on girls, girls pretending they didn't like it, a lot of texting, and a lot of foul language shouted at the top of pubescent lungs. It looked like it might rain, but not one kid was dressed for even the possibility of bad weather. My gaze continuously shifted from the sidewalk to my rear-view mirror to the school's front door, where I watched a portly guard scan everyone quickly through the metal detectors.

Had Cesar rediscovered his faith? Is that why he chose to break from the Scorpions, or had he just grown tired of disappointing his mother? Had he chosen Mass at St. Brendan's because it was well outside of his neighborhood? Was he deliberately trying to avoid Hector and the others? Pop worked with at-risk kids, and Cesar certainly qualified, but so far, the fact that Pop worked in a church and Cesar had visited it, were the only things that connected them. Had Pop and Cesar met that night in secrecy? If so, why? What were they hiding?

I perked up when I spotted Marisol a half block up, walking toward the school in a purple sweater, gray hoodie, and tight jeans. She strolled along with another girl, both of them teetering on heels too high for sixteen-year-old feet to handle, books cradled in their arms, knockoff designer purses slung over their shoulders, and chattering a mile a minute. When the pair got closer, I got out and trotted over to intercept them. "Marisol!"

She stopped and turned, then frowned when she recognized me.

"I'd like to talk to you," I said.

Marisol groaned and shifted her weight to one foot in a show of adolescent pique. "I can't talk to you. I got homework to finish before first period. It's freaking history, and Mr. Beatty is a real tool. These questions are hard, too."

"I only need a few minutes."

"Hector said not to talk to you, anyways. He says you're trouble."

"You do everything Hector tells you to do?"

She thrust her chest out. "Hector's not my boss. I do what I want. But if he found out I was talking to you after yesterday, he'd lose his shit. He's got some serious anger issues. He threw a wrench through the window after you left."

"Better the window than my head," I said. "Five minutes. That's all."

She angled her head. "What's in it for me?"

I glanced at her friend, who stared at me with dark, lifeless eyes. She was shorter and thinner than Marisol, but it was her hair that got my attention. Her dark bangs were severely cut on the diagonal; the rest of her hair had been violently assaulted by long streaks of bright magenta. It was quite a statement, of what, I couldn't quite make out.

Did no one do anything nowadays just because it was the right thing to do? When did that stop? Why had it? I was tired of deals and going tit for tat. Marisol stared at me blankly, probably wondering what my malfunction was.

"Fine. You give me five minutes, and I'll give you the answers to your history homework. Even trade."

Marisol brightened. "For real?"

I nodded. "That's what I said. Tit for tat."

Marisol frowned. "What's tits got to do with anything?"

I screamed inside. "Let's do this, Marisol."

She leaned over and whispered something to the girl. "So I'm gonna be a minute," she said, pulling away from her friend's ear.

"Whatever," the girl snapped. She walked off reluctantly, turning back every couple of steps to watch us.

Marisol rummaged around in her purse, pulling out a nubble of chewing gum, which she popped into her mouth. "I like the deal, but like I said, I don't know nothing about Cesar. He was Hector's friend, not mine."

The girl hesitated at the door, still watching. I was curious as to what she found so fascinating.

"What'd you tell her?" I asked.

"I told her you were my *papi's* new girlfriend come to spread the drama."

Marisol waved her manicured fingers at the girl in an effort to shoo her inside. Besides the wild red fingernail polish, Marisol sported a shiny ring on each finger, and each wrist was tricked out with rows of gold and silver bangles. Whenever her arms moved it sounded like we were surrounded by fairies in flight.

"So now she's waiting for the show. But there ain't gonna be no show, Josephina!" Josephina, denied satisfaction, pulled a face, flipped us the bird, and then disappeared inside. "Sometimes I don't know why I'm friends with her," Marisol said, smoothing nonexistent wrinkles from the front of her sweater. She took a moment, then her eyes narrowed and her mouth turned up into a slow smile. "So, you know history, huh? You probably graduated college and everything. I mean, you got to at least be halfway smart to be a detective."

I nodded slowly. I didn't like the deal, though I'd proposed it. The whole thing felt predatory, but I needed her cooperation, and altruism wasn't going to get it for me. I had a pretty solid grasp of history. My mother had been a teacher, and I'd gotten my degree before the Peace Corps and joining the police department. I felt pretty confident Marisol couldn't stump me, but I didn't have time to waste.

"Sure. You at least have to know how to read and write and count to ten," I offered facetiously.

"That's what I figured," Marisol said, the snarkiness of my response sailing right over her head. She opened one of her books and pulled out a sheet of paper. "So this'll be one hand washing all the other hands, like they say."

"Or you could decide to come up with the answers on your own. For the sake of your education," I said, though the minute my words hit the air, I realized how futile they were. This little exchange didn't actually rise to the level of contributing to the delinquency of a minor, but it still wasn't sitting well. She stood blank faced, the paper in her hand, waiting for me to wrestle with the moral complexities. "Fine," I said. "You first."

Marisol shot me a victorious smirk. "Okay, question one. Who's that old, black dude who invented peanut butter?" My brows furrowed; she'd stumped me right off the bat. Black dude? Peanut butter? She waited patiently, chewing, while I searched my internal database for peanut butter-related factoids. "You mean George Washington Carver?"

Marisol grinned. "Yeah, that sounds about right. I think it was three names like that." She plucked a pencil from her hair and wrote the answer down.

"But he didn't actually invent peanut butter," I said. "He—"

"Bub-bub-bub!" she said, waving her hand to ward off further explanation. "Whatever, all right? All I need is the name. I don't need to get all into it."

I looked around to see who might be listening. No one was.

She blew a bubble, then quickly sucked it back into her mouth in one seamless move. "And when did that slave war stop? It like happened two hundred years ago."

I searched her face for a sign that she was putting me on. Sadly, she was not. I pressed my lips together to keep from saying something indelicate and paused before answering. "The Civil War."

Marisol stared at me flatly.

"It was a pretty important conflict," I offered gently. Marisol blinked, waited. I should have stopped, but didn't. Something in me just couldn't. "It determined the direction of the entire country." She cleared her throat, drummed her pencil against the book. I stared at her; she stared back. "1865."

She wrote it down. "Okay, now I guess you can ask me something, but then I get to go again. That's how the deal works."

"Tell me about Cesar's girl," I said.

Her eyes slid away from mine. "I told you I don't know her."
"You recognized her picture. Tell me."
"What makes you think that?"
"Everything you didn't say yesterday."
She squinted. "Huh?"
I slid my hands into my back pockets fighting the impulse to shake her. "You liked Cesar, didn't you?"
"He was okay, I guess. With him and Hector it was like having two brothers instead of one, and one's enough, feel me? They were always in my business. Still, I'm sorry he's dead, especially for his mom." Her eyes narrowed. "Hey, maybe the girl had something to do with it, you think?"
My hands itched to get out of the pockets. "I won't know till I find her," I said calmly. Marisol thought it over. While I waited, it began to drizzle. Marisol pulled her hood up over her head. I just got wet.
"My turn again," she said. "Some guy who was supposed to be hot like Johnny Depp, shot the president and then hightailed it like The Flash. The president was Lincoln, like the car, but what's the name of the Depp dude?" All I could think of was how much of my tax money was going toward public education and how little I, apparently, was getting in return for it. I wondered if I could sue to get any of it back. Could I sue Marisol specifically, or would it make more sense to sue the system? The girl was a junior in high school, for mercy's sake. What were they doing inside that massive building? Weaving baskets?
"John Wilkes Booth," I said, my patience slipping. "Now you. You saw her. Where? Go."
She pulled in a deep breath. "All right! I was downtown looking for some cute earrings because I didn't see nothing good over on Commercial where I usually go, and I was trying to bump up my look. See?" She jiggled her earrings playfully. "Cesar and her was at the McDonald's on State where I stopped

to get me a Quarter Pounder with Cheese and a medium Coke before I got back on the bus. I was ditching, so I had to get back by the time school let out so it'd look like I was in it." Marisol stuck her lower lip out in a childish pout. "Only the bus was late, and I got detention."

"Did Cesar see you?"

"Oh, he saw me. He almost lost his shit." She winked. "I gave him one of those when I passed the table so he'd know he was busted. When I passed again on my way out, I was gonna do it again, but they were gone. I was kind of looking forward to it, too, busting him twice, I mean. Now you. Who was the army general on the loser side of the Civil War?"

"Robert E. Lee," I shot back. "Do you remember when this was?"

She shrugged. "Around New Year's. School had just started back after the holidays. It was a Friday, I know that. Oh, and it was cold. I was wearing the ugly green coat with the black buttons I got for Christmas, even though I asked for the kickass purple bomber with the real rabbit collar that I saw in the window at—"

I interrupted the flow. "Did you ask Cesar later about seeing him and the girl?"

Marisol shrugged. "Didn't have to. He knew I saw."

The school bell rang. "Damn! I gotta bounce," she said, getting panicky. "One more late mark and I get detention again, and I don't get to go to the dance, and that cannot happen, you feel me? Anyway, it's my turn. The Civil War ended in some apple field somewhere. Name it."

I squeezed my eyes shut, then slowly opened them again to find Marisol watching. "Appomattox Court House, not an apple field. It's in Virginia."

She wrote it down. "That does it," she said, shoving the pencil back into her hair and slipping the paper back into the book. "Josie's so gonna want to get her hands on these. They're worth twenty points each, can you believe it? It's sorta cool you knew this lame shit right off the top like that. But just so you know, I could've come up with 'em myself, if it wasn't for the fact that I had to do my nails last night."

"I have a couple more minutes," I said, racing the clock. "Did you tell Hector or anybody else about seeing Cesar with this girl?"

She hesitated. "Nah, 'cuz it was my chip, you see? And it evened us up." I looked a question. She rolled her eyes. "Cesar had something on me I didn't want everybody knowing about, okay? That's why I didn't say nothing yesterday about seeing her. Hector would have been all over that. So, Cesar keeps my crap, I keep his crap, and all's cool with us two. Remember the wink? You get it, right?"

"What was the girl wearing? Do you remember?"

"I guess. Hey, you're getting more answers than I got questions."

"You have any more homework?"

"No, that was it."

"Then don't worry about it."

"You could even it up with money?" Marisol suggested happily.

"No. I can't," I snapped. "Maybe she was wearing a school jacket? Something distinctive you remember?"

Marisol gave me the full-on teenager sad face—tucked-in chin, baby pout. "Just doesn't seem fair, is all."

My hands left my pockets. "Marisol!"

"All right! Here's what I know. I know she wasn't from the neighborhood. I know she looked way too goody-goody for Cesar. And I know if I told anybody about him being with her, he would have gotten all kinds of shit for it, especially from Hector."

"Because she was black?"

"Hell yeah, not that there's nothing wrong with being it, but

Cesar never used to hang around with black girls." The bell rang a second time. The final warning. Marisol shot an anxious look toward the school building.

"So anything stand out about her?" I said hurriedly.

Marisol frowned. "Besides her being black?"

"Yes. Yes." I nodded violently, a headache blooming behind my eyelids.

"Kinda skinny. You can't tell that from the photo. She was kind of medium dark, a lot darker than you, okay looking, I guess. Nice jeans and a bitching leather jacket. She was eating a salad, so probably real healthy." Marisol's eyes shifted upward, while she recalled the particulars. "She had on a gold necklace with the letter *D* on it; I guess her name starts with it. I've been trying to get one for myself, only with my whole name, but they cost big bucks, you know?" She exhaled. "Oh, and she was wearing a green baseball hat with a rat or a dog on it, and it was pulled way down like she was hiding from the cops. And she acted kind of nervous. That's it. That's all I got."

The hat rang a bell. "Marisol, do me a favor. Wait right here. Don't move from that spot. I'll be right back." I bolted across the street, popped my trunk. I kept all kinds of things in there, a change of clothes, a pair of binoculars, tools, warm blankets, work gloves, emergency flares, even an old pipe about the length of a baseball bat that I'd picked up from somewhere. I'd never had occasion to use it, but if I ever needed something to defend myself with on the fly, it was there. I burrowed in deep and grabbed up an old St. Brendan's baseball hat, green with an image of a badger on it, and ran back across the street clutching it as though it were a precious bird that might fly away. "Is this the hat she was wearing?" I held it up for her to get a good look at, my mouth dry, my hands beginning to sweat.

Slowly, she began to grin and nod. "Yeah, that's it. See? A rat!"

"It's a badger. It's the St. Brendan's badger."

Marisol's mouth hung open Maybe she didn't know what a badger was? "Looks like a rat, though, right? Doesn't matter. I'm done with this. I bought new shoes and a dress for that dance. I'm not missing it!" She sprinted off on her hooker heels.

"Thanks!" I yelled after her. I clutched the hat in my hot little hands, nearly giddy with excitement. "Yes!"

Chapter 16

I rang the rectory bell, then rang it again before the peel of the first ring even had a chance to fade away. Cesar had a girl not from his neighborhood, a black girl in a St. Brendan's hat. Cesar connected to the girl, the girl connected to the church, and the church meant Pop. Who was she? Where was she now? What tied Pop to the two of them? I rang the bell again, but still no one answered.

Pop noted everything of importance in a small datebook he always carried in his breast pocket. That book was almost his second Bible. He wrote down birthdays he didn't want to forget, appointments, Mass schedules, his grocery lists, goofy doodles, hospital visits to the sick and dying, our chess sessions. He'd start a new datebook every January first and when the year was done, he'd file it away and buy another just like it. The book he was working on at the time of his death was missing from his personal things gathered at the morgue, so it had to be in his room at the rectory. I wanted that book. I wanted it bad. If the girl was here somewhere, if Cesar had been, Pop would have made note of it. The rectory door opened just as I was about to ring again.

Thea stood there, startled, drying her hands on a dish towel. "What on earth?"

I stepped inside without being asked. I didn't have time for niceties. "Pop's office. I need five minutes." I rushed though the foyer and opened his office door, stopping cold at the sight of his empty desk and boxes stacked against a wall.

Thea followed me in. "Father Pascoe decided to work in here," she explained almost apologetically. "It's bigger."

I swallowed a lump. Already he'd taken over, pushed Pop aside. Couldn't he have waited just a little while longer before boxing up his things? Had he craved Pop's job so much that he couldn't at least pretend to mourn his passing? It felt disrespectful and unfeeling not only toward Pop, but also toward the people who loved him, like me. A slap in the face is what it felt like, and I didn't much care for the sting of it.

I began pulling open desk drawers. "I'm looking for his datebook. The last one." The first two drawers were completely empty. The third held Father Pascoe's stuff. He'd begun to move in everything he needed. "He didn't have it that night. I didn't come across it when I checked last time, but I could have overlooked it. It has to be here."

I checked every drawer, but it wasn't there. I eyed the boxes. Father Pascoe had packed Pop's things, but hadn't yet taped up the boxes. I began picking through them one by one, as Thea watched. I could feel her sympathetic gaze on my back. It wasn't her fault, any of it. Her job was to take care of Father Pascoe and the rectory, and that's what she was doing.

"I want his umbrella," I said, clearing the first box, but finding only old office papers in it. It was interesting how much clutter one could accumulate in a lifetime. We held on to paper and bits of nonsense that in the end didn't mean a thing. "It won't mean half as much to Pascoe." I didn't much like the man, and I doubted he held any great affection for me. He was a little too rigid, a little too standoffish, and always two steps off the pace. He and Pop were polar opposites. Pascoe, a company man who followed the rules, Pop, a man who didn't give a fig about them and had no qualms about bending a few when they offered no real-world application. The two were constantly at loggerheads.

The last box held framed photographs of Pop's kids—kids he mentored, kids from the school's sports teams, kids from his outreach program. Pop stood with them, smiling, his arms around them—their protector, their mentor, their light through dark times. They wouldn't find the same light in Father James Pascoe, that was for sure. I turned to Thea. One of the photos was of Pop taken just this past Christmas. We'd done ugly sweaters and could barely keep it together long enough for someone to take it. "And these photos."

"I'll make sure you get them."

I heard the front door open and close. Father Pascoe appeared in the doorway, lean, vulture-like, his mouth twisted into a disapproving scowl. He was twenty years Pop's junior, but double his age in outlook, a poor substitute all the way around.

"What's going on in here? What are you doing?" He met me at the boxes, seemingly surprised by my forwardness. I turned to face him. Thea had disappeared from the doorway. Pascoe's eyes scanned over the boxes, over more than twenty years of Pop's life, as though they were nothing. "This area is off limits," he warned.

I ignored the posturing. "Father Heaton's datebook. Do you know where it is?"

Father Pascoe slid by me and took a seat behind the desk in Pop's chair, steepling his long, thin fingers, his bony elbows propped up on the desktop. "Detective Farraday warned me that you might try to bulldoze your way in here. I hoped you wouldn't. You've disappointed me."

I stepped away from the boxes, faced the desk, and leaned down on it. "You know the one I mean. He carried it everywhere. It wasn't found with him. There may be useful information in it."

He leaned forward, his thin neck swimming inside his clerical collar, every vein and cord in his neck pronounced. He smiled, but there was little warmth in it. It was irrational to want to dump him out of the chair, but I wanted to do it all the same.

"You and he were close, I understand that. Perhaps not the wisest decision on his part, or yours, but he was not a man who accepted sane counsel. He chose instead to make his own rules as he went along, however much that may or may not have contributed to his tragic passing."

"Look, I didn't come here for a cage match. I need the book. It's not in the boxes. Is it in his room? Can I check there?"

Pascoe shot up. "Absolutely not. This is a rectory, not a crime scene, and you are not with the police. I'm the pastor now. The business of the parish must move forward. If the book is found, I'll pass it along to the proper authorities. I think it best if they handle the investigation. I'll address the issue of the boxes and his other possessions once I've had time to go over his written instructions for their distribution." He sighed, an angelic smile on his face, which didn't seem to fit with what I knew of the man. "We needn't be adversaries. We've all suffered a great loss. We should part ways amicably, don't you think?"

I smiled back, but it was just a mask. "You're absolutely right. He would want me to be respectful of your new position." I pulled the photograph of the girl out of my pocket. "So, respectfully, do you recognize this girl?"

Pascoe's lips pursed, but he looked at the photo. "I don't."

"She's somehow connected to the boy who was killed here. She's likely too old to be a student, but she may be a member of the parish."

Pascoe frowned. "If so, it's a police matter."

I took a step back. "Where were you the night Father Heaton was killed?"

Pascoe's eyes widened. "You can't be serious?"

I was serious. Where had he been? Why did Thea have to break the news to him over the phone, and why had it taken him until midmorning the next day to make it back?

"I'm sure the police asked about your whereabouts," I said, watching him.

He straightened. "As a matter of fact, they did not. Not many people would accuse a priest of murder, even fewer would do so to his face. But I understand that you're grieving, as we all are. I harbor no ill feelings. In fact, I'd like to invite you to a memorial that we're planning for Father Heaton. This Sunday, one o'clock. We'd love for you to join us. Now if you'll excuse me, I have pressing business to attend to."

"He had some trouble with a parishioner," I said, ignoring his attempt to dismiss me. "George Cummings. What do you know about that? Did he tell you what was going on?"

Father Pascoe straightened his jacket. "Good day, Ms. Raines." He smiled. "Sunday. One o'clock, if you wish to pay your respects."

I turned and stormed out, eyeing the stairs to the second floor on my way out. Pop's book had to be in his room. I could take the stairs against Father Pascoe's refusal to let me look, but they'd have me for trespassing, and I could kiss my license, freedom and livelihood good-bye. I glanced back at the office. No, I wouldn't give Father Pascoe the satisfaction of seeing me hauled off in cuffs. Farraday would just love that. I sighed and slowly stepped out onto the front stoop. If I wanted that datebook, I was going to have to break in and take it. Surprisingly, I had no problem with that at all.

*   *   *

Nancy was sitting at her desk when I walked into the school office. Her inbox was full, her out-box empty.

"Back again?" She looked better than the last time I saw her—no red eyes, no crying—but there were bags under her eyes, and as she rose, she moved as if every step was an effort, every facial expression a chore.

"I won't keep you. I've got a photo of a girl. Would you mind taking a look and telling me if you've seen her before?"

Nancy reached down and grabbed for the eyeglasses that dangled from a chain around her neck. "Sure. Does this have to do with Father Ray?" I nodded. She took the photo, studied it. While she did, I listened to the lively chatter of children as they changed from one classroom to another, and wondered where Anton Bolek was at that moment. "She looks kind of familiar, but I can't place her. There are so many children, new ones every year. Down here in the office we usually get just the troublemakers." Nancy's brows knit together. "She looks at least fifteen, sixteen. She's too old to be a student here."

I took the photo back. "Someone saw her wearing a St. Brendan's hat, but no one I've asked so far seems to know her."

Nancy eased her glasses off, let them dangle from the chain again. "Is she important?"

"She may be."

Nancy smiled. "I was just about to get a bit of fresh air. Want to tag along?"

We walked out onto the front steps, surveying the quiet street. At the curb, I watched as Anton Bolek jacked himself up into a beaten-up Chevy S10 truck. Once in, he shot me the monster of all stink eyes. I returned it.

"Where's he off to?" I asked.

Nancy's eyes narrowed. "He said he had an appointment."

He started up the truck and chugged up the street, spewing muffler exhaust in his wake, and I bid him a silent good riddance, watching as the truck turned the corner and disappeared. I wondered how he'd get along with Father Pascoe now that Pop was gone. Knowing the both of them, I had a feeling they'd get along just fine. Pop's death had certainly been fortuitous for the both of them.

"What do you think of Bolek?" I asked.

"Not much," Nancy said, and the look of contempt on her face told me all I needed to know.

"There was something going on between him and Father Heaton. Do you know what that was?"

In my experience, office managers and administrative assistants everywhere knew where all the bones were buried. I didn't think Nancy would be the exception. She shook her head. "I knew there was something, but Father Ray kept pretty tight-lipped about it. I could tell he was worried, though. It seemed to come to a head right before he died. I heard them arguing in the inner office, muffled voices only, nothing specific. After that, he asked for Anton's personnel file. That's the first step toward termination. It looked like Anton had run out of chances with him, and I think he knew it."

"And now?"

Nancy shrugged. "Nothing. Father Pascoe hasn't mentioned Anton, the file's back where I had it, and he's still here."

Pop was gone. The exhaust was gone. The truck was gone. I stared after it. "And Anton's still here."

I ran the last half block to Deek's Diner, dodging a light rain that for no good reason suddenly gave way to an angry downpour. I made the door just as a clap of thunder rattled the plate glass, sliding inside on slippery soles to shake the wet off my slicker.

I'd asked Whip to meet me for breakfast. Retrieving Pop's datebook was now priority number one. I hadn't yet come up with a plan for getting past Father Pascoe, but maybe Whip, given his illegal past, might have a few ideas I didn't. Besides, he'd want to know about the memorial.

I wasn't in my usual back booth more than five minutes when Whip ducked in the door, soggy from the rain. When he slid in opposite me and shimmied out of his jacket, I told him about my run-in with Father Pascoe.

"Who gets asked out of a rectory?"

"I do, apparently." The thought of it did little to lighten my load.

"Hell, you want me to go get it?"

"No!"

"Then you're going to need a good second-story man. I know one." He repositioned his bulky body in the tight booth. "His name's Wendell. I did a stint in Joliet with him."

"Don't you know any people who haven't been locked up?"

He smiled mischievously. "Yeah, you. So what are you going to do? And where do I fit in?"

"I don't know yet. I'm still thinking it through." I told him about Anton, and the vibe I got off the creepy little man.

"He's rotten. Take it from me. He's got something going on in that church nobody knows about."

The sinking feeling in my stomach plummeted to new depths. "Yeah, that's what I'm thinking."

Whip cracked his knuckles loudly, which set my teeth on edge. "You're going to have to break him. No low-life scum's going to walk up to a cop and say, 'Excuse me, officer, I'm running a meth lab in the church basement, would you mind taking me in?'"

I reveled in the fantasy for just one moment. It was a beautiful dream. "That would make the job so much easier, though, wouldn't it?"

"Dream on. So, how're you going to come at him? Because I

got guys I can call who'll scare him so bad he'll roll over on his own mother."

"Let me think about it. And while I'm thinking, I'll think about finding you some new friends."

Whip grinned. "No thanks. The one's I got are just fine by me." He read through the laminated menu deliberately. He was a cook, after all, and seemed to analyze it like a wine connoisseur would a rare wine list. Finally, he slid the menu across the table to me. I didn't need it. It hadn't changed since the diner opened. Everything on it was grease and carbohydrates.

"Kinda shitty Pascoe not telling you about the memorial till now. What did he think you'd do? Show up dressed in a bear costume?"

"He's afraid I'll ask too many questions. Pascoe's all about the official, so he's firmly on Farraday's side. I'm unofficial. Add to that, Farraday's got them all cowed. The archdiocese, no doubt, wants this to disappear fast, under the radar. A priest committing suicide, or so they think, no, they don't want to even think about that. As far as Father Pascoe's concerned, things are working out just peachy for him. He's got a new job, a new office. He doesn't want me rocking the boat."

Whip unfolded his napkin and spread it across his lap. "Then we're just going to have to disappoint him. I'm going to be at that memorial, whether he likes it or not."

I smiled. "Everyone will be there, which means no one will be in the rectory."

Whip shook his head, smiled. "You may have been a cop, but you've got the mind of a criminal."

I shrugged. "You gotta know 'em to catch 'em."

"Cass, what're you having?" Muna's booming voice came from across the room. Warily, I turned, smiled, and watched as she snaked her ample frame around the closely placed tables; she headed straight for me. "Your usual?" she asked when she reached me, her Southern drawl conjuring up images of slow-rocking porch swings, tall glasses of sweet tea, and the smell of talcum. She eyed Whip with a mixture of lust and circumspection. "And who's this strong, dark, mysterious man?"

Whip extricated himself from the booth to shake Muna's hand. "The name's Charles Mayo, ma'am. Friends call me Whip." He glanced at the nameplate on her chest. "Pleasure to meet you, Miss Muna."

It looked as though Muna might faint dead away. The two stood there staring at each other way too long to suit me. I cleared my throat loudly, hoping to break the spell. I'd been thwarted by a career-climbing priest already today, and Muna's love life was low on my list of concerns. I wanted buttered toast. Whip squeezed back into the booth, looking very pleased with himself. I rolled my eyes.

"Well, well," Muna managed. "A gentleman. What can I get for you, Mr. Mayo?"

Whip scanned the menu again and placed his order, a full breakfast fit for a fairytale giant.

"And I'll have toast," I said, though Muna hadn't yet gotten around to me. "And a cup of tea." I was too keyed up to eat much; besides, if I planned to squeeze through Pascoe's windows on Sunday, I needed to keep it wiry.

Muna drew back as if I'd slapped her. "Toast and tea?" She slowly smoothed the creases out of her white apron. "No, ma'am. You need some meat on you, and I'm not walking all the way out to that kitchen and all the way back over here with just no toast and tea. When you see old Muna Lee Steele again, darlin', I'll be carting back bacon, eggs, and some hash browns with that toast, and you'll drink a glass of whole milk with it." I started to protest, but her hand went up to keep me quiet. "Hush! And you better eat every bite of it, too." She smiled and winked at Whip, then turned on her heels, scowling at me over her shoulder, though there was no heat in the look. "Come in here looking like a stick woman. No, ma'am." She yelled into the kitchen. "T.J.? Work up a full plate for Cassie. And express it. Toast and tea," she grumbled. "Don't that just beat all to Hell and back?" She disappeared into the kitchen. I massaged my forehead and daydreamed of faraway places.

"I like her," Whip said, smoothing his napkin. "Sturdy. Sassy. That's my type."

I glared at him.

He stared at me innocently. "What?"

"Find your own sandbox," I said.

"Still territorial, I see. Never did want to share your marbles."

I stuck my tongue out at him.

"And it wouldn't hurt for you to dip your toe back into the sandbox. Seems a shame to waste all that good-looking on the guy who delivers your paper in the morning."

I narrowed my eyes. "I get plenty of sand, thank you."

"Because I know a guy."

I balled up a napkin and tossed it at him. "Stop talking!"

Our orders arrived quickly. Thanks, no doubt, to Muna's desire to get back to Whip in a hurry. He had the Plowman's Special—eggs, bacon, hash browns, grits, and biscuits. I was presented that, plus a bowl of Wheaties, a glass of milk, OJ, and three chocolate doughnuts. Muna had to haul it all in on a big, round tray that looked like an oversized pizza pan.

I looked up at her. "You're kidding, right?"

She glared at me, unbowed. "Does it look like I'm kidding?"

Whip rubbed his hands together in gleeful anticipation of an artery-clogging feast. I sat quietly watching Muna unload everything.

"Now eat," she commanded, tucking the tray under her arm and moving away quickly on rubber-soled shoes.

"Man, this looks good," Whip said. He leaned over and took a whiff. "Smells good, too."

Reluctantly, I picked up my fork, speared scrambled eggs in its tines, and pushed the eggs around planks of bacon on my plate, managing one small bite per lap, my progress monitored by Muna's watchful gaze from across the room. This went on for a time with Muna's eyes narrowing whenever my fork stopped moving. Hopefully, the rectory window would be wide enough for me to shimmy through.

Chapter 17

When I got home, nearly every parking spot on my block had a car in it, which wasn't unusual. Free street parking in Hyde Park was hard to come by without a residential permit, and even if you had one it wasn't easy. I parked a half-block up from my building and walked back, taking my time, jangling the keys in my jacket pocket, replaying my encounters with Marisol and Father Pascoe and wondering what I was going to do about slimy Anton Bolek. I was slow to spot the unmarked cop car with the two detectives inside, double-parked at the curb. By the time I did, it was too late to turn around and fast-walk in the opposite direction.

I turned briskly into my yard, head down, and barreled on, knowing that it was futile. The familiar crackle of the police radio and the ominous thwack of car doors opening and closing behind me stopped me in my tracks. I sighed, giving in to the inevitable, and turned to watch Farraday and his partner amble toward me as though time meant nothing and they had oodles of it to burn. Already, I was impatient with their intrusion. I needed time to think and wanted a hot shower and a long nap,

thanks to Muna's food orgy. I didn't want cops, especially these cops, on my doorstep.

Farraday barely rated a second glance, but his partner was a new experience, so I watched him closely as he walked up to meet me. Black, mid-forties, gym-fit, tall. Battle veteran, I decided, as he drew close enough for me to see the years of filthy streets etched on his face. Both were dressed like you'd expect—trousers, button-down shirts, ties, and blazers—everything rumpled from sitting in the car too long. I glanced surreptitiously downward, sure of what I'd find—two pairs of dusty, hard-soled cop shoes.

Ben had told me the partner's name was Weber, and I watched with great interest as he flashed his ID, and then tucked it back into his pocket. He wasn't bad looking. I recalled Whip's crack about dipping my toe in the sandbox, then reeled it back in. "Sand" was a complication I didn't have time for at the moment. Farraday didn't bother flashing anything. I knew him, he knew me. No smile, no nod, nothing. Weber wore dark sunglasses, hiding his eyes.

Farraday glared down at me, ego personified, with his eyes fixed intently on me as though he expected a challenge. "I ought to arrest you right here and now. I say mind your own business, you ignore that and go about leaving your PI prints all over my case. Would you mind telling me, just for the hell of it, what your problem is?" The question was blunt, instantly off-putting. I stared at him for a moment, taking in the disdainful look on his face and the remnants of the uneven shave he'd given himself that morning, deciding instantly that I wasn't going to play along. I stood silently. "Or maybe you'd rather take this inside and we can talk about it in there," Farraday said, more order than suggestion. I imagined his brusqueness got him pretty far with dodgy suspects and witnesses prone to shading half-truths, intimidated by the possibility of jail time. For me, it did squat.

I managed an icy smile. "Here's fine."

I didn't want Farraday in my house. I didn't want him in my yard, either, but better here than there. Farraday stretched his body to its full height and width, which reminded me of an animal that puffed up and out to scare off anything big enough to eat it. There was a button missing on his shirt. I glanced again at Weber. Still stoic, still not bad looking. I wondered what was going on behind the sunglasses.

"We went by Irma Luna's," Farraday said. "Name ring any bells?"

"One name," I said. "One bell."

Farraday's thin lips curled into a flat smile. "You two hit it off real good, apparently. For us she's got zero, but you she likes. You're the only one who gives a rat's ass what happened to her kid, a goddamn champion of the people." He grinned, amused by his own cleverness. He was enjoying himself, which made me dislike him even more. "We're on this case full swing, and I know what went down. That's me telling you three times now. But what I want to know is—what the hell do you think you're playing at?"

I tightened my grip around the keys in my hand, pressing tender flesh to jagged metal until the impulse to be indelicate subsided. Farraday was a bully; bullies made lousy cops, and I'd had my fill. I eased out a breath, took my time pulling it back. "I offered my condolences to Mrs. Luna. We talked. Talking's legal. I think you know why I have an interest." I unloosed my grip on the keys. "And I know where the lines are. I used to walk them, remember?"

Farraday glared. "I remember lots of things." He took a step closer to me, leaned in. "This is what you're going to do; you're going to knock it the hell off. You're going to step so far back off of this that they'll need to send out a search party to find you."

Our eyes locked. "This is the third time you've threatened me. I'm beginning to take it personally."

"I didn't hear a threat." He turned to Weber. "You hear a threat?" Weber stared at his partner, but said nothing. His face never changed. "What's the matter, Raines? Do you have nothing better to do than prowl the streets looking for fresh bodies to poach? Is business that slow?"

I smiled at Farraday. "That the best you can do?"

Farraday looked as though he might implode. "You always did think you were better than the rest of us, the ace detective, smarter than the average."

I pulled a face, feigning empathy. "I never knew you had an inferiority complex. It explains a lot, though."

He bristled, his hand traveling down to tap the star clipped to his belt, almost as though he were reassuring himself that it was still there.

I said, "If there's a point to this, and I seriously hope there is, I wish you'd hurry up and get to it."

The veins in Farraday's neck danced as he bit down on his lower lip hard enough to blanch. It was impressive, really. I flicked a look at Weber. Still nothing. The man could have been made of marble for all the animation he showed. No one spoke for a time.

"Well, as pleasant as this has all been . . ." I turned for the door.

"Did I say we were done?" Farraday barked.

I felt my composure slipping, but quickly pictured myself making my one measly phone call from the women's lockup, and instead internally skipped on along to my happy place. "No, I'm saying it." I kept my voice low, calm. I had neighbors. It was bad enough I had cops in my yard; I didn't need to elevate the situation by causing a scene. "Either arrest me for talking or get out of my yard."

It looked like Farraday didn't know whether to arrest me for nothing or pummel me with the butt of his gun.

"Why don't I jump in," Weber said, breaking his silence. "Give me a minute while you call in and check on that report?"

Without another word, Farraday broke off and stormed back to the car, slamming the driver's door behind him, as though he were a petulant child denied a candy bar at the grocery store. He sat there, his arms folded across his chest, his eyes trained straight ahead. I wondered if he was in there stomping his feet against the floorboard.

Weber reached into his pocket and pulled out his card, handing it to me. "That was interesting."

I read the card. "By all means, jump right in, Detective Eli Weber."

He smiled, slipped off his glasses. Nice eyes, I thought. The color of almonds, with flecks of yellow. "I've heard stories about you. I wanted to see for myself. You hold your own, that's for sure."

"Stories? From who?" I didn't know if I liked the idea of stories about me floating around the cop houses. Weber grinned, but didn't respond. He just stood there looking at me. Finally, tired of the staring game, I picked my door key out of the jumble on my key ring and headed for my front door. I was done. I didn't have time to waste on a silent cop and an imbecile having a hissy fit.

"You started out at the Fifteenth under John Bergen," he said, calling after me. I stopped, turned, and eyed him warily. Bergen had trained me. "I worked a task force with him a few years back. Real old-school cop—but sharp. I heard about the lymphoma, hoped he'd beat it." He read my look, then shot me a smile that seemed to twinkle like diamonds. "Relax, I'm not working you. Bergen was one of the good ones." Weber's eyes tracked a mufflerless car as it sped down the street. "You don't always get to pick your partner. Maybe this sticks, maybe it doesn't. Farraday's not an easy one to latch onto. You took that a lot better than I would have."

"Only a dumb fish rises to slow-moving bait."

Weber nodded, slipped his glasses back on. "Well, if you come across anything else while you're out there 'talking,' I'd appreciate the heads-up. I'm all about teamwork."

"Uh-huh."

He frowned. "That didn't sound too promising."

I glanced at the cop car to make sure Farraday was still in it. He was. "How perceptive of you."

"I know there's something. You trained with Bergen, and he didn't pull dead weight along behind him. He sure as hell didn't, suffer fools gladly." I narrowed my eyes, certain he was shining me on. "No bull. Just fact."

"Sounds like bull," I said.

"If you went to Luna's, you had a reason. I don't think you came out empty-handed, either. In fact, I'd bet good money on it." His eyes held mine. "Teamwork works, if you work it."

"I've had Farraday on my team," I said. "It didn't work out so well for me." I took a step toward him. "I want this case solved. It's important to me. I can't depend on Farraday to follow through."

"So give me what you've got," he said simply.

I hesitated. I didn't know Weber, or what kind of cop he was. Pop was mine, not his. Nobody would care more about him than I did. But CPD had resources I didn't have, manpower I didn't have. I studied Weber's body language, searched his face for evidence of deception. Could I trust that he'd stand for Pop, even if Farraday wouldn't?

"About Bergen?" he said. "He recruited me for that task force. You knew him. You know what that says."

He was right. I did know. It said John trusted Weber. It meant Weber was good police. A nod from John Bergen was all the endorsement any cop would ever need. I slid my hands into my pockets. "All right. I'll give you this. Cesar Luna knew that church. He'd been there before. That means he knew Father Heaton. He didn't just happen by looking for things to steal. The night he died? He'd been jumped out of the Scorpions. That explains the bruises."

"Most times quitting a gang is fatal," Weber said.

"Maybe it was this time, too. Hector Perez and the others weren't too happy with Cesar. Try rousting some of them. I also found out that Cesar had a girl, someone not from the neighborhood. A black girl who a witness saw wearing a St. Brendan's hat. She and Cesar were seen at the McDonald's downtown on State in early January, on a Friday. Maybe security cameras picked them up. She might hold a piece to this."

Weber looked satisfied. "Anything else?"

I thought of the girl's photo, Pop's Bible, but decided to keep them to myself for now. I'd see how Weber held up his end first, then decide how much I'd share. "Just this tip. You'd do well to watch your back. Farraday never learned how to cover anything but his own ass."

Weber thought about it for a moment, and I could tell from the pensive look on his face that he heard and understood me. "I'll do that, Ms. Raines." He then doffed an imaginary hat and walked away.

On Saturday morning, the sun pulled me out into the yard, where I spent some quiet time hand tilling the soil in my grandmother's flowerbeds as though it were my life's passion. I didn't much like gardening. It had been her thing, not mine, but I wanted to preserve the beds. It helped that the air was crisp, the sky cloudless, and somewhere, the early birds were chirping their little heads off, though that was bad news for anyone trying to sleep in on their day off.

Pop's memorial was a day away, and while I knelt in the moist earth working my fingers through dirt that felt clean, I was busy formulating a plan to ruin Father Pascoe's day, and lift Pop's datebook from what I hoped would be an empty rectory. I would get in and out as quietly as the proverbial church mouse, or I would spend the night in jail. I'd have to be ready for either scenario.

"Morning."

I turned to see a man of about sixty dressed in a dark suit and tie standing just inside the yard. I returned the greeting and watched as he stood there grinning like an idiot. "You looking for someone?" I asked.

"Not exactly."

I waited for him to say more. He didn't. I glanced at the suit. It was a nice suit—well cut, business appropriate. "You missed the bank by a couple blocks. Up a block, right at the corner." He chuckled, and my blood froze. I'd heard the laugh before.

"You look so much like your mother." As recognition dawned, I slowly got to my feet, and stepped away from him. "Theodore Raines," he said gently. "Your father."

In an instant, nearly all the air seemed to whoosh out of my lungs, leaving me next to zip to draw on. He moved forward to shorten the distance between us; I backed away again to lengthen it.

He stopped, mindful of my retreat. "I took a chance you'd still live here. Grace and Frank left you the building, I see?" He eyed the flowerbed. "She loved those flowers. I'm glad you're keeping them up." He looked disappointed, as though he'd had his heart set on something other than stunned silence. "This is a surprise, I know, but I couldn't think of an easier way to do this other than to just do it. Pull the Band-Aid off, so to speak?"

I stared at him, but didn't say anything. It'd been over two decades—a lifetime—since I'd seen him last, and now here he was again, older, grayer, a stranger, but not. What did you say to someone you'd let go of and never expected to see again?

"I'd like to talk." He said it plainly, as though he'd just returned from the corner store, not from Lord knows where after twenty-three years. I couldn't take my eyes off him. Of course, I saw it now—the hazel eyes, more green than brown, his face the color of warm caramel. My eyes. My face. The very same doorstep he'd left me on was just a few feet behind me. I turned to look at it, seeing it now as it was then, me on the step holding my suitcase, listening to the lie.

"It's only for a little bit," he said, crouching down to my level. "I'll be back before you know it."

I turned back to face him now, mystified by his presence.

"I need to explain myself," he offered tentatively.

"No, you don't." The calmness in my voice surprised me. I didn't feel calm. I didn't exactly know what I felt, not yet. "You don't get to do this. I'd like you to go."

He drew back. "I realize I'm the last person you want to hear from. I get that, but if you would just give me a minute."

My mind clicked rapidly through half a lifetime of missed Christmases, birthdays, and childhood traumas, which left a void my grandparents and Pop had tried their best to fill. I hadn't believed he'd come back, but a part of me still hoped. I was a kid, that's what kids do. I'd waited dutifully before finally letting him go. I watched as he wiped sweat from his brow, almost too ashamed to look at me.

"I made a terrible mistake, one I'd like to try and make up for."

I said nothing. What was there to say? It could have been worse, a lot worse. I might not have had grandparents to raise me; I might not have had Pop. I was lucky, luckier than others. I turned out all right. I turned out just fine.

"I've moved around all over, lately it's St. Louis," he began hurriedly. "This is not the best way to do this, I realize." He moved to take another step toward me, seemed to think better of it, and stopped. "If we could just go inside, maybe? Talk?"

Somewhere down the block someone started a mower. Slowly, I let out the breath I'd been holding. The sound was reassuring, a reminder of the normal, a confirmation that the Earth still turned and the bottom hadn't dropped out of my life again like it had the last time the two of us stood here. I shook my head. "I don't think we need to." I eyed the suit. "What are you? A banker, or something?"

He brightened at the question. "Insurance adjuster, actually. It's not very exciting, but I'm good at it."

My entire body trembled, but it wasn't anger. It'd been too long for that, the break too complete. What was it? He tried a smile, but didn't pull it off. He managed instead just a pained grimace. "Maybe you could tell me a little something about yourself?"

I took a step toward him. I no longer needed the distance. I'd discovered, standing by my grandmother's flowers in front of the home I owned, that I was okay, solid, and that he'd long ago lost the power to hurt me. The shock was over. That's what it was, I thought, the trembling. Not anger, shock, like seeing a ghost in a dark room, like suddenly turning a corner and bumping into someone coming the other way, a startle, a surprise. "If people knew better, they'd do better," I said. "That's how they explained you to me."

"Your grandparents?"

I nodded. And Pop. "I could accept that. It made sense in the end."

"There's a lot more to it, though," he said.

"Does any of it matter now?"

He looked at the building, the flowers, the street, and then me again. "I'd like to hope it might."

"Okay, I'll give you ten seconds to nutshell it for me." I watched him, my eyes holding his, no play in them. Maybe there was just a little anger percolating down deep.

"I have no excuse," he said.

"I agree. Eight seconds."

"I'm here to ask for your forgiveness."

That was a tough one. If Pop were here I might be able to work on forgiveness, but I was on my own. Forgiveness was going to take some doing. "Six seconds."

He appeared confused, like he didn't know what to say or do next. "I want to make amends."

We were silent for a time.

"How many seconds do I have left?"

I didn't answer.

"I'll just keep going then, okay? I remarried. A couple times, actually, but I have a family now. You have a brother. Family's important; I know that now. I still miss your mother and think about her all the time. I went by the cemetery to see her. Do you go?"

"She's not there," I said.

He nodded. "You deserve an explanation."

I really looked at him. I had no idea how old he was when he last celebrated his birthday. You forget things like that over time. I knew he was an only child, so was my mother, so was I, but I knew nothing about his parents or how he grew up. What I did know, what I could feel, was that there was no emotional connection between us. There was nothing, except a slight fit of pique, mine not his. But anger was easy. Anger passes, if you let it. What do you do with nothing?

"Time's up," I said, my tone gentler. There was no point in working myself up, no sport in kicking a man at his most vulnerable. It was done, dead. He left. I went on without him. *Move on, Cass, move on.* I quietly gathered up my garden tools. "Nice seeing you again."

His face fell. "I'm at the Fairmont, if you change your mind and want to talk, and I hope you do."

"I won't."

"Well, I'll wait all the same. I'm not giving up."

I nearly chuckled. He'd promised much the same twenty-three years ago, right before he turned, walked away, and never came back. "I don't believe you."

He hung his head, nodded, and then turned to leave without another word. I stood there and watched him go. He'd remarried. He had a whole new life, a family. I went inside, leaving the garden for another day.

Chapter 18

The church was packed, as I knew it would be. I was sitting in the next to last pew on the aisle next to Whip, both of us dressed in black suits, though Whip looked very uncomfortable in his. He kept tugging at his collar and loosening his tie as though he were trying to wiggle out of a hangman's noose. He caught me looking.

"I hate ties," he griped. "You know who wears ties? Corporate raiders and aldermen on the take, that's who. You cannot trust a man in a tie, and you can take that to the bank." He scanned the pews. "Jeez, looks like everybody he knew is here. Good for Father Ray." He glanced over at me. "And for you." He sat quietly for a time. "Funny how a place can seem smaller than you remember."

"Yeah." I glanced up at the vaulted ceiling. The church could accommodate over a thousand sinners, and every spot of pew had a person sitting in it—young and old, wealthy, not wealthy by a long shot, black, white, homeless, VIPs, and average Joes; they were all here for Pop.

I watched as people moved slowly up the center aisle, fanning out at the foot of the altar, searching for a spot to squeeze into, everyone's voice lowered to reverential tones, as though they were afraid to wake the saints. Above the altar table hung the figure of the crucified Christ reproduced in alabaster, his dying body flanked by stoic disciples painstakingly chiseled from Italian marble. I wondered where they had all been when Pop needed their intervention.

Whip leaned over to whisper in my ear. "I can pop a lock in twenty seconds easy." I narrowed my eyes at him. "Just saying."

Inwardly, I was impressed with the time. It took me more than triple that to pick a quality lock. I stared at the confessional, my mind on Pop's last moments, wondering if I'd ever be able to look at this church, or any other, as places where bad things did not happen. Like I'd done at Pop's funeral, I checked around for Anton Bolek, Maisie Ross, and George Cummings. I didn't see Maisie. She was likely done with Pop at this point anyway. You couldn't harass a dead man. There was no sport in it. Surprisingly, I spotted Bolek, not in a pew, but holding up the side entryway, dressed not in a suit, but in his janitorial greens. Why was he here? I watched him for a time, then my eyes slipped away to find Thea sitting up front weeping. When I turned back to Bolek, he'd gone. Someone tapped me on the shoulder. George Cummings. Whip eyed him suspiciously, but said nothing.

"I just stopped by to say hello," Cummings said, "And to ask if you've been able to come up with anything new."

"Not yet. Still digging."

"I get the same answer from the police. I never realized how slow moving this kind of thing can be. Since we talked, I've been keeping my eye open for a few of those homeless people that used to hang around here, but I haven't seen them. Maybe they got scared off by all the trouble."

"That could be," I said.

"Well, I'll keep looking. I had this thought, too. We keep sign-in sheets for when we open up the hall for the free meals. I'm not saying it's one of them for sure, but if you ever need to take a look at who was in and around here about that time, I'd be glad to give you a look. There could be something there, you know?"

"Thanks. That's a good idea."

He reached into his pocket. "You gave me your card; here's mine. Call if you want that look." Cummings slowly moved away in search of a seat. I tucked his card into my bag.

"What's his story?" Whip asked the second he was gone.

"Parishioner. He could be a good source of information."

Whip studied the back of Cummings's head. "Smiles too much. Happy people make me nervous."

"When did you get so cynical?"

"Halfway through my first stint in the joint."

We watched as Father Pascoe made his way slowly up the center aisle, greeting those on the aisle with a handshake and a regal smile. I caught his eye as he passed and offered a small wave. He smiled back, but I could tell his heart wasn't in it.

Whip leaned over and whispered. "Is that him?"

My eyes tracked Father Pascoe all the way to the altar. "Yep."

"Does he always look like he swallowed a bat?"

"Yep."

Whip shook his head. "Probably a sin wishing you could push a priest's face in, right?"

"While actually sitting in church? I'm almost sure of it."

Whip thought for a moment. "I think I could sell it to St. Peter."

There was another tap on my shoulder; this time it was an old woman in a church hat sitting in the row behind me. When I turned around, she pointed toward the front doors.

"That young lady's trying to get your attention."

I looked where she pointed, shocked to see an old friend, Sister Barbara Covey, standing there waving me back.

"It's Barb!" I whispered to Whip as I eased out into the aisle. He turned and waved. "You said she was in Africa?"

"She is. She was." I eased out of the row. "Guard my seat with your life."

"Like you even had to ask. I'll even make enough room for Babs."

I chuckled. "The last time you called her Babs she chased you three blocks with a two-by-four."

"We were thirteen!"

"Yeah, but she's still a Covey."

In fact, Barb was the youngest of nine rambunctious Coveys, all of them tough as nine-inch nails and not a bit shy about showing it. In school, she questioned everything and broke every rule just to prove she could. She rode the nuns like rodeo horses all the way to graduation day, and then surprised them all—and the neighborhood, too,—when she turned around and became one of them. No one saw it coming, especially the beat cops who knew the Coveys all too well, having picked up every last one of them at one time or another for breaking curfew, bloodying noses, busting streetlights, or spray painting the sides of mail trucks or neighborhood dogs.

"I've been signaling for you for ten minutes," Barb said, pulling me into a hug. She looked as though she'd flown ten thousand miles folded up in an old steamer trunk, her unruly red hair pushed under a battered Cubs hat, her pale skin tanned and freckled by the African sun. I'd called her to tell her about Pop, but, though we talked by phone regularly, it had been a year since I'd last seen her. She was supposed to be in Tanzania teaching English to little African children, not standing here dressed like a safari guide, a dusty rucksack slung over her shoulder.

I pulled her over to a quiet corner of the drafty vestibule.

"How'd you get here? Why didn't you tell me you were coming?"

She held up a scarred flip phone that looked as though it had been used as a baby chimp's chew toy. "I tried, but I couldn't get you. When I couldn't, I figured you were busy giving the cops the business."

"You didn't have to come. I would have called."

"I know. And I tried sitting it out, but I couldn't sleep for worrying. Then I got mad, and prayers weren't helping. Finally, I just had to be here. He would do the same for me."

"How'd you know about the memorial? I just found out about it myself two days ago."

"Happy accident. I've been traveling for over a week. There was a bumpy truck ride to the nearest township, then three dodgy prop planes to get me to Zanzibar City, then Lufthansa to O'Hare, stopping twice to switch planes. I'm jet-lagged, and I'm covered in dirt and mosquito balm. I hitched a ride from the airport to your place with a kind man named Sharif. Don't give me that look. He was perfectly nice. But when I got to your place, you weren't there. Mrs. Vincent filled me in and was nice enough to drop me off. Her car is massive, by the way, and built like a freaking tank. They really don't make them like that anymore, do they?" She peeked into the church. "Great turnout. So what do we know so far? Who are we after? Which Covey do I have to call?"

Whichever one she called would be trouble, I thought. Barb's brother, Sean, once stole a squad car right out of the district lot and then drove his girlfriend around town in it all night. He was now a detective working out of the Twenty-second, but everybody still called him Booster. Even Barb's mother had an edge. She once cussed out a monsignor.

I led her inside. "We'll hold off on calling the Coveys, and I'll bring you up to speed later. Whip's saving our seats."

Her face lit up. "I can't believe Charlie's here. Where's he been?"

"Long story. I'll tell it later over a cold glass of milk."

Barb pulled back. "Milk? After the odyssey I've been on? I'm going to need something stronger than that."

"Fine. I'll swipe some Communion wine. Let's go."

I waited for Communion to make my move, while those who wanted it were out of their pews and heading toward the altar, their hands clasped in prayer. Farraday and Weber had slipped in just before the start of Father Pascoe's homily and had wasted no time scanning the church to find where I was sitting. What did they think they were doing? Did they really think Pop's killer was going to stand up in a crowded church and confess to double homicide? I nodded to Weber. Farraday I ignored. When the time was right, I slid Whip a knowing glance and moved to get up. Barb grabbed my arm. "I saw that. What's going on?"

"I need to stretch my legs. I'll be back in a bit."

She didn't believe me. "Try again. Where are we going?"

The row ahead of us emptied as people headed toward the altar. "*We* are not going anywhere. I'm going to stretch my legs. You and Whip are staying here until I get back."

Whip leaned over. "Look, Babs, we'll explain all this to you later."

Barb glared at Whip. Whip grinned. It was 1996 all over again, sans the two-by-four. I eased out of the pew. I'd have to thank Whip for the diversion later.

He grabbed my wrist. "Anybody heads that way, I'm right behind them. Just so you know." He angled his head at Barb, who sat pinch-faced beside him. "I'll fill Barb in. Go."

I opened my mouth to argue, but closed it again. Truthfully, I could do a lot worse than Whip as backup. I slipped out of the pew, eased around the Communion line and made it out of the church, hopefully, without anyone noticing. Standing out on the front steps, I took a good long look at the street. A line of black limousines sat parked at the curb, each with a bored driver behind the wheel. At the mouth of the street, two squad cars sat idling, protection and transportation for all the VIPs inside. News vans, their satellite dishes raised and ready, sat behind the limos with reporters cooling their heels inside, waiting for the church to let out. Pop had been a big deal. He might have had a lot of enemies, but he had an equal number of powerful friends.

I strolled toward the courtyard as though I were out for a contemplative walk, feeling for the picklocks in the pocket of my suit jacket. I had intentionally worn slacks instead of a skirt, and flats instead of heels, in case I had to go to Plan B and climb through a window. Whip had boasted he could pick a lock in less than twenty seconds. Only I would take that as a personal challenge.

Rousing organ music wafted out of the church's open windows, accompanied by tinny voices mumbling their way through "Amazing Grace." I climbed the rectory steps like I belonged there, but stopped when I caught sight of the door, which stood ajar. The fact that I wouldn't need the picklocks should have delighted me, but instead it lifted the hairs on the back of my neck. I checked the lock. It hadn't been busted or forced. There were no outward signs of tampering. It simply looked as though someone had failed to shut the door behind them, which didn't sound at all like Father Pascoe or Thea. Neither would have been so careless, not in this neighborhood, not after what happened to Pop, not even with two squad cars parked across the street.

The wisest thing would be to flag down one of the cops and have them check the house, but then I'd lose my one shot at getting inside to look for Pop's datebook. I gently pushed the door open, stepped into the foyer, and listened for sounds that didn't belong. Had someone wandered in? Somewhere toward the back of the house a clock ticked loudly and coffee was brewing, the smooth aroma of it filling the entire downstairs. I slid my gun out of the holster just in case, holding it down at my side. I slipped quietly into Pop's office. The boxes I'd checked were still there, but new ones had been added since I'd been here last. There was no one hiding behind the door; there was no other place anyone could hide.

I tiptoed back into the hall and headed toward the kitchen. I checked inside the utility closet as I passed it. Nothing but brooms, and mops, and boxes of Hefty bags. The kitchen was clear; a full pot of coffee sat waiting for whoever had brewed it. Back up the hall, I eased the door open on what used to be Father Pascoe's office before he took over Pop's. He hadn't completely moved all of his things, and what was left behind had been frighteningly arranged, stacked and placed in such a manner as to suggest that Father Pascoe might suffer from some form of OCD.

A line of religious figurines sat on the desk, each one a different saint. I devilishly toyed with the idea of moving each of them a millimeter off its mark just to send Father Pascoe reeling, but squashed the petty urge. I slipped out of the room, closing the door behind me, reholstered my gun, and double-timed it back to Pop's office, suddenly mindful of the fact that the church music had stopped. There was no telling how much time I had left. I had to move quickly.

Six new bankers' boxes with HEATON stenciled on the lids sat on the floor against a wall. I started there. On my knees, I searched the first four boxes without finding anything useful, only more parish forms, office supplies, and a few new photographs. I'd have to tell Thea that I wanted those, too. I found Pop's datebooks in the fifth box, each one labeled by year, the earliest dating back to 1993. Two years before he came to St. Brendan's. I stopped my search, held the book. I wanted the datebooks, too. Setting the book aside, I searched the box for the 2018 book, but it wasn't there. The last book was for 2017, way before Pop got into whatever trouble he'd gotten into, way before someone began following him and Cesar showed up. I checked the box again, hoping I'd just overlooked it, but again I came up with nothing. The book wasn't there.

Singing started up across the way. Good sign. I checked the closet, but it held nothing more interesting than a black overcoat hanging from a wooden hanger. I checked the pockets, but found only half a roll of Lifesavers. I headed upstairs to Pop's bedroom. It was forbidden territory, and every step I took on the stairs felt like I was breaching the entrance to some sacred sanctum, but I kept moving. This was my first time past the first floor, my first time seeing where Pop had really lived. There were name plates on the walls outside each room. I found Pop's. His door was open. I eased inside. The room smelled of sandalwood and Ivory soap, like Pop had, but it was barely big enough to accommodate the twin bed he'd slept in. I could have swung a cat by the tail and hit all four walls. The man hadn't been fussy, but how could he possibly have slept here without feeling like the walls were closing in on him? It appeared as if everything was as Pop had left it. I drew in a breath, and got a whiff of something besides sandlewood and soap. It was must, as though the room had been locked up tight for months without any circulating air. I padded over to the window and opened it just a crack, then checked my watch for time. I'd been in the house about twenty minutes. I wouldn't have too much longer.

The book was not in any of the drawers in the night stand or taped beneath them; it wasn't hidden under his mattress. His dresser drawers just held clothes. I walked the floorboards, but they were securely nailed down. No hiding places there, but why would he need to hide it? There was nothing else in the room but a cane back chair, a small TV pushed into a corner and an old lamp. I reached over and turned the lamp on, but it barely gave off enough light for even me to be able to read by. I wondered how Pop managed. I glanced at the wooden crucifix hanging over the bed, but if Jesus knew where the datebook was, he wasn't saying.

My hand was on the knob to the closet door when it flew open and a blur of gray and green barreled out at me, knocking me backward, sending me crashing to the floor. I landed hard, the back of my head slamming against the floorboards, dazing me. The room was so small that my torso and legs landed inside the room, and my chest and head in the hall. I lifted my head to identify the blur. It was a man with wild eyes. I tried scrambling up, but before I could, rough hands fastened around my neck, squeezing hard. Dark face, strong hands. Skull cap. Dirty jacket. He knelt on top of me, his weight pinning me down, his knees hemming me in.

At my back, my gun pressed against my right kidney, but I had no chance of getting to it. The immediate problem was breathing. I struck out at him, my fists bouncing off his chin, his cheek. My eyes began to water, my vision grew cloudy. I had seconds, if that. At least two hundred pounds of crazy now stood between me and a good, deep inhale. An image of my first two-wheel bicycle flashed before my eyes. I loved that bike. It was red with white fringes on the handlebars. Funny where your mind wanders when you have a crazy man sitting on your chest, and your lungs are crying out for oxygen.

The wild man grunted as he bashed my head against the floor again, sending white-hot stars dancing behind my eyelids. "I won't let you get me!" he shrieked. "Tell him! The evil bastard!" I threw an elbow to his stomach, then his throat. No effect. The man was rock solid. I slugged him in the jaw, jamming my knuckles. No effect. His hands gripped tighter around my throat. "I saw. I lost my candles. You can't have me!"

I dug my thumbs hard into his eye sockets, kicking out with my legs to try and buck him off. When he yelped and let my neck go, I gasped for air, coughed uncontrollably, and scrambled away from him, only to have him recover too quickly, grab me by the foot, and drag me back. I kicked wildly, twisting away, flipping over on my back so he couldn't disarm me. There is no greater indignity than getting shot with your own gun.

I landed a solid kick to his solar plexus, then skittered away again, diving for the bed, sliding under it, rolling up on the other side to use it as a buffer. He stood, a massive tree with legs and arms, and headed for me, tossing the bed aside as if it were nothing, roaring like an animal. I drew my gun, my fingers fumbling on the grip, but before I could raise it to aim, he was on me again, knocking it away, sending it spinning under the night table beyond my reach, but thankfully, beyond his, too. We both lunged for it at the same time, knocking over the lamp, stretching, clawing, both of us desperate to get to it first.

Chapter 19

We met in a tangle just inches from the Glock, both of us pawing for it. I elbowed him again. He punched me in the head, stunning me again, but there was too much adrenaline flowing through me for me to give way. If I did, I was dead. I kneed him in the groin, which gave him something else besides the gun to think about. It also gave me enough time to grab the gun and roll away.

I didn't want to kill him, not in Pop's room, not on the day of his memorial, but I would if it came down to him or me. I scrambled to my feet, turned, and assumed a shooting position—knees flexed, one foot forward, arms out, sights to the eyes—but he wasn't where he'd been. He was halfway out the door, running like a maniac. He bounded down the stairs, his heavy feet sounding like the hasty retreat of stampeding buffalo. I took off after him, the room spinning, my legs wobbly, tumbling down the steps, seeing double as two of him cleared the bottom riser and tore out the front door.

The sun's glare hit me like the blast from a klieg light, blinding me for a moment, flooding my eyes. The loud murmur of many voices told me that the service was over. I tumbled out into the courtyard and ran toward the front of the church, my head pounding, squinting into the sun. A crowd milled around on the front steps of the church, and the man I was chasing shoved his way right through the middle of it, soliciting rude remarks and shocked expressions. I holstered my gun. I wouldn't need it. If he'd had a weapon, I would be dead now. My throat burned, my airway felt constricted. "Stop him!" I weaved in and out of the crowd, eyes on the fleeing man ahead of me. "Move! Watch out! Move!"

The stunned crowd parted, but no one stopped the man. As I ran, I could feel blood trickling from my forehead. I kept running. I cleared the crowd just as the man barreled across the street and disappeared into the gangway of a row of pale, squat apartment buildings. I dashed into the street, narrowly avoiding getting mowed down by a car. The driver lay on his horn, and the noise bore through my brain like the assault from a hundred rusty spikes.

I heard Whip's voice behind me and multiple sets of feet bringing up the rear, but I didn't stop to look. I raced ahead, jumping over garden hoses and sprinklers, tripping over uneven sidewalks. My head throbbed; my eyes were trained ahead, scanning the parking slots and gangways, searching frantically for the man who'd tried to kill me.

"Freeze! Police!" a woman barked from behind me. I stopped running. "Hands up! Turn around!" My eyes desperately searched the lot, but the man I'd been chasing was long gone. He'd slipped into some nook or cranny and disappeared into shadows like a wisp of lazy smoke, but I wasn't going anywhere. I stood still and waited for instructions. "Hands up! Face us! Slow!"

The female cop had been joined by her male partner. It sounded like they had been joined by a crowd. I raised my empty hands. I turned around slowly. The cops had their guns pointed at me, and behind them stood a gallery of onlookers from the memorial. I checked for Farraday and Weber, but luckily they were not among the spectators.

"I'm a PI," I announced to the cops. "There's a gun in my holster. I've got a valid FOID card, and my PI license is up to date."

The cops were hyperalert, cautious. I didn't blame them. Whip and Barb stood well back, both winded from running after me and poised to jump in and assist if needed. Practically everyone in the crowd had a cellphone camera trained on the scene. Cummings was there and Father Pascoe, stiff and sanctimonious in his starched vestments. I could tell he was going to make a stink about my trespassing in the rectory. The triumphant smirk on his pinched face gave it away. And Anton Bolek, standing off to the side, his eager, hateful eyes taking it all in. Again, what the hell was he doing here? I stared at him until he turned and walked away. There was something there, something for later. Turning back to the cops, I sighed and resigned myself to an afternoon of questions, red tape, and complications. Some days it just didn't pay to get out of bed.

It took three hours to convince the police that I was not John Dillinger on a rampage. Since I hadn't technically broken into the rectory, they couldn't get me for breaking, only entering. And since the church crowd witnessed the crazy man bolt out of the house with me in hot pursuit, they went along with my version that I, Cass Raines, being nothing if not civic-minded, spotted the rectory door ajar and went to investigate, thereby encountering a strange man hiding in a closet. I engaged said crazy man; a fight ensued and was followed by a very public, very well-attended foot chase that ultimately led to my current predicament.

Did I know the man? No, I did not, I told the cops. Did I take anything from the residence? On my honor, I did not, I responded, giving them the Scout's salute. The blood on my face and the bruises around my neck were evidence of the conflict, and they also got me a little sympathy, so when they ran my credentials and found that I was, indeed, an investigator in good standing, my paperwork was current, and my gun had been legally procured, I was allowed to leave without charges. I had the feeling that Father Pascoe had come down to the station just to see them lock me up, but, thankfully, he left unsatisfied.

It had been a rough day, made more so by the fact that I was still without Pop's datebook. Where could it be? Had someone gotten there before I did? Was it the crazy man? Why did he think I was after him? Who did he think sent me?

It was nearly seven when I got home, and everything on my body hurt. Whip, Barb, Ben, and I sat in my kitchen on the red vinyl barstools pulled up to the center island Monday night quarterbacking the last few hours. The stools matched nothing else in the room—not the wallpaper with yellow roses, the chrome appliances, or the kitschy rooster clock above the fridge that I bought from a street vendor in Ixtapa—but I liked how everything didn't go together. I especially liked the clock. Its hour and minute hands were fashioned to look like the legs of the rooster, and they moved around the clock face marking the time, becoming particularly amusing at 3:45 AM and again twelve hours later in the late afternoon. Blue cotton eyelet curtains hung at the window over the sink, which faced the kitchen window in the building next door. The floor was a patchwork of alternating black-and-white tile. My head throbbed like a mother.

From my refrigerator and cupboards, Barb and Ben had cobbled together sandwiches, a salad, fruit, and chips. It was an unimpressive dinner after such an inauspicious day. It hurt to open and close my mouth too wide or turn my head too far to the left or right, so I stuck with iced tea and small fruit slices that were easy to slide down my swollen throat.

"You're really not going to the hospital to get checked out?" Barb asked.

I slid in a tiny wedge of pineapple. "Not necessary," I croaked, my voice hoarse, raspy.

"You've got a goose egg the size of Pittsburgh on the back of your head," Whip said. "And a gash on your forehead. I'm not going to even mention the neck bruises."

"I appreciate that," I said. I reached for the bottle of aspirin in front of me and took three.

"What the hell were you thinking?!" Ben asked.

"When?" I asked.

"From the time you woke up this morning and decided to break into a rectory." Our eyes held. He shook his head. "You telling them about your civic-mindedness? A real Hail Mary. We're cops, not morons."

"And the book wasn't even there?" Whip asked, glancing nervously at Ben. I felt for him. He was sitting at a table eating a crappy dinner with a cop, a nun, and a PI. It was the beginning of a bad bar joke, and a situation no ex-con could ever prepare for.

"Not in his office," I said. "I didn't have a chance to check the closet. For obvious reasons."

"You don't think he killed Father Ray and that poor boy, do you?" Barb asked. "From what you said, it sounds like he could actually be a witness." She shot a pointed look at Ben.

I shrugged, then winced. My shoulders hurt, my chest hurt, everything hurt, including my pride. "I won't know until I find him."

"I could make some calls," Whip volunteered. "I know people."

"Or maybe we should let *him* find him?" Barb said, cocking

a thumb in Ben's direction. "I don't think you should tangle with him a second time."

I narrowed my eyes at her. My eyes hurt, too. "This, coming from you?"

Barb smiled. "Coveys are bullheaded and scrappy, not stupid. That guy was twice your size."

I turned to Ben. "The techs found candles at the crime scene."

Ben eyed me skeptically. "And? It's a church."

"He mentioned losing his candles."

Ben's mouth fell open. "And you're saying he came back for them? C'mon, that's one hell of a leap, even for you."

"It wouldn't hurt to run the candles you found for prints. It might give us a name."

"So he's some crazy dude with a fetish now?"

"He was in the rectory," I said. "In Pop's room. That can't be a coincidence."

Ben ran his hands through his hair. "Nobody knows what it is. You've got this thing all muddled up in your head, and you won't let go of it."

"I'm not some idiot going off all half-cocked on a wild goose chase. The guy was in that church. I'm sure of it. He saw what happened. He said as much."

"Or he's just crazy," Ben shot back. "Out of his mind nuts."

No one spoke for a time.

"All this and your old man, too, " Whip said, shaking his head. "Strolling back now like he just ran out for smokes. That's some brass balls right there." He glanced over at Barb, made a face. "Sorry. I keep forgetting you're a nun now." My grip tightened on my glass. In all the excitement, I'd almost forgotten about my father. Almost.

Barb's eyes shifted from Whip to me. "What do you plan to do about him?" she asked.

"I told him to get out of my yard. He got out. We're aces."

Barb said nothing. I sipped. Ben assaulted his sandwich. Whip grabbed a handful of chips from the bag and began popping them one after the other into his mouth. "Where's he been?"

"All over, apparently. Recently, St. Louis," I said.

Whip pulled a face. "That's cold. You can practically spit on St. Louis from your back door."

It was close, wasn't it? Close enough to visit, close enough to mail a letter from, close enough to be sent for if he'd had a mind to do so, which, obviously, he hadn't. I could tell by Barb's sympathetic expression that she also thought St. Louis was pretty damn close. I plucked a cherry tomato from the salad, avoiding her, my mind on candles and wild men. "The man I'm after is obviously homeless." I was speaking to Ben, working my way back to talking. "He was dressed in an old Army jacket, and wearing a black skull cap. It looked like he hadn't had a shave in weeks, and he smelled of BO and smoke. When I talked to George Cummings, he mentioned that a homeless man matching that description hung around the church regularly. He disappeared after the murders, now he's back. I wonder if I can track him down through some of the local shelters."

Barb emitted a faint sigh, but said nothing about the change in topic. She would give me my feeble attempt to divert the conversation, I knew, but she was only biding time.

"Homeless," Ben sighed, meeting me halfway. "One of the cases I'm on now, the one I told you about? Some guy's going around beating the crap out of them. Six attacks so far, and almost every night a new one. Whoever it is comes up on a guy, flashes a light in his face, rousts him, knocks him around, and then repeats the whole thing with the next unlucky fella down the line. The last vic took the beating, but suffered a heart attack during. He didn't make it. Now we're looking for a killer. We've got zero pattern—different nights, different times. I may be able to give you some coverage on the shelters. I'll let you know."

I socked him gently on the shoulder. "Thanks."

He socked me back. "No problem."

Just like that we were good again.

Barb groaned. "That's horribly sad."

"Well, it isn't good, and that's a fact," Ben said.

"No one's been able to give a description?" I asked.

Ben smirked. "Sure. One witness swears it was Santa Claus. The people we're dealing with aren't exactly all there. Best we can do is keep at it and hope we catch a break before somebody else dies."

"What about the victims?" I asked. "Any pattern there?"

"Homeless men. Sleeping rough. That's it."

Barb folded her napkin neatly. "I hope whoever's doing this gets the help he needs."

"Oh, he can get it, but it won't change the fact he's a nut-ball," Ben said. "People don't change, sister. They are who they are till the wheels fall off, take my word for it."

Barb tucked her napkin in beside her plate, giving it a finishing pat. "If I believed that, Ben, I'd be out of a vocation."

"Maybe, but if I *didn't* believe it, I wouldn't last two seconds on the street. You got to go with what you're given. A cop's got no time for nuance."

"That's why we run when you chase us," Whip said.

Ben stared at Whip, who'd been sitting quietly, pulling uncomfortably at his tie, hoping to avoid Ben's close scrutiny. Truthfully, it was a strange dynamic going on. Cops by their very nature distrusted criminals, and criminals distrusted cops right back. Ben and Whip were sitting and eating together, and neither seemed comfortable with it. Ben's eyes narrowed. "You been running anywhere lately?"

I tossed a strawberry across the table at him. "Knock it off."

Barb crossed her arms across her chest, sat back. "All I'm

saying is, people are almost always more than what they present. And change comes in big and small ways. Life has a way of forcing the issue." Her gaze shifted to me. "Anyone can change, and everyone is redeemable."

Ben and Whip's eyes locked onto their empty plates as though they were reading tea leaves hidden in the floral pattern. I found a spot on the wall across the room where the wallpaper was beginning to peel away. Maybe if I stared at it long enough, Barb would find something else to talk about. I flicked a look her way. She sat motionless, her arms still crossed, her gaze confident, infuriatingly sure and patient.

"Redemption's above my pay grade," I said. "Not that anyone's paying me these days."

"God redeems," she said. "We forgive."

Ben shot up from his seat. "I'm going to the can."

And just like that he was gone.

"I'm going to queue up for when he comes out," Whip said.

And he was gone, too.

"Something I said?" Barb asked.

I frowned. "That'd be my guess."

I began to stack plates at the table for no other reason than to give my hands something to do, hoping that the more I moved, the less it would eventually hurt when I did. I stood. "I know you mean well, but I don't want to talk about my father, and I know that's what you're angling for. I've got other things to deal with right now."

Barb slid her plate toward me. "I know."

I only had four plates to clear. The stacking didn't take long. I walked the plates over to the dishwasher to give myself some breathing room, but Barb followed me over with the glasses. She placed them gently onto the top rack of the machine, then backed up and leaned against the counter to watch me fiddle. I could feel her watching me and knew she'd keep at it until I turned around and faced her. The longer I didn't, the sillier I felt, until finally I pushed the washer door closed, turned, and, leaning against the opposite counter, faced her, my arms folded, the only defense I had remaining. "You aren't going to let this go."

She grinned. "Do you want me to?"

"Words cannot express how much. I'm fine with things the way there are."

"Poppycock." I looked a question. "Nun word for load of crap."

"I forget sometimes how earthy you can be."

She shrugged. "At your own peril. . . . It was a surprise seeing him, I imagine."

"Surprise would require at least a hint of recognition on my part. I thought he was just some guy looking for directions." I stared down at my bare feet, warm against the cool linoleum.

"And when you found out he wasn't?"

"I had a garden spade I thought about using for an alternate purpose." I gave her a wan smile and padded back over to the table. She sat across from me. "I don't need this right now, I really don't," I said.

"I've never seen a convenient complication, have you?"

"There's that."

"How did he seem? Did he look well?"

I shrugged. "He looked like an old man in a nice suit."

Barb drummed her fingers on the table. "You know, some people can handle upheaval, some can't. Your Mom's illness came out of nowhere, I remember, and blew everything up."

I nodded. It was true. Practically overnight, she was gone, and I was left with the one who didn't know how I liked my mashed potatoes or what my favorite color was or on what side I parted my hair. My father was in the house, but not intimately familiar with my life, with me. He was a stranger even then. My care, the feeling of being cared for, was my mother's domain. Then, just like that, she was gone; then he was gone. I grieved for her and for the sense of security I'd lost, but not so much for him. I didn't know him well enough to miss him.

"I can't imagine who he thinks he's coming back to."

"You should have asked him."

"That would have required having an actual conversation. Besides, I only gave him ten seconds. He doesn't feel like my father. Your dad stuck around. You feel differently."

Barb chuckled. "He had nine kids! Where could he go that my mother couldn't find him? That little spitfire would have hounded him to the ends of the earth. But, you're right, I feel differently. He was a great dad. That didn't stop him from grounding us or whacking us when we needed it, though."

"Or leaving one of you in jail overnight to teach you a lesson," I said.

Barb smiled wistfully. "Ah, those were fun times, weren't they?"

"Not if you ask your mother."

"I still don't think she trusts any of us to this day. She proves it by staying in touch to a maniacal degree. She called me every other day in Tanzania."

"Go see her," I said.

Barb scowled. "She'll want to trim my hair and buy me a new dress like I'm six. I'll go soon. I'll have to go. She knows I'm back. If I don't go, I'll find her camped out on your front lawn."

I sighed. "Well, there, I've talked."

Barb sputtered. "Barely. I did most of it."

I started to rise. "My bit still counts. Thanks for the ear. You're a peach."

She waved me back down. "Nuh-uh."

"I'm feeling a little sorry for those Tanzanian children. You're a bossy nun. That's the worst kind, by the way."

"Quit your whining. Just this, then I'll drop it. Whatever your father came to say, you owe it to yourself to listen. Then decide what, if anything, you'll do about it." She shrugged. "Maybe nothing. But what you have now is not a good place to end things. 'Nothing is ever settled until it is settled right.' That's Kipling, not me, by the way."

"Which part?"

Barb blinked. "What?"

"Which part was Kipling?"

"The part about nothing being settled. I could have gone with the parable of the prodigal son, but you would have expected that one." I stared at her. "See him. Listen. Talk if you have something to say. Make the effort."

"He doesn't get a do-over. He left, fine. I dealt with that. But now he comes back and thinks that's perfectly okay to do? That's what burns me, the audacity."

Barb sighed. "He's not an idiot. He knows he can't change the past. He's got to be working on the next chapter."

"He's a bastard."

Barb leaned over and patted my arm. "I wouldn't lead with that. It starts you off on the wrong foot. Settle it right." She clapped her hands together with an air of finality. "Now that that's done, which one of us gets to tell Ben and Whip it's safe to come out of the bathroom?"

Chapter 20

I gave up all hope of sleep around four AM. The fight in Pop's room and the ensuing chase played over and over in my head all night like a lousy movie that just wouldn't end. My blankets lay twisted and rumpled at the foot of my bed from all the tossing, as though I'd spent the night wrestling an alligator. I'd have had the wild man were it not for the slippery grass and the jittery cops. A couple more strides, one lucky break, and I'd have had him. Who was he? Who was he afraid of? What did he see in that church? Maybe I'd spooked him and he wouldn't come back. Maybe I hadn't, and he was there now. I couldn't relax thinking about the possibilities. I had to get up.

Every muscle in my body protested, but I slowly sat up in bed and slid my legs over the side, drawing in a cautious breath as I got to my feet. My head felt like a slab of concrete—leaden, blockish—and the aspirin I'd taken had done little to lighten it. I squeezed my eyes shut as jabs of molten dagger points seared their way up and down my spine. My lungs seized up and sweat beaded on my furrowed brow, but I slowly made it to the shower. I'd live, I decided once there, but for a while it wouldn't be at all graceful.

I left Barb sleeping in my spare bedroom and a note I'd written telling her where I'd be tacked to the door. I had no idea when I'd be back. Make yourself at home, I'd instructed her. I had a lot to do, and I had to get it done before Farraday decided it was past time to toss his weight around. Anton Bolek. He was hiding something. I was sure of it. But I couldn't tail him twenty-four hours a day, not solo. I called Whip, hoping he was an early riser, hoping he had a friend or two.

"How many do you need?" he asked. "And do you want just straight-up surveillance or scare-the-shit-out-of-him surveillance, because I got guys for both."

"Just curious," I said. "What's option *B*?"

"We eyeball him, but he sees us doing it. Day in, day out, relentless, we're there, like a bad smell, but he doesn't know why. He worries about that. Where he goes, we go. By the end, he's jumping at shadows and hiding under his own bed, ready for a padded cell. All depends on how far you want to push this."

I thought for a moment, thinking how nice it might be to put a good scare into the oily Bolek, but settled for option *A*. I just needed to know what he was doing that he didn't want Pop knowing about. I didn't want to scare him to death. "I want to know what he's up to without him knowing he's being watched."

"Option *A* it is then." He sounded downright giddy over the phone, happy, I guess, to finally be given a task, which gave me momentary pause. Was I really going to sic a bunch of ex-cons on Anton Bolek?

"You saw him at the memorial. You know what he looks like. He drives a dark blue Chevy S10 with a shoddy muffler. There's a faded MAKE AMERICA GREAT AGAIN sticker on his rear bumper."

Whip sputtered. "Shit, he's due a good spooking just for that."

"No one gets hurt. Promise me."

"I'll get back. Sit tight." He ended the call. I held the phone in my hands for a moment, worried, just a little, about what I'd just done.

In the dark, I trolled the neighborhood around the church, cruising down alleys, scanning the sidewalks and gangways. I was still at it when the sun came up, but the man from the closet was nowhere. For lack of anything else to do, I pulled up into a spot a few doors down from the rectory and sat watching it until kids began flooding into the school next door. Sitting in my car, watching, began to feel a little predatory. I drove once more through the alley and was about to give up, when I caught sight of a woman picking through a garbage cart. I ditched my car and approached her slowly. "Hello?" I called. "Excuse me?"

The woman jerked around, letting go of the cart lid, which landed with a reverberating thud. She rooted excitedly into layers of clothing, finally coming up with a battered metal rod about the length and width of a golf club. One end was wrapped in duct tape, I assumed, for a better grip. The other end, the business end, well, no tape needed there. That end was for bashing. "Mind your own! Ain't doing nothing here that's any of yours!" She thrusted and parried with the rod, impressively nimble on her feet. "Get on! I move along when I'm ready to, no sooner. Free country."

I took a step back, well out of striking range, my hands up. "When you move along is up to you. I'm not here to hassle you. I'm looking for a little information." I gave her what I hoped was my most disarming smile. While in uniform, part of my job was moving the homeless along. I was a defender of the peace, the arm of the law, and the law said no vagrancy. Nothing in the law, however, forbid me from feeling for them, or taking a moment to realize that only the grace of God separated me from them. Most of the time, I let them be, often passing a few bucks their way for a hot cup of coffee or a meal. Many did more harm to themselves than they could ever do to anyone around them. They were ghosts who walked the streets alone, and people looked right through them as though they were invisible.

The woman was of indeterminate age, dressed in threadbare layers of disparate fabric, some suitable for cold weather, some for hot. Behind her sat a bedraggled shopping cart adorned with long strips of colored ribbon worn dull by time, weather, and rough use. The cart held her meager possessions—clothing, plastic bottles, discarded toys and trinkets, and on top of all that, a stack of old magazines tied neatly in filthy twine. The woman smirked and lowered the rod a little, not much. "You got it right. I come and go as I please. If they throw it out, their loss. Mine now."

"My name's Cass. I'm looking for someone. Maybe you know him?" She just stood there. Had she heard me? "What's your name?"

That got a rise. She reached back and grabbed the cart handle, as though I were going to snatch the cart from her. One hand held the cart, the other her makeshift sword, which she aimed at me. "Don't talk to Social Services. Nothing good ever comes of it."

I eased my arms down primarily because it hurt to keep them up. "I'm not a social worker. The man I'm looking for is dark, about two hundred pounds, tall. He wears an Army jacket and likes candles. Maybe you know him?"

The woman blinked rapidly, then shook her head. "Don't like candles. Too witchy. I go flashlight—lasts longer, burns bright. Go with the bunny batteries, too, not the crap kind. The ones that go on and on and on and on. Get them from the church bins around donation time. That's all you need to know about that."

I didn't have my bag, but I reached into my back pocket for the case I kept my driver's license and credit cards in and pulled out my emergency twenty dollar bill. I held the money up for her to see. "Maybe you could think about the man I described a little more? I'd like to pay you for your time—for keeping you from what you were doing. Dark, about two-hundred pounds, Army jacket. Maybe he hangs around here."

Her eyes darted around the alley as though she expected a sneak attack. "Ha. Know that old trick. Where they hiding? Are they out there parking the crazy wagon?"

"No trick," I said. "Just another moment to think about it and the money's yours."

I could tell she didn't believe me. Trust was just one of the many things she'd lost along the way. "Whether I seen him, or not?"

"That's right," I said. "Either way." I waited while she thought it over.

"What do you want him for?"

"Just to talk," I said. "Like I'm doing now with you." She eyed the money, but didn't move. "I was a friend of the priest who died here. I think the man I'd like to talk to knows something about that."

The rod fell down to her side. She smiled. "Father Ray?"

The tension between my shoulder blades relaxed some, not a lot. "He was real nice to street folk. Kindly."

"Yes, he was. So, please, is there anything you know that might help?"

Her eyes narrowed. "Money first."

I stepped forward slowly and handed her the twenty, watching as she deftly slipped it into a hidden pocket. "What should I call you?"

She jumped back. "Why?"

"You've got a name. I'd like to use it."

"What'd you say *yours* was?" she asked.

"Cass."

She grimaced, shook her head. "Like mine better. Cleopatra."

I took her name at face value. Maybe it was real, maybe she'd just adopted it for herself. Her prerogative. It was clear she had very little else to call her own, but at least she had the freedom to cling to a name that suited her. I stood quietly as Cleopatra reached into her fuzzy memory bank. After a time, she let out a loud, triumphant snort.

"Sure. I know him. Name's Old Sarge. Army man." She made a broad sweep with her arms. "Walks all around here, up and down, night, day. And he can do it, too. He's always got new boots. It's magic, or something. Haven't seen him. Used to, now I don't."

"Old Sarge? You're sure?"

She glowered. "You heard. Now you best be getting on the get and leave me to myself." She backed away.

"Wait! Do you know where he'd go?"

She sighed heavily. "I just told you. Here!" She yelled the last bit.

"Besides here."

She spread her arms wide in a gesture of profound annoyance. "How would I know? I'm in this place, and he's in some other place. I can only see what I see. See? But if it was me looking for Old Sarge, I'd check where the food's at. Everything living's got to eat."

She turned and double-timed her cart down the alley. "Free to do my business," she shouted back over her shoulder. "Free to come and go."

While I watched her round the corner and disappear, I dug my phone out of my pocket. Following the food wasn't a bad idea, and food meant checking shelters and soup kitchens, and in this neighborhood that meant Bear Burgett. She ran the Sanctuary out of a repurposed dental clinic, well within wandering distance of the church's back door. Hers was the closest free meal around. Bear had a spooky gift for memorizing names and faces, a gift she'd perfected as a prison guard at Logan Correctional. If she'd ever served Old Sarge a meal or offered him a bed, she'd remember him.

I'd punched in the first three digits of her number, when I heard the rectory door open and shut. I trotted over to the gate just in time to see Father Pascoe slide into his car and drive away. I put the phone back in my pocket. Bear could wait. I eased open the back gate, slipped through the courtyard, crept up the rectory steps, and rang the bell. No one answered. I leaned on the bell. Nothing. I pressed the bell to the tune of Jingle Bells, then waited a few seconds more. All clear.

"Hot diggity." I dug out my picklocks, ducked behind the evergreen bush, and went to work on the tumblers. No alarm to worry about, thank goodness. I'd often urged Pop to get one, but he never felt the need—something about trusting his fellow man and fostering a sense of openness, blah, blah, blah. I had the lock beat in less than three minutes. Not as fast as Whip's record, but breaking and entering wasn't my day job. "Just proves I was right, Pop," I muttered, just in case he was listening. I slipped inside and closed the door behind me. "Flimsy locks leave you wide open for all kinds of squirrely vagabonds. Present company excluded, of course."

I bypassed the office. I'd searched it already and hadn't found anything that got me anywhere. I took the stairs two at a time headed for Pop's room, to the closet, which last time had held a nasty surprise. I didn't expect lightning to strike twice, but just in case, I unholstered my gun before easing the door open, exhaling deeply when I found it empty of anything with a pulse. I put the gun away and got to work. Time flies when you're breaking the law.

The contents of the closet proved less than revelatory. Nothing inside but Pop's black suits, a couple of cardigans, and a St. Brendan's baseball jacket hanging on the rod. Every pocket I slid my hand into was empty. No book. No proof of Cesar and Pop's connection. The fact that I wasn't finding the book anywhere led me to believe its absence was deliberate, that someone had taken it, but for what purpose? What secrets did it hold?

A cardboard box about the size of a kid's lunchbox sat on the top shelf. I pulled it down and opened it, but there were only white clerical tabs inside. I shoved the box back, frustration getting the better of me. Reaching up to feel around the back of the shelf, my foot bumped up against something on the floor. I looked down to find a battered green duffle bag pushed under the hanging suits. Down on my hands and knees, I slid the bag out where I could see it and quickly unzipped it.

Men's clothes. I pawed through the bag, feeling along the lining for hiding places, upsetting the sweaters, turtlenecks, and such. Winter clothes, brand-new with the tags still on them. Nestled into a side pocket someone had placed a pocket Bible, a small laminated prayer card slipped between the pages. I turned the card over in my hands. ST. BENEDICT JOSEPH LABRE.

It meant nothing to me. I was a lapsed Catholic in good standing, and had long ago lost the ability to identify obscure saints. Fluttering the Bible's pages yielded nothing else.

I thought I heard a noise downstairs and froze, waiting to be caught, my hand in the bag. When the noise didn't repeat, I resumed my search, mindful of the time I was taking.

These clothes were all for someone twice Pop's size. Who? Beside the duffle sat a new pair of boots, size eleven and a half wide. Also, not Pop's. I shoved everything back inside the bag, pushed it back inside the closet and stood, brushing the dust off my pants. If the contents of the bag were meant as donations, since when did people give away brand-new clothes? And why were they all the same size, as though meant for someone specific? Heavy sweaters, warm socks, all the things someone would need to get through a cold winter outdoors. Were they for Old Sarge? The man Cleopatra said wore the magic boots?

I quickly checked the hall, then raced for the stairs, then stopped. Maybe Father Pascoe had helped himself to Pop's book? Thea, maybe? But I quickly dismissed her. She wouldn't have. I eyed Father Pascoe's bedroom door and for a second contemplated searching it, too, but that would be pushing my luck. Reluctantly, I let it go. Instead, I trotted down the stairs, through the entry hall and back out the front door, pulling it closed behind me. I stood there for a second, my back to the courtyard, breathing a sigh of sweet relief until a man chortled behind me. Startled, I whipped around to find Detective Weber standing at the foot of the rectory steps, his arms folded across his chest. He had me dead to rights for unlawful entry, illegal picklocks in my pocket. I would be the easiest arrest he'd ever make in his entire career. I sighed, slowly raised both arms high, the universal sign of surrender, and wondered how long they'd make me wait before I could make my one phone call.

Chapter 21

"Father Pascoe inside?" Weber asked.

I shook my head.

"The housekeeper?"

I squinted at him. "Are we really going to play this game?"

Weber removed his sunglasses and hooked them onto his belt. "This is the part when folks start bargaining and coming up with fantastical tales. Some people even start to cry or offer to make generous donations to the Policemen's Fund. You want to give any of that a shot?"

I stiffened, affronted by the very idea of stooping so low. Never in a million years, I thought. Two million even. Our eyes locked. I stood tall, defiant. In that moment, I was Rosa Parks on that Montgomery bus, Norma Rae atop that factory table, a stubborn two-year-old refusing to eat her peas and carrots. "Absolutely not."

He grinned. "Aw, go on. It might be fun."

I held my wrists out for the cuffs. "Look, if we're going to do this, let's do it. I've got things to do. If I can get processed by noon, I can arrange bail and be out in time to sleep in my own bed tonight. Chop, chop."

He chuckled. "Man, you're something else."

He was having way too much fun with this, which was beginning to irritate me. "I assume I can put my hands down now?"

He nodded. "Your idea to put them up."

"Yeah, well, it's usually safer that way."

He motioned for me to lower my arms. "I'm not taking you in. You wore the star. Far as I'm concerned, you still do."

"Heh, don't let Farraday hear you say that." I lowered my arms, grateful for the professional courtesy. "Thanks."

Weber's eyes swept over me. "Besides, I don't see the rectory's TV under your jacket. Also don't see a door key. Do I want to know how you got in?"

"I wouldn't think so."

"Takes a lot of nerve to break into a holy place."

I flicked a thumb toward the church. "The holy place is over there. This is just a house. You're not Catholic, I take it."

"Methodist. When I feel the urge to be anything. Did you at least get what you came for?"

I shook my head. "I was looking for Father Heaton's datebook. He always carried it."

"And it's not inside?"

"No."

Weber smiled. "Took a big chance going for it, though."

I shrugged. "No guts, no glory."

"What's so important about a datebook?"

"It should verify that he knew Cesar Luna. It might identify Cesar's girlfriend and the homeless man who almost choked me to death. The fact that I can't find it anywhere, I believe, is significant, don't you?"

"I heard about that guy. He popped out of the closet." Weber's eyes traveled to my neck. "You're working up some nice bruises there. Hope you gave as good as you got."

I shrugged. "I walked away. That's good enough."

Weber scanned the rectory. "But you came back. . . . I'm liking the initiative. But if I were a different kind of cop, you'd be on your way to jail right now, and that would be a real shame."

I narrowed my eyes. I'd been a little slow on the uptake, but was quickly catching on. "What kind of cop are you?"

"I could tell you over coffee." He stood there, an amused grin on his face. I blinked and stared back. He really wasn't bad looking for a cop. I liked the eyes, the intensity of his gaze, the way he met you head on, calmly, assuredly. My eyes traveled to the ring finger of his left hand, and that's when the wheels of possibility screeched to an abrupt stop. The finger sported a narrow band of skin a few shades lighter than the rest of his hand, which bore witness to his having recently removed a ring. And I had a pretty good idea what kind. I hadn't thought to look the first time we met. I blame Farraday. He distracted me.

"Separated," he said when he caught me looking. "The job's tough on marriages."

"Newly separated."

"Almost a year. The papers are filed. It's over."

I scanned the courtyard. No Farraday. He was probably out there stomping on a litter of puppies with his big cop feet. "Farraday's not crouching under a bush waiting to Taser me, is he?"

"He's working another angle, and he's working it hard, determined to show you up. I had a couple more questions for Father Pascoe, so I thought I'd stop by and ask them. It keeps us out of the same car."

"The bloom fell off that rose pretty quick." I smiled, feeling vindicated. It wasn't just me who found Farraday a repugnant little toad. Besides, Weber would be far safer away from Farraday than he would be closer to him. I just wasn't sure yet why that even mattered to me. "What do you want with Father Pascoe?" Weber looked a question. "I told you why I'm here, in the spirit of full cooperation. It's your turn."

"I came across some additional information. I want to talk to him about it."

I paused, waiting for him to elaborate. He didn't. "Seriously?"

"That's all I can say at this time," Weber said. "And you're one to talk. You've been stingy with the facts from your end."

He was right, I had to admit. Cops were trained to ferret out information and hold it close, not trade it as freely as Pokémon cards at a ten-year-old's birthday party. Weber's reluctance to show all of his cards matched mine.

"All right then. What about the surveillance from the McDonald's that Marisol mentioned? Any movement on that?"

Weber shook his head. "Not yet. It's slow going. Too much tape, not enough eyes. Good tip, though."

"What about the guy I chased yesterday? Any leads on him?"

"It's been less than twenty-four hours," he said. "Who do you think we are? The Justice League? You have anything besides this datebook?"

I held out my empty hands. "Nothing. My best angle is the guy who tried to kill me. I have a contact at one of the shelters. Maybe she can help. Where was Father Pascoe the night of the murders? I know he told Farraday."

Weber turned to watch cars drive down the narrow street. "His alibi's solid."

"That tells me nothing. Are you guys not looking too closely at him because he's a priest?"

"I'm rethinking the cuffs," Weber said. "Anybody ever tell you that talking to you is like playing a verbal game of ping-pong?"

"If they did, I wasn't listening. I told you why I was here."

Weber's eyes widened. "You were backing out of a locked door! What choice did you have?"

I bounded down the stairs, headed for the alley gate. "I've got to go."

"Hey, what about that coffee?"

I turned back. "Why?"

Weber looked confused. "Why do people drink coffee?"

"No, why coffee with me? Farraday must have given you the 411 on me already. Wasn't that enough to scare you away?"

Weber watched me closely. "Your eyes turn colors when you're riled up, you know that? I like that you give as good as you get, and you're easy to look at. I like that you're giving me a hard time right now about drinking a friendly cup of coffee. You could probably kick my ass, and I don't even care. I might even learn to like it once I know you better. You're not typical, and I like that, too. Full of piss and vinegar, as my grandmother used to say, but there's a soft side, too. People think a lot of you. I've asked around. That's just some of the reasons why you . . . and there they go again."

"What?"

"Your eyes."

The whole thing took me by surprise. He held my gaze until I looked away, and then peddled backward. "See you around, Detective Weber."

Weber let out a frustrated groan. "Really? That's how it is?"

I smiled, then slipped back into the alley, headed for my car, aware that he was watching me go. The flutter in my stomach told me that Detective Weber could be the right kind of trouble, but he was off limits. Separated was still married, ring or no ring. Besides, Pop came first. Every minute that ticked by, Old Sarge burrowed deeper underground. Coffee would have to wait. I started my car and dialed Bear's number.

She answered on the half ring, as I expected her to. "Speak," she barked.

"Cass Raines." I said. You didn't waste time with idle pleasantries when talking to Bear. Small talk wasn't her thing.

"Raines. Long time. Spill it. I'm up to my tits in broccoli flo-rets." Bear Burgett was a mighty tugboat of a woman, short, stout, able to pull twice her weight and half of yours. She didn't waste time; she didn't waste anything. She'd spent way too many years trying to stretch stores of turnips and cheap rump roasts so they'd last until the next donation came in. In the background, I could hear the clattering of steel pots and metal utensils, and over that, the confusion of too many voices at-tached to bodies in motion confined to too small a space.

"I'm looking for a man—African-American, tall—maybe dealing with some mental issues. He goes around in a field jacket. People call him Old Sarge. He's been known to cruise around St. Brendan's Church, but hasn't been seen there for a while."

There was a long silence on Bear's end. "Why're you asking?"

"You heard what happened there. I think he may know something about that."

"Hey, hey, hold it. Those potatoes need to be blanched first. Blanch. Blanch! Hold on." Bear muted me, but quickly re-turned. "Papers said it was a robbery-suicide thing. Maybe gang-related."

"I think it was murder," I said.

"Uh-uh. So, you're looking at Old Sarge for that?"

"I'm looking at him as a possible witness, that's all."

"What's your stake?"

"Unofficial, and personal," I said.

There was a long silence.

"I've seen a guy in an Army jacket once or twice, but I don't know the name. I'll ask around. Get back in touch."

"Thanks—"

Bear ended the call abruptly, cutting off my thank you. I punched END, though at that point it was merely for formality's sake. I eased out of the alley, thoughts of broccoli and compli-cated coffee rolling around in my head.

*   *   *

My chess set sat forlornly on the side table in my office. It wasn't half as nice as Pop's lucky board, but we'd played plenty of lively matches on it. It pained me even to look at it now, knowing Pop wasn't here to take me on, knowing he never would be. I still hadn't figured out the notes in his Bible, deciphered the significance of the underlined passage, or learned anything new about the girl in the photograph, and I was exhausted from the effort and from grief. I got up from the chair, padded over to the chessboard, and began removing the pieces, laying each one gently into the chess box. My fingers gripped the last rook tightly before I tossed it in and shut the lid, perhaps for the last time.

I walked over to the window and glanced down at the street watching the cars pass. Deek's was at the corner, apartment buildings across the street, a bookstore two blocks up. It was just midday, too early for anything truly interesting to happen outside my windows. The missing datebook weighed heavy on my mind, along with the identity of the black girl and the whereabouts of Old Sarge. I'd heard nothing from Bear yet, but it'd only been a few hours. I had the real sense that time was slipping away from me and that I was failing Pop somehow. What could I do next? What had I missed? My office door opened and I turned around to see my father standing in the doorway. I would have thought it impossible for my heart to sink any lower, but it did. He'd ditched the suit, opting this time for a casual sweater and slacks. He was the last person in the world I wanted to see, but I was done fighting. It was exhausting dredging up old hurts. "Yellow Pages or Google?" I walked the box over to the closet and slid it onto the top shelf.

He eased farther in, his eyes sweeping over the small room. "What do you mean?"

"You had a good shot at finding where I lived. I mean, that's where you left me. You'd have had to look up this address."

He nodded. "Yellow Pages."

"I'd rather not lace up for round two, if that's okay with you." I'd just packed away memories of the father I'd inherited. Now I hoped someone, anyone, would rid me of the father I'd gotten by biology.

His brows furrowed. Was I seeing concern? "What happened to your face, your neck?"

There was nothing I could do about the goose egg on the back of my head, but I'd done my best to cover the cut on my forehead and the bruises around my neck. Still, concealer only went so far. None of this was something I wanted to discuss with Theodore Raines. I sat. "Nothing for twenty-three years, now twice in one week. Lucky me."

"You don't have to talk. I'll talk," he said in a rush, as though an alarm would sound when his time was up. "Just give me one hour." I rolled my eyes. "Thirty minutes then." He straightened defiantly. "I'm not going away, Cassandra. I swear I'll stand here till I either grow roots or shrivel up and blow away."

I sat watching him, thinking of chess and loss and, strangely enough, Kipling. I could test his resolve and let him stand till he fell, a satisfying prospect in my current state of mind, or I could settle it as Barb, and Kipling, had advised. Life was all about choices—the ones you made and those you let slip away. "Tomorrow," I said finally. "Deek's. It's at the corner—"

"I know it," he said, cutting off my words. "Nine? Breakfast?"

"Ten. And I'm not eating with you."

He frowned, then shot me a slow smile. "I'll take what I can get." He took one final look around, then left, easing the door closed behind him. I watched the door for a time, then attended to the overdue paperwork on my desk.

Kipling was beginning to be a pain in my ass.

* * *

"Cassie, wouldn't you like to unpack that suitcase?" I sat rigid on the twin bed covered by a spread of circus clowns; my grandmother sat beside me. My hands clasped in my lap, ankles crossed, legs too short for my feet to touch the carpeting. Waiting. *"You're home,"* she said, watching. She had my mother's smile, her kind eyes. The suitcase had stayed packed for weeks. I needed to be ready in case I had it all wrong and my father was actually coming back. We could learn to be a family. *"I can help, if you want?"* she offered in her quiet way. *"Or we can leave it packed for as long as you need it to be."*

I looked up at her, down at the big blue suitcase with the red vinyl handle, a three-year-old sticker from Disneyland plastered on the side, hating it, wishing I could burn it. As long as I needed it to be? I stood, stopped waiting, and grew up. *"No, thank you. I can do it myself."* I took a breath, opened the case, and without a fuss put my things away in drawers that were now mine.

He was sitting in a booth when I got to Deek's. Thankfully, not the one I preferred. He stood when I reached him. "I was worried you wouldn't come."

I removed my jacket and slid in across from him. "I said I'd be here. I keep my word."

He said, "Unlike me, you mean."

I watched, said nothing. He pushed his half-empty coffee cup away. "Coffee?" He raised his arm to signal for Muna, who was across the way dropping off a plate.

"Tea," I said.

"Tea." He repeated it, as though it were an insight into my personality, one he needed to file away for future reference. He caught Muna's attention. "Tea, please. Thank you."

Neither of us spoke for a time. When Muna walked over with the small pot of hot water and a caddy full of teabags, she found the two of us staring at each other, not talking.

"Nothing to eat?" she asked, a suspicious look on her face. Maybe she could feel the tension, my trepidation.

Ted Raines looked at me, hopeful.

I shook my head. "Nothing."

He looked up at Muna and smiled. "I guess nothing for me, either."

Muna stood there for a time watching the both of us. "Everything okay over here?"

I didn't answer, neither did he; she placed a hand on her hip. "Well, somebody better say something, or I'm going for the bat behind my counter."

"Everything's fine," I said.

She fixed my father with a withering stare. "Better be."

When she charged off, he stared after her, his mouth slightly open. "What just happened? Does she really have a bat?"

"At least one," I said.

"Your water's getting cold."

I hadn't touched the pot or the cup. I didn't touch them now. He rubbed the back of his neck. "I guess I should just start, right?" He glanced over at Muna and found her staring at him. "Is she going to do that the whole time?"

"She is," I said.

He took a sip of cold coffee, grimaced, then braced himself, the silence between us threatening to go on indefinitely. I didn't have time for it. I had leads to uncover, leads to follow up on.

"So?" I asked, hoping to get things moving. "You wanted to explain yourself."

He nodded. "I did. I do." He toyed with his cup. "I ran. That's the long and short of it. Your mother, her illness, it was all so horrible. I loved her so much. I love you, too, though up till now I've had a terrible way of showing it. After she was gone, I knew I was over my head. I had no idea what to do next, so I ran."

"And you weren't coming back," I said.

"I told myself I was coming back, but you're right, I managed to convince myself that you needed more than me, that you'd have more of a chance in a loving home with your grandparents." He took another sip from his cup. "Grace and Frank, apparently, felt the same. They lost your mother, but they made it perfectly clear to me that they weren't about to lose you, too. We never really hit it off. I was never good enough, and they let me know it. I provided, sure, I loved your mother and you, but I was never quite good enough." He offered a half smile. "It's good to see you again, to see that you're well."

"I am well."

He nodded, watching me, looking a little shaky and tense. This wasn't easy for him. I could see it. It shouldn't be. "I got married again, twice, but I told you that already. I had to learn to be a good father. It's important to me that you know that. I'm even a little bit overprotective, like I should have been with you. . . . Your brother's name is Whitford, we call him Whit. I mean, his mother and I do. She's Sela, my second wife. He's going on seventeen. . . . Maybe you two can meet soon? . . . I'm rambling." He drew in a long breath, blew it out, settled. "The longer I stayed away, the easier it got." He picked up his cup again, but put it down without drinking. "Aren't you going to say anything?"

"I promised I'd listen."

He exhaled noisily, disappointed. "You did, yes."

"Well, after so many years, it was the guilt and shame that kept me away. I moved in and out of a lot of cities, had a lot of different jobs. I was drinking, though I eventually got a handle on that. Seventeen years clean, come August. I stopped right before Whit was born. I didn't want to fail another kid." He wiped his forehead with a napkin he'd twisted to near shreds. "Do you remember that I drank?"

"We weren't that close, were we? You worked, you came home, I was in my room."

"I regret that now. Well, I did drink, and I lost control over it when your mother got sick. When we found out she wouldn't get better, it got bad, then worse."

Muna returned to top off his cup. She eyed my untouched teapot and mug, scowled at Ted, then left again without attending to either. Just checking in. In addition to the bat behind the counter, I knew she kept a switchblade tucked in her waistband. Deek's wasn't a rowdy place, but Muna had worked a lot of dodgier places before here, and old habits die hard.

"I'm not the same man today. You have every right to push me away. I'm just hoping you won't. Haven't you ever done anything you wished you hadn't? Something you'd sell your soul to take back, if you could?"

I thought of Jimmy Pick, then quickly pushed the thought away. "I'm not exactly sure what it is you want from me. I'm not a child anymore. I grew up. I'm too old for the circus. I scrape a knee, I bandage it myself. I vote and drive, pay my own bills, kill my own spiders. I can run perfectly well with scissors. Besides, why now? Why not ten years ago? Five?" He didn't answer. I watched as his face clouded over with shame. "Guilt? Is that what's eating you?"

"Partly," he said.

"And the other part?"

"I read about what happened to Father Heaton. I still get the hometown papers where I live."

At the mention of Pop's name, I folded in on myself, immediately guarding whatever door he'd managed to ease open. I didn't want him talking about Pop. Pop was mine. Pop stuck, as fathers are supposed to. He didn't run off when I needed him. I shot my father a look of warning.

"What's he got to do with you?" I asked.

"I know how important he was to you." His eyes searched mine. "I thought that you might need someone."

"By someone, you mean you?"

"He and I weren't exactly friends, but I saw how you took to him, how easy it was for him to get through to you when I couldn't. You bonded with him like you never did with me. I held a lot of resentment toward him, I guess. The drinking didn't help any."

I watched as his hands balled into fists on top of the table. Obviously, the feelings weren't all behind him. "So when I read about what happened, I knew you'd be grieving. I thought maybe you'd be open to talking. That maybe there was room for me now."

I sat stunned, staring at his hands, listening to the undertones of anger in his voice. "You hated him."

He shook his head. "I envied him because he had you, but I was blaming him for my own failings. Sobriety gives you a truer perspective on things."

"So you came back because his spot was suddenly vacant? You came back to make sure Pop was dead?" My voice rose.

He leaned back, as though I'd slapped him. "Of course not. I gave you my reasons for coming."

I shook my head, anger rising. "I don't believe you. He took your spot, and you've hated him this whole time for it."

He jutted his chin out, his expression resolute. "You're wrong. If anything, it's the opposite. I realized that instead of resenting him, I owed him for what he did for you. I'm just sorry I got here too late to tell him to his face."

I searched his eyes, looking for truth, not certain if I was seeing it or something else. I didn't know the man well enough to tell. But I was getting a sinking feeling, one I didn't like, one that threatened to blow the top off of the conciliatory calm I'd managed to keep on top of ever since the man wandered into my front yard.

"You called him Pop? I'm not sure how I feel about that."

My eyes narrowed, my defenses, now miles thick, were firmly in place. "*Were* you too late?"

He looked confused. "I don't understand."

"You said you were too late to tell him you owed him a debt. Were you too late? You've really not seen him in over twenty years?"

He stared at me, still not getting what I was asking. Then he got it. His eyes widened. "Wait a minute. Are you asking me if I had something to do with how he died?"

"Did you?"

"How could you think such a thing?"

I had to know. "When did you get here? In town."

"Cass, look. You've got this whole thing twisted."

"You wanted to talk, we're talking. Answer the question. When did you get here?"

"He was already dead when I got here. I told you I read about it in the paper."

"How long?" My voice rose higher, quivered. "How many days exactly?" Could he have killed Pop? How much did he resent him? How deep did it go? What would I do if he was the killer I was looking for? What would I do?

He didn't answer. He didn't do anything, just sat there stunned, wounded.

"I'm your father," he said. "I may not have a right to the title, but I *am* your father."

"So you're refusing to answer?" I stood, fumbled with my jacket. "Fine. Then I'll find out on my own." I punched my arms into my jacket sleeves. "And I will find out. Oh, and for the record, *he* was my father, not you. Pop did more for me than you *ever* did. He cleaned up the mess you left behind. If I find out you had anything to do with . . ." I couldn't even finish the sentence. I needed to get out and away. "Go back to your family. Go protect the hell out of *them*. We're done." I turned to leave.

"Wait. Please," he said. "If this is all I get, then I may as well get through it all." He reached into his back pocket, pulled out his billfold, and set it on the table. I watched, wondering if he intended to pay me for my time. God help him, if he did. He opened the billfold and pulled out what looked like an old photo folded in quarters, which he unfolded and laid beside the wallet. "This is you accepting your high school diploma. I left before you or your grandparents saw me." He reached back in and pulled out a second photo and laid it next to the first. "College graduation. I sat in the back row, nearest the door." He reached into the wallet for a third time. "The police academy." He smiled. "You looked so determined." He looked up at me. "I didn't let go."

The photos unnerved me. I didn't know what to feel about them, about him. What right did he have to monitor me, but not parent me? "You were a ghost hiding in shadows. No good to me then, no good to me now. I'd say I'll see you around, but I doubt I'll lay eyes on you again." I turned again to leave. "Thanks for the tea."

"I was here," he said calmly. "Two years ago."

I turned back. "You're free to come and go as you please, obviously."

He pulled a small folded square of blue paper from his wallet. Not a photograph this time. He slid the paper toward the center of the table. It was a hospital visitor's pass. There on the face of it was the name of the hospital I'd been in, the letters ICU, and the date—two days after the rooftop shooting. "I prayed every day, harder than I ever have before, or since."

I felt a flutter in my throat. I wanted to stop him from talking, to turn tail and run, like he had done all those years ago, but I held the spot. I'd learned from Pop and from my grandparents that you held up your end no matter what, you didn't run, you didn't back down, no matter how painful it was, no matter how difficult.

"I had nothing to do with your Pop's death. I wouldn't do that to you. And I'm not giving up this time. That's a promise I intend to keep."

I sneered, seething. "Still don't believe you."

I reached into my pocket, placed a five-dollar bill on the table next to the contents of his wallet. "And just so we end this clean, that's for the tea." Halfway to the door I stopped, turned, and went back.

I could feel the other diners watching me. I was making a scene and didn't care. I wanted to look into my father's face one more time to see if I was looking into the face of Pop's killer. He stood up to face me.

"I'm going to ask you one more time. How long?"

He tossed his napkin down on the table, a dejected look on his face. "Four days." He kept his voice low, but it was too late for that. The entire diner was already engaged in our drama. "I came by train. The ticket's back in my hotel room, if you need to see it."

"Yeah, I need to see it."

"My word's not good enough?"

I laughed in his face. "Are you serious?"

I could feel Muna beside me now. She had my back. Why couldn't he have killed Pop? Killers didn't always look like deranged lunatics. Some of them showed up on your lawn with bright smiles, dressed in good suits. Cesar Luna could have been in the wrong place at the wrong time, maybe seeking Pop's counsel when Ted Raines showed up.

I took out my cellphone and snapped his picture. I'd need it to show around the church. I'd find out where he'd been if it took everything I had. If he killed Pop, he'd pay, and the fact that we shared blood wouldn't factor in.

His eyebrows knit together. "What's that for?"

I shook the phone in his face. "If anyone around that church recognizes you, I'll be back, and God help you then."

"I'm not going anywhere," I heard him say as I turned and headed for the door. I didn't believe that either.

Chapter 22

I paced the sidewalk outside of Deek's to try and steady myself, thinking of my father, the ghost, wafting in and out of my life like a restless haint, resenting Pop, envying him. When I'd had enough and could think straight again, I walked to my car and slid my key in the driver's door. My mind was not on the street.

The four-door, rimmed-up, drive-by special with tinted windows rolled to a slow, menacing stop at my front bumper, boxing me in at the curb. The front passenger door flew open, and a sumo-sized Hispanic man lurched out of the front seat, his dark, flat eyes trained on me, his black jeans sagging, the short-sleeves of his white T-shirt rolled up over heavily tatted biceps. The gaudy gold chains around his thick neck jingled like dog chains when he moved. The look on his face seemed to issue a challenge. Go ahead. Try to get past me. No gun that I could see, though I was sure he had one tucked somewhere. Mine would have come in handy, but I'd left it at home in the lockbox. I didn't think I'd need it for coffee with my father.

The big guy cocked his fat head toward the back seat. "Get in."

I checked the street, though now it was a little late for that. There was no one walking or driving along. Figured. It was just me, the car, and the gruff offer of a dicey ride I had no intention of taking. I slid a glance toward the diner. No help there. No one was looking. I thought of Muna's bat tucked soundly under the counter. My father was probably still in the booth ordering breakfast.

I turned back to Big Guy and we stared at each other until finally the back window rolled down to reveal Hector Perez sitting in the back seat. "We don't got time for no pissing match here, Ignacio," he said. The sight of Hector Perez sitting in the back of a banger car hemming me in at the curb was not reassuring, considering he was a known thug, and we hadn't exactly parted the best of amigos. Still, my shoulders relaxed some. Better the banger you know than the banger you don't. He said, "We been sitting out in front of your office down there for a long time, Five-O. We got to talk, but not in the open like squatting ducks."

"What do you want?" I asked, eyeing the giant, paying close attention.

"Let's go for a ride," Hector said.

I shook my head. "Not a chance."

He smirked. "You don't trust me?"

"No," I said. "Move your car."

He shot me a greasy smile. "Or what?"

It was a good question. There wasn't much I could really do. Ignacio advanced a couple steps. "He gets any closer and we're going to have a problem," I said.

Hector chuckled. "He won't, but maybe you will." His eyes traveled over me, as though he were a hungry man eyeing a pork chop. "You're not carrying." He shrugged. "No gun. No nothin'. That's stupid."

He was right. It was stupid. Ignacio laughed, then took another step forward. "Kneecaps. Groin. Eyes. Ribs. Throat. Groin first," I said.

Ignacio blanched and stepped back, his beefy hands cupping his privates.

Hector laughed. "Smart move, Iggs. Look Five-O, I maybe got some information you want. But I'm not hanging around out here like this to give it to you. Things could get, how you say, messy." His smile disappeared. "I figure I owe Cesar."

"Why now?"

"Call it change of heart, eh?" He eased the back door open.

"Still not getting in," I said. "I don't trust you, but I do trust Mrs. Luna. You want to talk? Let her set the date and time, and the three of us will discuss that information you have. She has my number. Now move."

Hector's eyes went cold, black. "I don't like your attitude."

"Tough nuts," I said.

For a moment there was only silence, then Hector nodded, and his smile slowly returned. "Wait for that call."

His door slammed shut; the back window rolled up. Ignacio slid back into the car, and then the car sped off. I was still on my feet, but the blood had well and fully drained from my extremities.

My father burst through the diner door. "Who was that? Are you okay?"

Muna rushed out right behind him, bat in hand. "Where'd they go?"

I opened my car door. "Everything's fine. It was nothing."

Neither looked convinced, but I climbed into my car and drove away, leaving them on the sidewalk watching me go.

"Hello?"

"Raines? Bear. Did I wake you?"

"Not a chance," I said.

"Why the hell not? It's four-thirty in the morning."

I ran the damp rag along my kitchen counter. After a day of coming up empty on the black girl and Pop's datebook, I'd spent the night sanitizing my kitchen instead of sleeping like a normal person. "Sounds like you were trying to wake me."

"Nah, I'm up to my buttercups in biscuits," she said. "Didn't realize till you picked up how early it was. Bad form. My oops. Anyway. We found your guy."

I stopped wiping. "How? When?"

"Nah, nah, nah, nah. Doesn't matter," she said, as if skipping over details so inconsequential they hardly seemed worthy of a mention. "He also goes by the name GI and hangs out around the Angel Arms Shelter on East Sixty-Third. Ask for Rashid. This GI's not an every dayer, but he stops in there enough for it to be kind of a thing. Hot meal, hot shower, a warm cot; he's never there earlier than ten, never after dark. After sundown, he bedrolls it in the park beside the beach house, but only when the weather's good. Nobody seems to know where he goes otherwise. Can't miss him. Stop by here before you head over to the Arms; I'll wrap up some biscuits for you."

"Thanks, Bea—" That's as far as I got. She'd hung up.

I checked my phone. No messages from Mrs. Luna. She'd vowed never to speak to Hector again, so it was likely he was having a hard time getting her to set up a meet. It was also possible Hector was full of crap and had nothing to offer. I wasn't sure what Hector's game was or what he wanted with me, but I didn't like the idea of him popping up when I least expected it. And I wasn't that hyped about seeing Ignacio again.

I plucked one of Bear's biscuits from the brown paper bag sitting on my passenger seat. I was starving, which was inexcusable seeing as I'd spent most of the night in my kitchen. The flaky biscuit, still warm from Bear's oven, melted into glorified nothingness as soon as it hit my mouth, the taste and smell of the palm-size medallion sublime. By the time I pulled up in front of the Arms, I'd eaten two without one single pang of guilt. I'd dropped a crisp fifty dollar bill into Bear's donation box. I should have left more. Her biscuits were a bona fide religious experience.

From the curb, the Angel Arms looked like a fairly new, one-story building. It sat on a double lot at Sixty-Third and Woodlawn. A storefront Baptist church—the Church of the Blessed Heavenly Gate—sat just to the left of it; a popcorn/candy/hoagie place sat to its right. Before getting out of the car, I grabbed the biscuits. They were too good not to share.

The Arms was a men's-only shelter, and I found a good number of them milling around inside, playing checkers in a corner, lounging on folding cots, or sitting transfixed in front of a large television set whose picture sputtered and rolled without anyone seeming to notice or care. I looked around for an office or a desk with somebody official sitting at it, but there wasn't anything like that here. I managed to politely snag a passing arm. "Excuse me," I said. "Where would I find Rashid?"

The distrustful eyes peering back at me cut toward the back. "Kitchen," their owner offered before he skittered away.

Double swinging doors with portholes in them led to the kitchen, where two black men bustled about, stirring huge pots and ladling some sort of stew into smaller pots before moving them to a counter to be served. I cleared my throat loudly then opened my mouth to ask for Rashid, and quickly found I needn't have bothered. The man stirring the big pot looked up. "You the one looking for GI? Friend of Bear's?"

"That's right," I said. "Cass Raines. Rashid?"

"Nah, Chester," he said. He pointed a sloppy ladle at the man at one of the smaller pots. "That's Rashid."

Chester was average height, average build; Rashid, wearing a pair of half glasses, was a little shorter and older by a couple of decades. Rashid waved me over, watching me closely. "You a cop?"

"Used to be," I said. "But I'm sure Bear told you that already."

He nodded approvingly, as though I'd passed some kind of test, and smiled. "She did. But I like to make sure. Cops and homeless kinda got a love-hate thing going."

Chester chimed in. "Yeah, they love to hate us!"

Rashid glowered at Chester. "Don't you have a pot to stir?"

"Stirring it, ain't I?" Chester said. He eyed the bag I was carrying. "You bring your lunch?"

I held it up. "A gift from Bear."

"Biscuits?!" Chester exclaimed.

I handed the bag to Rashid. "Biscuits."

Rashid pulled a stool up to the counter for me, then he and Chester each plucked a biscuit from the bag. Rashid emitted a blissed-out sigh, his eyes shut, a smile on his face as he bit into flaky perfection. "God, that woman can bake a biscuit, can't she?"

"She sure can," Chester said as he popped the last bit into his mouth. "I wonder how she does it."

"Don't matter how," Rashid said. "Only that she keeps them coming."

When they were done, Chester went back to his pot, a little happier than before, and Rashid went back to his in much the same way.

"Any friend of Bear's is a friend of mine," Rashid said. "And them biscuits just got you unlimited access to all I know about GI."

"Goes for me, too," added Chester. "I'm an open book."

Rashid cut a look his way. "That's gotta be one small book, you ask me."

Chester flipped him the bird. "Don't recall anyone asking you."

I chuckled at their friendly banter as the pots got stirred. I wondered briefly what had landed them both in a homeless shelter, but that was their business, not mine. I just hoped they were getting what they needed. "So, what can you tell me?"

"GI ain't been around here for a good while," Rashid said. "Don't even come in for the stew no more. He likes the stew. Right, Chester?"

"I know that ain't you asking me to talk, is it?"

"Man, shut up," Rashid said. "Quit playing the fool."

Chester held up a ladle. "All right, the man liked the stew!"

Rashid peered over the top of his glasses. "What did GI do to get you looking for him?"

"I heard he hung around St. Brendan's church. There was some trouble there that he might know something about. Someone else I talked to said he also goes by the name Old Sarge."

"You can't go by names with street folk," Rashid said. "What folks call you, or what you go by yourself, ain't always the name your mama gave you. This trouble you're talking about. You think GI's the cause of it?"

"I don't know, but I'd like to ask him."

"GI ain't really the talking kind."

Chester chuckled. "Yeah, he's king of the antisocial."

"When's the last time he came in here?"

Rashid tapped his ladle on the side of the pot and gave my question some thought. "Maybe two, three weeks."

Chester shook his head. "Longer than that. More like a month, I'd say."

"But he came in pretty regularly before that?"

"Regular enough," Rashid said. "Not like you can forget some big dude marching and chanting. But he wasn't an everyday fella. GI would come and go when the mood struck, I guess, and that's all there was to it. We come in regular, Chester and me. Shower up. Get our feed on. Then work in here fixing meals for the other guys. Even trade."

"GI ever tell you anything about himself? Maybe he had a friend here at the shelter?"

"No and no," Rashid said. "The man ain't never dropped a hint of personal information. Sometimes he bunks at the beach at Sixty-Third. I know because I bunk there sometimes myself. It's peaceful, and the cops leave you be, for the most part."

"Guess he likes the sound of the water," added Chester. "It's too loud for me. All that in and out. But GI squats under the trees over there. He swoops an old funky blanket over the top of a big crate, making himself a cabin. Whittles sticks like a son of a—" He stopped, went back to the pot. "Almost forgot it was mixed company. Anyway, don't know what he's gonna use all them sticks for." He chuckled. "Maybe he's making a picket fence to go 'round his property line."

"When's the last time either of you saw him there?"

"Been a good while for me. Rashid?"

"About two weeks for me. I found a different spot." He shook his head at Chester. "Got nothing to do with the loud water, though."

"Anything else either of you can think of that might help me find him?"

I watched as both men stopped to consider the question.

"He's on meds," Rashid said. "Don't know what kind. He's almost okay when he's on his pills. You got to keep your distance when he's off them. That's like a lot of the guys in here."

I stood, pushed the stool back where it'd been.

"Thanks for talking to me. I appreciate your taking the time."

"You going over there looking for him by yourself?" said Chester.

I nodded. "Sure."

Rashid readjusted his glasses on the bridge of his nose. "It looks like you can handle yourself all right. But watch your back."

Chester went back to his stirring. "Better watch your front and sides, too,"

Chapter 23

I headed to the beach house to find GI, but I couldn't get my car anywhere near the park. Flashing blue lights, the sound of sirens, and traffic cops shooing cars away from the lot entrance told a story I knew wouldn't have a happy ending. I did a U-turn, parked in the lot across the street, and walked toward the lights. There was no great sense of urgency, only dread. Blue wooden barricades blocked off the parking lot. I stopped there. Inside the cordon, squad cars, unmarked units, evidence vans, and a CFD ambulance and fire truck, their lights flashing, clogged the lot as cops moved about in antsy cliques waiting for their call to action. No one had to tell me. Someone was dead. I hoped it wasn't my guy.

News crews had fallen back to the old beach house, and reporters readied themselves in front of high-def cameras. Above them, on the balconies of the old structure, a few intrepid photographers craned themselves out over the stone railings, zooming long lenses past the crime scene tape in search of money shots.

A young black cop stood at the line, as did a handful of

hearty onlookers pulled from the bike and jogging paths, lured by the promise of someone else's tragedy. Everyone stood bundled up tight against the cold wind blowing off the lake. I searched the faces of the cops, hoping to find one I knew. I waited stoically, my fingers stiffening in the cold, my mind on a different line, a different death. It grew colder while I waited. Bitter wind skimmed off the water, and iron-handed gusts bit at my cheeks and seeped into bone, forcing my hands into my pockets. Time moved slowly. I watched the onlookers, one by one, tire and move along. I watched the reporters and photographers get what they needed and then do the same. Finally, it was just the rookie and me at the barricade.

The cop yanked up the zipper on his jacket, eyed me. "Down to two."

I looked around. "Looks like it."

"Cold," the cop said.

I nodded. "A little bit."

"You can't get any closer."

I eyed the barricade, then the cop. "Not without climbing over or under." The rookie turned. He scanned the lot, probably looking for his training officer, then looked at me, right in the face, as he assessed my threat level.

"Not that I'm planning to do either. Who'd they find over there?" I said.

His eyes narrowed. I could almost feel his defenses go up. He wasn't supposed to disseminate information, only hold the line. He was a patrol officer, low rung on the totem pole. And he was new to the job, so that put him two rungs below the bottom rung. I could almost hear him tick through his academy training for the takedown of a persistent civilian at a police line. He stared at me. I stared back, then glanced down at his name plate on his right breast pocket. His name was Billings.

Billings adjusted his belt, checking the positions of his gun, radio, cuffs, and Mace, just in case. "I'm going to need you to back up, ma'am."

"Your cuffs are in the wrong position. That'll cost you a few critical seconds when the chips are down." I held my hands up and out. "Just a tip. Take it or leave it." I could tell he wanted to stare down at his belt, but didn't dare. He was a rookie, but he wasn't stupid. I burrowed into my jacket, but left my hands free. "I used to be on the job."

He squeezed his lips tight, his eyes distrustful. Despite the cold, sweat formed on his forehead. "That so?"

I rattled off my star number and watched his face go from scared shitless to thank God I won't die today. "They've got a body. I don't see any witnesses warming up in the squads. Were there any?"

Maybe he was bored, maybe curious, maybe just trying to stay warm by keeping his mouth moving and his brain alert. Barricade duty was grunt work. Right up there with Dumpster diving for body parts and walking a line looking for spent shell casings.

Billings nodded. "You said 'used to.'"

"I went private." Billings blanched, but didn't respond. Cops and PIs had a weird dynamic. "Any idea what time the call came in?"

"Probie!" A gruff voice called from across the lot. I watched as a cop who must have weighed three hundred pounds labored toward us, the buttons on his uniform blouse straining to do their job, his red pie face twisted into an unpleasant scowl, part anger, I assumed, part distress from the physical exertion needed to make the trek. "Billings, you got time to shoot the breeze? I told you to observe and hold the line, and by observe I meant the crime scene, not the thrill junkies that side of the barricade."

Billings drew himself up to his full height, his back straight. "Yes, sir. I'm holding the line, sir."

He surveyed me. "Then tell your girlfriend here you'll catch up with her when your tour's over, and get back to it."

"Yes, sir," Billings responded, his feet already moving him toward the opposite end of the barricade.

The fat cop stood blocking my view. I stared at the knit cap on his head longer than I should have; it barely covered the crown of his head. No way could he pursue or apprehend a fleeing suspect without keeling over from a heart attack. "Unless you got business here, young lady, I suggest you move it along. Nothing here that concerns you. Police business." He turned to leave, certain that his warning was all that would be needed to get me on my way.

"How do you know?"

He turned around, surprised. "What's that?"

"How do you know nothing here concerns me?"

He positioned his massive arms akimbo, straining the threads on his bulletproof vest. "You trying to crack wise?" His jowls wobbled like a turkey's.

I glanced at the rookie, but he kept his eyes trained forward, his back straight. Little fish up against big fish? Big fish always won. The name plate on the fat guy's chest read TOMLINSON. He looked to be about forty, but he'd never make it to retirement age in his current condition. I doubted he could even reach around his sizable waist to put chubby hands to his own handcuffs, not that I planned on taking it to that level.

"I'm a PI working a case." I resigned myself to the snarky retort coming. I didn't have to wait long.

"That's supposed to impress me, Magnum?"

I shrugged. "Not trying to impress you. I was hoping to get a little information about the victim you found under those trees there. What happened? Are there any witnesses?"

Tomlinson chortled. "Your best bet would be to catch it all on the news tonight. Now move it!"

"Who's the detective in charge?"

"Lady, you don't listen too good, do you?"

My cellphone rang in my pocket. I answered it.

"What are you doing here? And what are you doing talking to Two-Ton Tomlinson?"

It was Ben.

I reeled around, searching for him. "Where are you?"

"I'm looking right at you standing behind the barricade talking to that twelve-year-old and Two-Ton. Look eleven o'clock." I followed his direction and spotted him standing off to the side of the trees, pointed in my direction. I wondered how I'd missed him. He waved. "Do not force him to exert himself in any way. He will surely die."

I sneered in Ben's direction, then stepped away from the barricade and turned my back to Tomlinson. "He's the one getting excited. If I took off running toward you right now, he'd never catch me."

"He could shoot you."

I slid a furtive glance at Tomlinson, who stood now plastered to the barricade as though I might actually try to wrestle him for it. "I'd bet good money it'd take him five minutes to get his gun out of his holster. Who's dead?"

"Me first."

"I'm following a lead," I said. "Who's dead?"

Ben stepped away from a knot of detectives. "I'm going to need more than that. Start talking," he whispered into the phone.

"The homeless man I chased out of the rectory? He beds down near that stand of trees you're looking at." Ben said nothing. Apparently, he wanted more. "He bunks in a makeshift tent? Likes to whittle sticks? He wears an old Army jacket. Goes by the name of Old Sarge, or GI, depending on who you talk to." Our eyes held across the lot. Still, Ben said nothing. "I can ID him," I said, growing a bit impatient. "I got a pretty good look while he was trying to strangle the life out of me."

"You keep trying to connect the church to this," Ben said. "You don't have the evidence, just a theory."

"That's why I'm here, isn't it? Looking for evidence? Will you at least give me the benefit of the doubt?"

Ben paused. "Put Tomlinson on the phone."

I walked back to the barricade and handed my cellphone to Tomlinson. "Detective Ben Mickerson. He'd like to speak with you." I pointed to Ben across the lot. He waved at Tomlinson, pointed to his cellphone. Tomlinson sucked in a wheezy breath and raised the phone to his ear. He listened for a time, glared at me, grunted twice, then handed the phone back. Slowly, he eased away from the barricade, taking the rookie with him. I watched them go, waiting to see if Two-Ton would make it before I eased the phone back up to my ear.

"What'd you tell him?"

"I told him there were doughnuts in the tech van. Wait right there. Do not cross that line."

I took it as a dare, but probably shouldn't have. I stepped over the line, just a shoe length, but stayed behind the barricade . . . for Ben.

They finally loaded up the body and drove it away. When the lot cleared, Ben walked over to me and held up his phone for me to take a look at it. He'd taken a picture of the dead man. "That him?"

I exhaled a sigh of relief. "No. Too old, too thin."

"You sure?"

I nodded my head. "I'm sure. Not him. What happened?"

Ben slipped the phone into the pocket of his trench coat. "Looks like somebody walked up behind him and drilled him one. Likely happened early this morning. No one noticed till a couple hours ago. Bullet went straight through the Army jacket. We found him dead by a stack of sticks. If he's not your guy,

I'm guessing he was in your guy's squat, and your guy decided to do something about it."

How'd you come up with that?"

Ben shrugged. "He came after you, didn't he? People have been killed for less."

I scanned the empty park. First, GI bolts from the rectory and outruns me, now I come this close to finding him and miss again. This was the place I knew to look for him, and he had slipped through my fingers. I was out of ideas.

"Where could he be?" I asked.

Ben unwrapped a stick of gum from his pocket and popped it into his mouth. "I'm going to assume that's rhetorical." He balled the wrapper up into a tight little sphere and rolled it in his fingers. "Just spit-balling here, but these attacks on the homeless started after the church, and they've been pretty steady since. Your guy could be my guy . . . and Farraday's and Weber's guy, too. . . . We're all of us rolled up together in the same mess, which is going to get real tricky for you from this point on. You know that, right?"

I frowned. "You're a blast of pure sunshine, you know that?"

He shrugged. "Don't shoot the messenger. Come on, I'll drive you to your car. And if I were you, I'd watch my back. Front, too."

"That's twice today somebody's given me that advice."

He grinned. "Then if I were you, I'd take it twice."

I stared at my bedside clock. It was two AM, and I couldn't turn off my brain enough to sleep. GI was out there some-where, and someone else was dead. It was just too much of a coincidence to think that the dead man just happened to meet his end in GI's makeshift tent the very day I got a bead on him. The attacks on the homeless started after Pop was killed and appeared random at first; now I wasn't so sure. None of the other homeless men who'd been attacked had been shot in the back of the head, only rousted, as though whoever was doing it was looking for someone specific. The dead man at the beach house was different. He was in GI's squat. It was dark. He was wearing an old Army jacket. Maybe the jacket, too, belonged to GI?

He sent you. That's what he'd said while his hands were clamped around my neck. *He knows I saw.* I was looking for a witness, not a killer. I was sure of it. And something else I was sure about now, I wasn't the only one looking. GI knew who killed Pop and Cesar Luna. He saw and he ran, and the killer knows it. And I had to find him first, before GI ended up dead just like the others.

I got up, got dressed, grabbed my stuff, and headed back to the park. Chester had said GI liked the sound of water. He felt safe around the old beach house and the trees. If he knew someone was after him, would he run or stay where he felt safe? I hoped it was the latter.

It was raining again, and the park was closed, no one in it but me. Nothing like a dead body to keep everybody away. A steady rain pelted the hood of my rain slicker, the muffled sound competing with the splash of waves lapping against the rocks in the lagoon. In the dark, the street lamps looked like tall birthday candles, the flamelike bulbs glowing yellow, casting eerie shadows over the trees. I flicked on my flashlight and started walking toward where the body had been found, the sound of my footfalls on the slippery grass magnified by the silence of the night. The crime scene tape was still in place, but there was little left of GI's squat, just a bare patch of trampled dirt and a few twigs the techs hadn't thought significant enough to take away.

The beach house, its granite bricks dulled by murky half-light, loomed imposingly just a few yards away. Its green-tiled roof, impressive in daylight, was now inky black, robbed of color by the waning moon. Facing me, the dark archways of the ground-level loggias and second-floor balconies looked as bottomless as a bogeyman's eye sockets.

The building had been a bathing pavilion back in the day when such things were the rage. Now it was owned by the Park District and rented out for the occasional charity soiree. I trained my flashlight on the gated entrance and walked over to check it out. Sweeping the small cone of light beyond the gates, I could just make out the stone steps leading up to the promenade.

"Sleep outside under the murder tree in the rain, or inside under a roof with a view of the water? He'd choose the inside." I shook the gates. Locked. But something about the way they rattled prompted me to try each iron bar individually, twisting each until I came across two loose ones. A quick glance behind me, a hasty sweep of the deserted lot, confirmed that I was still alone, so I set my flashlight down and fiddled with the loose bars until I was able to lift them up and out one by one, near elation overtaking me when their removal opened up a space just wide enough to slip through. Easing through to the other side, I heard a loud rip and felt a sudden rush of cold air on my left thigh. I looked down to see bare flesh beneath the six-inch tear in my jeans. "Great," I muttered. "Just great." I reached back through the bars and retrieved my light, then headed for the stairs, moving fast before a squad car swung by on patrol and ruined what was left of the night. Cold air swirled around the dank, hollow halls as I crept up the sandy steps, the darkness sending a shiver through me. All my senses stood at attention as I squinted into the dark, watching for movement, listening for quiet footsteps other than my own.

"GI?" There was nothing but the sound of lapping waves, rain hitting the roof overhead, and my heart leaping out of my chest. "Old Sarge?" No movement. Which name should I call him? Did he answer to both? Would he answer to either? "GI!" I called out again, this time louder.

I stopped at the top of the stairs and stood there staring at a dozen dimly lit votive candles set around the floor in a circle. GI's candles. Inside the circle there was a dark mound that I couldn't see clearly. Slowly, I swept the beam of the flashlight over the mound. Blankets. The light finally landed on the soles of a pair of boots.

"GI?"

Suddenly, the blankets moved, and a man leapt to his feet, reeled around, and landed squarely in my beam. It was him.

Chapter 24

I'd found GI. I felt like rushing forward and grabbing hold of him so he couldn't run away again, but I didn't. I didn't dare move for fear he'd spook and strike out. Instead, I stood quietly watching. Behind GI was the beach below; behind me were the stairs I'd just climbed up. There was just one way in, one way out. If GI made a run for it, he'd have to go through me, and no way was I going to make that easy for him. He'd talk or he wouldn't, but he wouldn't get past me walking, not again. He stood poised for a fight, his face strained with fear and befuddlement, a pointed stick and a pocket knife gripped tightly in his bearlike hands.

I backed away and thought carefully about what I'd say. "Is it GI or Old Sarge?"

He said nothing. It looked as though he was barely breathing.

"I may know some friends of yours. Cleopatra? Chester and Rashid?" Nothing. "Father Ray?"

He blinked. There was a moment of recognition, I was sure of it. The knife and stick lowered just a little. My heart raced. Maybe he would be lucid enough to understand the questions I asked. Maybe he'd even answer them.

But the moment quickly passed. The knife and stick rose again. He stared me down, his eyes intense. He still said nothing. He looked confused, as if he'd long ago lost the ability to understand the world around him. He slowly rolled the stick in his right hand, the knife in his left, playing with them, testing them. The stick had been sharpened to a lethal point. I watched the stick, the knife, and his eyes, which darted around the promenade as though he were searching for somewhere to hide.

He ducked his chin. "Don't know you. You don't know me."

I took a step forward, stopped. "I'm Cass. Cass Raines. Father Ray was my friend." Distrustful eyes searched mine. I chanced it and took another step, slipping my right hand into my pocket, palming the Glock. Last resort. "We've met." I took a half step forward, the soles of my running shoes scratching across the concrete. "Remember? In the rectory."

He didn't respond. He was wearing a dark parka instead of his Army jacket, the one that had somehow ended up on the dead guy under the tree. His hair was hidden under a black skull cap pulled down low on his forehead, as it had been the last time I'd encountered him. None of his clothes looked worn, even the soles of his boots, which I'd seen sticking out of his blankets, looked as if he'd barely broken them in. I flashed to the bags of clothes in Pop's closet. They weren't random donations. The clothes were specifically for GI. Why? What connected them? "Can we talk about Father Ray, about the church?"

He shook his head violently. "No talking."

I swept the flashlight over the tangle of blankets again, spotting a well-thumbed copy of *The Grapes of Wrath* half hidden in the tangle. He saw me looking and braced himself to defend his property, as though I might try and poach something from the pile.

I smiled, hoping to make a connection. "Steinbeck. Heavy stuff." Again, I got nothing back. "Hungry? Maybe after we talk, I can get you something to eat, maybe find you a warm bed, meds, if you need them?"

"Took them." He began to pace, keeping his back to the lake, the sticks pointed at me. "Said I would. I did. I am. I know the day, the place, the president."

"And Father Ray, too."

He squeezed both the stick and the knife tighter. I was upsetting him. And the fact that I was upsetting him, upset me as I stood yards from him, one sweaty hand on the grip of my gun, the other on the flashlight. He was a big man, solid, mid-fifties, maybe younger; it was hard to say for sure. The street aged people quickly. He was at least six two to my five seven, and strong, as the bruises around my neck could attest. I certainly didn't want to tussle with him again.

He began to fidget, his eyes wandering.

"GI," I barked, drawing his attention back to me. I let go of the gun, shoved the flashlight into my pocket, and held my hands down by my sides. "Let's talk."

"No talking. I want you to go."

"I know." I took another step forward. It was the opposite of going, but I was hoping he wouldn't notice. "But I can't go, not without talking." I hesitated for a moment, glancing at the stick and knife, then took a tentative half-step forward. I was an idiot. I knew it, but I couldn't stop now. He hauled off and kicked one of the candles over, sending sparks of white light rolling along the floor of the promenade. My hand went back into my pocket, back on the grip of the gun. "At least tell me your real name. I told you mine. It's only fair." He didn't answer. "I'm Cass. I grew up not far from here. I used to go swimming right down there on that beach. You like the water, the ebb and flow of it. I'm not wild about the seaweed. You?" We stood silently. "Just your name."

He angled his head. "Father Ray's friend?"

I saw light at the end of a very long tunnel and ran for it. "Yes. A dear, close friend."

"I take the meds. I promised."

"Who did you promise?"

He took so long to answer, I didn't think he would. "Our friend."

"Let's talk about him," I said, "then I'll go." Slowly, he slipped the knife and stick into his pocket and moved to warm his hands under his armpits. It was a promising sign. I didn't dare move, or breathe, or hope. I just held my place and waited, knowing everything hinged on what happened next and how wrong it could all still go. Our eyes held, his dark face mottled by the glow of small candles. Then I remembered what I'd brought with me, slipped my hand into an inside pocket, and retrieved two candles, much like the ones on the floor in front of me. The man's face brightened when he saw them. "I thought maybe you might like these."

He reached out for the candles, moved toward me, offering up a thin smile. "You brought me light?" He cradled the candles in his hands almost reverently. "God's in the light."

I didn't dare speak, or even breathe. I stood stock-still on the verge of knowing, waiting for what came next.

He backed away again. "Yancy," he whispered finally, as though someone might overhear. "Yancy Gantt. That's my name."

I grinned like an idiot, feeling as though I'd just won the lottery. "It's a pleasure to meet you, Yancy."

He lit the candles I'd given him, and we sat cross-legged on the blankets facing each other, the glow of a low light flickering between us. I still kept a good distance. Yancy seemed lucid enough now, but there was no guarantee he would stay that way. I huddled against the cold, wondering why he preferred this desolate spot to a warm shelter. As we talked, it became clear he didn't remember me from the rectory. Maybe he hadn't been on his meds then. He'd never been military, he said. He'd come across the jacket at a charity giveaway somewhere. He was simply another lost soul trying to find his way. Pop was helping, as he'd helped so many others. I wondered what would happen to Yancy now that Pop was gone. I wondered the same about me.

"They found a body in the park today," I began, mindful of the space separating us, more than ready to lengthen it quickly if he became combative.

He paused. "Traded my squat for Ernie's knife. Mine broke. Too many sticks. I told him it wasn't safe, but still he wanted it."

"Why wasn't it safe?"

Yancy looked away, turned back. "The wolf."

Surely not a real wolf, I thought. Did he have the real and the imaginary mixed up in his head? "What wolf?"

"I can't talk about him." A person, not an animal. Good to know. "You saw this wolf?"

Yancy made a face, looked away, then back again. "Never said I did."

"But you did. That's why you ran." I scanned the promenade. "That's why you're here in the dark alone. Who is he? Can you tell me what happened?"

He held his head in his hands. "Sometimes I mix things up."

"Then tell me what you *think* you saw."

He hesitated before answering, leaning over to slowly pass his hands over the candles, the light illuminating his misery. "I saw a wolf pretending to be a sheep. And he saw me."

Yancy stood to pace, agitated now at the recollection. I stood, too. I wasn't sure what he'd do, and I needed to block the stairs. I couldn't lose track of him again. Not when I was this close. Not after learning I'd been right. Pop and Cesar Luna were killed by the wolf. Farraday was an idiot. I hadn't been wrong. I did know Pop as well as I thought I did.

"What happened? Who is he?" Yancy paced quickly. His eyes were wild again, confused. I'd stirred up something I didn't think I could rein in. I watched helplessly as Yancy quickly disappeared into a place I couldn't reach. The stick came out, the knife. He began to nod at nothing, as though he were talking to someone who wasn't there, pacing like a big cat, captured and caged. I was losing him.

"Stop," I said.

Yancy stopped moving. He turned to me, stared right through me. After a time, he clicked back to lucid. I could almost see the shift take place in his eyes. I kept my voice low, steady, though every impulse in me wanted to scream out and shake him until whatever he knew tumbled out. For Pop. "I need to know. You have to tell me."

Yancy backpedaled, leaning against the stone balusters. I was afraid he might fall or, worse yet, jump. I drew closer in case I had to catch him. "He was helping. Father Ray. But the wolf didn't want it. He came to make it stop. That's what he said."

"Make what stop?"

He shook his head again, shrugged hopelessly. "It's gone."

"Close your eyes, Yancy. Think."

He stared at me strangely, his head angled.

"I won't move, I promise. Close your eyes, try to remember."

Moments passed, but he finally closed them. I stood waiting, hopeful, desperate for any scrap of recollection.

"I came for my candles, the ones he saves for me. The angry voices woke me. I saw the wolf, and the one he brought with him, our friend, too, and the boy." Yancy threw his arms up over his head, then covered his head in his hands. "Clean the slate. Move along. Next. That's what he said. But he had to have the girl first." He shook his head. "But our friend wouldn't tell. He knew he didn't want peace. He said so. 'Much too late for that,' he said, 'much too late.'"

I moved to step forward, then remembered my promise and held back. This was torture. "What happened, Yancy? Do you know his name?"

He frowned, his eyes opened. "If I ever did, it's lost now." He tapped a finger against the side of his head. "Nothing stays. My squat's not safe. I told Ernie."

I held out a hand, trying hard to hide my disappointment at not getting more. "Come with me. I can make sure you're safe." He opened his mouth as if to speak, and it looked as though he might agree to come, but then the curtains fell swiftly, and he was gone again. With a frenzied look in his eyes, he barreled past me and bolted for the stairs. "Wait!" I ran after him, yanking the flashlight from my pocket, flicking it on as I hit the stairs, just in time to see him take the last few steps two at a time, hit the ground floor, and head for the iron gate. My light bounced around like a drunken fairy as I chased after him. He slipped seamlessly between the bars. He'd obviously had a great deal of practice at it. I followed, squeezing through clumsily, tumbling out into the empty courtyard and into a hail of bullets.

Chapter 25

I felt a zip of air move past my left ear, a bullet barely missing me. I gasped and dropped to the asphalt, burying my head in trembling hands. Yancy lay a few yards away doing the same, both of us fastened down by a shooter we couldn't see. I could feel the weight of the gun in my pocket, but couldn't get my arms to move enough to reach for it. I was frozen to the spot, cringing each time a bullet flew past me and ricocheted off the beach house's façade. Eventually one of the bullets would land and hit one of us.

Get up! Get up! Get up! I shouted the words in my head, willing myself to obey. But I couldn't get up. I was back on the rooftop, Jimmy's bullet having found its target. I couldn't move. I was going to die today. My eyes squeezed shut. I saw his face again, Jimmy's, and the exact moment he decided to kill me. I smelled my own blood and recalled how the world fell away. I grabbed for it then. I needed to grab for it now. I needed to move. *Now*! A bullet pinged off the dirt inches from my head. I reached inside my shirt and grabbed onto the ring at the end of the golden chain. I opened my eyes, focused.

Move, goddammit!

I let the ring go, pushed myself to my knees, forced myself up into a squat. The bullets kept coming, but I scrambled toward Yancy, reached him, and took hold of the back of his parka and rolled us both into the shadows behind a pair of garbage cans. I pinned him under me, then grabbed my gun and aimed. But there was nothing to shoot at. The lot was empty. The shots were coming from somewhere in the park. The sound of the bullets hitting the metal cans reminded me of a shooting arcade at a traveling carnival, all pings and dings and thuds—fine if you were the shooter, frightening as hell if you were the target.

Suddenly, I heard the sound of police sirens and the shooting stopped. I stayed put. I didn't trust it. I hoped the police were heading here. I rolled Yancy behind me and carefully peeked out from behind a can. Nothing. How long had it been since the last shot? Five minutes? Five hours? I listened for the sound of approaching footsteps, but there were none. Then a car with a faulty muffler started up somewhere close, followed by the sound of squealing tires. The park fell silent. The shots had scared even the crickets away. It felt like the worst was over. Well spent, I leaned my sweaty forehead against the can and took a moment to breathe, my hands taking on a life of their own. I turned around to check on Yancy, but he'd taken off. I couldn't believe it. He'd slipped through my fingers again.

"Son of a—"

Blinding light suddenly hit my face, watering my eyes. It was too early for the sun. Was I dead? My brain sputtered, firing synapses that didn't quite connect, as I, like Yancy, worked to separate reality from nightmare.

"Police!"

Voice. Male. A flashlight, not the sun. *Get it together, Cass.*

"Hands up! Do not move!"

Do. Not. Move. The words pinballed around my sputtering brain before slowly registering.

Finally, a command I could follow.

Detective Farraday stepped into the interview room. I was sitting at the perp table in handcuffs. The cuffs, of course, were unnecessary—kind of like using a ball-peen hammer to pound down an office staple. Farraday made a dramatic show of slapping a file folder down on the table and slowly pulling out a chair to sit across from me. I didn't know what time it was, but it felt like I had been in the small, hot room for hours. That too was Farraday's doing. I glared at him as he folded his arms across his chest and plastered a wide grin on his stupid face. I groaned inwardly as I took in the deep lines at the corners of his eyes and the spider web of broken blood vessels creeping along his fleshy cheeks.

"What'd you do with the other gun, Raines?"

I didn't bother answering. What did he think I'd done? Shot at myself, then raced over to the beach and tossed one of the guns into the lake? I wondered, truly, what world Farraday lived in, because it was painfully obvious to me now that he didn't live in mine.

"I'm guessing whoever shot it, took it with him, or her," I said.

I scanned the yellow nicotine stains on his fat fingers and his greasy hair. I had a monster of a headache. The pounding behind my eyelids was relentless and the harsh cop light hurt my eyes. I didn't have the energy for another go-round with Jim Farraday, or the time. I had to find Yancy. I needed to know if he was okay, and I needed him to tell me more about the wolf.

"The unit heard shots and went to check it out. POs found you crouched behind a garbage can." He smirked, obviously amused, as though my dodging from bullets was some big joke. "Park closes at eleven. Signs are posted everywhere. Target practice, maybe?" He chortled. "We've got guys out there looking, of course, but what do you say you save us all some time and tell me what you were playing at out there?"

I watched his lips move but tuned him out, my mind drifting back to the park and the sound of bullets pinging off the cans, the smell of my own fear, and the dirt I cowered in for a time.

"Hey!" Farraday pounded a beefy fist on the table, setting my teeth on edge. "Wake up!" I tuned back in, watching as he whipped open the folder, then leaned over to sneer at me. "I knew we'd end up here, me sitting across the table from you, and you in cuffs. I knew you wouldn't let any of this go. That's how you are, isn't it? Digging, digging, but with no sense of how it goes, how I say it goes. So, let's have it. Who were you shooting at?"

Still I didn't answer.

Farraday grinned. "Don't tell me . . . some other kid got in your way?"

My heart seized, but I fought hard not to show it. Some other kid, as if Jimmy Pick weren't kid enough. He wanted me to strike back. I could see it in his eyes. He was hungry for it. I folded my hands in my lap. Farraday pounded another fist on the table, hoping to rattle me. I didn't flinch. I'd expected it. Pounding fists on things was what lousy cops did when swagger and bluff didn't get them what they wanted.

"I've got you," he hissed. "Breaking and entering, trespassing, damage to public property, not to mention the gun charges. You know what else I got? I got all damn day to sit here and watch you sweat. Then I'm going to toss you into a box and leave you there." He leaned back, prepared to wait me out. "So I suggest you start talking, and if I were you, I'd make it real good. Impress me." His eyes held mine. "I bet those cuffs are uncomfortable. Up to you how long you stay in them."

I smiled, ignoring the pain in my arms, my numb fingers. Giving in to the discomfort would only make Farraday think he'd won some twisted battle of wills. Under the table, I flexed my fingers, trying to bring sensation back. Cowering in the dirt hadn't been my finest hour, I had to admit. Good thing the shooter had been a lousy shot, or I'd be dead, Yancy, too. I'd hoped I'd put the worst of Jimmy Pick behind me, but tonight made it clear I still had work to do. And where would I look for Yancy next? He'd never go back to the beach. He knew he wasn't safe there now. But I had to find him. He saw who killed Pop.

"I'm prepared to make a statement."

Farraday leered at me, confident he'd won. "Now that's you being smart, for once."

"But not to you. I want real police."

Farraday shot up from his chair and leaned over the table, nostrils flaring . . . "You deal with me right now, or I swear to God I'll bury you in a cell and swallow the key whole."

I turned my back to him, facing instead the two-way glass. "Who's behind the glass?"

"I asked you a question!"

I ignored him. "I assume the lieutenant in charge, maybe Weber, a couple more cops? If I'm wrong, one of you tap on the glass."

No one tapped. I'd pegged it right. Farraday had an audience. I also had one, which meant pounding fists was all Farraday was going to be able to get away with. I stood, addressing the glass.

"I found a witness. He was there that night at the church. He may also be connected to the attacks on the homeless. Someone unknown shot at the both of us. You have my gun. You know by now it hasn't been fired. You've also checked the beach house, so you found the blankets and the candles. I wasn't alone out there. The witness is in the wind, and so is the killer." I lifted my cuffed wrists, angled them toward Farraday. "This is doing nothing but wasting time."

"This is my case," Farraday barked, maneuvering himself so he stood between me and the glass. "Mine."

I stepped around him, inches from the glass now, close enough to fog it up with my breath. "I'm more than willing to talk, but not to him. Not if he were the last man standing after the bomb drops, and I want that on the record. This is not a murder-suicide or a robbery. It's personal, it's close. It's got something to do with Cesar Luna and a girl and Father Heaton and somebody in that parish."

I backed away, reclaimed the chair. Farraday looked as if he wanted to throttle me. I hoped he'd try. I really wanted to take a shot. I'd regret it immediately, of course, as serious consequences would rain down on my head, but for two glorious seconds it would be sheer bliss to clamp my hands around his throat and squeeze till my fingers gave out. "Unlike you," I said calmly, "I don't have all damn day. Neither does the next homeless person unlucky enough to get it in the back while you sit here fiddling with yourself on company time."

He grabbed one of the chairs and slung it across the room. It looked as though he might make a charge, but he stopped suddenly before he got to me, no doubt remembering the peanut gallery. Instead, he made a great show of straightening his tie, then walked over and leaned in, his face way too close to mine. "You know what your problem is, Raines? You don't respect the star."

I stared up at him, my cold eyes boring into his hot ones. "I respect the star just fine. It's you I don't think much of."

He hesitated, the veins in his neck straining. He kept his voice low, his back to the glass. "Let's get this straight; you killed that kid, not me."

I both loathed and pitied him. He hadn't taken a life. He had no idea of the weight you had to carry afterward. He didn't know I saw Pick's face everywhere, always. He didn't know the nights were the worst, and that there'd be no end to it. We were linked, Jimmy Pick and I, and always would be. The back of my neck got suddenly hot, my headache worsening. "What was his name?" I watched the blank expression on Farraday's face. He hadn't a clue. "You have no idea. He was just another black kid to you, and that's your problem."

"I don't need to remember their names. All I have to do is bring them in."

"But you weren't going to bring Jimmy in, were you? You were going to kill him right there on that rooftop. That's why you rushed up after we told you to hang back. You saw your chance slipping away, and you wanted the takedown. You wanted it more than you wanted that kid down safe. You didn't care who got hurt then, you care even less now. That's who you are. That's who you'll always be."

Seething, Farraday slid a furtive glance toward the glass, his lips curled back into a ferocious snarl. "There will always be a cloud hanging over my head because of you and that damn kid. You're going to pay for that. Maybe not here, maybe not now, but it's coming, you have my word on that."

I took a moment to steady myself. Just because Farraday didn't know how to conduct himself didn't mean I didn't. Sometimes you had to bury heat and hate; sometimes you had to bide your time. I watched as Farraday drew back, retrieved the tossed chair and set it right again.

I asked, "Am I under arrest?" He wouldn't answer. He'd gotten to the end of what he could do with me with the others watching. He'd always be there seething and waiting, and I'd have to be ready for him. But for now, we were done. I approached the glass. "Someone tap once, if I'm under arrest."

Again, no tap came. My hands in cuffs, I turned the knob on the door and surprisingly found it unlocked. I stood in the hall waiting for the room next door to empty. As I'd assumed, the lieutenant, Ben, and Weber filed out. I held my wrists out to Ben, and he reached down and used his cuff key to free me.

The lieutenant, Fisher according to his nameplate, spoke up. "You're free to go, Ms. Raines."

Weber nodded, then eased into the room with his partner, shutting the door behind him. Ben held me by the arm and led me through the squad room. As we walked, I let out the breath I'd been holding. I drifted off to my happy place. There were clouds there and cute baby chicks. We stopped at a small room with no mirrors. I slumped down into a padded chair, an improvement over the metal one I'd just spent hours in, and rested my head on the table. Ben sat beside me.

"What do you need?"

I lifted my head up off the table, but before I could scream for aspirin, Weber walked in with Farraday's file folder, the one he'd tried to intimidate me with. He dropped the folder on the table. I opened it. Why not? What more could they do to me? There was nothing inside but a skimpy incident report. Farraday didn't have enough to justify holding me for hours, interrogating me. It had all been a ruse, a cheap show of force. The interview, the cuffs, the sweating it out in the tight room, all of it was Farraday flexing muscle, digging screws into tender places.

I held the folder up. "Really?? How does he still have his job?" I held up a hand. "Don't bother answering. I know."

"Back in a sec." Ben eased out of the room and came back carrying a bottle of Tylenol and water in a CPD coffee mug.

I nearly lunged at him as though he held the antidote to a poison I'd just ingested. I downed the tablets, the water. "Thank you, partner."

He nodded. "I saw the signs."

I sat there, my eyes closed, waiting for the medicine to take hold. When I opened them again Weber was sitting, too. The last time we'd met on the rectory steps, he'd wanted coffee and mentioned my eyes.

He grinned. "I'm real police."

I glanced at Ben. "And you know I sure as hell am," he said.

I started talking.

*   *   *

I spilled out details of the previous night's events. Weber took notes while I talked. Ben sat there nodding, taking it all in. He wasn't the only one who could read the signs. He was upset with me, and I had a pretty good idea what about. Since the rooftop, he had taken it upon himself to mother hen the heck out of me, and my putting myself in a vulnerable position in the park, I knew, wasn't sitting well with him. I could almost feel the heat of his disapproval radiating off his skin. I would hear about it later, but not yet.

"He didn't ID this wolf?" Weber asked.

I shook my head, avoiding Ben. My headache was letting up. It took three Tylenol, not the customary two, but I didn't need Ben's disapproval counteracting the medicine. "He's mentally unstable. Something spooked him and he ran."

Weber tossed down his pen. "Then how do you know you can trust what he thinks he saw?"

"He said he's on his meds. He seemed clear for most of our talk."

Ben straightened up in his chair. "How many shots were fired at you?"

"What's that got to do with anything?"

"I know you know. You counted every one of them. How many?"

"Fourteen," I answered begrudgingly. "All misses, obviously."

There was a knock at the door. A cop in uniform stepped in and handed Weber a computer report. He scanned it.

"Yancy Gantt. We picked him up a few times. Vagrancy. No surprise there. I'll see if we can't get some units out there looking."

I had a thought. "Does he have any connection to LA?"

"Yeah. Last pickup was in LA, again for vagrancy, about a year ago. Does that mean anything to you?"

"It just confirms a connection," I said, thinking of Pop's receipts for airline tickets. "Meds. He has to get them from somewhere. Wherever it is, it has to be close to his squat. Free clinics?"

Weber peered at me over the top of the papers. "And what'll you be doing while we do all that?"

"No one's looking at the school janitor, but something's off there. He's being watched. He's into something. We just haven't caught him at it."

Ben's eyes narrowed. "We?"

"Freelance operatives. Don't gnaw on it."

Ben rolled his eyes and let out an exasperated groan. Weber went back to the report, and I watched as his expression slowly changed from slightly amused to deadly serious.

"What is it?" I asked.

"They found fresh blood trailing off from the parking lot. It follows the path leading to the underpass a couple blocks away. Looks like Gantt was hit."

I sat stunned, the thumping in my head instantly back. I was aware of Ben and Weber watching, but I kept my eyes on a small spot on the far wall. I'd been slow to grab my gun, unable to get myself unstuck and moving. If I'd reacted faster, maybe . . .

I stood up, left the room.

If Weber or Ben said anything, I didn't hear it.

Chapter 26

It was Yancy's blood.

Back at the park, I retraced my steps from the night before, finding in the light of day, the cans I'd crouched behind for cover. The droplets of dried blood trailed off down the pedestrian path leading away from his squat. I followed the drops as if they were bread crumbs, my eyes trained on every crimson dot as they grew fainter and farther apart. How frightened he must have been, I thought, how frightened he still must be. I turned my collar up to ward off the chill from the lake. It was blustery today, and the biting wind blew right through me. Still, I kept on the path. I didn't have a choice. Yancy was in trouble, and I had to find him.

The blood snaked north along the path rimming the now empty beach. It was too cold for swimming, too cold for Yancy to be without a warm place. I headed for the underpass, following the dots, walking every inch, kicking aside every sodden leaf blown in on a lake breeze. I stepped aside as bikers, dog walkers, and runners blew past me, then went right back to it. Following the dots. The rain the night before had stopped long before the shooting started. It was my one lucky break in a long night of unlucky ones. If not for it, there'd be no blood at all to follow.

I stood at the mouth of the underpass, dug my flashlight out of my pocket, and eased inside. The tunnel was dark and cave-like and smelled of dried urine, wet dog, and rancid lake water. I sucked in a breath and held it for a time, then made my way slowly through, sweeping the ground with my light. I took two slow passes, my footsteps echoing off the stone walls covered by faded murals and graffiti, decades old. I found nothing. Maybe that was a good thing, I tried to convince myself. If he made it through the underpass without bleeding, perhaps that meant he hadn't been hurt too badly. Or maybe he'd staggered up to the crossing, changed his mind, and doubled back across the grass without passing through. I couldn't know for sure. Either way, this is where the trail ended.

I scanned the street. Where could he have gone? Where would I go if I were frightened, bleeding, and unsure of the world? I couldn't begin to hazard a guess. I trudged back to my car, exhausted, with no idea where I might look next. Guilt hung like heavy stones in my pockets.

There were eleven messages on my phone when I checked it—eight from Barb, three from Whip. I sighed. Somehow I'd acquired a Scooby gang, and I didn't quite know what to do with it. I was used to going it alone without having to account for my time or explain where I'd been. Having a posse was new. I dialed my home number, expecting to get it with both barrels. Barb snatched up the receiver on the half ring.

"Where are you?" Her panicked pitch was that of a frightened parent. "I thought you were dead. I called Whip. The three of us have been out looking for you."

I could count. Barb and Whip made two. "The three of you?"

"Pouch. He's a friend of Whip's. We needed another set of eyes. You'll like him. You'd never guess he was in prison for killing a man. Hey, don't change the subject. Ben called. He said you were shot at and arrested. We didn't know what to think." Her voice was so loud and fast that I had to pull the phone away from my ear. Even still, it came through like thunderclaps. When I pulled the phone back, she was still at it. "What is going on? Who shot at you? Why were you arrested?"

"I was detained, not arrested."

"What the heck's the difference?"

I massaged my forehead and smiled in spite of the situation, remembering a similar conversation I'd had with Pop. "Arrested lasts longer." I rolled down my car window for some air, wishing I could fly through it. "Look, I'm heading to the office. I have some calls to make, hospitals to check. If you and Whip and this Pouch person want to meet me there, I'll fill you in and prove to you all that I'm not dead."

"We're on our way. And you'd better be there."

"I said I'll be there, I'll be there. Why are you so agitated, anyway? This can't all be about a few missed phone calls."

Barb went quiet on the other end. Then I remembered her visit with her mother. "You saw your mother," I said. Barb said nothing. "You know, given your vocation, you'd think you'd have the patience of Job. Did she trim your hair?"

"Oh, shut up, smartass."

She hung up on me.

I stood in the dim hallway ten feet away from my office door. From here I could see glass, shattered like jigsaw pieces in front of the door. Maybe if I stood in this one spot long enough, I reasoned, I'd discover that my tired eyes were playing tricks on me, and someone really hadn't smashed my window in. I listened for Dr. Gupta's drill, but didn't hear it. Any other day he's drilling away, but not today when my door gets taken out. I was still standing there when my Scooby gang climbed the stairs and joined me.

"Aww, man, that doesn't look good," Whip said.

Barb gasped. "Tell me that's not your office."

I turned to get a good look at the new guy.

He grinned and extended a pudgy hand for me to shake. "Pouch. Pleased to make your acquaintance."

He was a short, stout white guy with dark, deep-set eyes that never quite landed anywhere. Everything he wore was gray— jacket, shirt, pants, shoes, knit cap. Maybe he was forty, or sixty. It was hard to gauge. He looked like a giant human rat.

"Pouch," I said, turning back to the glass.

Looks like you got a break-in there," Pouch said.

I nodded. "Yep."

Whip let out a frustrated howl. "So, are we just going to stand here and do nothing?"

"Whip's right." Barb took a step forward. "Let's go check it out."

"Everybody stop. You three downstairs, out the front door. Wait for me on the sidewalk."

Whip groused. "Like hell."

Barb grabbed hold of my arm. "You can't go in there alone. Not after last night. What if somebody's in there waiting?"

"I mean it. Down the stairs. Out the front door." I felt for the gun in my pocket and waited till the three of them had descended the stairs. I listened for the sound of the front door screeching open and slamming shut before I moved. I'd put enough people in danger already; I had no intention of adding to that number. I couldn't take on any more weight.

I headed off down the long hall, keeping my back to the wall. When I reached my office, I stepped forward, crunching fallen glass under my Nikes, and peeked through the gaping hole. Someone had made quite a mess of things. There was paper everywhere, chairs overturned, even my window blinds had been slashed to ribbons. That was a lot of rage, I thought. Who had I gotten on the wrong side of besides Farraday? What wrong button had I pushed? I wondered seriously about Farraday, but then dismissed him. He was an incompetent blowhard, but surely he wouldn't jeopardize his career by trashing my place, no matter how angry he was.

I slipped my key out of my pocket and unlocked the door, which seemed silly seeing as I could see the inside of my office from where I stood. It reminded me of Maisie's place. I crept in, stepping on and around squares of white paper strewn about the floor. It was like playing a monochromatic game of solo Twister. Right foot, glass. Left foot, paper. Everything I owned had been manhandled and thrown to the floor. What did they think I had?

My desk drawers had been pulled off their casters and rifled through, their contents turned out. My file cabinets were completely gutted, folders strewn everywhere, drawers gaping open and dented, as though someone had hauled off and side-kicked them all. The only thing left unmolested was the safe under my desk, probably because whoever ran amuck didn't have the know-how to crack it. Amateurs. I carefully checked the closet. All fine. Obviously, nobody cared about ripping up my change of clothes and extra shoes.

I plopped down into my chair, the hairs on the back of my neck tingling. This was hateful and personal. Somebody out there wanted to send me a message I couldn't miss. In a fit of anger and frustration, I slid the few papers left on my desk over the side and onto the floor. Why not? I didn't have to worry about making a mess.

Whip's head appeared in the doorway. "I called the police. They should be here by Christmas." Whip's head was quickly joined by Barb's and Pouch's, the three of them framed in a ruined door frame.

"I said wait outside."

Barb walked in, kicking papers aside with her foot. "We figured when you didn't scream or anything, the coast was clear."

Pouch's eyes widened. "Wow, this is rough. Amateur work, though. I knew a guy once who could break into your place, make himself a sandwich out of stuff in your fridge, then take what he wanted, and you'd never know anything was amiss till you went looking for whatever. That there's a professional at work." He scanned the office. "This looks like a kid just went apeshit. Unless we're dealing with crazy. If it's crazy, all bets are off."

I just looked at him. "Why do they call you Pouch?"

He grinned. "Funny story there. I started out as a knuckler, see. You know what that is, right?"

I was losing patience. "Yeah, you're a pickpocket."

"Okay, right. Well, even as a little kid, see, I had nimble fingers. I could lift practically anything without anybody knowing it—jewelry, wallets, purses, dogs, whatnot. And you always gotta have a place to stash the stuff, right?" He opened his gray jacket to reveal a gray fanny pack. "Pouch. Get it? The name stuck."

I slid Barb a sideways glance, then turned back to the gray rat. "Barb said you were inside for murder."

Pouch frowned, his rodent eyes skittering away from me. "Unfortunate circumstances. Self-defense, all the way. Totally. Like I said, a knuckler from way back."

I tried a smile. "Got it. Thanks."

I dug down into the pile of debris at my feet and came up with the Yellow Pages, slapping it down on the desk. I needed a speedy glazier . . . and a vacation, though that would have to wait.

"Who would do this?" Barb moved around the office picking things up, trying to put them back where she thought they belonged. "Am I the only one worried about this?" She searched our faces. She was not the only one. I felt sick. I'd assumed last night the shooter was aiming for Yancy, but what if he'd meant to kill me instead? I glanced at Whip and Barb. What if something happened to them while they were standing next to me? I didn't know Pouch, but I couldn't be responsible for him either. I had to get them away from me somehow.

I opened my mouth to stop Barb from tidying up. Technically, this was a crime scene, and nothing should be touched, but let's get real. There was no way the police were going to do much about this. Nobody died. No state secrets were stolen. The best I could do would be to get my glass replaced and call my insurance company. I'd likely have to eat the losses.

Whip stood my hat rack back on its legs. "Somebody's trying to put a scare in you. Who?"

I leafed through the Yellow Pages. "I don't know." I looked up, remembering something. "Barb, St. Benedict Joseph Labre. I found his prayer card attached to clothes in Pop's closet. The one's meant for GI. Who is he?"

"He's the patron saint of the homeless and mentally ill."

That fit, I thought. Adding the card would have been Pop's attempt at adding just a little bit more solace. I went back to the Yellow Pages. "You guys should go now. I can handle things from here. I'll wait for the police, if they show up, and for the glass guy. I'll meet you back at the house. We'll order pizza or something."

Barb stared at me. "I'm not leaving. Deal with it."

I turned to face Whip, but encountered the same stubborn expression. I even got it from Pouch, and I didn't even know him. It was no use. I was stuck with them and maxed out on worry. I simply couldn't worry any more than I already did. I ran a finger down the page looking for a glass guy who sounded legit. That simple task was the only thing keeping me from screaming. I looked up in time to see Pouch strolling furtively around my place as though he were walking the aisles of a high-end department store.

"Pouch, just so you know, I'm frisking you before you leave here."

His gave me a startled look, a rat caught exposed outside of his little rat hole. "Sure. Sure. No problem."

He turned his back to me, but I could still see him as he slid an office stapler out of the gray pack.

I swallowed the scream.

The glass set me back $105 even. I'd have to hire someone to stencil my name on it again. Until then, I was the nameless PI on the third floor. I finally got my new posse to leave, but only after they helped pick up and refile every piece of scattered paper. It took almost three hours, but by the end of it, my office looked like it did before someone did their crazy tap dance on it, except for the ruined window blinds. I frisked Pouch on his way out, but he didn't have any of my stuff on him. I was sitting at my desk feeling sorry for myself when there was a knock at the door. It was Father Pascoe, dressed in his clerical garb, cradling a banker's box as though it were a twenty-pound baby. My mood went immediately from dark to deadly.

"Not today, Father. I haven't the energy." I grabbed for a Post-it note, a pen. "What say I pencil you in for the twelfth of never? That work for you?"

His thin mouth twisted into a scowl. He walked slowly over and set the box gently onto my desk. "This belongs to you."

I eyed the box, wondering if it might explode or spew toxic gas all over the place. I stared up at the priest, saying nothing. It was a box. Unless it came with an explanation, I wasn't about to get overly excited about it.

"Father Heaton left a detailed will. Most of his things he donated to charity. These personal items he bequeathed to you."

I perked up, stared at the box, suddenly interested in it.

"I'm delivering them to you, along with an apology. I could have been . . . less obstructive." I said nothing, just stared at him, wondering where the old Father Pascoe had gone. "Thea mentioned that you wished to also have his umbrella and some of the photographs. I couldn't carry it all with me today, but those are yours, as well. I'll make sure you get them."

I stood, placed my hands on the box, then slowly opened it. Inside was Pop's watch, his eyeglasses, a few personal papers, and a black leather-bound diary. I ran my hands over the cover. I never knew he kept one. A diary. Better than a datebook. I smiled, then looked up at Father Pascoe standing there more contrite than I ever thought possible. "Thank you," I said.

He nodded. "You're welcome."

We stood for a time, the box between us.

"Where were you the night of the murders?"

The look of shock on his face lasted only a moment, then he began to laugh. I'd never seen him do that before either. It was a little disconcerting, but I was willing to go with it.

"You are relentless."

"You've given me the box. You don't have to pile the flattery on, too"

"Hospital," he said simply, his expression suddenly serious. "Overnight stay. Chemo." He smiled weakly, reading the shock on my face. "Not what you expected, I see?" That explained his ill-fitting clothing, maybe even the irritability, the aloofness. He shrugged. "My chances are good. I have my faith. I don't need sympathy."

I smiled. "You thought you'd get sympathy from me?"

He shook his head, amused. "Perish the thought."

"What was going on with Anton Bolek? Did Pop tell you?"

"He did not, but I knew he suspected something. I assume he preferred to handle whatever it was in his own way."

"The same way he handled his argument with George Cummings?" I watched the priest closely.

"That Father Heaton did mention, though he offered nothing specific. He said simply that he was praying for Cummings' acceptance."

I frowned, disappointed. What kind of acceptance? About the homeless at the church?

I pulled my cellphone out and showed him the picture of my father. If he was a killer, I needed to know it. "Have you seen this man before?"

Father Pascoe pulled out his glasses and took a long look before sliding them back into his pocket. "I don't believe so. Who is he?"

"An acquaintance." I put the phone away. "Yancy Gantt. You know him?"

Father Pascoe shook his head. "Seems I've walked into the lion's den here."

"Well, if you had answered my questions the first time I asked them back at the rectory, we wouldn't be doing this now. Please, Father. Yancy Gantt?"

He sighed, nodded. ""We inherited Yancy about a year ago. Father Heaton promised his mother before she passed away that he'd watch out for him, make sure he was safe. He did that."

"Even going so far as to retrieve him from LA?" I asked.

"You know about that? Well, obviously, you do. He hired a detective out there. He found him, but he was in a bad way. Father Heaton brought him back here, kept him warm, fed, clothed, and, when he could get Yancy to agree, he got him psychiatric help. I wasn't completely onboard at first, but Father Heaton prevailed. Unfortunately, we haven't seen Yancy since that night."

"I've seen him. I talked to him. He's a witness to the murders, and now he's running. Besides the church, where else would he feel safe?"

Father Pascoe gave it some thought, unsettled, it appeared, by Yancy's role as witness to a double homicide. "I don't know. But in honor of Father Heaton's promise, I asked everyone in the parish to keep an eye out for him and to let me know when they found him. I also contacted the police, but they couldn't commit to much."

"You've actually got people out looking for him?"

He nodded. "The search has been organized through our outreach committee. I'm confident we'll know something soon. Well, I must be going." He turned to leave. I stopped him. "Father Ray knew his killer. That person was harassing him, following him. Who could it be?"

"All he would say was that it was someone in need of great healing. But, perhaps, there's something in the diary that will shed some light? I haven't read it. It wasn't my place, but it now belongs to you . . ."

"Father? One more. Who heads your outreach committee?"

"Our most ardent organizer, of course, George Cummings."

As Father Pascoe slipped quietly out, I stood there transfixed for a time, thinking things through, ordering the puzzle pieces in my head. I nearly missed the ringing phone, picking it up just in time. It was Mrs. Luna. I'd almost forgotten about running up against Hector Perez and Ignacio in the street. Today was the day of our meeting with Hector. Her church. Neutral ground. Noon. I stared at Pop's diary, anxious to study it. Reluctantly, I told her I'd be there.

Chapter 27

Hector glared at me across the long Formica table in St. Teresa's school hall, a basement room that apparently doubled as the kids' lunch room. The table was low, the chairs lower. I couldn't get my knees underneath the table and had to angle them sideways to keep from losing all feeling. I felt a little like Gulliver among Lilliputians. Hector and Mrs. Luna looked perfectly fine in their seats, Hector leaning over casually as though he were a bored kid in math class, Mrs. Luna sitting stalk straight, her hands folded in front of her, her dark eyes holding worry.

She'd washed her hands of Hector, but agreed to the meet if it meant learning more about Cesar. Hector's friends, including the Mack truck I'd threatened, hadn't been allowed past the door—by Mrs. Luna's orders. Father Vasquez, a jittery little man with big brown eyes and thick black hair, stood a distance away, his face devoid of all color, his eyes flitting nervously from table to door and back again. He had gangbangers in his church hall. I could almost hear him praying to Jesus.

I repositioned my legs, trying to find a good spot. "You

made yourself perfectly clear in the garage the other day. You said I'd get no help from you. Did I miss something?"

Hector sat slumped in baggy jeans and a black jacket, the logo of some band I'd never heard of emblazoned on the front, an unsmoked cigarette tucked behind his right ear. He was wearing sunglasses, though the sun was outside, not here in the church hall. He sat up in his tiny chair and offered a sly grin, as though he knew the secret to life itself and was bent on with-holding it until the oceans ran dry.

Mrs. Luna watched him closely, hopeful, but sad. Maybe Hector would tell her something that would give her peace, maybe he wouldn't. Either way, her son was gone forever. She'd gain little when it was all said and done.

I leaned forward as much as I could without my knees folding up under me. "Would you mind taking the sunglasses off, please? I like to see who I'm talking to."

Hector smirked. "You don't see me sitting here?"

"Your eyes. I'd like to see them."

He turned to Mrs. Luna, as if to protest, but she nodded almost imperceptibly, and he reached up and slipped the glasses off.

"Better. Now, tell me why I'm here."

"I'm here to offer you a deal." He shrugged. "Something for you. Something for me."

I said nothing, just watched. It wasn't often you were offered a devil's deal by an actual devil.

"What's for me?" I asked warily.

He shook his head. "Information."

"And what's for you?"

We stared at each other. "Cesar was my *hermano*. Some ass-hole offed him. It wasn't none of us, and it wasn't none of them . . . you know the them I mean." He slapped an angry palm down on the table. "I want the guy. Blood for blood. No one offs un *Escorpión* and gets away." He leaned back, satisfied he'd made his point. "So we make a working arrangement. I give you information, you find the guy, you give the guy to me. I get what I want, you get what you want, and it's all good for everybody."

Mrs. Luna caressed the gold cross hanging from a chain around her neck, her expression pained, her mouth a thin, tight line. "When did you lose sight of God, of goodness?"

For a split second, I thought I saw a glimmer of shame in Hector's eyes, but whatever I'd seen was quickly gone. He'd lost the battle for his soul a long time ago. He'd die as he lived, lost. "This is how the world works," he barked. "This is how it's done."

"You and your boys went out looking and came up empty," I said. "Now you need what I know, so you can do what it is you do."

Hector grinned. "Something like that."

I scanned the room, the overhead fluorescents, the cheaply tiled floor, the petrified priest in the corner. There would be no working arrangement, of course. It was justice I wanted, not revenge, not blood. It would cost me whatever information Hector claimed to have, but it'd just have to be that way. Justice for Pop and Cesar would be a hard-fought battle, but I'd fight it in the light, not in the dark.

I let out a slow, even breath. The meeting was over, as far as I was concerned. I moved to stand. "I don't think I actually need to say the words, but I will, just so I make myself clear. No deal."

Hector stopped smiling, his eyes went colder and harder than I'd ever seen them. "That's a mistake."

I could see Ignacio and his pal start to get jittery at the door. My gun was in my pocket, my hand close to it. "I'm sure it won't be my last."

Hector nodded, an oily grin on his mean face. He was furious. He'd likely expected me to jump at the deal. "Then we do this the hard way."

Mrs. Luna shot up from her chair. "Stop." She turned to Hector, pain and fury in her eyes. "The information. For me." She beat her fists against her chest. "For me! For me!"

Hector flicked a look toward the door. I stayed quiet, my eyes holding his. I watched as he swallowed hard, and thought things through. If he had the resources or the skill to find Cesar's killer, he'd have done it already. He needed me, but with me he wouldn't get the revenge he wanted. He'd have to decide if he could live with that.

"She steps out, you stay," he said to me finally. Mrs. Luna opened her mouth to object, but Hector nodded. "What I got, she doesn't hear from me. That's it."

I turned to Mrs. Luna and nodded for her to leave the table. I sat down again when she reluctantly stepped out of the hall.

"I'm listening," I said.

Slowly, Hector reached into his back pocket and pulled out a Ruger .22 semiautomatic, placing it on the table where it landed with a chilling thud. He then slid it toward me, fingertips only. I turned to watch the priest. I could see his knees shaking. I eyed the gun, then Hector. I was as alert now as I'd ever been in my entire life.

Hector frowned. He'd lost his gambit, done in by a mother's grief. "Cesar's. He never went nowhere without it, till he got jumped out. He left it with me saying he wouldn't need it no more."

I picked up the gun, hit the magazine release, and let the magazine drop into my hand.

"It's empty," Hector said. "Do I look like a fool to you?"

I looked over at him, but kept my mouth shut. It was a loaded question, which I wisely ignored. Instead, I concentrated on the Ruger. I slipped the magazine into my pocket, then racked back the slide. No rounds flew out, but I eyeballed the chamber and the magazine well, anyway. Satisfied the gun was unloaded, I set it back down on the table, away from Hector. The gun likely in his pocket, I couldn't do much about.

"Doesn't mean he didn't have another," I said.

Hector shook his head, pointed at the gun. "You're not getting me, lady detective. *This* was Cesar's one and only. His signature, right? See the pearl grip? The initials in silver? His father's."

"This didn't require a car ride or a face-to-face. If you have more, I need it now. Not in dribs and drabs, all of it. Now, or I walk, and I won't be back."

I could hear his foot tapping under the table. "I knew about the girl, okay? Cesar told me. She's why he wanted out. They were planning on running off. I told him he was loco, but he wouldn't listen. There's a baby coming. That's not something his Moms needs to hear right now, you feel me? I know her name. I've seen her, okay?"

I pulled the photo of the girl out of my pocket, slid it across the table to him. "This girl? The girl I asked you about that you swore you'd never heard of?"

Hector didn't look at the photo, didn't need to. I felt like lunging over the table and slapping the crap out of him. He'd cost me days of searching and coming up empty. He shrugged, slid the photo back across the table. "He was sneaking around. That wasn't like Cesar, so I followed him. He was with her in front of some community place. She's with some group, or something."

"What group?"

"How the fuck should I know? Some do-gooder group. They bus them in from all over to hook little brown kids into going to church, learn to read, and shit. The place is way out of the neighborhood, which is why Cesar thought I wouldn't scope him."

I flicked a look toward the door. How would Mrs. Luna handle learning she had a grandchild on the way? Would it make Cesar's loss easier or more difficult? "Where's this center?"

Hector paused.

"You're either all in, or you're not," I said.

He scowled. "By the Ford plant. On Torrence. The sign had some kind of bird on it."

"And you said nothing to Cesar about following him, and seeing this girl?"

Hector harrumphed. "Said a lot of things, but he wasn't hearing none of it. The girl's family's not the kind that'd want a gangbanger at the table. Her Pops was a real prick, Cesar said. All over her like a cheap suit, like he was scared she'd get dirty, or something. Real Romeo and Juliet shit. I said, 'Hey, Cesar, for old times, let me go over there and break his neck for you.' But he said he had somebody else working the old man, and before you ask, he didn't tell me who. He just said it was somebody he listened to, somebody he met while he was stepping out on us."

Somebody he listened to, somebody he knew? Pop? "What's her name?" Hector hesitated, as though reluctant to play his last card, even though he'd offered it. "Hector?"

"Deanna. He called her Dee Dee. He should have stuck to his own. Maybe he wouldn't be dead now."

I sat back in the tiny chair. Finally. Deanna.

The Ford assembly plant was in Hegewisch, a tough, blue-collar neighborhood built on a foundation of wetlands, sand, and immigrant grit. It wasn't that far off Cesar's turf, but far enough that he could avoid running into people he knew. I idled at the corner of 130th and Torrence, at the plant's gate, scanning the sprawling complex, its blue Ford sign looming. Other factories had dried up and blown away long ago, taking with them secure jobs and good pay, but Ford stayed put, its line still moving, union workers now rolling out Explorers in place of the Model T's the company started with.

I headed south first, rumbling over bumpy railroad tracks,

driving slowly, the stench of diesel fuel hanging heavy in the air. Torrence was four long, straight lanes of even road, a street-racer's dream. When cops were elsewhere, drunken lead foots, tumbling out of the bars at closing, raced the road, cocksure they could beat it. I passed quite a few candles, stuffed bears, and white crosses set out along the scraggly berm, memorials to the ones who'd lost the bet and ended up dead. There would be more crosses, more bears. The road always won.

I drove all the way to 159th, past the nature preserve, on the off chance Hector had no sense of direction, but I found nothing but burger joints, liquor stores, and auto garages. I turned north next, driving miles, finding the same. It wasn't until I rattled over the steel bridge spanning a narrow ribbon of the Little Calumet River that I spotted the bird, a white dove, attached to a hand-lettered sign outside the Gentle Peace Outreach Center. The small storefront wasn't much to look at; I'd have driven right past it were it not for the dove. What caught my attention, what tugged at my gut and gave me a sick feeling of déjà vu, was the old man out in front sweeping up shards of plate glass, the handful of teens helping him do it, and the gaping hole in the front windowpane where, I assumed, the shattered glass used to reside. I pulled into the lot and got out.

"Help you?" the man asked cautiously as he peered through thick lenses, his guard immediately up. This wasn't the neighborhood for curious strangers stopping to pass the time, and it didn't look as though the smashed window had put him in a trusting mood. The kids ignored me. Instead they chattered away, brooms in hand, listening to music from an iPhone and speaker someone had propped up on an upturned garbage cart, oblivious to the adult world around them.

I eyed the glass. "You've had some trouble."

The old man leaned on his push broom, his bald head gleaming. He'd passed his sixties a good decade ago and stood a bit unsteady, favoring his right side, as though he were in pain. Bad knees or bad feet, I figured. Either way, sweeping was probably something he shouldn't have been doing. "They busted clean through the front and ransacked the place last night."

I felt his pain. My office toss had taken four people to set straight. I peered inside the center at a wide room painted in primary colors. School desks, tables and bookshelves were tossed about, books thrown to the floor and trampled over. "What'd they get?"

"A computer. We had two. I don't know why they didn't take them both, but I confess I don't understand the criminal element." He squinted up at me. "But I told the lady all that over the phone. You're with the insurance company, aren't you?"

"Sorry. No. I'm a private investigator. I'm looking for a girl who might be a volunteer here." I held out a hand for him to shake, though he seemed reluctant to at first. "Cass Raines."

He stood fastened to the spot, the push broom between us, but I could almost feel him retreat. I glanced down and noticed the outline of a brace underneath his pant leg. I'd been right. Bad knee. "Reverend Ellis Crowell," he offered. "I thought you were from State Farm. Detective, you said? Who're you looking for?"

I dug the photograph out of my pocket. "Her name's Deanna. I'm hoping someone here can tell me more about her. Her last name for starters, or where I might find her."

Crowell ignored the photo, his eyes never left mine. He didn't look like an easy one to pull something over on, bad knee or no bad knee. I could tell he was going to make me work for it.

Chapter 28

Reverend Crowell went back to his sweeping. "I don't have time to talk. I got to get this up before somebody cuts themselves."

I looked around and saw another broom leaning against the front door. I grabbed it and went to work forming my own pile of shattered glass.

Crowell turned. "What's this?"

"One more broom can't hurt," I said. "Maybe while we're sweeping we could talk a little."

His rheumy eyes held mine. He didn't know what to make of me, I could tell. "You're hoping to soften me up with a good deed, that it?"

I stopped sweeping. "I don't think you soften up that easily."

His eyes widened in surprise, and he began to laugh. "You seem like good people, and I thank you for the help."

We smiled at each other and went back to work on the glass.

"Have you been broken into before?" I asked.

"This is a first. We don't have anything anyone would want that badly."

I smiled. "Except a computer?"

He snorted. "A very old computer, donated to us and loaded up with nothing more than reading games and math exercises."

"No cash inside?"

"If we had cash, our computers wouldn't be so old." He stopped sweeping and turned to face me. "Whatever you think she did, she didn't."

I gathered a pile of glass onto a dustpan and lifted it into a nearby cart, glass shards landing at the bottom with a loud crash. "I just need to talk to her."

"We have good kids here. They may come to us a little dented, but we straighten them out in good time, and we do it with love."

"I believe you, but this is important. I'm asking for your help."

Crowell's gnarled hands steadied the broom handle. "I don't like the idea of somebody looking for one of my kids, even a nice young woman like you. I'm here to protect them, to see they get what they need. Anybody wants to get at them has to go through me. Maybe you're a detective, but you could just as easily be something else. I read the papers. I see what goes on."

I smiled. He reminded me a lot of Pop. I put the broom down, pulled my PI's license out of my back pocket. I'd anticipated the once-over. Crowell watched me as I did it, giving me a full-body scan, head to toe, as though he were committing me to memory in case he had to pick me out of a lineup later. I held up the license, close so he could read it through his thick lenses.

"Does this convince you?"

I waited while he read it through the laminated plastic. I couldn't blame him for being distrustful, the world was crazy and people could be cruel, but that didn't make the waiting easier.

"Could be fake," he announced after taking forever with the fine print.

"You can verify it with the state. I have the number, if you'd like to call. I'll wait."

"What about a business card?"

I slid the license back, pulled a card free. If I could fake a license, I could fake a business card, I thought, but I was in no position to argue. If I pushed too hard, I'd get nothing. If I didn't push, I'd get nothing. It was a delicate and slow dance. I watched as he scrutinized every embossed letter. He finally nodded and tucked the card into his pocket for safe keeping.

He smiled. "Guess that proves it. Can't be too careful."

"I understand. So, where can I find Deanna?"

Crowell shook his head. I was moving much too fast for him. "Wait a minute now. You still haven't said what you want to talk to her about."

I groaned inwardly. "She knows someone involved in a case I'm working on. I'd like to ask her about that."

He took the photo from me, but again didn't look at it. Plenty of time for that, apparently.

"Sounds like a lot of tap dancing to me. What's the case?"

I sighed. "That's all I can say. Sorry."

Crowell pulled a face. "Wasn't much." No more smiles from my end. I was growing old, and Crowell had already beaten me to it. "Dangerous work for a woman, isn't it? Traipsing all over looking for people. I've seen those shows, nothing but killers and drugs and such. Pardon me for saying, but you don't look like the type that would go in for all that."

I was a little curious to find out what type he thought I looked like, but decided it would only get him revved up and running down the wrong conversational track. I still had to find Yancy, if the police hadn't already. I was buried neck deep under a pile of disparate bits of detail that were leading me in circles. I was literally drowning in nothing and everything and didn't have time for small talk. I didn't want to be rude; as my elder he was due my respect, but he was literally killing me.

My pile of glass was gone. Crowell still had half of his. I went to work on that, as he stepped aside to watch. "The work's pretty routine," I said. "A lot of paperwork, a lot of sitting, a lot of waiting for people to tell me things I need to know." I looked up at him. He squinted over at me. He got that I was referring to him. He was old; he wasn't a fool.

"And what if they don't tell you?"

"Then questions go unanswered, and bad things are allowed to happen."

Crowell pursed his lips, thought about it, then finally glanced down at the photo, taking time to study it. Slowly, his eyes shifted from idle curiosity to warm recognition. He shot me a doleful look and handed the photo back. "That's Dee Dee."

I stopped sweeping. "What's her last name?"

Crowell shrugged. "Don't know it. We don't go in for a lot of formality around here. It's easier to get the kids to trust us that way."

"Where's she from? What school?"

Crowell shook his head, frowned. "Don't know that either. The kids volunteer. They come. They stop coming. New ones take their place." He fished into his pocket and pulled out a checked handkerchief, the kind my grandfather used back before Kleenex made everything disposable. He wiped at his nose and eyes. "Hay fever."

"Someone saw her wearing a hat from St. Brendan's," I said, pushing, looking for an angle.

"We have a bin inside with all kinds of T-shirts and hats and such that we exchange with other places. A kid is free to take whatever they want."

I'd counted on the hat to make the connection, and fought hard to hide my disappointment that it'd gone nowhere. "When's the last time she was here?"

Crowell thought for a moment. "Winter, but whenever she comes back we'll welcome her with open arms." Crowell smiled.

"What about Cesar Luna? Do you know him?"

Hector had followed Cesar to Gentle Peace. He'd seen Cesar out front with Dee Dee. I could tell Crowell knew the name. "Tough one there. Not so good to begin with, but he was trying. Dee Dee was helping him study for his GED."

"He was killed," I said, watching him for a reaction.

"I read about it in the papers. That was a real shame."

"Did either of them mention knowing Father Heaton, or having any connection to St. Brendan's?" Crowley scratched his head. "Don't think so. What's all this about?"

"Cesar and Dee Dee were seeing each other. She may know why he ended up where he did. I'd like to ask her about that."

Crowell smiled shyly. "Seeing each other? Well, I wouldn't know. That's not something they'd talk to me about. Dee Dee came in a van with other kids a couple times a month. Their schools give them community service points for volunteering with us. I never met her parents, and she never talked about them, at least not to me. Cesar came on his own, parking his car out back instead of in the lot. I thought that was strange, but I didn't press him on it. We mostly take them as we find them, regardless of where, or who, they come from."

Frustration gave my voice a near-desperate edge. "You don't talk to these kids at all?"

He smiled calmly, as though he'd been asked to explain The God Particle to a circus mule. "About the important things— self-respect, decency, personal responsibility. That's what we teach here, along with the three Rs."

I eyed the kids standing around, sweeping a little, but mostly flirting and passing the time. "Would one of these kids know more about either of them?"

Crowell searched the group. "Trina might. She was pretty friendly with Dee Dee." Crowell called over a cute girl dressed in tight jeans and a pink sweatshirt. Petite, wide eyed, and looking as sweet as a teacup poodle, she appeared to be about sixteen.

She ran over smiling, but eyed me shyly. "Yes, Reverend Crowell?"

"Trina, this is Detective Raines. She has some questions about Dee Dee."

Trina's eyes got big. "What's Dee Dee got to do with the police?"

"I'm a private investigator. My name's Cass," I said, extending a hand for a friendly shake, hoping to ramp our encounter way down. People tended to get nervous around detectives and clammed up tight, which was the opposite of what we needed. The kid looked like she'd rather be anyplace else but here talking to me. "I hear you and Dee Dee are close."

She shrugged as though she wasn't interested, then stared down at the tops of her shoes, absentmindedly kicking at the dirt around her. "We talked. She was nice."

"When's the last time you spoke with her?"

Trina shrugged. "A few months ago, I guess. She stopped coming, then she stopped answering my IMs."

"Around wintertime?"

Trina looked up at me. "She was at the Christmas party. Did something happen to her?"

"Why would you ask that?"

"It's like she just disappeared, or something."

"Any reason why she would?"

Trina frowned, looked away. "Guess not."

"Do you know her last name? Where she lived? What school she went to?"

Trina shrugged. It was a teen thing. "Her last name's Baxter, and she was homeschooled. She didn't talk about her parents a lot. She did say they were really into her business, very strict, way stricter than mine. She had to like, check in all the time, every minute almost, and get permission for every place she went, even to use her own cellphone. It sounded like jail, or something."

"But her parents let her come here?"

"You have to have volunteer work on your college applications, or else you don't have a good chance." Trina slid an embarrassed glance at Crowell. "It's fun here, though."

"She met Cesar here," I said. "Her parents weren't happy about that."

Trina shuffled some, avoiding Crowell's steady gaze. Hanging out and hooking up were not things you discussed willingly with an old reverend present. Crowell got it. I got it, too.

"Well, it doesn't look like you need me," he offered. "I'll get back to my sweeping. Holler if you need anything." He drifted away, back to the glass. I could almost see the tension in Trina's body drain away.

"So Cesar and Dee Dee were hanging out?"

"Man, I'll say. It was like one day they don't know each other, the next they're like stuck together with glue. No way could she tell her folks *that*. They would have gone crazy, especially her father. Dee Dee said he told her she wasn't allowed to even talk to boys . . . *at all*, especially a boy like Cesar."

"What else do you know about her?"

"Not a lot. We mostly talked about music and stuff. It was like she was afraid to say too much. I know her dad would drive by and make sure she was here. She'd look out and see his clunky van in the lot and go all weird. It made her nervous all the time. I mean, he was real into the parenting thing. She hardly mentioned her mom. I guess she was cool with her."

"Did you ever meet her dad?"

Trina shook her head. "I mostly saw him as he cruised by outside. He never came in, but I guess I got a good look. He just looked like somebody's dad."

I pulled my phone from my pocket, scrolled to the picture of Ted Raines. He said himself he was an overprotective father, that he'd moved around. Could Dee Dee's father be mine, too? He said he lived in St. Louis, but I only had his word on that. Maybe it was a long shot, but still I couldn't just dismiss the possibility. He resented Pop taking one daughter away from him. Could he have tolerated him taking two? "Does *he* look familiar?" Trina studied the photo, but shook her head. "The man I saw wasn't so old." I put the phone away. "Tell me about Cesar," I said. "How'd he feel about Dee Dee's parents?"

"I guess he was kind of mad about how her dad was treating her, and he wanted to do something about it, but I don't think Dee Dee wanted him to, you know? The IMs stopped right before the party at Christmas; I do remember that. I just figured they got busted, and her folks grounded her and took her phone away. Her *phone*!"

Trina made a gagging noise as though her airway had been cut off. The cellphone was a teenager's lifeline, practically another appendage. "I was real shocked when she showed up. Then when Cesar walked in, too, it made sense. After that, though, poof, nothing, and then we heard about what happened to him. Dee Dee must have gone crazy."

"Do you still have her number?"

"Yeah, but it's disconnected now." Trina reached into her pocket and pulled out her phone, scrolling through it, her nimble fingers moving as fast as lightning. "Here it is." Trina held her phone up for me to see, and I jotted the number down.

"Did you save any of her texts?"

Trina shook her head no. "My parents check my phone, too."

Crowell drifted back. "That photo you have of Dee Dee's pretty old. We have newer ones inside, if you'd like to take a look? Ones of Cesar, too."

"I'd appreciate that," I said.

Crowell led me inside, both of us stepping around the debris scattered over the floor. Around the large room, every wall was covered in corkboard that held hundreds of photographs of children. Trina followed us in, invested now in what I found out about her friend.

"We put their pictures up to show we're family. There's even a few of us old folks up there somewhere."

We searched the images, moving deliberately from one board to the next and back again. We went all around the room twice, studying every smiling, freshly scrubbed face, but there were no photos of Dee Dee or Cesar anywhere.

"That's strange. I know they're here." Crowell took off his glasses, blew on them, and put them back on, as though a speck on the lenses was the cause of our futile effort to find what we were looking for. "Could just be these old eyes."

It wasn't the old man's eyes. I couldn't find the photos either, and my eyes were just fine. I took another slow pass, using the photo I had as reference when I found a girl on the wall who looked a lot like Dee Dee, but wasn't. I turned to Crowell. "They're definitely not here."

Confusion blanketed his face. "Where could they have gone?" He looked to me for the answer. I didn't have it. Trina, too, looked to me for an explanation. Still, I had nothing. But I was beginning to get a bad feeling about the whole thing. An overnight break-in, a stolen computer, missing photographs of two kids—one dead, one vanished. This was not coincidence.

Crowell patted his pockets, reached in, and pulled out a cell-phone. "Wait. I've got the pictures from our holiday party. I know they're on there."

I watched as he hunted and pecked at the small screen.

"My grandson was supposed to transfer these so we could print them out and put them up, but he hasn't yet." Crowell grimaced. "You know how kids can be." His thumb swiped across the screen as he scrolled through his photo gallery. I stood in the sea of chaos, glancing around at overturned chairs and shredded kiddie artwork. "Ah. See? Here they are."

He handed over the phone. He was right. There they were—

Dee Dee and Cesar together, standing close, obviously besot-
ted, Cesar looking much younger than in his mugshot, Deanna
much older than in the photo I had.

"May I look through the rest?"

Crowell waved a dismissive hand. "Of course."

I found at least a half-dozen more of the couple caught at
candid moments, their heads close, staring at each other as
though they couldn't bear not to. The final photo was a group
shot: kids dressed in red and green crowded in, arms around
each other, facing an unknown photographer. Their backs were
to the front picture window, which now lay shattered on the
sidewalk outside. Everyone in the photo was smiling, except
for Dee Dee and Cesar. Why? What had happened between the
time the first photograph was taken and this last one? "They
don't look happy here," I said. "What happened?"

Crowell had no clue. Trina leaned over to see. "I remember
that. They were having a good time, then all of a sudden they
freaked out. I asked Dee Dee what was going on, but she just
walked off like she didn't even hear me. Right after that, they
ducked out the back."

"And you have no idea why?"

"Oh, no, I know why," Trina said. "Right after they left, her
dad's van pulled out of the lot and followed them."

"You saw Mr. Baxter in the lot that night?"

Trina's face crinkled into a confused frown. "Who?"

"Dee Dee's father."

"His name's not Baxter. He's her *stepfather*, not her real one.
I don't know what his name is, really, but I know it's not Baxter. Whatever it is, she never ever used it, but he was trying real
hard to get her to, so they could be like a real family. He wanted
to adopt her and everything, but she thought he was real creepy
and didn't want him to."

My stomach began to flutter, part excitement at feeling I was
close to something important, part foreboding. Where was Dee

Dee? God, don't tell me I was about to stumble upon another dead kid.

"Mind if I copy these photos to my phone?" I asked Crowell.

"No, go ahead. Did you find something you could use?"

I handed the phone back to him. "I hope so."

Chapter 29

I headed north, calling Ben from the car. "I need a favor," I said when he picked up.

"Where the hell are you? I've been calling you all day, so has Barb. I know this because when she couldn't reach you, she called me. And what in the Sam Hill is a Pouch? She said she and Whip and this Pouch were backing you up on this thing."

I checked my watch. It was after five. "No, no, no! Did she say what they were doing?"

"Not to me. Try returning a call once in a while, and you might find out yourself."

"All right. I'll call. Happy now?"

"Huffy, really? That's a lot of nerve, even for you."

"You done?"

"Not even close, but we can talk about it later. What's this favor?"

"I need whatever you can find on a Deanna Baxter. She's maybe about sixteen. No address, but I have a cell number. She's the girl in Cesar's photograph. I found a community center where she and Cesar hung out, but he's dead and no one's seen her since December. She could be important."

"Now I'm tracking down teenagers?"

"She's the mother of Cesar's unborn child. If anyone knows what he was up to before he got killed, it's her, but all I've got is a disconnected cell number." He grumbled on the other end of the line. I couldn't blame him. It wasn't much. I heard paper rustling on his end.

"All right, give it to me."

I rattled the number off. "Thanks."

"Yeah, yeah. Just answer your damn phone."

He clicked off.

Dee Dee and Cesar were together in December. Where was Dee Dee now? Had she run away? Did her stepfather have her under lock and key? Was she dead somewhere, too? I shuffled through the disparate bits of information I had—Pop's Bible, the sticky note, 430/HWY, 150-DB. DB. Deanna Baxter. That fit. What about the rest of it? God, I hoped Dee Dee was still alive.

Yancy was moving. He had to be, otherwise, why couldn't the police find him? Moving was good. Moving meant alive. I checked, but there had been no reports of unidentified homeless men brought into any of the nearby hospitals or the morgue.

I drove away from Gentle Peace not nearly as excited as I should have been. Yes, I had a name. That was something. But I had little else so far. I hit the expressway headed north and when I hit Stony Island, I took it all the way to the Midway before turning for the Drive where I slowed and scanned the lakefront for signs of Yancy. It was raining again, and Lake Michigan was a mass of gray, undulating water, bleak and gloomy. It was easy to see why Yancy found it comforting even like this, the rocking of the waves, the soothing comfort in the ebb and flow. You could watch it for hours, as Yancy undoubtedly did, if one had the time and the temperament. At the moment, I had neither. Before I knew it, I was parked and back at Yancy's squat, looking up at the sky, wishing there were stars pointing in his direction. It was almost six p.m. but because of the rain, the sky was dark, and the park was deserted. I noticed that the beach house had a new gate across the entrance and a new lock securing it. The garbage cans Yancy and I had cowered behind had been removed. There was nothing like a late-night shooting to goose slow-moving bureaucracies into fast action. I headed north up the path toward Promontory Point just a half-mile or so away, ducking into the pedestrian tunnel as I passed it, to make sure Yancy wasn't huddled inside. As I walked, I listened to the beat of the rain bouncing off my slicker, breathing in the scent of wet rubber, my flashlight dry in my pocket. It was too early for the streetlights to come on, even though the sky was murky, but I made my way along the slippery path by the light of passing headlights on The Drive, rainwater squishing in my shoes.

Through a thin curtain of rain, I could just make out the Point's castlelike building sitting at the head of a lonely peninsula jutting out into the lake. It was surrounded by a tumbled seawall of limestone blocks that stair-stepped down to the shallow water below. In summer, sunbathers sprawled on the rocks like Catalina seals awaiting high tide, and intrepid swimmers used them as jumping-off points for daily laps in the choppy water. Bike riding, kite flying, and Tai Chi on the lawn at dawn, kept the spot humming. Would Yancy feel safe here?

I trudged up the trail, headed toward the darkened building, slogging over the wet grass to avoid the parts of the path that had flooded over with muddy water. The path veered away from The Drive here. There were no more headlights to guide me, so I grabbed the flashlight from my pocket and turned it on. The sound of the waves crashing against the craggy rock competed with the drumbeat of rain echoing in my ears. It had been a long day, and I was exhausted, though it was more mental than physical. I'd been shot at, almost arrested, had my office broken into and on top of that Pop had left behind a puzzle I couldn't solve. Someone wanted me to stop digging, that was for sure, but whoever it was didn't know me. It would take far more than a broken window and a trip to the police station to turn me back.

Squinting past raindrops, I thought I saw a light, a flicker inside the building. I stopped cold and waited for it to come again. There. It was definitely something. I raced forward, the beam from the flashlight dancing, and my feet slipping on the sodden grass. I careened into the building's French doors, my muddy shoes skating along the stone veranda. I emitted a sound, half expletive, half prayer, but managed to keep my footing.

I rattled the doors. Locked. I peered through the windows, but it was too dark inside to make anything out. Then I saw the light again. It was not inside the building, but around the back, something shining and reflecting off the wet windows. I picked my way around the side, feeling along the stone walls, my fingers digging into narrow niches in the stone to keep me from falling as the rain beat down and gusts of disgruntled wind threatened to blow me over.

I saw the candle first, its low light sheltered by a tiny alcove and overhang. Next to it, lying on the damp ground—Yancy Gantt. I recognized the parka, the skull cap, his boots. I breathed a sigh of relief, but it was short-lived. Near panic soon overtook it. It didn't look like he was breathing. I looked around, but there was nothing here but Yancy, the lake, and the one solitary candle flickering. I drew closer, mindful of where I placed my feet. Nothing moved but the candle flame.

"Yancy?" I gently pulled back the collar of his coat, fingertips only, and placed two fingers to his carotid, feeling for signs of life. I felt nothing. I pressed harder, my own breath holding, then nearly jumped out of my skin when I felt a faint throbbing. He was alive. Barely. I wiggled out of my slicker and placed it over him for warmth, then dug my phone out of my jeans pocket to call 911. "Hang in there," I said, shivering against the cold.

He looked up at me, puzzled, and I knelt down and leaned in, shielding him from the pelting rain. "Hey, remember me?" Yancy nodded, a glint of recognition in his eyes. I couldn't tell how badly he was injured. I didn't want to move him or exert him, but I needed to know about the wolf. What if this turned out to be the only chance I'd get? I placed a gentle hand on his shoulder. "Yancy? Can you talk?"

He moaned. "Hurts."

I scanned the park in desperation, looking for flashing lights along the Drive. Nothing yet. It was too soon. "Can you try just a little?"

He squeezed his eyes closed, nodded once.

"The wolf, Yancy."

For a time, he said nothing. I checked him again, afraid that he'd slipped away, but his eyes were open again. He was staring at the lake behind me. How much time did I have? How much pain was he fighting against? I felt like a heel pressing him, but he was the only witness, the only one who knew.

There was a slight shake of his head. "Two . . . wolves."

Two? I agonized over what to ask next, searching for a way to phrase a meaningful question that could be answered by a simple flick of the head in hopes of minimizing his discomfort. "Who are they, Yancy?"

"Black heart. No soul." His voice wheezed out like air through a bellows, his tone and pitch frighteningly low. He began to chuckle lightly, shallow breaths only. The sound of it was alarming, air rushing in and out of his lungs, rattling and gurgling as it did. "Saints and sinners. Soft. Hard."

He wasn't making any sense. If he'd been on his meds at the beach house, he was certainly off them now, after wandering around aimlessly with a bullet in him. Was any of this real? I frantically searched the Drive again, but still there was nothing. What was taking so long?

"Ran. Hid," Yancy muttered.

I rubbed his hands to work some of the cold out of them. "You're done running now. You're okay. Just lay quietly. They're coming."

He went quiet again. The silence felt like it would last forever. Then he broke it. "Deanna, Cesar, Buddy, Boss. . . . He hid her. He came looking." Yancy drifted off. He'd gotten to the end of what he had. I sat stunned by his offering. The sound of sirens came first, then the lights. I watched as they grew closer. Help had arrived.

"Hold on, Yancy," I whispered.

His lips moved. I leaned in. "The beads." His voice was so low I could barely hear it. "Fell like rain."

I watched as the ambulance a quarter-mile away, slowly turned off the Drive and gingerly moved up the narrow path that was just perfect for bikes and joggers and strolling baby carriages, but not so perfect for first responders in cop cars, fire trucks or ambulances. When the rig finally slid to a stop in front of the building, two paramedics jumped out, saw me signaling them, and quickly went to work on Yancy. Buddy and Boss? Beads? I had no idea what to make of any of it, and Yancy was likely dying. The paramedics checked Yancy's vitals and started an IV. I followed it all, my eager eyes taking it all in, the sound of police sirens getting closer. I jumped when a hand came down on my shoulder, and turned to find Ben there. "What happened?" he asked.

"I found him. I don't know how bad it is, but it looks bad."

"You get anything?"

I retrieved my slicker from the ground. "I don't know. He says there were two in the church. He heard names. The girl's, Cesar's and two new ones—Boss and Buddy."

Ben sighed, a look of skepticism on his face, but he didn't say anything.

"He got the first two names right," I argued, in hopes of convincing him. "I have to believe he got the others right, too. Anyway, it's all we've got."

I watched as the paramedics loaded Yancy onto a gurney and slid him into the back of the ambulance; the back doors gaped open, revealing all manner of medical paraphernalia.

"Where are you taking him?" I asked them. "U of C. You family?"

Reluctantly, I shook my head no.

"Then you'll have to meet us there."

The back doors banged shut and the rig sped away, spinning tires spitting up the grass on the soggy lawn. The hospital was just blocks away. I hoped Yancy made it. I moved to leave, fumbling for my keys.

"I'm following them over," I said.

Ben blocked me. "You think that's a good idea?"

"Why wouldn't it be?"

"When's the last time you slept?"

"What's that got to do with anything? This could be the break I need."

"If it's a break, I'll handle it. He's alive, thanks to you. Now go home, get some rest, let them work on the guy. Did you call Barb?" I hadn't. I'd forgotten. She wasn't going to be happy. "See? You're running on empty. I'm saying this as a pal, as one who gets you. Put it down for a night and walk away."

A part of me knew he was right, but I still bristled at the idea of being sent home like a naughty child caught out past curfew. Yancy could be the difference between knowing what happened and not knowing. There was no way I could back off and let it go.

"Is that friendly advice or an order?"

Ben narrowed his eyes. "You need it to be an order?"

Even in the rain, a small crowd had gathered along the pedestrian trail, drawn by the emergency lights and the promise of a spectacle. The ambulance gone, they now tuned into our conversation. I could feel them watching. Maybe they were waiting to see if the wet woman facing off against the big cop would get Tased, carted off to jail, or both. I was dead on my feet, though I would cut off my own arms before admitting it. I should shut up and go home, I knew it, but I was too wired, too worried, too pig-headed to comply; the fact that Ben was perfectly calm and nonconfrontational only made me dig my heels in even more.

We faced off for a time, neither of us letting it go. He was just as stubborn as I was. That's what had made us such a good team back in the day. Neither of us ever gave up on anything no matter how hard fought the battle. I kept telling myself to stand down, even as my blood boiled, even as I wanted to scream the building down. But I couldn't win, and I finally accepted it.

I broke the stare down first, punching my arms into my slicker. "I'm going home."

"Good idea."

He didn't dare smile. I was waiting for a smile. One smile, one indication that he thought he'd won, and I'd walk back my concession. "But I'll be at that hospital first thing in the morning."

"I know."

I slid him a dangerous look. "We're not done with this, you and me."

"Know that, too."

I walked off. He followed.

"Stop following me!"

"Where's your car?" he asked calmly.

I stopped. My car was in the lot half a mile away. I squeezed my eyes shut, mouthed an expletive.

I turned to face him. "You think this is funny, don't you?"

"Nope," he said smiling. We stood in silence on the inky

path, rain pelting down on us, Ben getting the worst of it. That was a good friend for you. Risking pneumonia to make sure you were safe, even after you'd told him to shove it."

"I'll drive you back," he said.

I melted instantly, and all the fight drained away. "Thanks."

"On the condition that you admit that I was right back there," he said.

I turned and walked off again.

"Say it. I'm right." I could tell he was grinning. I could hear it in his voice. "I want to hear the words."

I burrowed into my jacket, smiled. "Like hell."

Chapter 30

Around ten the next morning, I planted myself in the hospital's lobby. They wouldn't let me up to see Yancy, and I couldn't badge my way through, so I sat quietly in a blue chair that, despite the padding, had no give in the seat or back. After only a short time, I felt as though I'd ridden the open range on a crookback horse. It didn't matter. I'd wait, though no one in charge would part with a single bit of information on Yancy's condition. I wasn't family, and they were serious about those HIPAA laws. Cesar and Dee Dee, I mused. Boss. Buddy. Baxter. Wolves? I pulled out my phone to scroll through Reverend Crowell's holiday pictures. Dee Dee and Cesar happy, then Dee Dee and Cesar not happy. The initials in Pop's Bible. One fifty? An amount of money? Part of an address? It could be a time, I thought, but Pop hadn't added a colon. "Ugh, Pop. Help me out here." I called Ben.

"You're at the hospital, aren't you?" he asked.

"I told you where I'd be."

He grumbled on the other end of the line.

"They won't tell me anything," I said. "They won't let me up. What do you know?"

"He made it through surgery, but he's still out of it. They plucked a round out of his lung, and he lost a lot of blood."

"Will he pull through?"

"They're guarded, but optimistic. We put a cop on his door." I sighed, relieved that Yancy had better protection than I could obviously provide. "Thanks. That's great. I believe him when he says someone's out to get him. They might keep trying till they do. The cop helps. Anything on Deanna? An address maybe?"

Ben let a beat pass, cleared his throat. "Still working on it. But Gantt did do more talking in the ambulance." I perked up. "What'd he say?"

"The paramedics said he kept muttering something about a roaring polar bear chasing him." My spirits fell. "You know all of this is probably bullshit, right?" He was treading lightly. "Maybe he's seeing things that aren't there?"

"I believe him. He's been running for his life, scared out of his mind. And those attacks on the homeless, the murder of the man in Yancy's squat? They're connected. Someone's out there looking for Yancy Gantt and rousting anybody who looks like him. Why? Because he was somewhere he wasn't supposed to be, and saw something he wasn't supposed to see."

"And you're basing all that on the ravings of a mentally un-stable man?"

I scrubbed my hand across my face, fatigue and exasperation battling for equal time. "How else would he know the names Cesar or Deanna?"

"Buddy and Boss? A roaring polar bear? C'mon, Cass."

"It isn't much, I'll admit."

"It's less than that and you know it."

"There's a connection. I just need to make it."

There was an uneasy silence on both ends of the line.

"One more link," I said finally. "That's all it'll take. Yancy knows."

I could hear Ben tapping nervously on his end, likely with a

No. 2 pencil, which he favored both for writing and gnawing. "Don't sit there all day. And eat something, for Christ's sake, will ya?"

I smiled and ended the call. Eat something? I was too wound up to eat. Yancy's life was hanging in the balance, and I hated hospitals. I didn't like the smells, the sterility, the fact that I almost died in one. Still, I'd stay until they threw me out.

"Are you up already? You just got in two hours ago." Barb said, shuffling into the kitchen wearing a pair of my fuzzy slippers, sporting a serious case of bed head. "You're going over the Bible again?"

I'd waited at the hospital all day, but heard nothing more about Yancy. When visiting hours ended, they cleared me out and I headed home. Now, for what seemed like the millionth time, I sat huddled over Pop's things, reading through the Bible passage, his sermons, turning pages in his diary, running my fingers up and down the pages, hoping something finally clicked. The diary was full of personal thoughts and observations, eloquent, heartrending, and all of it precious to me, but he hadn't mentioned Cesar or Dee Dee. He hadn't said a single thing about someone following him or hearing a stalker's confession. "I've cleaned everything. It was either this or retiling the bathroom."

Barb grabbed milk from the fridge, poured herself a glass. "It's almost midnight."

I looked up. "Then what are you doing up?"

She sat across from me, yawned. "I'm still on Africa time." She eyed the books and papers spread out in front of me on the table. "Anything?"

"If somebody confessed to him, he wouldn't have been able to tell anyone, but could he have written it down?"

Barb shook her head. "Nope. Not a word, not a hint, nothing."

I reached over the sticky note. "Then this can't be about his killer. It's got to be about something else. 430/HWY. There is no 430 highway in this state." I stuck the note on top of the Bible. "Assuming that's what HWY stands for." I clawed my fingers through my hair, then shoved the mess of papers away, tired of looking at them, frustrated that I wasn't getting it.

"Okay, this is what I think I know. Pop was being Pop. He somehow met and befriended Cesar, maybe through one of those youth programs he headed up, maybe during one of the Masses Cesar attended on the sneak. Cesar trusted him. Maybe Pop even introduced him to Reverend Crowell at Gentle Peace and that's how he met Dee Dee. Maybe Cesar met Dee Dee some other way, I don't know. But now they have a problem, right? They're in love, pretty soon they're expecting a baby. Her folks are going to go nuts about the whole thing. Who would they rely on to intervene, smooth the way? Pop, that's who."

"That's what I'd do," Barb said, sipping her milk. "So Pop goes to the church that night to talk it over with Cesar, and something horrible happens?"

"Buddy and Boss happened," I said. "Yancy's there. Maybe he came to get more candles, maybe he came just to get warm. Whatever, he's in the church. He hears angry voices and sees two men arguing with Pop and Cesar. It gets out of hand. Buddy and Boss are unknowns, but one or both of them has got to be connected to either Cesar or Dee Dee. One of them confessed."

"And you can't fill in the blanks until you talk to Yancy. Meanwhile, there's nothing else here?" She reached for the diary and began to leaf through it.

I got up to pace. "Nothing in that diary that I can see. I focused in on the months and weeks leading up to his death. He told me in my office the stalking started in January. There's nothing about any of that in the book. Everything is in cryptic

bits and pieces. There's no pattern, at least none that I can see."
I faced her. "I admit I'm not at the top of my game here."

Barb smiled. She understood. "Two heads then." She pushed
her glass away. "He purposefully tried to keep Cesar and Dee
Dee a secret, so whoever he was trying to hide them from had
to be someone close, right? Which, I think, lets out your father."

I stiffened. "It doesn't. I only have his word for where he
was when Pop and Cesar were killed. He knows that church.
He knows Pop. It could very well have been him sitting beside
him in that confessional, the one threatening him. Even if he
could have, Pop wouldn't have wanted to tell me that."

"So you're thinking he waited all this time to do something
this horrible? And he just happened to stumble in on the other
situation? The star-crossed lovers?"

"It's possible." I picked up the sticky note from the table, my
eyes bleary from overuse. "Letters. Numbers. It's like algebra."

She grinned. "Yeah, which you flunked."

I stopped suddenly, my mind niggling at the edge of something I didn't dare scare away by moving. Algebra. Numbers
and letters. What about letters for numbers? Pop would go for
that, right? I reeled. "Romans. Maybe it's not about the verse,
but the title of the book? Romans. Numbers. Roman numerals?"

Barb glanced at the Bible. "But he hasn't written any Roman
numerals."

"One fifty. That's a number. You're the teacher. What's that
in Roman numerals?"

"CL," Barb said.

CL dash DB. "CL, Cesar Luna. DB, Deanna Baxter."

Barb stood, excited. "The kids."

My eyes held hers, afraid to blink. "What about 430?"

She shook her head. "That'd be CDXXX. That's not on the
note. It could be a date, though. April thirtieth?"

I rushed back to the table, fanned through the diary, concentrating on the entries for April, but like the first hundred times through, nothing jumped out at me. "Or a time, maybe," I said, getting a niggle of recollection. "A time, not a date."

Four-thirty every day, no earlier, no later. Howard's got a bladder that runs like clockwork. Lillian Gibson. I could practically feel my brain power into overdrive. "I think I know what it means."

It was sheer agony waiting for a decent hour to pay a call on Lillian Gibson. Now on her front porch, I laid on the bell waiting for her to answer, hoping she could confirm what I had a sinking feeling was true. There was no answer. I checked my watch: 9:15 A.M. Was she already up and out this early? I peered in through the window, but the place was dark. I trotted over to Cummings's place, slipping into his backyard, looking for an easy access point, but in addition to his sound-proofing improvements, he'd also added a pretty decent security system. Why was Cummings's early morning departure with his family in tow written in Pop's note. Had he planned to meet them someplace? Where the heck was Lillian Gibson? I walked back to my car, pulled Cummings's business card from my console, and dialed his number, getting voicemail. I left a message. I wanted to talk, I told him, about his family's trip. Then I waited.

Two days. Bad vending machine food, the chair from Hell. Whip hadn't called in yet to report on Bolek. George Cummings hadn't returned my call regarding his family's whereabouts. My father hadn't shown up to produce his train ticket as evidence of his innocence. Ben couldn't find Dee Dee, and I could no longer stand the suspense. My nerves were fried. But Yancy held the key, so I was here. My phone rang in my pocket, and I lunged for it like a crazy person.

"Are you kidding me?" Ben barked.

"I'm here till I talk to him."

"You know this is obsessive, even for you."

"Did you call just to chastise me, or do you have something important to say? Anything on Dee Dee? Bolek? George Cummings?"

"We've got cops on it, all right? I called to tell you Yancy's awake. I just got a call from the floor. I'm on my way over there now to see if I can get a statement. Get a visitor's pass from the security desk and wait for me at the nurses' station. The cop on the door knows we're coming. You can thank me later with expensive booze." He clicked off, and I popped up from the chair and raced to the security desk. Things were finally looking up.

Yancy was in room 807, and I rode up to the eighth floor pressed into a crowded elevator, anxious for the car to make its way up. When the elevator doors finally whooshed open on eight, I heard a god-awful commotion coming from the far end of the hall and turned to see a small crowd of people standing there.

"Get the wheelchair off her," a nurse yelled into a small group of onlookers blocking the corridor. Ambulatory patients in hospital gowns were outside their rooms watching, glued to the action as nursing staff and orderlies attended to an old woman dressed in hospital booties and a chenille robe, who appeared to be pinned underneath a collapsible wheelchair, the front wheels pointed upward, spinning.

The old woman wailed. "Somebody shoved me! My back is broken into a million pieces!"

A short, blond nurse reached into the cluster of bodies. "Mrs. Strickley, stop struggling, please. Let us help you." She scanned the hall frantically. "Did anyone see what happened?" She reached out to the old woman. "Lay quietly so I can see if you're hurt."

"Of course, I'm hurt. I've been assaulted. Pushed over and out like a sack of spuds!"

A tall male nurse worked to move people back. "Please, everyone, go back to your rooms. Let us work."

I watched from the nurses' station as the crowd slowly thinned and I could get a clearer look at poor Mrs. Strickley, blue hair and all. She didn't look as though she'd been injured too badly, but I was no doctor. She appeared to be about a hundred, but also sturdy enough to last that much longer or more. I smiled, but shouldn't have.

"Please, everyone, step back." The harried nurse blew a corkscrew curl out of her flushed face. This obviously was more work than she'd planned on for the day. As everyone moved back to give Mrs. Strickley room, a man in blue stood up, revealing the familiar CPD patch on the sleeve of his uniform sweater. Yancy's cop? No way. I peered down the other end of the hall toward room 807. There was no one on the door.

I yelled. "Officer!" He reeled, heavy jowls waggling. He looked like a human-bulldog hybrid. "Are you supposed to be on the door to 807?"

He pointed to the old woman at his feet. "Emergency here."

I turned and ran full speed for Yancy's room, my back stiff from sitting so long. Maybe the cop had gotten a clue and was right behind me; maybe he hadn't and wasn't. Either way, I couldn't wait for him. Nearly there, the door to 807 eased open, and I watched as a black man with short dreadlocks furtively poked his thin head out. He wasn't wearing a lab coat or scrubs, but a black fleece jacket and jeans. He was no doctor, orderly, or nurse. He didn't look like he belonged in the hospital at all, let alone in Yancy's room. When he turned and saw me, he jolted back, then tore off down the hall toward the stairwell.

"Stop!" I screamed. He kept going. I pushed open Yancy's door and stepped into a cacophony of deafening bells and beeps. Every machine Yancy had been hooked up to was either beeping, flashing, blaring, or hissing. His still body lay on a mass of rumpled sheets, as though he'd been involved in a horrible struggle. There was a pillow over his face, IV tubes pulled free, blood on the sheets. I knocked the pillow away and hurriedly felt for a pulse, but couldn't find one. I pulled the emergency alarm, setting off another loud alert. I felt again for a pulse, but got nothing back. He was gone. The jowly cop ran up behind me, frantic nurses running in behind him, pushing their way to the bed. I turned to the cop, screeching. "You left the door! He's dead because you left the door!"

He swallowed hard, and his face lost all its color as the reality of his situation hit him. He was no rookie, but he'd just made the mother of all rookie mistakes. And he was going to get dinged for it.

"No one passed me," he argued, grasping for anything, hoping authoritative bluster would mitigate the damage done. "I had the door in my sights the entire time. The old lady . . . Who the hell are you, anyway? Let me see your pass."

The special visitor's pass had my name on it. I yanked it off my jacket and flung it at him, then ran for the stairwell. A code blue blared over the PA system, but it'd be too late. Yancy was dead. I gritted my teeth, kept moving. I reached the end of the hall and skidded around the corner, but the corridor was deserted. He couldn't have gotten that far ahead of me. The hall went on forever, and there were at least twenty rooms on each side of it. I slowly crept along, peeking into rooms at patients sleeping in their beds, listening for anything that didn't sound right. Two rooms up, a woman screamed.

"Get out. Nurse! Police! Get out!" That's what I'd been waiting for; I ran toward the wails. Fleece Jacket dashed from his hiding place and took off again. He was a good thirty yards ahead of me, barreling through nurses who appeared out of nowhere, knocking over meal trolleys and medicine carts. An oblivious woman walking an IV pole toward the restroom waddled out in front of me, and I nearly knocked her over. She screamed bloody murder, but I couldn't stop. Fleece Jacket hit the stairwell door, pushed it open, and disappeared, but seconds later the door wouldn't budge for me. I rammed it with my shoulder, but felt no give in it at all. I tried again, and the door gave just a fraction of an inch before slamming shut again. I peeked through the small square of glass just above eye level and saw the man hunched down behind the door, leaning all of his weight against it.

I rammed again, harder. The door gave again, but again fell back. Peering up through the glass a second time, I could see him mocking me with a cocky smile. I checked the hall for something, anything to break the glass; my eyes landed on a fire extinguisher in a narrow glass box. I ran over, pulled it out and threw it through the glass without a moment's hesitation, sending jagged shards raining down on the guy's back. He pushed away from the door and took off down the stairs. I chased him, taking two stairs at a time, gaining some ground. I could hear him gasping for air. He was tiring; I was, too, but I wasn't going to stop. He killed Yancy. Maybe he killed Pop and Cesar. Hell would freeze over before I gave in and let him go.

Down the stairs, seventh floor, sixth. When we rounded the landing on six and hit the next flight of stairs, the guy turned back to see if I was still there, hope in his eyes. I was. I wanted him bad and not in a good way. I hoped he could tell. "Stop!" I yelled, though I knew he wouldn't. If he were going to stop, he'd have done it two flights up.

"Fuck off!" he yelled back, his voice echoing off the walls.

I picked up the pace, though I had little left in the tank. I wanted to kill him. I wanted to plunge my fists into his chest and yank out his beating heart with my bare hands.

"I hear you breathing hard," he taunted.

I ignored him and dug in again, pushing myself well past empty, my legs buckling. If he got to the first floor he'd be long gone, lost in a crowd of visitors and staff. Fleece practically flew off the fifth-floor landing. I was a half flight up, but gaining. Just then the heavy door on the fourth floor opened, and a pair of chattering doctors in gray lab coats stepped into the stairwell, oblivious to the runaway train headed their way.

"Move!" I screeched, half-crazed and nearly despondent at the possibility of defeat. Startled, the pair did the exact opposite and planted themselves like oak trees, over-educated deer caught in the glare of oncoming headlights. I didn't have all day to think about what to do next. I had just enough time to clench my teeth, brace, and throw my body down the last few steps onto Fleece Jacket's back. The impact sent the both of us tumbling down the last few steps, slamming hard into the wall. We ended up on the floor in a tangle, each of us trying to get a hold on the other. One doctor flew past us headed up, leaving his stunned companion high and dry. The doctor left behind to fend for herself, flattened out and glued herself to the opposite wall like a panel of wallpaper. Her eyes wide, her mouth agape, she stood there, knees shaking, suspended like a dinosaur jawbone in a slab of amber.

"Get out of here!" I screamed, hoping to unstick her. "Go!"

She bolted back through the door. It was now just me and Fleece amid the wailing drone of security alarms. It sounded as though the entire hospital had been put on notice. Surely someone—the police or hospital security—would show up soon.

We rolled around on the landing, grappling like a pair of howler monkeys, knees ramming into vulnerable places, elbows slamming into bone. There was no way I could outfight him. He had me by at least fifty pounds, and his hands were as big as baseball mitts. The best I could do was slow him down and protect myself. I managed to land a strong kick to his groin on my way out of the scrum. The sound of the air whooshing out of his lungs as he folded in on himself gave me a great deal of satisfaction. The kick was for Yancy. I scrambled to my feet to loom over Fleece, gulping for air, my legs as useful as overcooked noodles. I watched as he whimpered like a child. If I'd had my gun I might have conked him with it. Lucky for him I had to turn it into hospital security before being allowed on the floor.

"Damn you." He managed to squeeze the words out, his sharklike eyes tearing, wide lips contorted into an agonizing grimace. He writhed around on the landing, all the air drained out of him, glaring at me. I glared back. He wanted to kill me, I could tell.

"You . . . got . . . nothing." He wheezed. "Less . . . than . . . nothing."

I sneered at him, breathing hard, sweating, my legs shaking, spent. "Shut . . . up."

He'd get his day in court, though at the moment it felt like more than he deserved. I kicked his foot away, then plucked his wallet out of his back pocket. "I have you coming out of a room you had no business in, a room where a man was killed. . . . Now I have you."

He squeezed his eyes shut. "Dammit."

"Which one are you, Boss or Buddy?"

He shook his head and clenched his lips shut like a child playing a defiant game of tick-a-lock. It only angered me more.

"Why'd you kill him? What'd he do to you?" I meant Pop, but the question also applied to Yancy and Cesar. They were linked; this man knew how.

"Go to hell," he managed to spit out.

"Maybe later, but since I'm here now . . ." I opened the battered billfold to reveal a few scraps of folded paper, money. My heart leapt at the sight of the driver's license sticking out of the narrow slot reserved for such things. "ID in your pocket. Real sure of yourself, weren't you?"

He made a play for snatching the billfold from me, but didn't come close. "Don't mean nothing."

"Not to you, maybe, but to me."

He smiled, despite his discomfort, like he knew a secret and found pleasure in keeping it to himself. It was a little freaky. I slid the license free to get a better look, but before I could, the stairwell door burst open, whacked me hard in the spine and slammed me into the wall again. I tried inhaling, but couldn't. The slam had knocked the wind out of me. Fleece's wallet flew out of my hands and landed at my feet. I turned to see two security guards tumble into the stairwell, wide-eyed, scared shitless, and braced for confrontation, each brandishing pepper spray and walkie-talkies.

"Nobody move," the flabby male guard barked, his tan uniform straining across his bulbous middle. "Faces in the dirt!"

His female partner was all of five feet and couldn't have weighed more than ninety-five pounds soaking wet. She was Cathy Rigby in regulation shoes. "You heard him. Hands against the wall." Her voice, almost as thin as she was, wobbled some when she spoke. She looked petrified. "I mean, behind your backs."

I stood there for a moment, stunned, my back burning, waiting for my breath to come back. "I'm an investigator," I said when I'd recovered enough to speak. "He killed the man in room 807. That's what the alarms are for."

"Hell no," Fleece bellowed. "She jumped me. Tried to steal my wallet!"

The guards looked at me, then back at Fleece, then me again. This was way too real for either of them to get their heads around. Checking visitors' passes and giving directions to radiology was one thing, two people fighting in a stairwell was something else entirely.

The flabby guard's eyes held mine. "I said down. Now!"

Fleece—recovered now from the kick—clambered to his knees, pawing for his wallet, which had landed just beyond his reach. I peeled myself away from the wall and lunged for him, and it, both of us desperate, both of us ignoring the guards' orders. Knotted up together again, we skidded down the stairs together, crashing painfully one level below. Fleece got his big hands on the billfold first, but fumbled with it, unable to get a firm grasp. I batted it away.

"Bitch!" he howled.

The wallet was all I could think about. I needed it. I could hear the guards rumbling down the stairs after us. I skidded over to where the wallet ended up and got my hands on it, clutching it as though it were life itself, but Fleece soon barreled in, working to pry it loose from my grip. I elbowed him in the ribs, and he briefly let go, but he was quickly back. I lobbed the wallet behind his head and pushed him off me. The wallet hit the wall, sending its contents scattering. Fleece now had a choice to make, take time to grab it all up and risk not getting away, or leave everything and run. Which would he go for? I didn't wait to see. I clawed for the ID. Fleece did, too.

"Stay where you are," Flabby Guard yelled, his gruff voice echoing off the metal railings.

"Both of you," Tiny Guard added.

I kept reaching, my fingertips just touching it. Fleece was right there fighting me for it. I almost had it. Suddenly, I felt a strong pull at the back of my jacket. I turned to look. It was Flabby Guard pulling me back. I roared out in frustration. "Let go of me, you idiot!" I lost my grip on the ID and watched horrified as my fingers got farther and farther away from it. I struggled to wriggle out of my jacket and free myself. "Stop him!"

Fleece snatched up his license, scrambled to his feet and ran down the stairs. I reached out to grab him, straining against the hold, getting nowhere. "He's getting away. Get him!"

Flabby Guard flung me onto my back and pressed his fat foot into my stomach to pin me there. I grabbed his foot and cranked it, which knocked him off balance. I watched as he struggled to right himself, his massive weight working against him. For a moment he teetered on the edge of the stair, his arms paddling, about to fall. I quickly swept my legs behind him and pushed him back toward the landing where he regained his footing. It was likely more than he'd ever do for me. I got to my feet.

"I'm a PI working a case. You're chasing the wrong person. Stop that man."

"Down on your knees," Flabby Guard barked. So much for my saving him from a fall.

"I don't have time for this." I barreled past him, took the stairs two at a time, heading for the third floor. The guards could stand there all day and bark orders at the wall. Fleece was on the move.

"Got a monkey on your tail, Raines," Fleece called from below me. "Why'd you kill that crazy man? What'd he ever do to you?" His booming laugh echoed in the narrow stairwell. His taunting was wearing thin. He'd get no response from me. I wasn't interested in goading him, just catching him.

"Stop," Tiny Guard yelled. She was close behind me, surprisingly fleet of foot for a jittery munchkin. Her lumbering partner was behind her. I could tell by the closeness of his wheezing.

"You want to help?" I yelled back to her. "Radio ahead. Tell them to lock the doors."

I peered over the inner railing and could see Fleece taking the stairs two at a time. He was almost home free.

"I said stop," Tiny Guard said. She was gaining fast. What'd she do? Run track in high school?

I tried stepping up my pace, but I didn't have much left. "Cass Raines. I'm a PI. Check with the cop on the eighth floor, or Detective Ben Mickerson. Now either help me catch this guy, or back the hell off me!"

"Almost there," Fleece said. "Sorry I got to bounce."

I wanted to take off my shoe and torpedo it down at him, but it would only slow me down. I hit the landing, turned for the last flight. Just then, something crashed into me from behind and knocked me to the floor. It was Tiny Guard. She landed hard, pressing her full weight down on me, a pointy knee gouging into my sore spine.

"Are you freaking kidding me right now?" I yelled.

"I said stop. I meant stop."

I could feel her fumbling for her zip ties. "Get off of me. I'm losing him!" I bucked and squirmed trying to flick her off, but she held on tight, as though I were a mechanical bull at Gilley's. I twisted around violently, a dangerous scream gurgling up out of my throat. I shoved her back full force, sending her sliding backward into the wall by the seat of her polyester pants. I came up off the floor nearly homicidal. She did, too. I didn't want to fight her. I turned for the stairs.

"Hey," she called out.

I turned my head. She blasted me with pepper spray. "Son of a bitch." My eyes clamped shut, stinging unbearably. I staggered back from the stairs, my face on fire. The howl I emitted was partly from pain and partly from outrage.

"Down on the ground," she ordered.

My eyes flooded over with toxic tears, and my nose began to run like Niagara Falls. The stairwell began to spin like a child's top. From below me came the sound of a crazy cackle. It was Fleece gloating.

"Better luck next time, PI Raines. I'll tell the boss you said hello."

The sound of the stairwell door slamming shut behind him echoed in my ears, along with the blare of security alarms. I coughed uncontrollably, the pepper spray coating my throat with chemical fire. "He's . . . gone!" I croaked, unable to see, to focus, to breathe. I knew not to rub my eyes. That would only spread things around. Instead I stood there stinging, burning, blinded, wanting to strangle something, someone. I could smell the spray on my skin, on my clothes, in my hair.

A hulking silhouette descended the stairs. I couldn't see detail, only a giant moving mass, but I knew it was Flabby Guard. He'd finally caught up. All I could do was stand there and blink and drip and whimper. Fleece was gone. I'd had him. "Good job, Lynch," Flabby huffed.

"You're . . . idiots." The coughing started then, and I slid to the floor. "Do you know . . . what you just did?"

"Quiet," Tiny Guard ordered.

I thought, 'quiet my ass,' but couldn't say it.

The stairwell door flew open. I peered through a flood of tears to see the cop from Yancy's room bursting through it. Had it really taken him that long to find us? "That's her," he said, his breathing ragged.

It hurt to breathe. The spray was in my lungs, gnawing at them.

"We got her," Tiny Guard boasted, reholstering the pepper spray. I squinted up at her, barely seeing her, but even Stevie Wonder couldn't have missed the self-satisfied grin on her gnome-like face. She looked as though she'd caught Public Enemy No. 1 and wanted to take full credit for it.

"I'll take it from here," the cop said. "She just killed a guy on eight."

Chapter 31

I shook my head, hoping to clear it. What did I just hear him say? *I* killed a guy? "Wait. What?" I croaked out between coughs. "Are you out of your mind?"

"I got you running out of a room with a dead guy in it," the cop said. "Let's go."

Up until then, all I could think about was Fleece. How I had him, and how now I didn't. How he knew my name, and how he all but flipped me the bird on his way out the door. This was a new wrinkle, a new worry. I didn't think it possible for me to get any angrier than I already had been. I was wrong.

One of the three grabbed me by the arm and marched me out the door, me straining against the hold, my lungs as dry as tobacco leaves. Quiet? They weren't going to get quiet. They weren't going to get easy either. I'd had him. I'd come as close as I'd ever been to finding out who killed Pop. Maybe it was Fleece, maybe not, but I'd never know now, thanks to these three. And Yancy was gone. I promised him I'd keep him safe, and I didn't. His death was another heavy stone in my pocket, another spent life I'd have the burden of carrying with me till forever. No, quiet was the last thing I was going to be.

* * *

The security office was about the size of a large broom closet, and I paced around it, fuming. The guards were gone. Spray and go, that's how they rolled. The jowly cop, too, had quietly melted away somewhere. They left me here, in the closet, the door locked from the outside. I was a prisoner, for all intents and purposes. I could still smell the pepper spray, taste it on my tongue. It stuck to my skin like a film of sticky goop. I wanted it off me, and I wanted out. I wanted to smash something, anything, into a million pieces. My head throbbed and my mouth was dry. I would have killed for a glass of ice-cold water.

I thought about Yancy. Would he end up in some potter's field somewhere? Was there anyone out there who even gave a damn? I told him he'd be safe with me. He wasn't. I'd promised Jimmy Pick the same. What was wrong with me? I massaged my forehead trying to loosen the headache's hold. Everything ached. I felt like shit and probably looked it, too. Fleece's cackling echoed in my head. The door opened, and I reeled around ready for a fight, but it was only Ben.

"I had him," I croaked before he could speak. My eyes felt as though someone had poured a bucket of sand in them.

"What the hell?" he asked, bewilderment blanketing his face. "I get you in here on the sly to talk to Gantt, and all hell breaks loose? I said meet me at the nurses' station. I get up there, alarms are blasting, he's dead, and you're hauling ass all over the hospital."

"The guy was coming out of Yancy's room. Your cop sure in hell wasn't going to chase after him."

"So you figured you'd do Pierce's job for him, that it?"

"He was off the door. Down the hall. He's a hack. He's less than a hack. He's . . ." I searched for a word, but my brain wouldn't cooperate. "He's a slug. You're assigned to the door, you stick to the door. Simple." I went back to pacing. It was a small office; my laps were short. "Yancy's dead because of him. Maybe because of me, too. But he'd have stood a better chance if Pierce had done his friggin' job!"

"Who the hell was the guy?"

"If I knew that, I wouldn't have had to chase him. He runs right out the front door. Me? They tackle and cuff. Pierce didn't stick, and don't even get me started on Frick and Frack out there. I ID'd myself. All they had to do was reach out and grab him. Pepper spray? Really?"

I kicked over a roller chair. I wanted to pick it up and fling it across the room, but there was no across. I marked off the width of an inch or so with my thumb and index finger. "That's how close I was. I had the son of a bitch!"

Ben scrubbed his hands over his face and sighed. "Done venting?"

"Then they lock me in here."

"Can you at least sit? Watching you storm around in a tight little circle like that is making me nauseous."

I plopped down in the chair and reached for the cold compress the ER nurses had given me to cool down my burning skin. I pressed it to my face and waited for relief to set in, my head suddenly too heavy for my neck. I'd coughed myself dry and sounded like a lounge singer after a midnight set.

"I was so close. I had his wallet in my hands. He's on the security cameras—on the floor, in the lobby. There has to be a good shot of his face."

"We're pulling video now. We'll get him." Ben studied me. "What happened to your clothes?"

I sneered and pointed to the clear plastic bag I'd pitched against a wall. My befouled clothing was inside. The pepper spray had eaten into every thread of fabric. I looked ridiculous in the green hospital scrubs they gave me to wear home, or jail, depending on where I was headed, but even they felt like burlap against my raw skin.

"It took me almost a year to break in those jeans. They were my favorite pair. I'll never get that smell out." I stood to pace again. "I'm sending this hospital a bill."

Ben snuffled. "Good luck with that. Right now? They're bucking for putting you in a cell."

I spun around to face him, my eyes narrowed. "*Me* in a cell?"

"Pierce says he found you standing over Gantt, the pillow in your hands. Nurses saw you running out of the room."

"Why would I kill Yancy and then hit the call button, bringing staff running right toward me?"

"I also talked to the guards and the doctors in the stairwell you scared the piss out of. All of them witnessed a piece of this thing. Now I need your side. Start to finish, from the pillow all the way to the pepper spray. And make it good. I've got CPD brass snapping at my skivvies, Farraday fanning the flames, and hospital suits wagging incident reports in my face."

I gave it to him straight—every kick, every slam, every tumble. The closer I got to the pepper spray, the angrier I got. When I was through talking, I slammed the compress down on the desk. All the cold had gone out of it anyway.

"He was right there. And you know what they did?"

"They grabbed you up instead?"

"Right! They grabbed me up instead!"

"And you're sure he said 'the Boss,' like a title, and not 'Boss,' like a name?"

"There's nothing wrong with my ears, Ben. He knew my name. He knew what I did for a living. He killed Yancy to shut him up. He had to be the shooter in the park, the one who killed the guy wearing Yancy's jacket. He rousted the others looking for Yancy. He has to be one of the wolves. It fits."

Ben shook his head. "Maybe, maybe not. It sounds logical, all of it, but it's not exactly rock-solid evidence. One thing's for sure, though, this thing is getting messier by the minute."

I began to pace again, running it through, searching for light where there didn't seem to be any. "What about the stuff out of his wallet?"

From his coat pocket, he pulled a sealed evidence bag with bits of paper in it. "It doesn't look like much, but we'll look it over."

I reached for the bag, he yanked it back. "Cop eyes only. We got it."

"Then what about the stuff from Pop's diary and Bible? The initials, the numbers I told you about? Neither Lillian Gibson or George Cummings have called me back. That could be important. And don't forget my father could be hooked up in all of this. He had motive."

Ben rolled his eyes. "Now you're fingering your own father? That's it. This is the end of the road for you on this."

"What?"

"You heard me. I've said it before. Hell, everybody's said it before. But you are absolutely stepping off this case, right here and right now."

I sputtered, unable to find words.

Ben held up a hand to ward off comment. "You moved the needle on this, no doubt. You tossed us some promising leads, found witnesses we missed. Great. But you've also been shot at, your office has been tossed, and two guys have tried to kill you. Besides, the department's close to going after your license, and Farraday's beating the drum loud and long on that."

"They can have it."

"Really? They can have it? C'mon, Cass, get your head in the game!"

"You know why I can't stop."

"I know it's personal. I know you've got a stake in how it shakes out, but from here on out, the loop doesn't include you. This bag, whatever we get from this Fleece character, it's all CPD."

"There's nothing legally keeping me from pursuing this, and you know it!"

"Legally? Not until you cross the line, which frankly you've done like a billion times since this whole thing began. Trust me, there's nothing more you can do on this solo." He stared at me. "And I know that look. You're thinking you're going to damn well do as you please, and I'm going to be put in the positon of having to cuff you and take you in, and I don't want any part of that. So take pity on my blood pressure and just go home, will ya?"

I heaved out the monster of all sighs, and chucked the tepid compress into the trash bin. I'd get nowhere arguing with him. He made sense. If our positions were reversed I'd say the same, but there was no way he was getting what he wanted. Surely somewhere deep within him, Ben knew that. He had to at least know me that well. "Where's my gun?"

Ben's eyebrows lifted warily. "Why? You plan on using it?"

"I'm going home. I want my gun."

"Now that's the first sensible thing you've said in days. I got it from the head of security. Fletcher. I knew you'd ask for it." He pulled my gun out of his pocket and handed it to me. "But no way are those scrubs going to hold it."

I looked around the small room, found a roll of duct tape and tore off a few strips. I taped the gun to my calf and pulled the leg of the scrubs down over it. Ben stood watching, his mouth wide open in disbelief.

He shook his head. "That's just wrong on so many levels."

"It's what I've got, all right? I'll worry about the aesthetics later." I headed for the door. "This door better be open when I pull on it, or I'm filing the mother of all lawsuits." I turned the knob. The door opened. "Know that's right," I muttered.

"Cass, I'm serious now."

I headed for the elevator. "Don't follow me. I'm done talking to you."

"Type A personality. Textbook case."

My eyes narrowed dangerously. "I'm flattered to know you've taken time to deconstruct my personality so completely."

Ben adjusted his belt, ignored the sarcasm. "I rode with you for five years. Shit presents itself."

I punched the button for the elevator more times than I needed to. I was in a hurry to get free of the hospital, and quite frankly, of Ben. Standing silently in the elevator car, Ben beside me, waiting for the doors to close, I caught sight of the two guards who took me down in the stairwell. They were holding up a wall at the other end of the hall. The doors began to close, but I reached out and held them open, glaring at the guards. They stared back at me with the same intensity.

"Nice day's work," I yelled. "What'll you do tomorrow? Hold the door open while some guy steals babies from the maternity ward?" I held up my bag of clothes. "And these are going to cost you. Favorite jeans. Pepper spray. Ruined." I pointed an angry finger at Tiny Guard. "The bill's coming to you personally, Half Pint!"

Fuming, she started toward the elevator. I took that as a declaration of war and moved to step off the elevator to meet her, but Ben grabbed me up by the waist, loosening my hands off the doors, which then closed with a quiet whoosh. When he put me down, I reeled on him.

"They're jackleg amateurs!" I said.

"That's right," Ben said. "Get it all out."

I squeezed my eyes shut and drew in a cleansing breath, but it came out as a hacking cough that doubled me over.

Chapter 32

I still couldn't sleep, even though I was dead on my feet and ached and burned all over. The encounter at the hospital ate at me and wouldn't let up, wouldn't let me rest. The old lady in the wheelchair had been a deliberate diversion. It, and the pretty nurse called to help, had drawn the cop away from Yancy's room; now Yancy was dead. I busied myself around the apartment in the wee hours, cleaning out my fridge again, sanitizing my counters, changing perfectly good light bulbs. Busy work. At one point, distracted, I picked up the phone to call Pop and talk things over with him, then remembered. How could I forget?

Before dawn, I went for a bike ride to clear my head of wolves and death and guilt for not being there for Yancy. Eventually, he'd have been able to tell me what I needed to know. That's why he was dead. He'd heard too much, seen too much. How many more lives would slip through my fingers before this was over?

I rode up to the zoo and back, along the path, the lake my only companion. My legs were tired from my mad dash hours earlier, my arm, still recovering from the damage caused by

Jimmy Pick's bullet, throbbed under the strain of keeping the bike steady. I got back home as the sun was rising, fell into bed and finally slept without dreaming, exhaustion managing to keep even good memories of Pop at bay.

The sound of a gunshot startled me awake. There was no mistaking the sound. And it was close. Too close. I checked the clock next to the bed. It was noon. I'd slept like the dead for hours. The blood-curdling screams came next. Marie's, then little Nate's. I bounded out of bed, no shoes, just sweats and a T-shirt. I grabbed my gun off the bedside table and raced for the door, taking the stairs three flights down at a panicked sprint to the street. I yanked the outer door open and tumbled out into the front yard just as a brown sedan sped down the block and turned the corner, black exhaust from a rusty tailpipe trailing after it.

"Cass!"

I reeled to find Marie and Nate huddled together in a small niche behind the front stoop. Their eyes hit mine, wide and petrified, their faces blanched of color, their bodies trembling. I couldn't believe what I was seeing. I stood there, stunned for a second. Surely this was a dream. This couldn't be what it was. Not here. Not Little Nate. Not my home. Mrs. Vincent and Barb raced out the front door.

"Don't! Go back!" I managed to croak out, holding them back with an outstretched arm. "Call 911."

They disappeared quickly, panic hastening their steps. The street came alive behind me as my neighbors filed out of their apartments to gawk at the scene. I heard the low hum of activity, but paid it no heed. My focus was on the huddle: the little boy, his mother. There was no blood that I could see. Their eyes were glassy, fixed. They were in shock. I slid the gun into my waistband, then knelt down and gently tried to separate them, to make sure they were both uninjured, but Marie had a death grip on Nate and wouldn't let go. I let her be. I stood watch instead, shielding them from the street and the onlookers, until the first squad car arrived. It was all I could do. I didn't allow myself to think about what might have been. I couldn't, not yet, or else I wouldn't have been able to stand at all.

The paramedics checked them both out. There were no nicks or wounds, no physical ones anyway. I stood close by, silent, my body freezing, afraid to look away for fear their status would change.

"The car just rushed up and the window came down," Marie told the officers. "And they shot. We ran. Thank goodness, the stairs were there. What if the stairs weren't there?"

I stared at Nate. He was small for his age, just four, full of life and bubbles just yesterday. Today, he sat stone faced, distant, his breathing uneven, labored. He was scared out of his mind. I wanted to cry. Then I wanted to kill the devils inside the brown car. Nate had been four, now he was older somehow. Marie turned to me, her eyes beseeching mine, pleading for answers I didn't have. She was angry, frightened, confused. "He shouted 'Back off, Raines.' That's what he said. He wanted *you*, not us. We could have been . . ." She began to weep. Nate clenched his eyes shut and leaned his body against his mother for comfort, and the rest of my heart, the parts still intact, broke.

Back off, Raines. I could feel Mrs. Vincent's hand on my shoulder and knew it was there to soothe me, but there'd be no solace for me, not soon, maybe not ever, because Nate would never be four again. And someone, me, surely, but someone else, too, would answer for it.

It took some time to sort it all out. The police took the report and canvassed witnesses, then I did a canvass of my own, walking the block, knocking on my neighbor's doors, looking for something, any scrap of information that might help. Marie and Nate went to stay with her mother. Stuart Kallish was downstairs packing up a few clothes and things to tied them all over for a time. I sat in my kitchen, staring at the rooster clock. It was well after three and I hadn't moved in over an hour. I wanted to check on Nate and Marie, but everybody said it was too soon.

Barb handed me a cold can of ginger ale from the fridge. "They'll be fine. You couldn't have known this would happen."

I took the can, but didn't drink. "I should have known. He's packing their things."

"They had a bad scare. They need some time to process it. Marie says they'll stay with her mother for a little while. See how things go."

"They won't be back. She couldn't even look at me."

"Time," Barb said.

I rose from the chair, leaving the soda. "I'm dead on my feet. I'm going to bed."

I went, but didn't sleep, couldn't sleep, and it was becoming a thing. I watched the bedside clock and wondered if Nate and Marie were okay. My brain hurt from pushing it. I kept seeing the car speeding away, kept hearing the screams. Pop, gone. Cesar, gone. Yancy, gone. Now little Nate was going. And Dee Dee was still an unanswered question. Where was she? *Who* was she? I rolled over and buried my head in a pillow to muffle the chaos in my head. One link, that's all I needed. I'd put Cesar and Dee Dee and Pop together, or thought I had, but what connected those three to Buddy and Boss? No, not Boss. *The* Boss. That's what Fleece had said. How did he know who I was? I finally drifted off to an unsettled sleep. There was a lot I had to do, but I couldn't do it yet. My heart hurt too much.

The phone on my nightstand rang, startling me awake. The room was dark, and it was dark outside my bedroom windows. I sat up in bed, picked up the receiver. "Yeah?"

"Cass, get over here. We got him."

I stood. "Whip? What?"

"Bolek," he said. "Me and Pouch had a hunch. Figured this guy wouldn't do his dirt in the light of day, so we started watching through the night. Three days, nothing, right? But tonight we got lucky."

Now I squinted at the clock. I hadn't thought to do it before. Eight-thirty P.M. That couldn't be right, I thought. I couldn't have let that much time get away from me. "Where are you? Where is he?" I searched along the floor for my shoes.

"The church. He got here about fifteen minutes ago. He's here with another guy and they're up on a ladder going after the gutters. Old church, I'm figuring they're copper. They also dragged some stuff out of the basement. Can't tell what. Me and Pouch are waiting till they really get going, then we're going to swoop in and grab their asses."

"No. Don't do that," I said, running for the door, one shoe off, one on. "Hang up. I'm calling the police. You and Pouch stay where you are. Do not move. Whip? Do you hear me? Whip?" He'd hung up on me. "Dammit." I grabbed my keys from the bowl and flew.

I slipped into the alley behind the church. It was dark, half the alley lights still not working. It was par for the course in this part of town. I knew Bolek was dirty. That's why Pop was riding him, keeping him close, likely trying to figure out what he was up to, and then giving him a chance to make the correction on his own. He wouldn't have wanted to turn him in to the police. I, on the other hand, didn't care one fig about Anton Bolek's immortal soul. I wanted him locked up. I wanted to see the cops knock that cocky smile right off his face.

I spotted the dark panel truck parked at the church's back door, well out of range of the two alley lights still working. Stealing copper gutters from a church. Most would assume a man couldn't get any lower. I knew better. There was always lower, like taking shots at a frightened four-year-old. But that didn't mean I'd give Bolek a free pass.

I saw the ladder and two dark figures, one on the ladder, one below keeping it steady. It had to be Bolek on the ladder because the man standing at the base of it was too thin to be him. I looked around for Whip and Pouch, but didn't see them. Maybe they'd done as I'd asked. Keeping to the shadows, I moved forward, watching as Bolek handed something down to his spotter, who then walked it over to the truck, slipped it into the back, and returned to the ladder. Suddenly, two more figures, one tall, one short, darted out from somewhere and grabbed the ladder and the man standing next to it. Whip and Pouch. Whip grabbed the spotter by the collar, pushed him against the church, and held him there. Pouch shook the ladder till it rattled, which forced Bolek to scurry down before it slid out from under him. I groaned, then ran toward them, hoping to get there before someone got hurt.

Whip clocked the spotter, dropping the man to his knees, then turned on Bolek, throwing a roundhouse punch to his face, connecting knuckles with jawbone, which emitted a sickening sound. "You thieving bastard," Whip said. Bolek yelped, fell backward, and slammed to the ground, out cold. Pouch, dressed in all black tonight, including the fanny pack, stood there holding a piece of gutter like a club, bouncing on the balls of his tiny feet, waiting for Bolek to bob up from the ground. He did not. These were petty thieves, not master criminals, and Bolek was in no shape to tangle with Whip, or anyone else for that matter.

When I reached them, I turned to Whip and Pouch, and shook my head. I eyed the gutter in Pouches hands, then narrowed my eyes. He slowly laid it at his feet and backed away. Whip, high on adrenaline, danced around like Muhammad Ali in Manila, itching for more.

"Got him," Whip said. "Lights out. Bam."

I stared down at Bolek and his accomplice. "I see that, though I'm pretty sure I asked you not to get him."

Whip's eyebrows rose unconvincingly. "Really? I must have misheard you. My bad, Bean."

Beneath us Bolek came to, moaning in pain. His companion just sat there and wisely kept his trap shut. Out of the corner of my eye I saw Pouch moving suspiciously, and I turned to face him. "Put it back."

"What's that?"

"Whatever you just palmed from the back of that truck, put it back."

Sheepishly, Pouch eased a shiny screwdriver and wrench from his fanny pack. He grinned. "Can't turn it off, apparently."

I walked over to Bolek, kneeled down in front of him, our eyes holding. "You stole from him. Still he tried to give you a chance, didn't he? You didn't take it. Your loss." The sirens came next. I stood and listened for them. This would be the second time in as many weeks that the police had to race to St. Brendan's in the dead of night

I looked up to find Whip staring at me. "You don't look right. You okay, Bean?"

I looked away. I wasn't, but I didn't want him to see it. "Sure. I'm good. All good."

His eyes bore in. "I know when you're lying."

I smiled weakly, placed a hand on his arm. "Later."

The piercing sound of the sirens grew closer.

"Man, they sure are loud, aren't they?" Pouch said.

"I feel sorry for the neighbors," Whip said.

"I'd invest in a little sound-proofing, myself," Pouch said. "Block it all out."

A beat passed. I turned to stare at Pouch. "What'd you just say?" I'd only been half listening, my mind instead on the things I still had to do. There was my father's alibi still to check out, Fleece, the missing Dee Dee. I'd been too involved in searching for Yancy, waiting for him to be able to talk to me. Now he wouldn't.

"I said I'd invest in some sound-proofing, cut down on all the noise," Pouch said.

Someone else had said much the same thing to me. It came to me in a flash. George Cummings. That's why he said he hadn't heard the sirens the night Pop died. I'd searched around his house, peeking into his windows. Hadn't the car in his garage been brown? A brown Cutlass. A speeding brown Cutlass.

I've got to go," I said to Whip. "You know what to say to the police, right?"

He pulled back, scowled, as though I'd insulted him. "Since I was twelve. Go. Do what you gotta do."

I took off for my car.

The Cutlass had been sitting in George Cummings's two-car garage. I'd seen it again as it sped up my street, after whoever was inside had taken a dangerous shot at my family. I called Ben.

"It's George Cummings," I said. "The brown Cutlass, the guy at the hospital, the assaults on the homeless, Pop and Cesar, all of it."

"I know. We finally tracked Dee Dee through her disconnected cell. It led to her address, which turned out to be Cummings's place. And, thanks to Father Ray's cryptic scribblings you showed me, we found Dee Dee and her mother at Hathaway House."

HWY. That's what it was. Not a highway, but Pop's shorthand for Hathaway.

"Cummings is Dee Dee's stepfather? He's the one Pop tried to make peace with. And you found her and her mother at a women's shelter?"

"Guess that says a lot about their home life. Anyway, we're rolling on his house now."

"He won't be there. He'll have gone under by now." I

wanted to kick myself for the time I'd wasted. What if that had been all the time Cummings had needed to get away? That pot-shot at my place could have been his last play."

"We still have to roll on it," Ben said. "Sit tight. I'll let you know when we grab him up."

A close friend of Pop's, he'd said. He'd offered his help in finding Pop's killer and then sat at his memorial weeping like a child. All the while, he'd orchestrated three deaths. He was Yancy's wolf in sheep's clothing, had to be. And now Yancy's roaring polar bear made sense. It was the white van from Cum-mings's yard, the one he was working on when I met him, the one Cummings drove to the lot at Gentle Peace to check on Dee Dee, the one Lillian Gibson said had the faulty muffler you could hear a mile away. I felt as though I might be sick. George Cummings had been one of Pop's pall bearers, hiding behind smiles and rosary beads while I ran all over town trying to figure it all out. And then there was Nate. A wave of fury overtook me, and I could barely contain it. I couldn't sit tight, or sit still, I just couldn't. I headed out looking for George.

I walked the perimeter of Cummings Contracting, studying the chain fence for weak spots. No white van this time. The bay doors were down. The lights were off. It didn't look like any-one was inside. Maybe I'd made the wrong choice. Maybe I should have gone to his house and waited with the cops. I switched off my phone and slipped it into my pocket, then eased out my standard equipment from the glove box—pick-locks, gloves, flashlight, chewing gum—the last item to steady my nerves. If Cummings wasn't here, then maybe he'd left something behind that would tell me where he went. I'd make it work. I had to make it work.

Sticking to shadows, I quietly jogged around to the back, looking for a way to get inside. I really did not want to have to scale razor wire. I'd had a rough night already, a rough couple of weeks, as a matter of fact, and had no desire to break my neck on top of everything else. The metal chain and padlock on the back gate matched the set out front, which dashed all hopes of my getting in without exerting any effort.

Resigned, I studied the fence for a good, dark spot to start my climb, but then quickly spotted a small section of fence where the links had come loose, creating a very small, but expandable breach. I searched the ground for something strong to pry open a wider gap, but there was nothing available. Then I remembered the pipe in my trunk and ran back to get it. The pipe was for emergencies. Maybe breaking into a murderer's business didn't exactly rise to the level of one, but I was going to use it anyway. Back at the fence, pipe in hand, I ran the plan over in my head.

Make a hole. Get in. Look for a hint to where he might have run. Get out without getting caught.

I slipped on my gloves and quietly got to work.

I peeled back more of the fence, looking over my shoulder, checking the street, chewing the gum, envisioning Cummings behind bars wearing an orange jumpsuit. When I'd made a big enough hole, I slipped through the gap, then slowly rolled the pipe back through to the other side to pick up on my way back to the car. I ran for the back door, then had a terrifying thought. What if Cummings had an alarm? Had I just worked up a sweat for nothing? I trained my flash along the glass in the back door, looking for wired circuits. I didn't see any, but that meant nothing. Alarms were getting more sophisticated every day.

I turned back and eyed my point of escape. If I picked this lock and the horn of Gabriel blew, I was going to have to haul ass. I mentally ran through my dash and scramble through the wire, then flicked the flashlight beam down to my shoes to make sure my laces were tied tight and offered up a prayer for safekeeping, not at all sure tender mercies extended to those willfully trespassing on another man's property.

Squatting down, I began to slowly tickle the lock's driver and key pins. Minutes went by, and I was still at it. I gasped in relief when I heard the familiar slide, slide, click. I was in. George Cummings's office wasn't much—desk, chair, another desk, another chair, a file cabinet. I slid a couple of desk drawers open, but they were empty. A bulletin board made of cork hung on the wall with colorful push pins stuck into it, but there was nothing on the board for the pins to hold up. On one of the desks there was a week-old newspaper gathering dust. I fanned through the pages on a desk calendar, but Cummings hadn't written anything down in weeks and there were no dates circled that would indicate he had anything pending. He was right. His business wasn't doing well at all. I shivered inside my jacket. The heat was off. A flick of the light switch yielded no result. The electricity was off, too.

I spotted the door to the vehicle bay and went for it. Get in. Get out. It was fast becoming my mantra. I turned the knob. The door was locked. Back to the picklocks, but this time, I managed to shave a good minute off my time.

I stepped softly into the dark, cold bay, which reeked of motor oil, old rubber, and rags. Sweeping my light toward the center of the room, the beam instantly bounced off the chrome of a brown car, a Cutlass Supreme. The car was just sitting there as bold as you please. On the other side of it sat the white van with CUMMINGS CONTRACTORS stenciled on the side, and beyond that, a door leading back out into the yard. I flicked off the flash. There was just enough moonlight coming in through the bay doors to navigate by.

I padded over and felt the car's hood, because that's what you did when you checked out a car parked somewhere you didn't expect to find it. The hood was warm. I drew back my hand, froze in place, the moment as chilling as watching someone pull back the hammer on a revolver pointed at your head.

"That's how you pick a lock?" The booming voice, part playful, part chilling came from behind me.

I reeled around to meet the source and watched as Fleece Jacket stepped out of the shadows and smiled. He took a step toward me, his right hand buried deep in his pocket, the pocket bulging. He was armed.

"Knew you'd make it here sooner or later."

I gripped my flashlight. I could maybe use it to bash in his head. My gun, unfortunately, was in my pocket, the butt gummed up with glue from the duct tape, safe and sound, and useless to me. There was no way in hell he was going to let me reach for it. He'd come to my home; he'd come after my family. I wanted to kill him.

"There are locks on the gates," I said.

He grinned, fished into his pockets and came up with a key ring. He jangled the keys.

"Lights off in the office?" I asked.

"Those little bulbs come right out of those sockets."

"And you're driving George Cummings's car."

He grinned. "Fair trade."

"And you are?" I asked. "You know who I am already. Seems only fair."

"Don't matter, does it?"

"They'll need something to put on your booking sheet."

He chuckled. "You're funny for a dead woman."

I scanned the room looking for an out. I turned back to find him staring at me. "Funny, I don't feel dead."

We locked eyes, neither of us saying anything for a time. He was wearing the same thing I'd seen him in last, the fleece jacket now ripped at the sleeve. I hoped I'd ripped it. "You flipped that lady out of her wheelchair."

He bowed his head slightly as if acknowledging a compliment. "Needed the big dumb cop to move."

"Then you killed Yancy Gantt."

"That his name?" He shrugged, appearing unconcerned with trivialities. "I got to do what the man says do."

I took a determined step forward. "And you shot at an innocent four-year-old and his mother."

He sneered at me. "That was for the hospital."

I was seething inside, but tried not to show it. Maybe I'd get my shot, but first I had to get out of here in one piece.

"George Cummings is your boss." *The* boss, not boss.

Fleece's gaze stayed even, cold. "If you say so."

"This is his business you're standing in."

Fleece looked around as if seeing the place for the first time. "Sure is."

I scanned the bay again without looking like I was doing it.

I stared at the van. White. Like the one Dee Dee's friend remembered, the one Lillian Gibson recalled being loud, the one that had spooked Dee Dee and Cesar at Christmas. Driven by her overprotective stepfather, the one who'd kept her a virtual prisoner, George Cummings.

He caught me looking. "You got a thing for vans?"

"Not particularly."

Fleece grinned. He was in no rush. Who would think to look for him here? Or for me? I furtively surveyed the bay. There wasn't much to it. Concrete walls. Concrete floor. Oil spots. Along the walls, hip-high work benches and storage shelves stacked with electrical wire in a variety of lengths and diameters, metal pipes (like the one I'd had before pushing it away outside the fence), and pipe connectors, things I'd normally designate as doohickeys. "So you're his henchman?"

He cocked a finger at me. "Hey, I like that. Yeah, I'm the henchman."

"You killed Yancy, Father Ray, and Cesar Luna?"

"You ask too many questions." He slowly pulled his gun out of his pocket and aimed it at me. It was a cheap automatic, nothing special about it. You could buy one on any street corner anytime of the day or night. "Banger was sniffing around the man's kid. Man didn't like it. The priest thought it was just fine by him. Man didn't like that either. It was personal for the boss, just a job for me."

I moved my hand toward the pocket with my gun in it, but didn't get far.

"Nu-uh. Slide it. Left-handed."

"I could be left-handed," I said.

"Don't matter." He motioned with his gun. "Slide."

I did as he instructed, wincing as I slid a perfectly good gun across the floor to him. Keeping his eyes on me, he moved to pick it up, faltering just a fraction of a second. Was it a lingering effect of our tussle in the stairwell? I didn't care. It was all I needed. I took off, flinging myself over the hood of the cooling Cutlass, smacking down onto the concrete on the other side. I hit the ground moving and duckwalked fast around the back of the van. I made it to the door and tried the knob. The door was locked.

In frustration, I pounded the door with my fist and was surprised at how flimsy it was. Now why invest in padlocks and monster chains and then hang crappy plywood on your hinges? Where was the logic?

"You tired of fooling around yet?" Fleece wanted to know from the other side of the room. He wasn't even bothering to follow. That's how cocky he was.

"I'll let you know when I'm tired of fooling around."

I crawled back over to the van and popped off its front hubcap. It was light in my hands. When did they stop making hubcaps out of heavy metal? Used to be, you kicked a cap, you risked breaking a toe. This cheap piece of plastic was an offense to the American auto industry.

"Don't know where you think you're going," Fleece said. "Door's locked. I checked this whole place out."

"Since we've got some time," I said, looking around for something heavier than plastic. "The cops are looking for you. They've got you on surveillance footage from the hospital. They're looking for Cummings, too, so the van and Cutlass are nonstarters as getaway vehicles. Needless to say, you won't get far on foot."

"I'll use your car. Keys are in your pocket, right?"

"I don't like strangers driving my car." I sneered at the hubcap, not at all satisfied with it as a weapon, but what choice did I have? "I have the driver's seat set just right, the mirror at just the right angle."

"Trust me, you'll be beyond giving a shit."

I took a quick bead and slung the hubcap, Frisbee-style, toward the bay door windows. The cap had a fat chance of shattering the glass, but the clatter the discus made startled Fleece enough that he was momentarily distracted. That's when I hit the flimsy door with all the force a desperate body could muster, popping it open with all the punch of a child's jack-in-the-box. Night air smacked me in the face as I tumbled out into the yard, scrambled to my feet, and took off in an all-out run, praising cheap building materials and giving thanks for over-confident henchmen.

It didn't take long for the chase to start. I could hear Fleece behind me. It wouldn't be long before he caught up. Of course, he now had two guns, his and mine. If he really thought about it, he'd discover that he didn't have to run after me at all, just aim and fire, but I tried not to think about that. I kept running, making a beeline for the hole.

A shot rang out and a bullet whizzed past my ear. Dammit, I was tired of getting shot at. I checked myself for pain. Nope. No pain, except for the pain I brought in with me. Guess he missed. I kept running. Almost to the fence now. Another shot and the sound of big feet coming up behind me. Still no pain. Hot damn. I was on a veritable roll. I touched the fence, slid my hand through the gap, then turned back to see how much time I had, discovering I had little to none. Fleece was just a few seconds off me. I knelt down. He rushed up. And when he got within range, I swung the pipe upward, beaning him hard along the side of his head. He was out before he hit the ground, the two guns skittering and spinning away from him like empty bottles in a kids' kissing game.

"That's right!" I said, taunting him, pumped up on adrenaline. I grabbed up my gun and kicked his far away from him. "Henchman, my ass."

I rolled him over and checked his pockets, flicking a cautious look behind me for clueless hospital guards. The wallet was empty, except for his ID. His name was Amon Jarvis. It was a dumb name. Who looks down at a cute little newborn and comes up with a name like Amon? I tossed the ID and the wallet down beside him. I had all I needed. I scrambled out of the fence hole and ran for my car. I called 911 so Amon wouldn't die before a jury sent him to prison, then I called Ben to tell him where he could find him. One down. One to go.

Ben didn't show up alone, of course; he came with Weber and a whole bunch of other cops. Amon was still out, which was just fine by me. He didn't look nearly as lethal out cold as he did while awake. Before long, there were a ton of cops crawling like ants all over Cummings's property, every last one of them eager to hear what happened to poor old Amon.

"That's the guy I chased out of Yancy's room."

Ben stared at me. He didn't look happy. He checked his watch. "I talked to you not an hour ago. Thought I said sit tight."

"I've just identified a murderer and presented him to you on a silver platter. Do you really want to quibble over tiny details?"

He bristled.

Weber jumped in. "So why were you two in Cummings's place?"

I took a moment. "Amon Jarvis is doing Cummings's dirty work. He was hiding out inside. You'll have to ask him why."

"And, again, how'd he get knocked out?" Weber pressed. He looked slightly amused, which, I could tell, wasn't sitting well with Ben.

"He fell," I said. It was absolutely true. I bashed him and he fell. He fell like a frigging tree.

Ben rolled his eyes. "How?"

"Pretty impressively, as a matter of fact. You should have seen it."

Neither one of them thought that was funny.

The questions continued long after the paramedics bundled Amon up and sped him off. Same questions asked by different detectives, each testing for inconsistencies. I told it backward and forward the same each time—excluding only the picklocks, the gloves, the peeling back of the fence, the pipe, and the chewing gum. I didn't need to draw them the whole picture. They saw the padlocks. I blamed the hubcap fling and the busted door on Amon. That's what he got for trying to kill me. Twice.

"But you still haven't explained why you're here and how you got in," Weber asked. I refused to look at Ben, but I could feel his steely gaze searing into the side of my head.

"I told you all the important things. Jarvis killed Yancy. He tried to kill me. He admits working for Cummings. He's who you should be looking for."

"You broke into the man's place," Ben said. "You knocked him out with that dumb pipe you keep in your trunk."

I scoffed. Dumb pipe? That pipe saved my bacon. "How do you know what I keep in my trunk?" Ben pulled at his hair, turned around in circles.

"Did you know the guy was there?" Weber asked. I looked

from one to the other. If Ben kept his dance up for too much longer he'd summon rain. I shook my head.

Ben stopped, faced me. "So, you went in there blind with no backup?"

"I repeat. I just caught a killer. Can we please just focus on the endgame here?"

"Sounds like he almost caught you," Weber said.

I zipped up my jacket. "Almost doesn't count. We've got to find Cummings. Our advantage is he doesn't know we've got Amon. He might still think he can pull this off, if he gets me out of the way. He doesn't like loose ends, according to Yancy, so he'll try to tie it all up. Or would you rather I just sit tight and wait for him to make his play, test the fates?"

Ben placed his arms akimbo. "How the hell do you know all of this?"

I shrugged. "Doesn't matter how. I know, now you know, so let's do something about it."

"No," Ben said. "Go home." I opened my mouth to protest. "Go home or go to jail."

"I'm supposed to just hang around at home twiddling my thumbs waiting for a phone call?"

Ben said, "Do you have a star?" I pulled a face. The question was obviously rhetorical. "Then the answer is yes. That's exactly what you're supposed to do. We have been doing our jobs, just so you know. We ID'd this guy an hour ago from surveillance footage at the hospital. He lives in a halfway house not far from here. Career perp, in and out of prison like they had a turnstile at the door. We even reached out to his parole officer. This Jarvis is, supposedly, enrolled in some post-prison mentoring program meant to ease the transition from prison to outside life. I guess we know how well that turned out for him."

"George Cummings volunteers all over the place," I said. "That's the link. Amon's an admitted murderer and a psychopath, and I want in."

"You're out," Ben said. "Good and out. One bullet's enough for one lifetime, wouldn't you say? Call it tough love. Call it whatever you want, but hit the bricks . . . or cool your heels in a box. Up to you."

I got in my car, started it, and drove away.

I knew the unit would sit on Cummings's place in case he came back. He was a murder suspect now. He had to know there was no place he could hide, I thought. All of this, all this time, hadn't been about a break-in or a stolen Bible; it hadn't been about a racist janitor pilfering copper gutters from the church. It had been personal, close, evil. It had been about George Cummings, his grip on the necks of his wife and step-daughter, his control over every aspect of their lives—what they wore, where they went, who they talked to. It was about one man's obsession, a futile grasp for the perfect family that had been threatened by the influence of Cesar Luna. Had Cummings tried to warn Cesar off, and he wouldn't go? Was what happened at the church a feeble attempt toward that end?

This is what Pop somehow got in the middle of; Jarvis said he interfered with the man's family, but that still didn't explain why he had to die. Was Cummings unhinged enough to mis-judge help for interference? Was he that far gone? Didn't mat-ter. The police had Amon. It was only a matter of time before they had Cummings, too.

It was well after midnight when I slipped my key into my door. I felt light somehow, as though a giant weight had been lifted from my shoulders. The lights were out. I tiptoed past my guest room, not wanting to wake Barb, but noticed that the door to her room was partway open. I flicked on the light, peeked inside. The bed was empty, still made. Her stuff was still here, her knapsack, the dust-caked hiking boots she'd worn halfway around the world. Where was she? Had she gone home to her Mom's? I slid my phone out of my pocket, hoping she'd left me a voicemail or text telling me where she'd be. The tiny

blue light flashing told me I'd missed some calls while Amon
Jarvis was chasing me around in the dark. I punched up the last
message.

"Yeah, it's me." It was Barb. "And my twentieth call. Anyway—*again*—George Cummings called. He says he remembered something that could be important. We're headed over to
the church now. Follow us. Call me. Bye."

I checked the time stamp. It had been three hours since Barb
had left the call for me. I doubled over, feeling as though someone had just kicked me in the gut. George Cummings. The church.
She said we. Who was "we"? I redialed, my hands shaking. Somewhere along the way I forgot to breathe. The phone rang and
rang, then someone picked up.

"Took you long enough." It was Cummings.

A ferocious rage that frightened even me bubbled up, blur-
ring my vision, setting my skin on fire. "Listen to me, you murdering son of a bitch!"

"No, *you* listen." His voice was calm, unhurried, as though
he had all the time in the world. "You just wouldn't let it go,
wouldn't stop. You're just like him, sticking your nose into
other peoples' business."

I slid down the wall to the floor, my legs suddenly too weak
to hold me. "The cops have Amon. It's over. Whatever you do
from this point, you'll have to do on your own. Are you up for
that?"

He paused. Was he reconsidering? God, I hoped he was. Up
to now, as far as I knew, Amon had been the one to get his
hands bloody. Was Cummings prepared to go it alone?

"Who's there with you? I want to talk to Barb. Now."

There was a long pause. "I'm up for it." The four words, de-
livered without feeling, sent a shiver down my spine. No feeling, no humanity. I was in trouble.

The flutter in my throat felt like I'd swallowed a nest of but-
terflies. "Put someone on the phone right now, George, or I

swear . . ." I stopped when he began to laugh uncontrollably, and I wondered if he'd suffered some kind of psychotic break.

"No police, just you. You're the last. Ten minutes."

The line went dead.

I shot up from the floor, snatched up my keys, and raced out of my apartment. Ten minutes. My tires squealed as I tore away from the curb. I ignored the stop sign at the corner and all the other stops and traffic signals along the way, tracking the time on the dashboard clock, sweating as time slipped away from me with blocks yet to go.

I'd been right. Cummings wasn't done killing. I was the last, but he couldn't get me without taking my friends first. It's what I feared would happen, that I'd put the ones I cared about in danger; now here it was. Who had he taken besides Barb? She'd said we. Whip? Mrs. Vincent? Why hadn't I checked to see if she had been in her apartment? I slammed a fist against the steering wheel and pressed my foot to the gas, my mind disordered by fear. I took the final corner on two wheels and dovetailed the car into a spot in front of the church with just seconds to spare. I ran for the front steps, slipping my cellphone back into my pocket. For a moment, I hovered at the door, my hands unsteady on the handles. I stood there, just for a moment, just to breathe, then pulled the doors free and walked calmly inside.

There was just enough light emanating from the gothic sconces running along the stone walls to cast an eerie pale over the altar table, the far ends of the wooden pews, and along the side aisles, but not nearly enough to do anything for the transepts. A glance there was like staring into a black hole. I dipped a finger in the font of holy water, mostly ritual, but at this point I needed all the help I could get. I coaxed myself forward, moving up the nave toward the rose window, my eyes slowly adjusting to the dimness.

An alabaster sculpture of the crucified Christ hung over the altar watching my progress; the thick scents of candle wax, incense, and wood polish mingled. This was Pop's church, and he was proud of it, proud of the beautiful mosaics, the gilded altarpiece, the statues of the twelve stoic disciples painstakingly chiseled in pink marble, proud of the people who called this church their spiritual home. He hadn't counted on George Cummings. As I walked, I slowly swept my eyes over the empty pews. Where was Barb? Where was Cummings? Who else did I need to worry about?

"Put your hands up." Cummings's strident voice bounced off the stained glass like an echo whipping around a deep canyon. I stopped cold, slowly raised my hands in surrender. "Keep coming. Join us."

I started again, but stopped again, startled, when the overhead lights suddenly came on and bathed the church in light. I could now see that Barb was sitting in the first pew, along with my father. I pulled up short, confused for a time. How'd he end up here with Barb? Both of them turned to watch me approach, both looked worried. I knew Cummings had to be at the light switch just inside the vestry door, so I waited for him to step out where I could see him. When he did, he slowly made his way toward the altar, a gun in his hand. My heart sank. I'd hoped we could end this easily; the gun dashed that hope. I started walking again, heading for the first pew. Cummings smiled, his eyes holding mine. He looked rock-solid, not the least bit jittery. When I made it all the way up the center aisle, inches from Barb and my father, I stopped.

"Sit," Cummings said. "With them."

I stared at the gun. It was a cheap throwaway, like Amon's. They must have gotten a group discount. Maybe he had seven rounds, maybe more. Whatever the number, he had more than what he'd need. "You took Father Heaton's keys," I said. "That was a mistake."

The church's back door had been jimmied the night of the murders to make Cesar's presence look like a break-in. It had been a ruse, a fake.

He grinned. "Amon's mistake. He was going to plant them on that homeless bum when he found him, but he got the wrong one."

"That homeless bum had a name," I said. "It was Yancy Gantt. He was here when you murdered Father Heaton and Cesar Luna. He saw you."

Cummings smirked. "How was I supposed to know he was sleeping in a pew? He ran out from the back there screaming about wolves. I almost had him, but he got away from me." He angled his head. "I tried to find him. I looked all over the neighborhood. In the end, I figured no one would believe him anyway. He was touched in the head. . . . I said sit."

"I'll stand," I said.

Cummings frowned and looked as though he might argue the point. I wondered how far I could push him, how far he'd let me go.

"Take it or leave it."

Cummings aimed the gun at me. "See? That right there? That's what got us into this mess. You just would not let this thing die. You kept picking at it and picking at it." He glanced nervously at the front doors as though he were expecting someone. I had a pretty good idea who.

"I told you the police have Amon. He's probably talking by now, telling them everything. He didn't strike me as the self-sacrificing type."

Cummings's lips curled into a snarl. "Or you could be lying."

I took a step forward, my eyes on his. "I'm not. I don't usually. I found Amon hiding out at your business. He tried to kill me. He didn't. Let them go. Let's end this."

Cummings didn't look at all like the jovial good old boy I'd met before. This was someone meaner, someone else entirely. Barb sat straight in the pew, outwardly calm. She didn't spook easily. George Cummings didn't know it, but he'd snatched the wrong Covey, not that there was a right Covey to snatch. My father was in a suit again, as though he'd dressed for dinner out and had had his plans diverted. He looked only at me, which made me a little nervous. We hadn't parted on the best of terms. I'd accused him of murder and had stuck to it. I guess I was wrong about that. Maybe that's what his look was for? A great big *I told you so*?

As compelling as the muzzle of Cummings's gun was, I glanced over at the empty confessional where I'd found Pop's body. He was the father I wanted and couldn't save. How strange it was to see the man who'd left me behind sitting in the front pew of his church. Someone, somewhere had a twisted sense of humor. I turned back to Cummings, willing him to drop dead, hoping he'd suffer on his way to Hell. My arms were still up, but getting tired.

I could tell Cummings was thinking things through, likely trying to find an angle that worked for him. He had to know that he couldn't get out of this, that there was no place he could run. I kept talking, looking for an angle of my own. I wondered if the side door was locked, or if the front door I'd just come through was the only way out.

"You trashed my office. Looking for . . . what?" My eyes swept over the altar, the marble floor under it as slick as glass. An ornate runner had been placed at the foot of it to keep parishioners from slipping down and breaking a hip when they came up for their Communion wafer. George Cummings stood there as still as a mountain, watching me, perhaps deciding if he had it in him to kill three more.

"I had to know what you were up to, how close you were

getting. I sent Amon." He grinned. "He had a real good time wrecking your place."

Up until then, I'd regretted beaning Amon with the pipe. Now I wished I'd beaned him twice. The gun didn't look comfortable in Cummings' hand. He wasn't used to holding one, I could tell. His aim wouldn't be steady, his shot wouldn't be sure. That made him all the more dangerous.

"Nothing like teamwork, I suppose. Mind my asking how you two got together?"

Cummings chuckled. "I gave him a job. Turned out he had some pretty impressive skills." He reached into his pocket and pulled out a string of black rosary beads, which he held tight in his free hand.

Hypocrite, I thought. Rosary beads in one hand, a gun in the other. He was a murderer. He'd taken lives in this church, right where he was standing now. Beads. The evidence techs had found beads under a front pew when they swept the crime scene. Hadn't Yancy said something about beads falling like rain?

"You tried to stop Yancy," I said. "That's when you broke your rosary beads."

He held the rosary up. "I have others."

"But the ones the police found," I said, "will have your prints on them."

He looked nervous, but tried not to show it. The gun wavered just a little. "That won't matter after tonight."

"Which one of you killed Father Ray?"

He didn't answer.

"The three of us are dead anyway, right? You've got the gun. What have you got to lose?"

Cummings looked down at the gun in his hand. I could see it made him confident he had the upper hand. I could see the smug satisfaction on his face, almost feel the surge of dominance in the set of his shoulders. "It doesn't matter how or who, only why."

"I already know why. You were trying to keep Cesar Luna away from your stepdaughter. How you did it, the lengths you went to, *that's* where you messed up."

"Father Ray started this. He said it'd be okay to send Dee Dee to Gentle Peace where she met that banger. I did everything, grounded her, took her phone, followed her, nothing worked. Then I found out he knew they were together!"

"That's when you argued in his office," I said. "It wasn't about the homeless."

"He tried to tell me that boy was okay, that he had changed, that everybody deserved a chance to turn their lives around. I told him he'd pay for what he did. I told him I'd *make* him pay."

My jaw clenched. "So you started harassing him, following him, but he wouldn't turn you in."

"He tried to shove that banger down my throat! He had no right!" His angry voice bounced off the church walls. I cringed. This wasn't the place for angry voices.

"So, you lured them both here and killed them," I said.

"Father Ray arranged a meeting. He called it his peace summit, if you can believe that. Like I'd trust him after what he did."

"He hid your family from you," I said. "So they'd be safe."

"They were safe with me! He waited till I wasn't there and snuck them right out from under me!"

So, it wasn't Cummings Mrs. Gibson saw leaving with his family that morning; it was Pop. Good for him, I thought, a slow smile creeping over my face. Good for him.

Our eyes locked. "Cesar's mother deserves to know who killed her son."

Cummings scoffed. "Amon solved that little problem for me."

"And *you* killed Father Ray. Because it was personal."

His eyes narrowed. "He *overstepped*. He put ideas in Janice's head, in Dee Dee's. He wasn't her *father*. He didn't know anything about being a *father*." Barb and I exchanged a look. She could tell Cummings's words landed hard. He grew agitated, began to pace around the marble floor, up and down the runner, tugging at his clothes, his eyes darting around the place.

"I don't believe you about Amon. You'd say anything to get them out of here. If the police had him, they'd be here by now, and you wouldn't be. No, I finish this, you and them, and the clock resets. I get my family back, or I move on and find myself another one" He flicked the gun in the direction of the first pew. "Enough talking. Get over there with them." He raised the gun when I stayed put. "You're not moving."

No, I wasn't moving. I wanted to divide his attention between Barb and my father and me. If I kept him off balance, kept him looking from them to me and back, maybe he'd make a mistake. I eased my arms down. He didn't notice. "One more question, then I will. Who dragged him into the confessional?" I wanted it all, every bit of it.

Cummings paced along the altar runner, up and back, onto the marble floor, back off it. "I didn't drag him; I made him walk there on his own. He needed to confess for disrespecting me. I couldn't get him to put the gun to his head, of course, the stubborn old fool. In the end, I had to do that myself."

I shut my eyes, trying to get the image out of my head, knowing I never would. When I opened them again, they met Cummings's. He laughed. "But you haven't heard the funny part yet. He forgave me. Right before I put his hand on the gun and pulled the trigger. *He* forgave *me*."

My breath caught, held. I stood there, out of the world, yet still in it.

Cummings stepped up to the altar, ran his hand along the table as though he owned it, as though it were his, not Pop's. "Janice is just confused right now, thanks to Father Ray, but I'll turn her around. I'll correct Dee Dee's behavior, too. I surely will." He stared at me, grinning. "You know where they are, I know you do, and you're going to tell me."

He was wrong about that. Hell would freeze over first.

He reached into his pocket and pulled out Pop's datebook. "You blame me. I can see it in your eyes." Cummings had helped carry Pop's casket, all the while knowing he'd been the one to end his life. No, it wasn't blame he saw; it was rage and sorrow. "But it's all in here, every meeting he arranged, all the advice he gave them for getting around me. He wrote it all down." There it was, I thought. I'd been searching for it all this time, and there was Pop's datebook right in front of me. Cummings held it up, smiled. "I took it off his dead body, slipped it right out of his pocket."

Cummings slid a gold plate toward him on the altar and placed the book in it. He eyed a candlestick, felt his pockets. "Anyone have a match?"

"Don't!" I yelled. It was Pop's. I wanted it. "Give it to me."

"It connects the banger to my house," Cummings said, "and to me. I should have burned it already, but doing it now in front of you feels like a better idea, since you seem to want it so bad."

My eyes stayed glued to the book. "Monster," I muttered, my voice carrying.

"What's that? Monster?" Cummings's eyes widened. "Not me, *him*. . . .

"Burning it won't do you a bit of good," I said. "You're done."

Cummings pulled a lighter from his pocket. He'd prepared for this. He meant to burn it, here, in front of me, just like this. "It'll do me a world of good. That's all that matters." He rolled the lighter in his hand playfully, taunting me with it. " Did I ask if you had a gun?"

I said nothing. He walked toward me, away from the plate, back toward the steps. "I didn't, but I should have, right?"

The answer, of course, was an obvious yes, but did he really expect me to suggest a frisk search? Slowly, Cummings pointed the gun at my father's head. Maybe he expected me to cry out, plead and wring my hands, and beg for the old man's life? My non-reaction seemed to confuse him.

"He *is* your father, at least that's what he said."

"You overestimate the depth of our relationship."

Cummings blew out a heavy breath and shook his head, a gesture that, from where I stood, looked an awful lot like pity. "See? Another disrespectful daughter; you're as bad as Dee Dee, thankless, disobedient, ungrateful. So it's okay with you if I shoot him, is that it?"

I glanced at my father sitting there, his eyes as still as death. I didn't see fear in them, as I thought I might; I saw resolve, which unsettled me more. Cummings quietly slipped his finger inside the trigger guard. That's as close as I wanted him to get.

"All right. It's here."

He swiveled the gun back and watched as I took my jacket off, moving in slow motion, not making any sudden movements. I then slowly walked the jacket over to the nearest pew and draped it over the back, as far away from him as I could get it. I lifted the bottom of my sweater and pulled a .9mm out of my tuck holster, held it up. "Come and get it."

Cummings wasn't going for that. "Lay it on the steps and move away."

I did as instructed, setting the gun down, pushing it away from me, and moving back out of reach of it. "Where's this going, George?"

He carefully picked up my gun, sneered. We both knew where it was going. "You're real hard to kill, you know it?" He returned to the altar and put my gun in the gold plate, as though it were a Communion offering. Did he intend to burn it, too? He was moving toward the front pew now, toward Barb and my father, and away from my jacket. I didn't dare look at it. I didn't want to get him thinking about it. I'd slipped my Glock in the pocket, a backup in case I needed it. It was looking like I might. "Maybe one of *them* will be easier."

"Real brave, George! There's not much challenge to killing an old man and a nun, is there? Or are they all you can handle?"

I hoped the taunts would make him angrier, draw him away from the pew. I mounted the altar steps, stood there on the top one, just shy of the runner, an easy target. "You got me here. Deal with me first."

He turned toward me. Good, I thought. That was good. "You shut your mouth!"

"Why don't you come and shut it for me, you murdering nutcase!?"

He didn't move, only watched. I smiled. "I didn't think so. You're just another bully. I'm tired, George. I'm going to sit. Let me know if you change your mind." I sat on the top step, watching him as he stood there, angry, confused, wondering what I was up to, figuring out what he was going to do about it. "All talk, no action. I see now Amon Jarvis was the brains *and* the muscle of the operation."

Barb looked as though she might faint. My father's expression never changed, but he'd folded his hands tightly in his lap, a little too tightly. Cummings headed my way, along the wide runner, the edge of it within arm's length of me. The gun in his hand was there to prove just how capable he was. I braced, biding my time till he got just a little closer. I watched his feet while I appeared not to watch them, then, when he hit the right spot, I reached down and yanked the runner out from under him, tripping him up. I bolted up, watching, as he fought unsuccessfully to regain his footing. His arms windmilled out; he teetered on his heels. When he hit the floor, his head bounced back, and the gun flew out of his hand, clattering to the marble and spinning away like a child's top, the fast-moving metal scratching, twirling across the floor.

I tracked the skittering gun, then turned to Barb, my father. "Get out of here, both of you!" Neither of them moved. "Go, I said!"

I searched the floor frantically, my hungry eyes sweeping right, left, and back again. I needed the gun. There. I spotted it. It had come to rest beside the organist's bench halfway between the vestry door and the altar table. I took off running for it, knowing Cummings was struggling to get up, to get his feet untangled from the runner. I knew two things at that moment: the one who got to the gun first probably wouldn't die, and the last one to get to it probably would.

Cummings was up now and headed for me. I dove for the gun and reached out for it, my hand clenching the grip. I had it. I wouldn't die. I heard a roar behind me and turned, horrified to find Cummings standing over me, reaching out. Before I could move, crawl away, or shoot, he stomped down on my right knee with his full weight, and I let out the mother of all screams, the ferocity of it bouncing off the walls, rattling the candlesticks. He grabbed for the gun, but I slung it away before he could touch it, sending it sliding again along the shiny floor out of his reach, and out of mine.

My knee was on fire, the pain white-hot and seering. I lay there waiting to get my breath back, looking up into the same face Pop had, finding nothing human, nothing decent in it. And then it began to rain hymnals.

The first hit Cummings squarely in the back of the head, stunning him. The second got him in the same spot, and he fell to his knees, shielding his head in his hands. The next barely missed my head. My right leg went numb, the agony nearly blinding, but still I thought it strange that it was raining hymnals. The next salvos, hymnals four, five and six, knocked Cummings off his knees. That was my shot.

I lifted myself up, muffling another scream. It was Barb pitching the books. She hadn't gone, as I'd told her to, and she had excellent aim. I flipped over on my stomach and slid along the floor, searching for the gun I'd tossed away. Sliding, dragging my right leg, I swam along the floor, my knee a throbbing mess of uselessness. I stopped a moment, nauseous, listening for the sound of the hymnals finding their target before starting up again.

It was slow going, my arms straining to do the work. I didn't see the gun. It wasn't where I thought it should be. I had to stop again, sweat beading on my brow and upper lip, my eyes watering from the pain. The gun was gone. It didn't compute. *Why* was the gun gone? Then I remembered the altar plate. My .9mm was in the altar plate.

I spun around, swam in the opposite direction, toward the altar table. It took forever, or felt like it. The hymnals kept coming. I pulled myself up, biting my lip, ignoring the fact that my knee wouldn't bend, balancing my weight entirely on the only working leg I had left. The plate was there, Pop's datebook, too, the gun was not. It made no sense. I grabbed the book and stuffed it into a pocket. Mine now. I glanced back at Cummings. He was lying on his back, heaving for air, done in by church books. Barb stood by, an armful more, waiting to hurl them too. And there was my father with a gun in his hands, the gun pointed at Cummings. It was my gun from the altar plate.

"Don't you move," he warned.

I hobbled toward him, hopped mostly. "No. Stop." I held my hands out. "Give me the gun."

My father's eyes smoldered with fury. It was a side of him I don't think I'd ever seen before. "No one messes with *my* little girl!"

I stared at him, not sure what to make of the display. Where'd that come from? What little girl? Who was this man? "He's done," I said, wiggling my fingers insistently. "Give it to me." He gave Cummings a final look, then reluctantly handed the gun over. "Now both of you, run! Get going!"

Barb didn't move. My father didn't move. "Barb. Drop the friggin' books and get out of here. Take him with you."

"Look at you," she said, her dander good and up. "We're not leaving."

I pointed toward the front of the church. "Someone has to call the police. Will you get out of here?!"

That did it. They raced down the center aisle, looking back every other step to check to see if I needed an assist, finally disappearing through the doors, finally safe. I bit my lip as a wave of pain shot through me. When I turned around, Cummings wasn't where I'd seen him last. He stood behind the altar table, fully recovered now from the hymnal missiles, holding the gun I hadn't been able to find. For a half second, I forgot my knee and wondered peevishly how he was able to find it when I couldn't.

He looked down at the gun in my hand. "Drop it, or I drop you, then I go after the other two." My hand tightened on the gun. His eyes narrowed. "You know I'll do it."

I nodded. I did know he'd do it. I lay the gun at my feet.

"Kick it to me," he said.

It took some doing on my part to kick it. My right leg felt like it didn't belong to me. Still, I managed to slide the gun toward him. "You ruined everything," he said through clenched teeth, as he kicked the gun farther away, making damn sure I couldn't get to it. He didn't need it, after all. He had the semi he'd brought with him. "I'm going to kill you."

I searched his face. It looked like he meant it. I limped backward, managing to angle myself along the side of the altar table.

"In this beautiful church," I said. "The one you said you loved so much? Look at that Italian marble."

Cummings' turned to look, and I took off in a crippled sprint, my knee barely holding me up, bone gnashing against bone with every step I took. I could tell it was wrecked, but I grit my teeth and dug into every quick, unstable step. It was a sickening sound, bone against bone, and I was pretty sure that whatever was going on down there, it wasn't going to be good—medically speaking. It was one more thing to hate George Cummings for.

As I brushed past the first pew, I grabbed my jacket from the back and hopped, trotted, and shambled quickly for the front doors. Cummings fired once and the bullet splintered the top of a pew near me. I ducked and slid into a row, landing hard, half on, half off a long, padded knee rest. The impact didn't do my knee any good. I muffled a scream as I clumsily worked the gun out of my jacket, listening for Cummings. I was drenched in sweat. I laid my forehead on the knee rest for a moment and closed my eyes, unable to feel my right foot.

"You're dead!" Cummings yelled.

From the sound of his voice he was still a good distance away. Regrouping? I popped my head up just above the top of the pew to check. It hurt to breathe, and every breath hurt more than the one before it. I couldn't stay where I was, and I hurt too much to want to move. Neither option left me in a good place. My mother's ring dangled in front of me like a lazy pendulum. It was supposed to bring me good luck. I wondered, as I hung out on the knee rest with a wrecked knee that felt like the Devil himself had done a demon's jig on it, when the luck would kick in.

"You may as well give up," Cummings said, getting closer.

Quietly, I lay my gun down on the kneeler under me, grabbed the ring, kissed it, then quickly flipped it back inside my sweater. Time to roll. I picked up the gun, gripped it, then as quietly as I could, eased off the kneeler and pushed it to its upright position, which gave me more crouching room. Then I reached out and eased up the kneeler in the pew in front of me, so I could crawl under the pew I was in, up to the next. I needed to put as much distance between the stepdaddy psycho and me, even if I had to do it one row at a time. My hand was sweaty on the grip of my gun as I crawled and slid toward the front doors, dragging my jacket along behind me. I might need it. Barb would have definitely called the police by now, but until they got here, it was just one-legged me and crazy George.

"I had this all under control!" he screeched, completely unhinged now. By the sound of his voice I could tell he hadn't covered much ground. What was he doing? Maybe he figured he had plenty of time to run me down. I cleared another two rows, even though navigating the low kneelers with a busted knee was tantamount to climbing the Himalayas with a yak on my back. "I'm going to enjoy killing you even more than I enjoyed watching that banger die!"

My pew crawl wasn't doing me much good. I was moving far too slow. There were way too many pews. It was only a matter of time before he found me. I pulled myself up into a one-legged crouch. I peeked up over the top of the pew. Cummings was checking pews no more than twenty feet away. It wouldn't be long now.

I braced, took a breath, and pushed off into a pathetic trot across the center aisle to the other side. Cummings fired twice, splintering more wood. I checked myself quickly for bullet holes. Free and clear, but my predicament hadn't much changed. I was across the aisle, but on another knee rest.

Shit, shit, shit, shit, double shit. I bit down hard on my lower lip, then squeezed my eyes shut trying to think beyond the pain. *Think. Think. Think.* Cummings has his semi, that's, what? Seven rounds? Nine? My .9mm's lying on the floor up there, thankfully, out of his reach, but, unfortunately, it's out of mine, too. I have the Glock. That's fifteen rounds. I wiped more sweat from my forehead, doing the rapid math in my head.

So, seven rounds fully loaded, and why wouldn't it be fully loaded, right? He'd fired three times already, hadn't he? I focused in, trying to recreate the rhythm of the shots in my head, but pain kept getting in the way. Had it been *boom . . . boom* or *boom . . . boom, boom*? I slid a glance toward the front doors, hoping Barb wasn't behind them waiting to burst in with hymnals.

I grabbed my jacket, got a good hold on it, then flung it up into the air. Cummings fired once, the loud boom followed by another. I cowered on the kneeler, not moving, listening to Cummings as he checked his ammo.

"Two bullets left," he said. He was close. I could hear him breathing. "I only need one."

"Moron," I muttered, though I was thankful for the confirmation. And he was right. He only needed one.

I wiggled out of my shoe, tossed it. He shot at it. One round left. "Too bad you kicked my gun away," I called out. "You could have used the extra rounds. Not to brag, but I'm a much better shot than you are."

My knee throbbed, I felt nauseous, and I didn't want to have to fire a gun in Pop's church, I really didn't. Cummings didn't answer back, but I could hear him moving. I got ready to make my stand. Unfortunately, it didn't sound like he was moving toward me. I peeked up over the pew top. I was right, he was racing up the center aisle toward the altar, toward the other gun.

I gulped in a quick breath, braced myself for the pain that was going to shoot through me, then scrambled up from the floor, gun drawn, limping quickly into the center aisle where I had a clear shot at Cummings's back.

"Stop!" I shouted. "Or I'll shoot!"

He stopped, turned, fired his last shot. I dropped to the floor, rolled, but he missed me by a mile. The drop to the carpet, however, didn't do my knee any good. I watched as Cummings kept pulling the trigger, his face contorted by hate and crazy, the hollow click of it echoing through the church. For me, it was the sound of salvation. For him, likely defeat. I scrambled to my feet as he turned for the altar again.

"Take one more step, and I swear I'll drop you where you stand!"

He turned slowly back and watched, grinning, as I hobbled slowly toward him, the Glock trained squarely at him.

He sneered derisively. "You won't shoot. Not in his precious church."

I gave him a moment to take a good long look at my face. The gun felt as heavy as a ship's anchor, but I held it steady. "Walk this way, then down on the floor." He didn't move. He was testing me. "I'm only saying it once."

He smirked. "You look like you're about to fall over."

"Then I'll shoot you on my way down," I said. "Move!"

Slowly, Cummings walked back, got down on the floor. I watched him closely while also looking for my jacket. My phone was in one of the pockets. I thought about sitting, but didn't think I'd be able to get back up, so I stood, teetering on one leg.

"It got out of hand," Cummings whined. "I liked Father Ray, but you don't interfere with family."

I thought I'd feel more, knowing I'd gotten Pop's killer. I thought that a weight would lift, but it hadn't. He was still gone. I wouldn't kill Cummings. He wasn't worth killing. He wasn't worth spending another moment on.

"A man's got a right to what's his!"

I tuned him out. I didn't have to listen. I hopped over to my jacket slung across a pew seat a couple of rows up. There was a bullet hole in the sleeve. I glared at Cummings. First, Tiny Guard ruined my favorite jeans, now this asshat put a bullet in my jacket. I briefly reconsidered shooting him. Suddenly, the front doors burst open and a horde of uniformed cops rushed in, guns drawn. When they saw me, they lasered in, and I found myself staring into a whole lot of gun barrels.

"Freeze!" they yelled.

I made like a Popsicle, dropping the jacket, raising my hands over my head. "Consider me frozen." I began to breathe again only when I saw Ben crash through the front lines and rush toward me.

"Not her," he said to the cops behind him. He pointed at Cummings. "That mope! Get him out of here before I lose my religion."

He hurried over to me, and I handed him my gun, glad to get rid of it, balancing on my one good leg, holding the other up.

"I'm fine," I said, taking in the look on his face. "But for the love of God do not touch me. My knee's busted, and I think I also stubbed my toe, but it's hard to tell because I have practically no feeling in my foot."

He grimaced as if my distress hurt him too. I appreciated the empathy, but no way did his emotional discomfort hold a candle to my physical pain.

He looked down at my knee, now twice its normal size. "He do that?"

"Forget it. I said I'm fine."

He walked over to the nearest uniform and whispered something to him, then watched as the cops cuffed George none too gently and then yanked him up off the floor. When Cummings was upright, Ben got right in his face, and, in a voice too low for anyone else to hear, told him a thing or two. When he was done, he made a slow show of straightening out Cummings shirt-front, his eyes flintlike. Whatever he said drained every bit of color from Cummings's face. He was uncharacteristically quiet as the uniforms escorted him out.

"What did you say to him?"

"Let's just say I made sure we understood each other."

I narrowed my eyes. "I want to know what you said."

"Too bad," he said. "Let's go."

I hobbled backward. "Where?"

"Let's see. I was thinking the hospital might be nice."

I opened my mouth to protest, then closed it again. There was no way of getting around a trip to the ER. "Normally, I'd bitch about going to the hospital."

"If it'll make you happy, bitch away, but you're still going." I hobbled a half step forward. The front door looked miles away. "Let me carry you," Ben said, making a move toward me.

I backed away from him. "Don't you frigging dare. Back up. I got this."

Ben arched an eyebrow, shook his head. "You have got some serious issues."

"Yeah, well, we don't have time to discuss them all now." I hopped forward, then stopped, remembering my .9mm. "I want my gun. Cummings kicked it away up there somewhere."

"Why are you always asking for your gun?"

"I paid good money for it. It's mine. I want it."

"I'll make sure you get it back. Now move. With any luck, we'll hit the hospital by Thanksgiving."

He slowly walked beside me as I limped along, hovering but being careful not to touch.

I slid him a look. "Are Barb and you-know-who okay?

"They're fine. Is that what you're calling him?"

"For now."

We walked a few more steps in silence. "Oh, hey, he gave me this to give to you. He insisted on it." He handed me a slip of paper. It was a train ticket from St. Louis to Chicago dated after Pop's death. "He says it proves his word is good."

"We'll see," I said, stuffing it into my pocket.

"You got him," Ben said.

I stopped, glanced over to the confessional box. Yeah. I did. "Where's Farraday? I want to rub his nose in it."

"He's suspiciously absent," Ben said.

I frowned, then winced. "Yeah, that sounds like him."

From the top of the church steps, I saw Detective Weber

standing at the curb with two cups of Starbucks coffee. He gave me a look, which told me one of the cups was meant for me.

"What's that all about?" Ben asked. "You don't drink coffee." He glanced at me, frowned. "And what's he grinning about?" Ben looked at Weber, then back at me. "Aww, c'mon! When did *this* start?"

"Are you taking me to the ER, or not?" I said.

"Not till you get that goofy look off your face, I'm not."

I picked my way down the stone steps and smiled.